W9-AZD-783

FANTASTIC HOPE

EDITED BY
LAURELL K. HAMILTON
AND
WILLIAM McCASKEY

BERKLEY
NEW YORK

BERKLEY

An imprint of Penguin Random House LLC

penguinrandomhouse.com

Collection copyright © 2020 by Laurell K. Hamilton

Pages 417–18 constitute an extension of this copyright page.

Library of Congress Cataloging-in-Publication Data

Names: Hamilton, Laurell K., editor. | McCaskey, William, editor.
Title: Fantastic hope / Edited by Laurell K. Hamilton and William McCaskey.
Description: First edition. | New York: Berkley, 2020.
Identifiers: LCCN 2019056339 | ISBN 9780593099209 (trade paperback) |
ISBN 9780593099216 (ebook)
Subjects: LCSH: Science fiction, American.
Classification: LCC PS648.S3 F288 2020 | DDC 813/.0876208—dc23
LC record available at https://lccn.loc.gov/2019056339

First Edition: April 2020

Printed in the United States of America
1   3   5   7   9   10   8   6   4   2

Cover image by ImpossiAble / Getty Images
Cover design by Judith Lagerman
Book design by Alison Cnockaert

TITLES BY LAURELL K. HAMILTON

Anita Blake, Vampire Hunter Novels

Guilty Pleasures

The Laughing Corpse

Circus of the Damned

The Lunatic Cafe

Bloody Bones

The Killing Dance

Burnt Offerings

Blue Moon

Obsidian Butterfly

Narcissus in Chains

Cerulean Sins

Incubus Dreams

Micah

Danse Macabre

The Harlequin

Blood Noir

Skin Trade

Flirt

Bullet

Hit List

Kiss the Dead

Affliction

Jason

Dead Ice

Crimson Death

Serpentine

Merry Gentry Novels

A Kiss of Shadows

A Caress of Twilight

Seduced by Moonlight

A Stroke of Midnight

Mistral's Kiss

A Lick of Frost

Swallowing Darkness

Divine Misdemeanors

A Shiver of Light

Specials

Beauty

Dancing

Wounded

Anthologies

Strange Candy

Fantastic Hope

TITLES BY WILLIAM McCASKEY

Fury's Fire Novels
Dragon Two-Zero

Anthologies
Fantastic Hope

CONTENTS

FOREWORD

You're holding hope in your hands. Stories of make-believe, let's pretend just like we did as children, except that a writer wrote it down and here it is, for you to read, for you to share the adventure. Science fiction, fantasy, and even horror are all about sharing the adventure, the dream. It's an escape, a glimpse of a better future or a better present. It's a place where the hero wins, the bad guy is punished, and the monsters are only real while you're reading the story. You can close the covers and be safe. Unlike the real terrors of the world online and in the news lately. It's like we're all on the front lines of whatever crisis or natural disaster is happening anywhere in the world, at any given time; there is no break in the stream of bad news, or so it seems. It has even infected our books and movies, so that dystopias where everything has gone as wrong as it can sit at the top of the box office or the bestseller list. Until I felt overwhelmed and in need of an escape, or at least a break.

If you are feeling the same way, welcome to a collection of stories where you can find hope, happy endings, loyalty, freedom, love, all the positive things that make the best of us. Welcome to thrilling adventures and a modern take on two-fisted adventure stories. Romance that travels lifetimes, or reaches beyond the grave for a happy ending. Travel to alien worlds, meet characters of all kinds, and learn that the end of the world may not be the end after all. Time travel to save the day and kill, just enough, but not too much. Have faith in yourself, in the people who love you, in magic, in religion, in Deity, in science, and in things harder to label with just one word. Believe that there will be smiles after the tears, joy after the pain, and that it will all work out, that good will triumph and evil will not win forever.

I had the privilege of editing these stories with my good friend William McCaskey. My thirty-seventh novel will be out soon. Will's first novel was published six months before this anthology. The rest of the writers in this anthology are the same, old pros and newbies. I love that about *Fantastic Hope*, because it's hard for new writers to get a foot in the door when there are no markets for their stories. When I started collecting my first rejection slips in the late 1970s, there were so many markets for short fiction that you could actually make a modest living at it, but now in 2020, not so much. One of the reasons I hope that this anthology sells well is that it could become a yearly market for new writers to start their careers alongside those of us who have been in the trenches since before the internet depressed and amused us all. You're holding people's dreams in your hands, dreams made real for you to read and share. I hope you enjoy reading them as much as I did.

—*Laurell K. Hamilton*

Fantastic Hope is a very personal victory for me. When I sat down to write my first book, *Dragon Two-Zero*, I didn't expect it to sell, but when your friend who has written multiple successful titles challenges you to write the stories in your head, you really don't have an excuse to say no. Laurell making that challenge showed me that there was another way to deal with the pain that I once used alcohol to cope with. On April 18, 2017, instead of reaching for a bottle, as was my custom on that day each year, I reached for a pen, and about six hours later "Ronin" was on the paper in front of me. I don't remember why I showed the story to my wife, but I did, and she cried. I sent it to Laurell with a thank-you note for giving me a way to deal with memory and loss that didn't end with a horrible hangover the next day. The next time I saw Laurell, she hit me for making her cry and then hugged me. Laurell is a big proponent of people doing their therapy and working through their shit. We sat over lunch and talked about the depressing stories that seemed to be everywhere, in the news and in fiction, and lamented that there weren't more uplifting stories. That is where the idea for *Fantastic Hope* was born. Laurell and I are both survivors, and we know that the world is not all unicorns, rainbows, and glitter. But we also know that there is light at the end of the tunnel and that the darkness can be pushed back, even if it starts with a spark.

I am honored to have been a part of this project, having the opportunity to work with authors that I read growing up and up and newcomers like myself that I am proud to see breaking into the industry. I hope that in this book you find a story that speaks to you, that reminds you that tomorrow is a new day with new opportunities.

—*William McCaskey*

TWILIGHT FALLS

A JOE LEDGER ROGUE TEAM INTERNATIONAL ADVENTURE

JONATHAN MABERRY

1.

PHOENIX HOUSE
OMFORI ISLAND, GREECE

"They're not *chem*-trails," I said with the last fragment of patience. "They're *con*trails."

We were in the briefing room and I was pretty close to throwing my cup of coffee at the smug little bastard who hosted the conspiracy theory radio show. Jim Peabody. He had a lean, oddly angular bird-like body and looked like an affronted egret. He had the kind of face you *wanted* to throw a coffee cup at. Even if you like coffee as much as I do. It was very hot coffee and it would hurt. So, the struggle was real because I wanted him to shut the fuck up.

"Just listen to him, sugar," said Joan Holliday, the head of our integrated sciences division. She looks like a six-foot-plus version of Dolly Parton. All the glam, glitter, curves, and sass of the singer, but thirty years younger and a shelf full of MDs and PhDs. She called everyone sugar. Or honey bunny. Or sweet cheeks.

"Why bother?" I demanded. "We've got some freaks threatening to release bioweapons in fifty countries. Fifty. Five-zero. We're standing on the brink of the actual apocalypse. We are a couple of very bad days away from living in either a disease-infested wasteland or a dystopia in which only those entitled assholes who can afford it are going to survive. That isn't the plot of a summer blockbuster, it's happening right now. So excuse the living fuck out of me if I'm not all that concerned about some crackpot belief trending with the tin-foil hat crowd."

Peabody actually recoiled from me, then took a half step forward. "Colonel Ledger, if you'd just listen to—"

"I've *been* listening," I said. "And all I'm hearing is bullshit."

"No, sir," said Peabody officiously, "you're hearing but not listening. You're not paying attention."

"'Paying attention'?" I had to smile. "Do you want to know what I was doing when I got the call to come in for this briefing? I was hunting for a group of terrorists suspected of smuggling a bioweapon delivery system into Athens. Do you know how many people live in Athens? Do you know how many people we're trying to keep *alive* in Athens? And Rome, and London, and Paris, and New York, and—?"

"Colonel . . ."

It was Mr. Church who'd spoken. A single word. Quiet, without emphasis.

I stopped my rant. We all looked at him. Church is a big man, black and strong. Somewhere in his sixties, but that isn't what made him the adult in the room. He was the adult in any room. You look at him and immediately want to check your fingernails to see if they're clean. I've seen generals and heads of state react that way, too.

"Every JSOC and private SpecOps team in the world is on the hunt for the bioterrorists. Our people, MHI, SEAL Team 666, Chess Team, Sigma Force . . . It's doubtful there's ever been a more concentrated hunt than what is currently ongoing. And, as valuable a field asset as you are, Colonel, cutting you out of that pack to deal with this is not likely to be the deciding factor in keeping the world on its hinges."

Doc Holliday pretended to whisper, but said, "You got spanked." And she said it in a little musical singsong. I glared nuclear death at her.

"Okay, okay," I said with bad grace and turned back to Peabody—who, for the record, *looks* like a Peabody. A classic example of the type. "Chem-trails. Sure. Fine. Explain to me how that's not a conspiracy theory."

Peabody pushed his glasses up his nose and said, "Well, Colonel Ledger, understand that I would normally agree with you. In all circumstances. Contrails are actually condensation trails. Line-shaped cloud formations created by changes in air pressure as aircraft cruise at certain altitudes and under certain atmospheric conditions. Water vapor in the engine exhaust interacts with low ambient temperatures, leaving lines of ice crystals. And some contrails are formed by changes in air pressure in wingtip vortices. Some disappear quickly and others can last for hours."

"Thank you, Bill Nye," I muttered. "Get to how that equals some kind of conspiracy."

"Regular contrails are harmless," said Peabody. "As you say, there are plenty of conspiracy theories about chem-trails. That nonsense got started after a 1996 air force report was published in which induced weather modification theories were discussed. Alarmists like William Thomas, Richard Finke, and Art Bell stoked the fires of the belief that some contrails were actually the release of ether chemicals or biological agents intended to accomplish a variety of goals. Mind control, pacification of the population for easier rule by the Illuminati, human population control, chemical warfare, and . . . well, the list goes on and on past into genetic seeding by reptilian aliens. Any notable outbreaks of disease, higher statistics of genetic disorders, cancers, and so on in given areas are then linked to these chem-trails."

I twirled my finger to indicate Doc Holliday, Church, and myself. "Choir," I said. And then pointed to him. "Preacher."

He flushed a little. "I had to establish certain things in order to tell you something that is *actually* happening."

Very quietly I heard Mr. Church say, "Ah."

Peabody had visual aids and sent images from his laptop to the big flat-screen in the conference room. The first image was a Google Maps satellite view of a stretch of nearly featureless desert. Endless sand dunes.

"This is Ténéré, a desert region in the south-central Sahara that stretches from northeastern Chad to western Sudan. One hundred fifty thousand square miles of nothing. It is ostensibly owned by Niger and Chad, but sparsely populated and of little value to anyone. You can't farm it and there is very little water. It is, for all intents and purposes, a dead land."

He clicked and a picture appeared of a pair of dark-skinned men dressed in white robes leading a string of starved-looking camels.

"There's a scattering of ethnic groups, but the area in question for us is used mostly by Toubou people, who are descended from the original Neolithic inhabitants of the Sahara region. They are genetically Ethiopians, and are regarded as a tough, nomadic, and noble people. Most of the Toubou are salt miners. They live at the very edge of poverty and starvation."

Click.

"This is one of the Toubou salt camps," he said. The image was that of several tents clustered in the lee of a vertical pillar of natural rock that stood up from the sand. A few pine trees leaned away from the sun's fists, and there were some handfuls of grass. "The oasis is called the Finger of God for obvious reasons. This photo was taken eleven days ago by a *National Geographic* photographer doing a story on nomad peoples."

We waited, and I found myself becoming invested now. There were people in the mix and I had a bad feeling this was not going to be a story with a happy ending. In my job we don't get to read a lot of those kinds of stories.

Click.

The next shot was of the same camp. Clearly days later. Had to be days, because even in the brutal heat of the Sahara, bodies don't bloat that much. They don't warp and expand into grotesque parodies of the human form. Doc Holliday made a soft gagging sound. I walked over to the screen and stood looking at it for a long time.

Men and women. Children. Even the camels.

All of them dead.

Sprawled in the sand. Covered in blowflies. Mouths thrown wide, but if with screams or prayers to an unheeding god there was no way to tell. Fingers knotted into fists on stilled breasts, or clutching handfuls of sand, or entwined with those of children. Reaching to each other for help, for support, or to make sure that when the darkness took them, they fell together.

None of us spoke.

Click.

The next image was of a plane flying high above, leaving a double trail of silver-white vapor.

"That was taken by the *Nat Geo* reporter the same day the first oasis picture was taken," said Peabody. "The other picture . . . well, that was forty-eight hours later."

I turned.

"It doesn't prove a connection," I said.

"No, no . . . but . . ."

Click.

It was an aerial view of another oasis. A substantially bigger one, with many healthy palms, a big pen of goats, and a sophisticated building whose pitched roof was lined with solar panels. Several pickups and Jeeps were parked in the shade of an angled canopy, and beyond the house were several acres of land covered with sand-colored cloth tarps. But what caught my eye was what was behind the building. There, at the end of a short, flat stretch of hard-packed sand, was an aircraft. A small, tidy jet.

Sticking out from beneath its wings were large chemical tanks.

"That's not proof," I said.

"Show him the rest," said Church.

Peabody nodded. "There are three other oases in the same area."

Click.

The same jet, flying at a height of maybe four thousand feet, dragging white lines behind it.

Click.

Another camp. More tents. More trees. More bodies.

Click.

That jet again.

Click.

The third oasis. The third horror show.

Click.

Click.

Into the silence I said, "Tell me about the people who own that jet."

2.

We had no idea what kind of tech our potential bad guys had. The days when a radar unit was some big obvious thing were long gone. Now that stuff was small, easily mounted on a Jeep or pickup.

So we did a HALO jump to get in.

High altitude, low open. That's three of us—Top Sims, Bunny, and me—throwing ourselves out of a perfectly good airplane at thirty thousand feet. Wearing goggles and breathing bottled air, and falling six fucking miles before we deployed our chutes. Yes, I was an Airborne Ranger in the army. Yes, I've done scores of combat jumps. No, I have never liked a single one of them. I have a good game face, especially in front of my men, but inside, my nuts crawl up into my chest cavity before I'm out the door, and they do not descend until about half an hour after I'm on the ground.

We didn't die, though, so . . . there's that.

We gathered up our chutes and kicked sand over them. Bradley "Top" Sims is the oldest member of Havoc Team. Pushing fifty, but clearly made out of boiler plates and scrap iron. Dark brown skin, eyes that missed nothing, and a patchwork of earned scars all over his tough hide. Beside him was Harvey Rabbit—sadly, that's his actual name. Everyone calls him Bunny. He's six and a half feet of Orange County white boy with a surfer tan and more muscles than anyone reasonably needs. They were my right and left hands. We'd joined Church's little gang of science geeks and shooters together. I trusted them more than anyone else I knew.

The equipment had landed a few hundred yards away, and we jogged over and uncrated three sound-suppressed dirt bikes. Very high-end stuff. Not as fast as regular motorcycles, their speed topping out at forty, but the engines purred like kittens. The cases were sand-colored and with the easterly wind blowing they'd be covered and invisible in a few hours. There were no markings of any kind on any of the gear we brought. No badges or rank insignias on our clothing. We were ghosts.

Top glanced at me, then up at the sky in the direction from which we'd come, and then down at the blowing sand. "World's going to shit and we're a long damn way from the fight," he said.

It was true enough. The bioterrorists had already begun limited releases on towns in Europe, Asia, and North America. A weaponized version of the Shanghai flu in Duoyishu, a village in southwest China's Yunnan Province. A superstrain of tuberculosis in Otranto, Puglia. And a dreadfully hardy strain of *Yersinia pestis* in a Navajo village in New Mexico. Right now the death toll was low. Comparatively low, anyway. Seven hundred infected, with seventeen deaths. No one was actually encouraged by those numbers. None of us believed that the death toll was going to stay low.

The threats about these attacks had been coming in via anonymous snail mail, social media posts from dummy accounts, and emails sent from internet cafés and fake profiles. The first one we knew about was nine months ago, and it wasn't taken seriously—except in retrospect. It was directed at the government of India and was filled with political and quasi-religious histrionics. All about how the current world is corrupt and that overpopulation is proof of a deliberate desire to pollute and destroy the world. The viewpoint of the group amounts to the belief that humanity has become a kind of thinking virus on the skin of the living earth. What was once a symbiotic relationship, back when humanity could be counted in the tens of thousands, has been thrown out of balance by industrialism and overpopulation. The group consider themselves to be the voice of reason.

Their "reasonable" suggestion, sent via email to the heads of state of the fifty most populous countries, was for the leaders to initiate a lottery to pick ninety percent of their populations and systematically euthanize them. Failure to do so would result in the group launching a program of bioweapon releases. How they planned to do that, and where they would get these bioweapons, was something we were working on figuring out.

The limited releases were incentives. Kicks in the ass.

That's why everyone with a gun was out hunting these freaks.

All we had for the group was a name—Silentium. Latin for "silence," which didn't tell us much. However, from the rhetoric in their messages it was pretty clear they were some kind of millenarian cult. Their rants were all about how mankind was corrupt and how a new age was going to dawn after the manufactured cleansing program. There were going to be seven years of violence, struggle, and death before the population was whittled down to a number in harmony with the earth.

Funny how these groups present a model of a societal golden ideal that is any rational person's concept of a dystopia.

And the three of us seemed to be in the wrong damn place for the fight. Church said this was worth doing, and I had to take him at his word. But it felt like we were throwing punches at the wrong chins out here. Top and Bunny and I shared a long look, each of us knowing what was in the others' hearts.

"Let's get it done," I said, "so we can go back to the war."

The target was twenty-nine miles south by east from the LZ. We saddled up without a word and were gone.

3.

FINGER OF GOD OASIS
TÉNÉRÉ
SOUTH-CENTRAL SAHARA

As we drove, we each reviewed the intel. Details were sent to the left lenses of our Google Scout glasses, a proprietary bit of tech designed for Mr. Church by one of his friends in the industry.

Our destination was called the Lab. Nice and generic. Whoever owned it was doing a pretty damn good job of hiding behind fake identities and shell corporations. Had to be some money in play for them to swing that. Had to be some sophistication, too. Our computer team, headed by Bug, usually brushed aside most obfuscation, but these people were tricky bastards. Bug chopped through the underbrush all the way back to a nonspecific start-up in South Africa. There were no computer records of any kind to explain what they had started up to do. And the identities of the key players were nearly perfectly hidden, as Bug explained to us via radio as we drove.

"We tracked down two of the people involved," he said. "Bongani Jiba, a woman from the Xhosa tribe, and Thabo Mahao, a man from the Sotho people. Jiba graduated from the University of Cape Town. Top of her class. Mahao earned a PhD in engineering from Stellenbosch University, having gone through school on a series of scholarships. Both of them are brilliant. Mahao's family were carpet merchants and the Jiba family were bakers. No known political connections."

"Anything suggesting they might be with this Silentium cult?"

"Nope. Not a whiff of that. No religious affiliation of any weight. No criminal records. And no clear connection between them."

"Two black twentysomethings with advanced degrees from white-dominated schools," mused Top. "Could have been radicalized on campus."

"Yeah, maybe," said Bunny, "but radicalized to do what? The Toubou were black, too. And poor as balls. What's the win in killing them?"

"To be determined," I said. "What else do you have, Bug?"

"Nothing. The facility you guys are heading to is on a patch of ground leased by the government of Chad to the dummy corporation. We can track some money exchanges, but it's from the government side. Cash deposits, so that's a dead end. All of the equipment must have been trucked in by private companies, or they did it themselves, because there's no record."

"What about the plane?"

"It's a ONE Aviation Eclipse 550," said Bug. "A light commercial jet. Cheap. About three mil. Top speed of four thirty. Fifteen-hundred-mile range, crew of one or two, with room for up to five passengers. Weighs thirty-six hundred empty and has a max takeoff weight of six thousand."

"Doesn't leave a lot for payload," said Bunny, "'specially if they're carrying full tanks of liquid. Water's eight pounds a gallon, and those look like fifty-five-gallon drums under the wings. That's another nine hundred pounds."

"So," said Top, "figure a pilot and a tech, plus the payload. Everything else stripped out."

"Sounds right," I said. "Bug, can we pin down who might have bought it?"

"Working on that. They only made thirty-three of them before they stopped production in 2017. I have someone running down ownership. Not a successful model, though, and a lot of them have gone to second or third owners. Get me some numbers off the engine house or tail and I'll get you some names."

"Roger that."

The photos of the oases and the compound where the jet was parked were taken by Buzz Clark, a seasoned photojournalist whose articles on African tribal cultures had won him three Pulitzers over the twenty-five years of his career. He was a pragmatic guy, by all accounts, and wasn't the type to merely be a witness to events but instead took some action when there was a need. Clark was discreet about it, though, because he didn't want to lose credibility with local contacts. That said, when warlords in Somalia were hijacking ship-ments of vaccines for a TB outbreak, he made a call. When he caught wind of a sex trafficking ring smuggling tween girls out of Malawi, he sent an email. He was stand-up. A lot of reporters won't for fear of ending a story they want to follow.

Clark contacted a buddy in the WHO, who contacted someone who contacted Peabody, who—despite my personal and totally un-founded dislike of him—contacted Church. Clark was nobody's idea of a ranting conspiracy theorist, so we all took him more seri-ously than we would virtually anyone else.

Since then, though, Clark had gone off the radar. He was sup-posed to be our man on the ground, but he hadn't responded to the last few attempts to reach him. None of us felt good about that.

The three of us drove on and reached the oasis called the Finger of God. A bunch of buzzards took reluctant flight, circling high above us as we parked and dismounted. We stopped upwind from the oasis and unpacked the backpack Bunny wore. In it were two lightweight hazmat suits, which Top and I pulled on. Bunny took a roll of duct tape and sealed our wrists and ankles. Then Top removed other items from the pack, including a BAMS unit, which he handed to me. He took a biological sample collection kit, and together we moved off, leaving Bunny well behind to guard our backs.

As we approached the bodies, I switched the BAMS unit on and began waving it around. The device was a bioaerosol mass spectrometer. It had a vacuum function that drew in ambient air and hit it with continuous wave lasers to fluoresce individual particles. Key molecules like bacillus spores, dangerous viruses, and certain vegetative cells were identified and assigned color codes. Most of the BAMS units on either the commercial or government markets were unreliable because they could only detect dangerous particles in high density. This version had been designed by Dr. William Hu, the former head of the DMS Integrated Sciences Division, and then seriously upgraded by Doc Holliday. If everything was copacetic, the little lights would stay a comforting green.

They were green until I got about four feet from the body of an adult woman, and then the lights all flashed red.

"Fuck me," I said.

Top stood next to me as I passed the unit over the body in order to capture as much of whatever was triggering the BAMS sensors. It was uplinked to a satellite and sent data to Doc Holliday all the way the hell back in Greece. I heard her gasp as if she stood between me and Top.

"Outlaw," she said, using my combat call sign, "discharge the filter and load a new one, then do a new scan." I did. Doc said, "Boys, this don't make any goldarn sense at all. I don't know whether to scratch my watch or wind my butt."

"Talk to me, Doc," I said. "Not feeling real comfy out here. Do you know what this thing is?"

"Well, I know what the sensors say it is, boys, but that don't make a lick of sense," complained Doc. "It's reading as better than ninety percent sure this is coccidioidomycosis. Shorthand is cocci or valley fever."

"We're not in a valley, are we?" asked Top.

"Even if you were," she said, "you're not in the right valley. The other name for this is California fever."

Top and I exchanged a look.

"Say again?" I said.

"Cocci is a mammalian fungal disease found in the southwestern US and northern Mexico. It has no damn reason at all to be killing people in the Sahara."

"Then why are we looking at about forty dead people?"

"Because someone is out there playing mad scientist," she said.

"Going out on a limb here," said Bunny slowly, "but am I the only one wondering if somehow we stepped into a big steaming pile of that millenarian bullshit out here?"

"How?" asked Top. "Those Silentium fucknuts are all about over-population, and these folks here are the exact opposite of that. Ain't many of them at all."

"You're right, Pappy," said Doc, using his call sign. "The Toubou are at cultural subsistence-level population growth, especially that far into the sand."

"But someone killed them with a disease from the States," said Bunny. "What the actual fuck's that about if it's not connected?"

"You got me, sweet cheeks." She paused. "Listen, whether or not it's connected is only part of the problem, and not the biggest part. The fact that these people *are* dead at all makes my ass itch, because cocci is rarely fatal."

"Looks pretty fucking fatal from where I'm standing," I growled.

"Well, no shit," she said in her mock-pleasant voice. Doc always sounded like she was asking for a cucumber sandwich at a church social, but that was all show. Inside she was as hard as any of us, and smarter than all of us. "Okay, the CliffsNotes version of the science is that cocci develops in certain ecological niches where you have hot summers and mild winters, and where there's very little annual rainfall. It's generally found in alkaline sandy soil. Not in pure-sand deserts where there is no rain worth talking about, because the fungus grows in the periods of wet weather, then dries out and is spread by arid winds. It's called 'grow and blow.'"

"We're in an oasis," said Top. "There's got to be water under the sand here and where the other deaths occurred."

"Sure," she said, "but not enough to do this. The growing cycle is wrong, and the location is mighty damn wrong. Also . . . the infection cycle is way too fast. Infection of cocci requires time, and generally an already compromised immune system. It might— *might*—explain this quicker and more pervasive infection rate if every single one of the nomads in those three groups were already HIV positive. But that's unlikely because these groups don't have a lot of physical contact with urban centers in that part of Africa where HIV is rampant. Maybe five percent of people exposed to cocci contract it, and of that group less than five percent fail to recover. None of the known infected die this fast. No, no, no. This isn't Mother Nature being a bitch. This is some true mad scientist bullshit here."

I glanced up at the sky as if I could see the jet and its contrails, but all I saw were buzzards circling, waiting for us to leave.

"Doc," I said, "put some people on this cocci stuff. Find out where samples can be obtained, and work out a scenario for how it might have been weaponized. Whether this is connected to the Silentium threat or not, if we can source this stuff, then we may have our first real lead."

"Oh, honey bunny," she said sweetly, "I'm already driving in that lane and calls are being made. Now get me some samples, and then go shoot some bad guys. I think we'll all feel better if you do."

Top opened the sample kit and we got to work. It did not take long, but it was an ugly task that left us feeling sick and stained and embarrassed to be part of the same species of biped as whoever did this. I glanced at Top, who was taking tissue samples from a little child. Unlike Bunny and me, Top was a parent. He'd already lost one child to war. He knew the pain of that. Just as he knew the fear. I could see a fever brightness in his eyes as he worked, and wondered how deep inside the heads of that child's parents he'd gone. They all died together, but had the parents watched their little one sicken and die before the disease took them, too? Or had the kid cried out to them for help, for answers, for protection as he crawled to where they lay? In either case it was an abomination.

Top caught me watching him and for a moment we stared at each other, saying nothing. Saying everything that needed to be said.

We walked out to where Bunny waited with a pressure can of disinfectant. We stripped out of the hazmat suits, stuffed them in a bag, and emptied the rest of the germ killer into it before burying it. The BAMS unit and samples were wrapped in plastic and sealed with tape. I took a transport drone from the saddlebag of my bike, assembled it quickly, fitted the samples into its undercarriage, and launched it. Our support team would track its transponder and do a pickup while we continued the mission.

We got onto our bikes and left. I glanced over my shoulder and saw the vultures dropping down again. The temptation to shoot at them was strong, but no matter how unsavory their appetites or grisly their meals, they were not the villains of this piece.

4.

As the miles burned away, I thought about the faces of the Toubou people who lay rotting in the sun. Innocent folks, going about a way of life that probably hadn't changed substantially in five or six thousand years. Good folks. Hardworking, uncomplicated, innocent of the cultural guile and corruption that was rife in the industrial parts of the world. Snuffed out.

Why?

As an experiment for some new kind of bioweapon? That was our leading theory, if this was the Silentium madmen. Had the Toubou lived on mineral-rich lands or good grazing pastures, there would be a different motivation. At least then you could build a plausible—if inexcusable—set of motives based on simple greed. But out here, in the vastness of the Sahara? The killers had to go out of their way to target them, which meant that it was a calculated evil or a specific cultural madness. A cult psychosis, like the Heaven's Gate group who committed mass suicide in San Diego in 1997, and the People's Temple nearly twenty years before them in Jonestown. Millenarian groups date back hundreds of years, and not all of them are corrupt or completely insane. My lover, Junie Flynn, believes in what early twentieth-century psychic leader Edgar Cayce called inevitable "earth changes," and there is a very real earth change movement within the post-hippie, post–New Age spiritual community. They're very gentle people. Historians, however, lump them in with the more radical millenarians like the jackasses who wanted to kill most of the world.

If Jiba and Mahao and whoever else was at the Lab were part of that group, and if they were responsible for these murders, then the isolation of this place would come back to bite them hard. There were no witnesses out here. There was no one *they* could call for help. Not in time. Not once Top and Bunny and I came for them.

And they could scream as loud as they wanted, but in the end they would give us the answers we wanted. My friends and I are good men, but we are not nice ones.

Not in places like this.

"TOC to Outlaw," came the call in my ear. TOC was the tactical operations center, where Church, Doc, and Bug were gathered to oversee this op. I raised my fist and we all slowed to a stop at the foot of a large dune, our bikes purring quietly.

"Go for Outlaw," I responded.

"We're tracking two vehicles inbound toward the target," said Bug.

"What do we know?"

"Two Humvees, both with civilian paint jobs. Older models, probably bought from military sell-offs. No visible armament. We don't have thermal scans, so no intel on number of occupants. ETA to target is twenty-five minutes."

Beside me Top cursed. That was going to be close to when we would arrive.

"What's the call?" I asked, and Church answered.

"The play is yours, Outlaw. If you ID them as hostiles, we can have a drone there in forty minutes."

"Copy that." I glanced at my guys and they each nodded. "We're going in. Soft approach, observe and assess."

"Very well. Proceed with caution," he said and ended the call.

Bunny looked into the distance, toward where the vehicles would be coming. "More of their team, maybe? Or bringing fuel for the bird?"

"Or coming to pick up the cocci bioweapon now that it's been proved," suggested Top. I nodded, because that sounded reasonable.

"Let's go find out," I said.

We headed out, pushing the bikes to their limit.

5.

As we drove we sent a drone ahead to surveil the landscapes, and the feed was sent to the Scout goggles and to the TOC.

"Hey," said Doc's voice, "what are those flat areas you just passed?"

I tapped the goggles to replay that portion of the video and saw what she meant. Way off to our left there were several areas that I first took for wind-smoothed sand, but when I zoomed in, it was clear that they were huge areas of ground covered with sand-colored tarps. Huge tarps, too. Maybe a quarter acre each, and we passed ten or twelve of them. No idea if there were others out of the drone's camera range.

"No idea," I said. "Not sure we have the time to check them, either. Racing the clock here."

"Whatever it is," said Doc, "I don't like it. Looks like camouflage for something, but whatever it is, it's flat. No sign of structures or vehicles under the tarps. Check it on your way back."

"I'll add it to my to-do list," I said, and kept driving. The Lab was ahead and we'd gained some advantage over the approaching Humvees. We kept going and then stopped two miles from the target.

Our approach vector had been picked so that the wind blew toward us, thereby carrying a good deal of the muffled engine noises away behind us. Even so, it was worth hiking the last bit to guarantee that no one heard us approach. The vehicles were still a few minutes out, but we had to move fast. The sun was rolling off the edge of the world, which gave us the shroud of twilight. The desert is dry and there isn't much moisture in the air to refract the fading sun's glow. It gets dark very fast.

Lights came on inside the Lab, but there were no perimeter spotlights. That was strange and it sent some minor alarm bells ringing in my head. Mass murderers and terrorists—if that's what these people were—generally went the extra mile in overall security.

I tapped Bunny's shoulder. "Let's get some birds in the air."

He unzipped Top's pack and they quickly unwrapped and activated a pair of eagle owl drones. They weren't exactly the right species for the Sahara, but it was night and they were close enough. Besides, we didn't think we were creeping up on a lair of evil ornithologists. Top and Bunny each tossed a drone into the air, and the little machines deployed their wings, flapped vigorously, and rose into the darkening sky. I pulled back the flap that camouflaged the small computer strapped to my forearm, and brought up the feeds from both birds. The screen split into two and gave me high-def camera feeds, thermal scans, and scans for electronics as the drones soared over the building.

On the first pass the thermals told us that there were eight people inside. No idea who they were, but they all grouped in one room. Electronic heat signatures suggested there were machines in there, and one of them was both hot and cold. A fridge. Then the drones circled and searched for the security setup, hunting for listening devices, infrared triggers, motion sensors, and other security systems.

Bunny leaned close and studied the display. "Well," he said sourly, "they got the whole package, don't they?"

"Yup."

And they did. The whole compound was wired six ways from Sunday, and all of it was networked through a very sophisticated computer system. I tapped my coms unit.

"Bug, you getting this?"

"Yeah."

"Talk to me."

"It's a pretty sweet setup. Absolute cutting edge. Very expensive. Looks like the computers are protected by a one-hundred-twenty-eight-bit cyclical random numerical coder. That's top of the line."

"And . . . ?"

"And we're in," he said simply. "Top of the line isn't 'us' now, is it?"

I heard Top laughing quietly.

Rogue Team International had the MindReader computer, which is arguably the world's most sophisticated super-intrusion software system. It's how we've been able to stay a couple of steps ahead of the bad guys—and some of our allies—even though we're a relatively small group. RTI works because we can spook our way into virtually any computer system, steal data, learn secrets, clone intel, and then sneak out again with no trace. MindReader rewrites the target system's security software, including time codes, to eliminate all traces of its presence. The next best systems—owned by the NSA, China, and Russia—could sneak in, but they left footprints, scars to mark where they'd been. Nobody ever knows that Mind-Reader was there. It makes our system the most dangerous in the world, which is why Mr. Church doesn't share it with anyone. That's a very deep line in the sand. His level of trust for other governments is nonexistent.

Bug said, "I own the security cameras and recorded a two-minute loop. You can stroll right up anytime you want. No alarms."

"Remind me to give you a big sloppy kiss."

"Please don't," he said.

We did not stroll up. We ran, quick and light, guns up and out. First thing we did was circle the building, looking for sentries. There were none, which was odd. Even with a couple of hundred thousand dollars' worth of security gadgets it was an oddly complacent attitude. In the back we checked the jet. The motor was cold, but that didn't mean much. I took our remaining BAMS unit and swept the mouth of the underwing tanks. The green light wavered and then turned orange.

"Doc . . . ?" I asked very quietly.

"You're weirding me out again, Outlaw," she said. "Whatever's in those tanks isn't cocci. It's some kind of chemical compound that isn't ringing any bells as biohazardous. We'll need samples for analysis."

"Can't do that now."

"Outlaw," called Top via the coms unit, soft and urgent. I turned to see that he had moved to a space to the left of the airstrip. I ran over while Bunny watched the building. He had a FN SCAR-L assault rifle with a sound suppressor in his hands and a drum-fed Atchisson Assault shotgun slung on his back.

I closed on Top and saw that there was another of the big dun-colored tarps stretching away into the gloom. Top had one corner of it up and raised it further as I knelt beside him.

Beneath the tarp was grass. Not sure what kind, but it was green and vibrant. Stiff stalks of it.

We looked at each other.

"What in the wide blue fuck?" I murmured.

Before he could even venture an answer there was a flash way off to our right. The vehicles were coming. Miles out, but coming fast.

We rose and turned and ran toward the house.

If we had time we'd pick the lock, go in quietly, listen, and learn. That ship had sailed. Bunny, Top, and I all pulled flash-bangs, picked windows where the drone thermals told us the inhabitants were grouped. We threw.

The grenades flashed and banged.

And we stormed in.

6.

We kicked in the doors and rushed through a lobby and a kitchen and into a big room that had to be a kind of rec room or lounge.

All eight of the inhabitants of the Lab were rolling around on the floor, hands pressed to their ears, eyes squeezed shut, screaming in pain and confusion. I saw the Xhosa woman, Bongani Jiba, and the Sotho guy, Thabo Mahao, right off. They were the only two black people. The other six were a mix of Asian faces—one Japanese, one mixed, and a variety of whites, one of whom had a distinctly French nose. They were all about the same age—mid-to-late twenties. All dressed in casual clothes, jeans, T-shirts. White lab coats were hung on hooks or draped over chairs. Only one of them had a gun—a small-frame 9mm in a Kydex belt holster. The plastic grips were a happy powder-blue color. There were no visible backup magazines, and the woman who wore it hadn't reached for the weapon. I know a lot of cops and soldiers who would have found a way to draw their guns even during the pain of a flash-bang.

Bunny took the pistol away and then gave cover, and Top and I searched everyone else. No guns. The only weapon—if you could call it that—was a Swiss Army knife. The one with the spoon. No locking blades.

Top cut me a look and I shook my head.

I knelt by Mahao because he was closest. I grabbed his shirt—his fucking Teenage Mutant Ninja Turtles T-shirt—and pulled him roughly to a sitting position. He was fighting through the pain to try to see me, to make sense of what was happening. I put the barrel of my Sig Sauer against the bridge of his nose.

"Thabo Mahao," I said, "listen to me. Tell me what this place is and what you're doing here. Lie to me and I will kill you."

He stared at me as if I'd stepped through a hole in the dimension. His mouth worked and took on about forty different word shapes before he managed to force out a reply.

"Who . . . who are you . . . ?" he gasped.

I tapped him with the gun. Hard. "That's not an answer to my question. Answer right now or I'll shoot you and ask someone else."

"This is our field lab," Mahao said quickly, his voice almost a yelp.

"For developing bioweapons?" I prompted, mindful of the cars on their way here.

Mahao's face took on the strangest expression. It's the kind of look someone gives you if you ask the weirdest or stupidest question ever. He said, "Bio . . . ? Wait . . . *what?*"

On the floor near him, Jiba was waving her hand back and forth as if trying to chase my words out of the air. "No . . . no . . ." she kept saying. "Are you crazy people? Bioweapons? *Us?* Are you mad?"

Despite being in pain and clearly terrified, Mahao gave me a crooked half smile. "Oh my god," he said, "you think we're *them!*"

As crazy as it sounds, he laughed. So did Jiba.

"No," she said, her streaming eyes going wide. "That's crazy. *Them?* You think we're them? You think we're those people who are trying to kill the world?"

"A lot of Toubou families are dead around here," I said. "Your jet's been spotted spraying something. Tell me what we're supposed to think."

Several of the people gasped, and two cried out in horror. Not at me, or even at our guns. They were reacting to my words.

"The Toubou . . ." breathed Mahao. "No . . . god . . . no. How did they die?"

I glanced at Top, who gave me a small shake of his head. Not a negation, but of confusion. So I said, "Coccidioidomycosis."

He stared at me in even deeper confusion and more profound horror. "Cocci? *Here?* Where?"

"Finger of God," I said, and told him the other locations as well.

Mahao seemed to ignore my gun. He touched my chest. And, for some reason, I let him. "Tell me what happened."

In my ear I heard Bug. "Incoming vehicles' ETA two minutes."

Bunny moved to the door, unslinging his shotgun. I gave Mahao twenty seconds of it. He was shaking his head the whole time.

"No, we weren't spraying the oases. Near there, sure, but not there. God, we would never hurt those people. They're good people."

"And what kind of people are you?" asked Top. "What are you doing with that jet? What are you spraying? And what's with that grass under the tarp?"

He actually smiled. "The people—whoever they are—are trying to kill the world because it's overpopulated. That's what the news says. But us—just a bunch of us—we're trying to *feed* the world."

"What?"

"You said something about grass? You saw it out back or at one of the test fields? That's *not* grass."

"Looked like it to me," said Top.

"It's not. It's something much better. Something we've bioengineered to grow even here in the desert. Something that is going to change the world. Something that will stop all those wars over natural resources."

"Ticktock, boss," said Bunny.

"What are you talking about?" I demanded. "What is it you're growing out here?"

There was such a light as I've never seen in anyone's eyes. Radiant, luminous, maybe even a little mad, but at the same time . . . there was a purity about it. A joy.

"It's wheat," he said. "We're growing wheat."

I stared at him. "In the fucking desert?"

"Yes," he said calmly. "In the fucking desert."

Jiba said, "And soon in every desert."

Mahao said, "Deserts make up one-third of the earth's total land mass. We can turn that into millions of square miles of croplands. We can feed everyone. Everyone. And all that green will drink up billions of tons of carbon dioxide and exhale oxygen. This project . . . we came up with it in college. All of us. Friends who saw that the world was in trouble. Our parents and their parents broke the world, soiled it, raided the larders. We decided to try and fix it."

"We *are* going to fix it," said one of the others. The Japanese man. "We cashed in our trust funds and raised money every way we could, then came out here to work. Away from our folks. And away from corporations who would try and stop us because abundance isn't financially useful to them. It will force the big banks and the multinational conglomerates to rebuild the global economy. That will take time, and while they're doing that, we'll provide the information on how to do this to everyone. Open source. Free to everyone."

"They don't want us to succeed," said Jiba. "The corporations and other people. We've been hacked more times than I can count. All nine of us had to buy fake IDs and go off the grid. We don't want this stolen, and we don't want to get hurt trying to finish this project."

"Nine?" I said. "Who's missing?"

"Gunter," said Mahao. "He's our resource guy. He went to N'Djamena, to the capital, to get some bulk materials we ordered. Seeds and a special chemical we need for the fertilizer. He was supposed to be back this morning, but he's late."

"Does he drive a Humvee?" I asked.

"No, why?"

"Do you know anyone who drives Humvees? Anyone you're expecting to arrive tonight?"

"Here? God, no," said Jiba, looking alarmed. "Gunter took a pickup truck. He'd never bring anyone else out here. We have a rule. Only the nine of us even know where this place is."

"Shit," said Bunny.

"Why?" asked Mahao.

Before I could answer, lights flashed through the window as the first of the Humvees swung onto the property outside the Lab.

I hurried to the window, and my heart sank. Men were scrambling out of the two Humvees. A lot of them. They were dressed in black, with body armor and weapons. Two of them dragged out a man who wasn't dressed for combat. He was a chubby blond guy wearing only boxers and a bloody undershirt. Had to be Gunter, and suddenly the whole story began falling into place for me. Gunter goes to Chad's capital, N'Djamena, to pick up chemicals and seeds. Either he said something to the wrong person, or our bad guys had people paying attention to anything out of the ordinary because *they* were conducting their own science experiments out here. I'm not good enough at math to figure the odds on how the Silentium goons wound up testing their cocci bioweapon in the same part of the goddamn Sahara as these earnest kids with their Lab. Million to one? People have bought scratch-off lottery tickets and become millionaires with worse odds.

From the damage I could see on Gunter's face, it was clear they'd worked him over. The kid was a scientist, not a soldier. He wasn't hardened to endure torture, and though idealism is often a sword, it is not a shield. They broke him, and I can only imagine how the Silentium cultists reacted to the news that a group of young nerds was cooking up something that would make a total joke of their entire argument. With a superabundance of food, overpopulation became a completely different thing. With deserts being turned to arable farmland, eight billion people weren't as firmly cheek by jowl. There was no substance, then, to a belief that enforced population reduction was necessary. The Silentium was about to become pointless.

And so they forced Gunter to betray his friends, and the cult sent a bunch of goons out here to kill everyone and burn it all down.

So . . . want to hear some more funky math? Work in these variables . . .

What if we'd gotten here an hour earlier or an hour later?

What if that *Nat Geo* journalist hadn't taken photos of a jet spraying something and tied it to inexplicable deaths . . . and had just enough of a conspiracy theory twitch that he thought he ought to tell someone about it?

What if the person he told dismissed it?

What if the story had not been told to the *right* person?

What if, what if, what if?

What if Top, Bunny, and I were not here?

I glanced at Top and Bunny. They nodded at me.

Here are some more numbers. There were twelve Silentium shooters and three of us.

Those odds?

Well, I like those odds.

7.

They swarmed the building.

Three of them kicked in the back door and entered fast, the barrels of their Kalashnikovs leading the way. They walked right past Bunny, who rose up from behind the big dining table. He opened up on them with the shotgun, firing 12-gauge buckshot from ten feet and cutting them in half.

Another group burst in through the front door. I don't know if they ever saw the grenade that Top threw. He timed it right, though, because it arced down between the lead guy and two on his rear flanks and detonated in the air. It blew parts of them out onto the driveway.

I had four come in through the shattered side windows of the rec room. They had to know something was up because the glass was already broken, but they came anyway. The Lab crew were in a storeroom and, I hoped, barricading the door.

I'd pulled the fridge out and turned it into a shooting blind. As the four climbed into the room, Bunny's shotgun and Top's grenade went off at almost the same moment. The shooters turned left and right. I was in the middle. Their guns were pointing the wrong way. Mine was not.

I hosed them with armor-piercing rounds. I emptied an entire magazine into them. You burn through a mag pretty fast. The tungsten-core cartridges didn't give a wet shit about Kevlar body armor. Not generally, and not at that range.

Then I was up and moving, hurling a flash-bang out the window because I didn't want to kill Gunter. I went out the window, tucked, rolled, and came up with my rifle, but damn it if one of the Silentium assholes wasn't down on the deck. The other shooter was. How the last man evaded the flash-bang is something I'll never know. He was three feet in front of me and tried to shoot me in the face, but he wasn't set for it. He fired a heartbeat too soon and the world seemed to explode inside my head. His own accidental version of a flash and bang. But I was already moving, bringing my gun up to try to stitch him from balls to brains. He swung at my gun with his own, which was not the brightest move in the world. He managed to knock my gun away, but the swing moved his barrel too far, so when he fired again he missed. Again.

Then we were chest to chest, our long guns too clumsy for that kind of fight.

In movies these fight scenes go on and on. Not in combat. You either end the bad guy or you get ended yourself.

I released my rifle and struck him in the throat with the open Y formed between the stiffened index finger and thumb. Before he could even react I kicked his knee and blew it apart. He dropped and I clubbed him down to the dirt with a pile-driver punch between his shoulder blades. Even through the body armor I could feel bones break. My rifle had slewed around on its strap, so I drew my sidearm and shot him in the back of his right shoulder and the back of his left thigh. Then I pivoted toward the other shooter, who was trying to get to his feet while shaking off the effects of the flash-bang. I had a clear head shot, but I needed to ask some questions. So, for the same reason I didn't kill the guy I'd just shot, I didn't kill this asshole, either.

He was nine feet away and I'm a good shot. I shot him in that gap between the protective thigh pads and the hard-plastic kneecap.

Aim at the center of the leg and you explode the base of each femur. Which I damn well did.

Top and Bunny came running around the building and into the driveway.

But our slice of the war with the Silentium was over.

Almost.

We took the weapons away from the two screaming men.

We even put field dressings around their wounds. Didn't want them to bleed out. This was in no way a kindness.

Bunny took Gunter into the building, and he kept the Lab crew away from the windows. Top and I dragged the surviving cultists around behind the lead Humvee. We used our knives to cut away their body armor. I heard the TV go on. Some kind of science fiction movie with loud dinosaur roars. The volume went all the way up. Bunny understood.

The wounded men were terrified. They were in agony. They cursed at us. They spat at us.

I knelt in front of the one I'd shot first. He was a white guy. Big and tough. His face was running with greasy sweat, and his eyes were jumping with pain.

"Silentium," I said.

I saw what that word did to his eyes. They widened. They shifted away. And I knew I was right.

"Do you speak English?" I asked mildly.

"Go . . . fuck yourself . . ." he growled. His accent was pure New Jersey. Fair enough.

"This is going to make it easy," I said. "I've got a whole bunch of questions, and I bet you know a whole bunch of really useful stuff. Names. Locations. Timetables. Stuff like that."

I think I was grinning. Not sure.

He wasn't. Top wasn't. And I doubted anyone inside the Lab or at the TOC was grinning. I probably was.

"We're doing . . . this . . ." he gasped, fighting the pain, "to . . . save the world."

I patted his cheek.

"Who gives a fuck?" I said. I drew my Wilson Tactical Combat Rapid Response knife from my pocket and with the flick of my wrist snapped the blade into place. That blade is only three and a half inches long. Length is relative, though. Scalpels are much shorter. It's all about *how* something is used.

"Names," I repeated. "Locations. And timetables."

He shook his head.

People think they're tough. They think they are able to endure. Gunter hadn't been able to resist them. This guy *knew* that. Why, I wondered, did he think he'd be able to resist me?

But . . .

He told us everything he knew. Every last bit. Who was running Silentium. Where the next strikes were planned. How they got the bioweapons. My friend there was very willing to talk. So, as it turned out, was his friend, who told the same stuff to Top.

As I said, we are good men, but we are not nice ones.

Nice ones don't save the world.

Nice ones can't.

8.

We sat in the mess hall back at Phoenix House, watching the news.

The lead story on every network was the dismantling of Silentium. It was, according to Jake and Wolf and Anderson and Sean and Rachel, a joint effort on the part of governments that set aside politics and fought for the common good. Sure. That's a good version of the story to tell. It'll be great when someone makes a movie. A feel-good story.

What's that old saying? When the legend becomes fact, print the legend. Sure. In the news, the only monsters were the millenarian cultists who wanted to destroy lives in order to create a version of the world *they* wanted. They were the monsters of the piece.

Top, Bunny, and I were not mentioned at all.

And that, I suppose, is how we all sleep at night.

NOT IN THIS LIFETIME

SHARON SHINN

Lili doesn't believe me when I tell her we were friends many times in the past, but she likes to hear the stories anyway.

"Where did we live last time?" she asks.

"New York City. We were waitresses then, too."

"When was it?"

"Nineteen sixty-five."

"So were we out marching for civil rights? Did we go to consciousness-raising sessions and burn our bras?"

I laugh. "No. We got stoned and listened to the Grateful Dead."

"Did we go to Woodstock?"

"That was 1969."

"Right, but we could have gone anyway. Were we still friends in 1969?"

I was dead by then, but I don't want to tell her that. "Not really."

"Why?"

I shrug. "Why do friends ever drift apart?"

Lili stops asking me questions for a minute so she can wipe down the last two tables while I refill saltshakers. It's Monday morning, the diner will open in less than half an hour, and there's still a lot to get done.

"How did we meet?" she asks. "Do you remember?"

"I was walking to work one day. You were standing under an awning, smoking a cigarette. I stopped and asked if I could borrow one, and we got to talking."

"Did you recognize me? You know, from before."

I turn to smile at her. Even in the gingham polyester apron that all Deli-Lishes employees have to wear, with her frizzy black hair pulled back in a ponytail so it won't get in the food, Lili is adorable. Bubbly as a cheerleader, friendly as a puppy. One of my best days, in every life, is the one in which I meet her again for the first time.

"Of course I did. That's why I stopped to ask for the cigarette."

"I can't believe I smoked back then."

"Everybody smoked."

"Did I recognize *you?*"

I laugh and shake my head. "You never do."

"Did we work at the same place that time?"

"No, I was at a bar down the street."

"But we became friends anyway?"

"We did. We found out we lived in the same neighborhood, so at night we'd wait for each other's shift to end so we could take the subway back home together. Felt a little safer that way."

"But we weren't roommates?"

"Nah. You were living with Adam."

"Adam," she says, trying out the sound of the name. I can see her nod of satisfaction when she decides she likes it. "Was he cute? Was he nice?"

"Really cute. Really nice. When we got to your place at midnight, we'd wake him up and then he'd walk me the rest of the way home."

"Did you have a boyfriend, too?"

"For a while. But we broke up."

"Why?"

"I don't remember." It's the first lie I've told her. This time, anyway.

"Was my name Lili back then?"

"It was, but you spelled it differently. With a *y* instead of an *i*."

"Is my name *always* Lili?"

"Mmm, no. Sometimes it's Lilah. Once it was Delilah. It's usually got a bunch of *L*s in it, though."

"Was your name Sasha?"

I shook my head. "No. I have a different name every time."

She's headed back to the kitchen, but pauses to poke me as she passes. "No wonder I never recognize you," she says playfully. "If you're always changing your name."

Changing my name, changing my appearance, doing everything I can to disappear or alter the course of events. Trying to make sure my life is different this time around. It never works. I just smile. "I like to mix it up a little," I say.

I follow her to the kitchen. We have to pass Armand, who's stocking the cash register and straightening the order pads and cups of pens laid out at the front counter. He wears his usual expression of brooding intensity, as if he alone has been told the fate of the world and it's a dire one. He casts me one long, measuring look and I know he's been listening to our conversation with a mix of scorn and incredulity. Armand has never said out loud that he doesn't believe any of the tales I've told Lili, but his expression has always made it clear that he thinks I'm either a liar or a lunatic or a little of both. But he's too aloof to say so to my face.

Well, he makes a point of saying very little to me at all. Fine with me. I have enough other things to worry about.

Back in the kitchen, Sanjay and Juwan are chopping tomatoes and cutting open bulk boxes of hamburger buns. Lili pauses to rinse her cleaning cloths in the sink while I get out the big ketchup bottles so I can refill the smaller ones on the tables.

"Did we know Sanjay and Juwan in New York?" Lili asks.

Both men look up in interest at that. Everyone who works in the place has heard some of my stories. I think Sanjay might actually believe them, while everyone else is too polite to say outright that they think I have an overactive imagination. Even so, with the exception of Armand, they all like to hear the tales.

I shake my head. "I don't think so. I don't remember them, anyway."

"My mother tells me I'm a very old soul," Sanjay says. "But I was probably in India in my last incarnation."

Juwan makes a kissy face from across the kitchen. "If you knew me before, you'd remember me now," he says in his deep voice.

I laugh. "I'll look for you in the next life."

"Plenty of this life left," he says suggestively, and we all laugh.

Armand pokes his head through the kitchen door. "Customers," he says, and backs out again.

We all look at each other, shrugging and rolling our eyes. No one can kill a mood like Armand.

"Time to go to work," Lili says.

It's my favorite kind of day. There's a steady stream of customers, no one is too much of an asshole, no one stiffs us on a bill, and no one I recognize comes through the door. Well, I mean, some of them I recognize—regulars who stop by Deli-Lishes two or three times a month. But no one I've known in a previous life.

Which isn't surprising, right? New York is almost eight hundred miles from Chicago. How many people would have made that migration in the past fifty or so years? Maybe I've left a lot of demons behind this time.

Maybe.

The only moment that gets a little weird is when an older woman, probably in her late fifties, takes a seat at my table around the dinner hour. She's big, a little flushed, as if the heat of early spring has made her remember how wretched it is to sweat. She sucks down the first glass of ice water I bring her, and thanks me fervently when I bring her a whole pitcher to keep at her table.

"Oh, you're a sweetheart," she says, gulping down another glassful. She's staring at me as she swallows, and when she sets the tumbler down, she's got a small frown on her face. "You look so familiar," she says.

"I've worked here two years."

"No, I've seen you somewhere else, I think. Have you ever worked in Evanston or Winnetka?" she asks, naming a couple of the northern suburbs.

"Nope. The Loop and Lincoln Park, mostly."

"No, that's not it . . . Maybe you were in high school with one of my kids."

"I didn't go to high school in Chicago. Maybe I just look like someone you know."

Her face shows dissatisfaction. "Maybe."

Lili's been close enough to hear this whole conversation, so she contrives to follow me to the kitchen. "Sasha! She remembers you! From before!"

"Well, I don't remember her."

"I guess you can't remember everybody you've ever met."

"I think she's just a stranger."

Armand, who is in back taking a fifteen-minute dinner break, glances over at us. "A bit of your past caught up with you?" he asks in a neutral voice.

For no reason, it's even more annoying when he says it. "No," I answer in a brusque voice. "She's nobody."

Armand shrugs. "Well, everybody's *somebody*," he says. "Even if she's not somebody to you."

I'm so irritated I don't even answer. I just grab a fresh pitcher of tea and go out into the dining area.

There are no more uncomfortable conversations with the unfamiliar woman. There are no other ghosts from my past who make their way to the diner. The day ends, we share out our tips, and Lili and I head for the L together. We don't live near each other, not in this lifetime, but we still catch the train together as part of our nightly ritual. It still makes me feel safe.

Though I know I'm not safe.

Tuesday is almost as crummy as Monday was fine. It's raining, Lili has the day off, I don't like the other two waitresses whose shifts overlap with mine, Juwan is in one of his rare bad moods, Sanjay has called in sick, and Armand is Armand. Because we're shorthanded, we're behind all day, so customers are crabby and everybody tips poorly. I have a headache by two and a blister on the back of my foot by four.

"Smile, sweetheart, it can't be that bad," says a smarmy-looking junior-executive type who manages to touch my hand three times as I lay silverware, napkins, and food on his table.

I feel my eyes narrow as I give him a cold, level stare. *You obviously have no idea how bad it can get*, I want to say, but I swallow the words. "Would you like anything else? A slice of pie?" I ask in a brittle voice.

He leans back against the seat and leers at me. "Pretty girl like you," he says. "I bet you have lots of boyfriends."

"Just the right number of boyfriends," I say. "So is that a no on the pie?"

"Sasha, that's your name?" he asks. It's embroidered on my apron; of course it's my name. "That's pretty. Is it Russian?"

"Nope. Just American. Do you want your check, then?"

"I'm Bill. I work down the street. I haven't been here before, but I think I'll be coming back."

"We're always happy to have repeat customers," I say.

"Are all the waitresses here as pretty as you?"

"Prettier," I reply. If I talk to him one more minute, I will break into a screaming frenzy. "Just pay me when you're ready," I say, placing the check on the table. Without another word, I turn and head straight to the kitchen.

I'm working hard not to let the fury get to me, so it takes me a second to realize Armand has followed me through the door. "Take your dinner break," he says quietly. "I'll handle his check."

Surprised, I look at him over my shoulder. "You don't have to do that."

He shrugs. "Guy's an asshole. And you're overdue for dinner. I'll take care of him."

I let out a long breath, deliberately unclench my hands, and then nod. "Okay. Thanks. But he says he's going to come back. Like, be a regular."

"We'll deal with him then," Armand says, and heads back out through the door.

Juwan looks up from the stove and gives me his first smile of the day. "He likes you," he says.

"Who, that creep at the table? He doesn't like people, he preys on them."

Juwan makes a scoffing noise. "No, you idiot. Armand."

Now I'm the one to whuffle with disbelief. "Uh, no he doesn't."

"Uh, yes he does."

"Because he's taking care of a jerk-off customer? That's his job. He's the manager."

"Dude looks out for you all the time. Don't tell me you haven't noticed."

I open the refrigerator to hunt up dinner. I'm starving, as it turns out. "Oh, for God's sake" is my only reply.

"You ask Lili. She'll tell you the same thing."

I'm halfway through a cheese sandwich and a side salad when Armand sticks his head back through the door. "He's gone," he says briefly. "And there's a new four-top at table five."

I cram the rest of the sandwich in my mouth and set the salad aside for later. "Thanks," I say. "I'm on it."

My shift ends at ten, and I have to admit I'm just slightly nervous as I take off my apron and hang it on a hook in the kitchen. I'm wishing I'd asked Juwan to work an extra hour so he could walk me to the L stop. Today's unsavory customer was pretty mild, all things considered, but something about him made my skin crawl, and I've learned not to ignore my instincts. Would he be the kind of man to hang around and follow a girl home? You hear stories like that all the time. Someone just catches a psycho's eye, and then it's all over. There's no reason for it. Just chance and misfortune.

I push my way through the kitchen door and back into the dining area, which is pretty full. The place doesn't close till midnight, and some of the biggest crowds come in after eight. I'm surprised to see Armand leaning against the front counter, talking to the night manager; his shift ended when Juwan's did. He breaks off his conversation when he sees me, and heads over to meet me at the front door. I don't wait for him to open it, because that feels stupid, but he's right behind me when I step outside. The rain has stopped, which is an improvement, but the air feels colder than it should in late spring. Well, that's Chicago for you.

Armand falls in step beside me without saying a word. I give him a sideways glance and realize I have to be the one to break the silence. "I thought you went home an hour ago."

He nods, then shakes his head. "Forgot my jacket and had to come back."

"Oh."

We walk most of a block in silence, except for the ever-present sound of traffic along Chicago's crowded streets. There's so much neon and street lighting and light pouring out from bars and restaurants that you could lean against any brick wall, pull out a paperback, and read the text with no trouble.

A few blocks away, I can hear the low rumble of a train pulling into a raised station and the scree of the metal wheels against the rails. Probably just missed my train and will have to wait twenty minutes for the next one.

"You live right off the Sheridan stop, right?" Armand asks.

"Yeah."

He nods and says nothing else. A few minutes later, we're at the station, and he's right behind me as I climb the open stairs to the platform where the rail lines run. "You don't take the Red Line," I challenge. "Don't you live in Irving Park?"

"Yeah," he says, and shrugs.

And that's it. He doesn't say another word as we wait with the dozen other commuters until the train arrives, as we find seats beside each other in the half-empty car, as we exit at another elevated station and make our way down the damp streets. I live in a residential block that's nothing but one U-shaped apartment building after another. Armand follows me up to my door and watches me get out my key, then nods.

"See ya," he says, and turns to go.

"Armand."

He turns back. "Yeah."

"You want—I mean—should I ask you up for coffee? Or a beer?"

He shakes his head. "Nope. Nothing I need."

I just stare at him. Much less lighting in this part of town. Much harder to read faces. "What do you want from me?"

"Nothing. Just wanted you to feel safe going home."

"But—"

"It's not a big deal," he says.

I stare at him helplessly a moment. "Thank you," I say at last.

He nods. "See you tomorrow."

And he's gone. Doesn't even wait to see if my key fits in the lock, if I make it safely inside, if the small apartment is clear of monsters. It does, I do, it is.

I still don't feel safe. But I do feel better.

The creep doesn't come back at any point over the next seven days. Lucky for him, because Juwan and Sanjay have appointed themselves my protectors. Sanjay has brought three cans of mace, one small enough to fit in my purse, and Juwan has brought a baseball bat. The bat and the largest can of mace have been left at the front counter, where anyone walking into the diner might spot them. Armand hasn't objected to their addition to the décor, and neither has Kenny, the night manager.

"We should take a self-defense class," Lili says Wednesday afternoon. "Karate or aikido or something. Maybe learn to use nunchucks."

"That's not easy," Sanjay comments.

She looks over at him. "You can fight with nunchucks?"

"Well, I took some classes, but—no. I never got any good at it."

"I think we should take karate," she decides.

"Maybe," I say. "I think there's a martial arts studio near me. I'll look up the schedule."

I pick up a tray of drinks to take out to one of my tables and see that I've got a new customer in the back booth. His head's down and he's focused on the menu as if it's a treasure map marked with caches of gold. When I've delivered the drinks, I pour a glass of water and take it over to him.

"Hi, I'm Sasha, I'll be taking care of you today," I rattle off. "Would you like to hear the day's specials?"

"Sure," he says, not looking up. All I can see is his hair, a tousled brown that looks like it should have been washed at least a day ago. "I'm hungry."

"There's meatloaf with gravy and fried onion chips for ten fifty. If you want the meatloaf platter that comes with mashed potatoes and green beans, it's thirteen dollars. There's also a fried-chicken special with mashed potatoes and mixed vegetables, also thirteen dollars. If you order pie with either one, it's only a dollar extra." Deli-Lishes does *not* pretend to be a place where healthy choices are paramount.

"I'll take the meat loaf," he says, finally looking up. "The platter."

I turn to stone.

His face is angular, with thick cheekbones and a pointed chin; a day's stubble covers the long jaw. One cheek is puckered by a narrow scar, while the other sports a tattoo of some unrecognizable glyph picked out in blue ink. But it's his eyes that are really chilling. They're dark brown, almost black, heavy lidded, incurious, cold. They seem like the eyes that you'd see on an assassin or a corpse. Someone whose soul or body is dead.

I can't tell if he recognizes me or not, but his expression doesn't change. "And a Coke," he adds, and hands me the menu.

My fingers are so nerveless I can't believe I actually manage to hold on to it. I nod dumbly and turn away, so distraught that I can hardly make my way across the room to the kitchen door. I shoulder it open and then just stand there, trembling, unable to speak. Any minute now, my legs will give way and I'll dissolve to the floor.

"Sasha? What's up, girl?" Juwan asks.

"I—" I shake my head. "I—he—I—"

Sanjay drops his spatula and sprints for the door, pushing it open just enough to peer out. "Did that creep come back? Should I go get the bat? I don't see him."

"Not him—not—" I can't explain. I can't form words. I'm incapable of taking an actual step, so I slide my feet along the floor until I am close enough to the wall to lean on it for support. My hands are palsied; I can feel my shoulders shaking. I might be going into shock.

Sanjay turns from the door and exchanges a look with Juwan. "Should I get Kenny?"

"Wish it wasn't Armand's day off," Juwan mutters.

Just then, Lili bursts in and comes straight for me. "What happened to you? Did that guy say something to you? The look on your face when you left his table—"

"She's freaked out about something but she won't say what," Juwan informs her.

"Did he say something to you?" Lili repeats.

"He's—he's the one," I manage to choke out.

"The one who what?" Juwan demands. By this time, they've all clustered around me in a semicircle. Lili's even taken my hand in a reassuring hold.

"He kills me," I whisper.

"*What?*" The word comes from all three of them at the same time.

I swallow and try again. "In every life. It's him. He kills me."

"Why would he do that?" Sanjay asks.

I shake my head. "I don't know. I never know. It's always random. He's a stranger. He shows up. He sees me." I try another swallow. "He cuts my throat."

Now there's another outcry, even louder. "What, you mean he follows you down an alley and just murders you for no reason?" Lili demands.

"Yes!"

"Is he some kind of serial killer?" Sanjay says. "Goes around killing women all over the country?"

"I don't know! I never learn anything about him! I meet him, and a couple of days later I'm dead!"

"A couple of days—!" Lili exclaims. "Oh, no no no. That is *not* happening to you this time."

"We should call the cops," Sanjay says. "Right now, while he's in the restaurant."

"Cops aren't gonna believe this shit," Juwan points out.

"Well, obviously we wouldn't tell them the truth," Lili says. "We'd say he looks like someone who harassed Sasha in front of her apartment the other day or tried to grab her purse or something. They come, they interrogate him—he says he was never anywhere near her place—but at least he gets on their radar. And he knows they're watching him. Maybe that'll make him nervous enough to skip town."

"It won't do any good," I say. I've stopped shaking now, but my body has turned so leaden that my bones can barely sustain my weight. He's showed up. That means my life is almost over. I'm not ready. I want more time. I want to live and live and live.

Not die and die and die.

"I think we should call the cops anyway," Lili says.

"There's no point to it. Even if they take him in and book him. He'll get out in a day or two, and he'll find me, and I'll be dead."

"No you won't be," Lili says firmly. "I'll stay with you, day and night, until this guy's gone. We can go somewhere! Up to the Wisconsin Dells, maybe."

"Yeah, if Armand lets two of you take a vacation at the same time," Sanjay says doubtfully.

Lili gives him a look of burning reproach. "If it saves her *life*, he will."

"It doesn't matter. This guy will find me wherever I go. I've tried everything. I've run. I've stayed put. I've tried to hide. And I think I'm safe, and then one morning I come around a corner and there he is. He kills me *every single time*."

"Maybe we should kill him first," Juwan says.

"Maybe," Sanjay answers. "But we'd have to be careful about it. He might be a drifter, but if a body turns up, someone's going to investigate."

My breath huffs out on what almost could be considered a laugh. Up until this point, I was never sure that any of them completely bought my tale of past lives. They listened, they indulged me, they acted like my story might be true, though they never came out and said so. But they're sure acting like they believe me now.

"You're not killing anyone, not for me," I say.

"Then you need to find yourself a gun," Juwan tells me.

"I can get you one," Sanjay offers.

"So can I," Lili and Juwan say in unison.

I am so deep into the funk of fatalism that I almost refuse. *What good will it do? I'm going to die anyway.* But then I pause to think about it. I've never had a gun before. Never had a way to defend myself. If I can change just one or two parameters of my story, could it have a different ending? Could he be the one to die, while I'm the one to live?

I might end up living in a jail cell after I'm convicted of murder, but at the moment that sounds like a most desirable fate.

Still. "I don't know," I say. "I'm not sure I can bring myself to kill anyone."

"Could you tase someone?" Sanjay asks. "Could you do that?"

I brighten. "Maybe. If I had a Taser."

"I'll bring one in tomorrow," he says.

"We still have to get her through tonight," Lili says. She crosses her arms and nods emphatically. "I'm going home with you."

"No, you're not," I say. "Then he'll just kill both of us."

She leans in closer to peer at me. "Has he ever? In the past?"

I shake my head. "No. But I never let you come with me before."

She settles back on her heels. "Well, then."

"It's too dangerous!" I exclaim. "I don't want to risk you just because I'm afraid."

"He can't kill all of us," Juwan says. "We'll all come home with you."

"What?" I say faintly, but Sanjay is nodding.

"Good idea," he says. "I have a change of clothes in my gym bag."

"Me too," Juwan replies. "In my car."

"I'll just wear something of Sasha's," Lili decides. "Oh, I know! That red shirt. I've always wanted to borrow it."

"You guys—" I say helplessly. "You can't—"

"Well, we can," Lili answers. "We're going to."

"Still gotta get through the rest of the shift, though," Juwan points out. "And that killer is just sitting out there, waiting for Sasha."

Sanjay is already smoothing down the front of his Deli-Lishes apron, making sure it isn't spattered with too much grease and ketchup. "I'll wait tables," he says. "Sasha, you can cook. At least until Our Friend the Murderer is gone."

Sanjay and I have traded chores before, on days he's too restless and claustrophobic to hunker down in the kitchen all afternoon, or I'm feeling particularly unsociable. Armand doesn't like it, because he's all about rules and predictability, but Kenny doesn't care as long as *somebody* takes responsibility for all the important jobs.

It's as if just by thinking his name, I've summoned him, because suddenly Kenny sticks his head through the door and exclaims, "What the hell, people! Get out here and take care of the customers!"

And we all scatter and take up our new or our accustomed tasks. I'm still a little dazed, but I'm able to focus on what I'm doing and I don't mess up any of the orders—at least not badly enough to cause anyone to send a plate back. It takes me a while to realize that my despair has lifted, not all the way, but enough to make me think I can see my way out of the darkness.

I've never faced the killer before with friends at my back. Maybe they can save me. Maybe they can help me save myself.

After our shift ends, the four of us climb into Juwan's ancient Ford. It's so old and decrepit that if I had known Juwan in my previous life, which I hadn't, he would have been driving the exact same car.

"The hell, J?" Sanjay says as he tries to avoid putting his foot through a rusted-out spot on the floor in the back seat. "How can this thing even *run*?"

"Don't see *you* with a car to your name," Juwan says as he starts the engine. The whole vehicle shakes so violently it seems like it's trying to vibrate into teleport mode, but it doesn't actually break apart into tiny pieces, as I expect.

"I'm taking public transportation till I can afford a *real* car."

"This is real enough to get us where we're going."

In fact, we make it safely to my apartment, which is much too small to house four people for the night, and which also doesn't contain any food. No one wants to make a shopping run because they don't want to leave me alone to face a crazed assailant. Eventually, we order pizza while Lili dashes out to the nearest convenience store. The men stay behind to guard me, and Sanjay explains how to use the weapon he plans to give me in the morning. Turns out it's a stun gun, not a Taser, but it still sounds like it will be simple enough to operate.

"Once he's on the ground, kick him in the balls," Juwan advises. "Then he'll never get up to follow you."

Dinner is pretty festive, since Lili picked up a couple of six-packs while she was buying breakfast food, and then I distribute people around the apartment for sleeping. Lili is sharing my bed with me, one of the guys gets the couch, and the other has to sleep on the floor. Sanjay loses the coin toss, so he makes a little nest out of all the blankets I can rustle up.

"Slept on worse," he says.

Juwan wriggles on the lumpy couch. "Not sure I have."

I blow them kisses from the doorway of the bedroom. "See you in the morning," I say. "And—thank you."

Juwan drives me and Lili to work on Thursday; Sanjay hops onto the L so he can swing by his apartment. As we walk from the car to the door of the diner, Juwan and Lili flank me on either side, shoulders close enough to touch.

I can't imagine they'll want to keep up this protective detail more than another day or two, but I am unutterably grateful for the effort they are making now.

When we push our way inside, Armand is behind the counter, restocking the register. His expression is severe.

"There was another creepy guy here yesterday?" he demands.

Kenny must have called him last night, which is surprising, 'cause Kenny and Armand don't really like each other. "Sasha's killer," Juwan says.

Now Armand's expression is thunderstruck. "Her *killer*?"

"From her previous lives," Lili explains. "All of them."

Armand is staring at me, incredulous, and I stare defiantly back. "They believe me," I say. "Even if you don't."

"Did he try to kill you yesterday? Did he threaten you? Did he say *anything* to you?"

I hunch my shoulders and head to the kitchen to get my apron. "He said he wanted the meat loaf," I say over my shoulder. "But I recognized him even before he said a word."

"Sasha," he begins, but I don't wait to hear what he has to say. I just push through the kitchen door and steady my mind for the day.

After all this, how does it happen that I am alone on the street not five hours later? Why do I think it will be okay if I make a quick, solitary run to the nearest ATM? Lili is taking care of a boisterous table of ten, the guys are busily preparing the orders, and I don't even think of asking Armand to accompany me. If the other three come home with me again, as they say they will, I want to be able to buy the pizza and beer. I want to show them how much I appreciate their help. And the ATM is only two blocks away. I can almost see it from the Deli-Lishes doorway.

I do remember to bring the stun gun. I carry it in my hand, hold my arm close to my body, try not to look like I'm expecting a monster to jump out at me from every alley and doorway. A cop car cruises by, and I just barely refrain from waving. *Hello, Officers! Glad to see you on duty this afternoon!*

The ATM is located inside a little glassed-in lobby that you can only access with a debit card, which makes me feel even safer. I'm the only customer, so I take a moment to check my bank balance—too low—before withdrawing a hundred bucks. Behind me, I hear the beep of the door lock disengaging as someone else swipes a card, and I spin around, suddenly flooded with adrenaline. But it's just some tall, well-made-up woman carrying a designer bag and wearing a resentful expression. I can't imagine anything going on in her life is worse than what's happening in mine, but I give her a sympathetic smile anyway as I sidle past. She nods, not smiling in return.

Outside the glass foyer, I shoulder my purse and turn back toward the diner. Maybe we won't get pizza tonight; I think everyone likes Chinese. Even Greek. There's a little place down the street from me that has cheap moussaka and spanakopita for takeout. Another six-pack, maybe a bottle of wine, and we're set.

I step past the dark, narrow space between two tall buildings, and a hand grabs my arm and yanks me into the shadows. I gasp and flail around, too startled to scream. Another arm comes around my rib cage and crushes me close, and now I can't draw breath to yell anyway. My assailant is behind me, so I can't see who it is, but the power in the grip makes me certain he's male.

Well, I'm certain it's my killer.

Not again not again not again.

The hand on my shoulder moves to take my throat in a choke hold, and the arm around my middle tightens even more. I can't breathe, but fear has gifted me with a lunatic strength, and I begin twisting and kicking wildly against him. I suddenly remember the weapon still clutched in my hand, and through my blurring vision and my frenetic struggling I try to remember how to engage the switch, even though I can't see it. I swing my arm back in a sloppy arc, feel the nozzle connect with his body, and press hard.

There's a buzz, a flare of light, and a howl from my attacker, who loosens his grip and staggers back against one of the brick walls. Panting, I whirl around, weapon raised and ready to use again. I'm also balancing on one foot, remembering what Juwan said. *Once he's on the ground, kick him in the balls.* But he's still upright, not even whimpering with pain, so maybe the charge has run down. Maybe the voltage hasn't disabled him at all, certainly not long enough for me to get away.

But as soon as I take a good look at him, I'm paralyzed. I couldn't run even if he were flat on his back, dead.

It's him. It's my killer. It's the last face I see, over and over, back through time, back through decades. He has come here to murder me, and no small toy will stop him, in this life or any other.

"Bitch," he says, and lunges for me.

This time I manage to scream as I fling my arms in front of me and try to scramble backward. I scream again, and he backhands me across the mouth before he grabs my shoulders and forces me to my knees. A second later, both of his hands are around my throat. I punch forward with all my might, aiming for his crotch but connecting with his thigh, and he hauls back and kicks me in the chest.

And then he slams against the wall as another body shoots between us and rips his hands away from me. I gasp and crawl backward as the newcomer punches my assailant again and again, each time bouncing his head against the unforgiving brick. But the killer is fighting back, and I see the flash of silver in his hands. A knife. The knife that usually cuts my throat.

"Help me!" I shriek, scrabbling out of the mouth of the alley, toward the street, toward sunlight, toward safety. *"Help me!"*

My vision is unreliable, but the sidewalk seems overfull of pedestrians. A woman screams, and a couple of men start shouting. A siren emits a single warning chirp, and suddenly two cops are charging toward me, guns extended.

"There! There!" I shout madly, pointing at the alley. "He tried to strangle me!"

They leap forward to position themselves on either side of the entrance. "Which one?" a cop asks. "There's two. One in a blue shirt, one in black."

I can still hear the sounds of the men punching each other, fists landing against flesh, grunts of pain puffing out of lungs. Still on my knees, I crawl over to peer into the alley. The man in the torn blue shirt is the figure from my nightmares.

The one in black is Armand.

"Blue," I manage, so stunned I can hardly get the word out. "The guy in black is my friend."

The cop nods once, then shouts into the mouth of the alley. "Hands up where we can see them! Both of you! Back off!"

Between the shadows and all the bodies in motion, it's hard to tell what happens next. But it looks like Armand reels backward, hands over his head, while the other man falls to a defensive crouch. The cops start forward, and the killer lets loose a guttural snarl. He grabs Armand, flings him in the path of the police, and takes off running toward the other end of the alley. The lead cop crashes into Armand, shoves him out of the way, and races off in pursuit.

The second cop curses, holsters his gun, and dashes back out, already shouting into his handheld radio, requesting backup. "You—stay here," he barks at me. Over his shoulder, he looks at Armand, who has stumbled out of the alley. "You too," he adds, then pounds down to the corner and out of sight.

Armand has one hand to the back of his head and one to his

waist, so I know he's injured. I jump to my feet. "Are you all right? What did he do to you? Let me see!"

"I'm fine," he says, but when his hand comes away from his waist, I see blood on his fingers.

"We should call an ambulance," I say, bending over to try to get a better look. On the black fabric, it's hard to tell, but he doesn't look like he's bleeding that badly.

"I'm fine," he says again. "What about you? Did he hurt you?"

I don't answer right away. I straighten up, and then I'm just staring at him. That serious face, just now purpling over with bruises. Those concerned blue eyes, focused on me as if they'd never been interested in looking away. "Did you follow me?" I ask wonderingly. "Were you watching out for me?"

Now his expression changes into something that might be pain—not a response to the physical beating, but to something worse. An emotional wound. "How can you not remember me?" he cries. "You remember everybody else!"

I am too stunned to speak.

He gestures at the alley, through which we can spot flashing lights and catch the shouts of police. I think maybe I hear a gunshot. Maybe not. "You knew *him* the minute you saw him! You knew Lili! How come you didn't know *me*?"

I shake my head and try to find my voice. "But you don't—you never—you've never remembered before," I whisper.

"New York," he says instantly. "The apartment in Greenwich. You embroidered the pillows on the bed. I hung green curtains in the window so the neighbors couldn't see in."

I gasp and almost double over. "Oh God," I say. I'm going to be sick, but I don't know why. Maybe because the world is spinning out of control.

He takes my shoulder, steadies me, pulls me upright. "You told me everything but I didn't believe you," he says. "I laughed at you when I didn't wish you'd just shut up about it. You were so mad that you kicked me out of the apartment. And then a few days later, you died. Just like you said you would. You died. He killed you. They caught him the next day, did you know that? Caught him and he confessed. He just wanted to know what it felt like, he said. It seemed right. The minute he saw you, he knew he wanted to take your life."

"Oh God," I say again. I'm even dizzier now, but it's all right, because Armand is propping me up, drawing me against him, giving me shelter. I know I should protest, because of the wound in his side, but it doesn't seem to bother him any, so I don't let it bother me.

"And I—I made a promise," he says. "To myself, to you. To him. I promised that if it happened again—if I saw you again in another life, if all of it was *true*—I promised that I'd remember this time. And this time I'd stop him."

"Armand," I say against his chest.

"I remembered you," he whispers. "But you forgot me."

I look up at that, all my dizziness disappearing in a wash of indignation. "I did not! The minute I walked into the diner, I knew it was you! But you'd never recognized me before. Why would this time be different? And I couldn't—" I made a hopeless gesture. "I couldn't go through it again. Falling in love with you. Telling you everything. Having you laugh at me. Not again. Not this time."

"It's all been different this time," he says, still in a whisper. "So what else might have changed?"

I don't have time to answer, because suddenly we're enveloped in a small knot of people. Lili, Sanjay, Juwan, who have apparently left the diner wholly unattended to come tearing down the street after us. They call out my name, they demand to know what happened, they snatch me from Armand's embrace to pass me from one to the other so they can crush me in a series of ferocious hugs. Somehow I end up back in Armand's arms, which feels so right to me and looks so right to everyone else that no one even bothers to comment.

"Why did you *do* that?" Lili cries. "Why did you go out by yourself?"

"I wasn't thinking—the ATM was so close—but then he was there, he saw me, like he always sees me—" The arms around my waist tighten so suddenly that I don't even try to produce more words.

I can see Juwan looking around. "Where's the dude now?" His hand is in the pocket of his camo jacket, and I wonder if he's carrying.

"Cops went after him," Armand says. "Maybe—" He shrugs and leaves the sentence unfinished.

Lili is staring at something behind me. "*That* cop, maybe?" she asks, and points.

Armand lets me go and we all turn to face the officer heading back our way. His face looks closed and forbidding, and it's clear something has gone very wrong this afternoon. Behind him trail three young men, shouting obscenities. He ignores them and comes straight up to us.

"My partner and I are going to need you to make a statement," he says. "About the man who assaulted you."

Armand puts his arm loosely around my waist. "Where is he? Did he get away?"

"The suspect is contained," the cop answers in a clipped voice. "My partner is with him."

One of the angry onlookers pipes up at that. "The suspect is *dead*!" he shouts. "Cops just go around shooting anyone they want!"

"Typical day in Chicago!" one of his friends yells out.

I stiffen with shock, and I feel all four of my friends react. "He's *dead*?" Armand demands. "For real?"

The officer's face takes on an even deeper scowl. "Paramedics are on the way," is all he says.

"Yeah, paramedics are gonna help when he's already *bled out* all over the sidewalk!" one of the protesters calls. "You *killed* that sucker! I got it all on my phone!"

I feel a strangled cry escape my lips, and then I turn in Armand's arms, hiding my face against his chest. I clutch folds of his shirt in my fists and press them against my mouth, trying to conceal the fact that I'm crying, but everyone can tell anyway. I hear the policeman saying, "Ma'am—ma'am—please—" I can feel Lili's hands patting at my shoulders while she murmurs that everything will be all right, really it will. Sanjay says, "I'd like to see this dead body," and Juwan answers, "So would I," so then the cop moves to head them off.

All this time, I'm sobbing. All this time, Armand is cradling me against him, kissing the top of my head. "It's over," he whispers. "Finally. This time. It's over."

It's maybe five minutes before I gather the strength to lift my head, and he kisses me gently on the mouth. "It's over," he repeats.

"No," I say, and I think that, even through my tears, my smile must be radiant. "My life. This time it's just beginning."

MR. POSITIVE, THE ETERNAL OPTIMIST

LARRY CORREIA

"Here, just take my money. I don't want to die!"

"Well, good," the man pointing the pistol at him said, "because I don't want to kill you."

"Okay." Stanley handed over his wallet.

"Thank you." The mugger opened it and scanned the driver's license as if to confirm something. Satisfied, he looked back at Stanley and smiled. "I still need to shoot you in the heart though."

"Wait . . . what?" Stanley hoped that he'd heard wrong, and that he would just take the money and leave him alone. "But if you shoot me in the heart, I'll die."

"Not if I do it *just* right." The mugger squinted as he aimed the little black gun. "So you need to quit shaking so much. Really, you're making this quite difficult for me."

Stanley looked around, desperate, but there weren't any witnesses. The two of them were the only people in the parking lot. The one single time in all the years he'd worked at this office building that it wasn't stupid crowded and lousy with traffic was when a nutjob came out of nowhere and stuck a gun in his face.

The thing was, his assailant didn't really look like a nutjob at all.

He was dressed the same as Stanley was, khakis and a button-down shirt, the uniform of boring business casual. While Stanley was short, pudgy, balding, and generally dumpy looking, the mugger was an average height, physically fit, well-groomed and clean-cut, fortysomething. He wasn't a crazy-eyed hobo or posturing teenage gangster, and Stanley had been robbed by both of those before because he was sort of a magnet for attracting assholes, but this guy seemed normal and rational. Like he shopped at Target.

"Just be cool, man." Stanley had to think back to all the previous times he'd been mugged, threatened, beaten up, bullied, pushed around, or otherwise victimized in his life, and . . . wow—there were a bunch—but calling on his copious experience, Stanley tried to calmly talk him down. "I don't want any trouble. You don't want to shoot me."

"No, really, I do. Sorry. This is probably going to hurt a lot."

He pulled the trigger. Stanley flinched.

Click.

When he opened his eyes, he saw that the mugger was looking down at his little gun, puzzled.

"Huh . . . there should have been a bang. Give me a sec. I'll figure this thing out."

Stanley turned and ran for his life.

"Whoops." There was a metallic clacking noise as the would-be assassin fiddled with his weapon. "I forgot to put one of the projectiles in the tube thingy first. My bad. I can shoot you now. Hey, come back here!"

This was the first time Stanley had exercised in several years, but it turned out having a lunatic try to murder you was a remarkably powerful motivator. He dashed between the rows of cars, shouting, "Help! Somebody help!" He looked back and saw that the mugger had started after him, and not having the lung capacity to call for help and sprint at the same time—Stanley wasn't really into cardio— he shut up and kept running.

"It's only a little bullet, I swear!" His pursuer was having no problem keeping up, talking as he jogged along.

Of course Stanley had to end up with an *athletic* psycho killer.

Red-faced and gasping, Stanley reached the row he'd left his car in. Even though he'd worked at the same giant data-entry company for six years now, he still didn't rate a designated parking space. Oh no, he had to park way out in Bumfuck, Egypt, and walk back and forth like one of the temp scrubs. If only he'd gotten that promotion to assistant manager—*then* he would've had a parking space up front and never even would've run into this guy, but he had been passed over *again*. Why did the universe hate him so much?

"Seriously, Stanley, you aren't looking very good. Don't have a stroke or something. If you die, I'm going to have a lot of explaining to do."

"Get away from me!" Stanley managed to gasp. But there was a glimmer of hope. He had almost reached his car.

Except his pursuer had easily caught up and was right next to him. "You're looking really red in the face there, buddy. I'm concerned about you. I wasn't supposed to do anything other than shoot you, but I'm going to have to restrain you now for your own good. I'll try not to break any of your bones in the process, I promise."

Before the killer could grab hold of Stanley's collar, there was a screech of tires as someone hit their brakes, but the driver had reacted too late. A red vintage sports car zipped past, narrowly missing Stanley but absolutely nailing his purser. The man went up the hood, cracked the windshield with his skull, and did several flips through the air before landing with a wet thud.

Stanley slowed down, stopped, and had to put his hands on his knees to keep from flopping over, because it turned out running while fat made you dizzy.

The car skidded to a stop, and the senior VP of marketing, Mr. Knudsen, leapt out. "Aw, not another pedestrian!"

The mugger-slash-pedestrian was lying in a crumpled heap, motionless. There was a whole lot of blood and white bits that were probably bones sticking out. Everything had happened so fast that Stanley was having a hard time wrapping his oxygen-deprived brain around it.

Mr. Knudsen was that type of senior management that had really nice hair and a trophy wife. "Did you see that? That wasn't my fault. You two came out of nowhere. Is he dead?"

"I think so." Stanley tentatively reached out and bumped one limp arm with his shoe. Nothing happened. He had never seen anybody die before. It was pretty messed up!

"I wasn't even drinking this time," Mr. Knudsen muttered. "My insurance is going to go through the roof."

"You saved my life. He was trying to murder me." Stanley pointed at the gun lying there.

"Really?" Mr. Knudsen mulled that over. "I can't possibly get in trouble for running down a criminal. Is vehicular self-defense a thing?"

"How would I know?"

"Aren't you Coopersmith from legal?"

"I'm Stanley from IT!"

"Oh." Mr. Knudsen wasn't very good at telling the underlings apart.

Then, like something from a horror movie, the assassin opened his eyes.

Stanley yelped. Mr. Knudsen jumped back. "Shit!"

"Wow. I've never been hit by an automobile before. That really does a number on the old spine." He seemed rather chipper, all things considered. "The guys at work are never going to believe this. Okay, back to business." Groaning, he reached for his gun.

It was pure instinct, but Stanley reacted and kicked the pistol, which went sliding beneath a nearby parked car, out of the gunman's reach.

"That was very rude, Stanley." He sighed as he crawled over, reached beneath the car, and began searching around for his weapon. Then he noticed the VP standing there. "Oh, hello, eyewitness person. Since I'm not allowed to violently silence anyone else, should any of your law enforcement authorities ask, this was just a simple armed robbery that went horribly wrong, resulting in Stanley receiving a gunshot wound to the chest. Very tragic, so on and so forth."

It would take the mugger a few seconds to retrieve his gun. *He had to get out of here!* Stanley's car was nearby. But it was a Kia Sportage with 120,000 miles on it. While Mr. Knudsen's restored custom Mustang was sitting right there, still running. Stanley hesitated. *Mustang. Sportage . . . Mustang. Sportage . . .* What the hell was a Sportage supposed to be anyway? So he ran over, jumped in the one named after a manly horse, and slammed the door.

"What do you think you're doing?" Mr. Knudsen demanded.

"Escaping." Stanley tried to shift into first gear, but it had been a long time since he'd driven a stick. "Call the police!"

"Fine. But don't *grind* the gears, you monster!"

Stanley burned rubber, literally. If he lived through the next few minutes, he was going to owe Mr. Knudsen a new set of tires. As the Mustang took off like a rocket, he glanced back in the mirror and saw that the killer had retrieved his gun and was looking a little disappointed that his target was making his getaway, but rather than give up, he sprang up and took off after the car on foot.

The dude was *fast.*

Stanley watched the mirror in disbelief as the mugger began to actually *catch up.*

He had to be on PCP or bath salts or something, but then Stanley had to tear his eyes off the mirror to keep from hitting any of the other parked cars.

By the time he skidded out of the parking lot and onto the street, he was doing fifty. Stanley spun the wheel to keep from hitting a passing garbage truck, but he managed not to wreck the VP's car. Once he was safely out in traffic, he looked back again but didn't see the guy who'd seemingly come back from the dead. Surely, he must have shaken his pursuer, but he wasn't about to slow down just yet.

And then something landed on *the roof.*

"What the hell?"

There was the *thump thump* of footsteps above him, and then the mugger casually hopped down onto the hood of the speeding car. Stanley screamed and swerved back and forth. He honked the horn. That part didn't even make sense.

The killer knelt on the hood and took careful aim through the glass. But then he frowned and held his fire. "All this bouncing is making it worse." He shouted to be heard over the wind. "You are making it really difficult to be precise here, Stanley. Would you please slow down?"

So Stanley floored it.

They were zipping down the street crazy fast, Stanley the IT guy screaming incoherently, and the guy on the hood calmly holding on.

"Okay, then. I'm just going to have to go for it. Don't complain to me if I hit you in the brain or something important." The killer aimed. Stanley instinctively ducked.

This time the gun did go off. Stanley didn't know much about guns, but the killer must have been telling the truth that it was just a little bullet, because it wasn't nearly as loud as expected. More of a *pop* as it punched a hole in the window glass and a *thunk* as the bullet lodged in the leather seat.

"You move pretty past for a chubby guy." Even though he was shouting, it still sounded like he meant it as a sincere compliment. "You've got to sit up though. I can't get a good angle if you're lying down like that."

Neither could Stanley steer, nor see out the window.

The Mustang clipped the back of a truck.

The killer went flying off the hood. Stanley hadn't had time to put his seat belt on, which was good in that it had kept him from getting shot in the heart, but bad that he wound up bouncing off the dash and getting squished against the floorboards as the car went spinning wildly through an intersection.

The Mustang rolled to a stop.

Wiggling, Stanley found he was mostly stuck, but the only thing truly injured was his pride. It took him a few seconds to scramble back up so he could see out the windows. There were other cars stopped in the intersection, and some immediately started honking angrily at the interruption. Other drivers were staring, concerned or surprised. Panicked, he looked around for the gunman, but there was no sign of him . . . until he spotted the lump lying in the road fifty yards away. The mugger had gotten tossed like a beanbag and, from the look of things, had bounced off the side of a bus hard enough to leave a man-sized dent in the sheet metal. Momentum was a hell of a thing.

Hands shaking, eyes blinking rapidly, Stanley just sat there, astonished to be alive.

And then the killer sat up again.

"Aw, come on!"

Despite being super messed up, the man took one look at his

surroundings, saw that he'd been flung into a bus, and then gave Stanley a very approving thumbs-up, as if to say, *Hey, man, good job eluding certain doom. Respect.*

"How are you so cheerful?" Stanley screamed.

The Mustang's engine had died. The right front fender was smashed, but the car was otherwise still in one piece. He tried the key, and surprisingly the engine started up with no problem. People had come running to see what was going on, some toward the Mustang and others toward the guy who was miraculously alive after being hurled down the street at ludicrous speeds. So Stanley laid on the horn to warn them to get the hell out of his way.

The thing was, since the bad guy was directly in his path, Stanley didn't really have a good way *around* him, but he could go *over* him.

Even though Stanley considered himself a peaceful, reasonable, nonviolent man, it turned out that when emotions were high, the decision to run over another human being was a surprisingly easy one to make.

So never laying off the horn, Stanley put the hammer down. Everybody else got out of the way except for the one he was aiming to squish. It turned out that even somebody who was seemingly indestructible still took a minute to shake off hitting a bus. Right before impact the guy actually smiled and shrugged, like *Oh well, that's how it goes sometimes.*

Bump bump.

Six blocks later, Stanley finally slowed down a little. His heart was racing, but at least it didn't have a hole in it. That had been close! Since he was in a stolen car and had just committed a hit-and-run, he probably really needed to call the police. So Stanley got his phone out and dialed 911.

"Nine one one. What's the nature of your emergency?"

"This maniac robbed me but then he tried to shoot me but the gun didn't go off so I ran but then my boss hit him with a car and he got really messed up and I thought he was dead but then he got back up so I stole that car and he jumped on it but then I hit a truck and he fell off and now I'm calling you!"

There was a long pause, as if the dispatcher lady needed a moment to digest that panicked run-on sentence. Only the voice that spoke up again wasn't the same one. This time it was a man . . . an annoyingly upbeat man. *"Wow, when you put it that way, Stanley, you've really had quite the adventure today."*

"You . . ." He stared in disbelief at his phone, but sure enough, he had dialed 911. "How did you reroute my call? No. How are you alive?"

"Both of those are excellent questions. But first, I just want to give you my compliments. Most people, when I have to do something painful or scary or fatal to them, they don't react nearly as decisively as you do. They hesitate. But you acted. The thing with the car? Bravo, Stanley. You are way tougher than you look. Let's face it. You are kind of a badass."

Stanley didn't get compliments very often and was momentarily taken aback. "Uh . . . thanks?"

"I still need to shoot you in the heart though."

"Oh."

"But I want you to know it's nothing personal. You seem like a really nice guy. After meeting you I am kind of surprised you have so few friends and such a negative and pessimistic outlook about quite literally every topic."

"How do you know that?"

"I checked your Facebook feed. But anyway, to answer your previous questions, the communications devices of this time are rather simplistic and easy to manipulate if you have a phased quantum field generator. And next, I am alive because I can't really die. Well, I could, and I have

before, but not here, or now. It's really complicated. Anyway, would you mind pulling over so I can catch up with you?"

"No!" Stanley reflexively mashed the red button on the screen to hang up. But nothing happened. The call wouldn't disconnect. His unrelenting assassin kept on talking.

"If you don't mind my advice—not that I don't think you're doing a terrific job on your own—but you shouldn't drive distracted. You might get in another accident. I'm going to put myself on speaker." And sure enough, somehow, now he was on speakerphone. *"That's better. This way you can keep both hands on the wheel for safety."*

Since he was an emotional wreck and trying not to plow into any other cars while violating the hell out of the speed limit and a whole bunch of traffic laws, that was actually helpful. Stanley almost reflexively thanked him, but that seemed inappropriate, so instead he shouted, "Who are you?"

"Oh, sorry. Normally I don't have a chance to introduce myself. I'm Chris."

Chris? That wasn't a very dramatic psycho killer name at all. "Why won't you just leave me alone, *Chris?*"

"This is my job."

"Going around shooting people?" Stanley was flabbergasted. Why would someone hire a hit man for *him*?

"It's not all mean. Sometimes, I get ordered to do nice things for them instead. But if I'm being honest, there is a lot of shooting. Stabbing too. And strangulation, sabotage, arson, spreading diseases, poison, that sort of thing. But it's been a really long time since I've had to use a projectile weapon. I'm pretty embarrassed about forgetting to put one of the ammunition thingies into the shooter tube."

"You are the worst hit man ever!"

"I'm not a . . . hit? Man? What is that? A man who goes around hitting people? That sounds barbaric."

Stanley was so very confused. "What do you normally shoot people with, then?"

"A graviton lance, obviously . . . Wait. Do you guys have those yet?"

Stanley tossed his cell phone out the window.

Except now Chris addressed him from the car's radio. *"That was really clever. You probably realized that I might be tracking you through your phone. Good job, Stanley!"*

That hadn't been what he'd been thinking at all, but it wasn't like he received positive affirmation very often. He worked in IT. "Yeah! You can't catch me that easy, Chris."

As Stanley searched for the off knob on the radio, he realized he had to think of something and fast. Not only was Chris apparently immortal, he also had access to some really high-tech gadgets. How did one escape someone so powerful *and* obnoxiously enthusiastic?

Stanley found his answer. Unfortunately, he found it by rear-ending a police car while he was distracted and messing with the radio.

Later that night, Stanley was lying low, or hiding out—or whatever you called it when you were trying not to be found by a homicidal maniac—at a bar. Because Chris had seen his license and knew his home address, Stanley was afraid to go back to his apartment. Though he had called his neighbor and asked her to feed his cat for him. Fluffles would be very upset if he didn't get his supper. Stanley couldn't go back to his office, because that was where Chris had already found him once, not to mention Mr. Knudsen was still really pissed off about his muscle car.

Home, where it was just him and Fluffles, and work, where it was a bunch of virtual strangers he never really had an actual conversation with, were the places he spent about ninety-five percent of his time. Which was kind of depressing when he thought about it.

So after the police had questioned him and then kicked him loose, he had fled to the place he spent the last few percentage points of his time, a sort of Irish-themed pub called Ox Knuckles that was midway between work and home, across the street from the hospital. He frequented this establishment because it had $12.99 bottomless loaded nachos and a weekly trivia night. Stanley loved nachos *and* trivia.

Now Stanley sat in a booth by himself, sullenly eating his nachos while holding an ice pack to the bump on his forehead caused by Mr. Knudsen's steering wheel, and feeling generally miserable. The police hadn't found any sign of his attacker. He'd told them about the trick with the radio, and how Chris had walked away from not one, not two, but *three* fatal car crashes, and so he had asked for protective custody, except the detectives had just kind of laughed at that. They'd said that Chris was surely just your run-of-the-mill, off-his-meds, lunatic stalker, who would most likely show up at an emergency room or morgue soon due to his injuries. Until then they'd just send a patrol car past his apartment once in a while. Other than that their hands were tied, budget cuts, so on and so forth.

Ox Knuckles was crowded with a happy, cheerful, Thursday after-work crowd. So if Chris did show up to murder him, at least there would be lots of witnesses. Plus, nachos.

But poor Stanley's head was still spinning. The more he thought about the day's events, the less sense everything made. There was no way he had imagined the weird bits due to stress, like the detectives had suggested. He was pretty sure Chris wasn't normal, and if he wasn't normal that meant he was abnormal, or maybe *paranormal*. And that idea really freaked him out, so he shoved it out of his mind.

"Hey, Stanley." He had been too distracted to notice the most beautiful woman in the world walking past his booth. "What happened to your head?"

"Lisa, hey. Yeah. Car accident." Because Lisa was basically a goddess, he tried to play it cool. "No biggie."

"Bummer. You doing trivia night tonight?"

"Trivia? What? That's tonight? No." As usual, when he saw her, Stanley struggled to form coherent sentences and turned into a stammering idiot. "Tough day. Tired. You know." He gestured at his nachos like an idiot. "Stuff to do."

"That's too bad." Her smile made him even dizzier than he'd been before, and that was saying something since he'd headbutted a steering wheel earlier. He didn't know what Lisa did, or where she was from, or anything about her because every previous attempt at conversation had degenerated into him being unable to use multisyllable words. All he knew was that Lisa was superhot, and that she was smart enough she usually dominated Ox Knuckles' trivia night. "You're my only real competition. Maybe next time?"

"Yup." And as with every time he talked to Lisa, his brain made it so he could not word good no more. "Bye."

Lisa left. He watched her go, then sighed and went back to ruminating on his inevitable assassination by a possible cyborg who might be from the future.

Stanley had started worrying that it probably wasn't a good idea for a man who only had three natural habitats to hide in one of them, and that was confirmed when Chris suddenly appeared and slid into the booth next to him.

"Hi, Stanley. Please don't scream again. That would frighten all these nice people."

Stanley realized he was trapped between Chris and the wall. Why had he picked a booth! Why hadn't he sat in a chair? Chairs had multiple escape routes! Stanley made a pathetic squeaking noise and started trying to slide beneath the table. Only he was too portly and got awkwardly wedged between the table and the seat.

"Wait. Please, stop sliding down. I'm not here to shoot you."

Stanley froze, halfway under the table. "You're not?"

"Not right now." Despite being hit by a bus and run over, Chris looked perfectly healthy. He had ditched his shredded and blood-stained clothing, and was now dressed to fit in with all the other bar patrons in jeans and a T-shirt. "My orders are to only shoot you between the hours of eight a.m. and six p.m., Monday through Friday."

"That's oddly specific. Why?"

"I do not know. But since it is almost seven, you are perfectly safe . . . for now . . . Ooh, what are *these*?"

Stanley peeked his eyes over the top of the table to see what Chris was marveling at. "You mean my nachos?"

"*Naw chows* . . . Fascinating." Chris reached for a chip, then paused. "May I?"

"Sure." Normally Stanley wasn't big on sharing, but he made an exception for people who were inclined to murder him. "Go for it."

"Thanks." Chris popped a loaded chip into his mouth and chewed. "Oh my gosh. That is literally the best pseudo-cheese by-product covered carbohydrate I have ever tasted."

"I know, right?" Stanley wiggled his way up until he was sitting normally. Maybe this psycho was telling the truth, and in whatever crazy delusional fairy tale Chris was living in, Stanley really was safe until regular business hours. "You promise not to shoot me?"

"I promise not to shoot you until tomorrow. I came to speak with you about my mission, in the hopes that you would quit being so difficult. May I have another? They are very good."

"Knock yourself out. They're bottomless."

Chris stared at the plate in disbelief.

"I mean, they are all you can eat. When these are gone they'll bring out more."

"Bottomless naw chows . . . amazing." Chris went to town on Stanley's dinner. Between bites he managed to say, "It always boggles my mind how in a time and location of such incredible treasures, so many of your people can have such a sour outlook on life."

"You were on Facebook again, weren't you?"

"Yes. It's how I discovered you often come to this establishment to engage in battles of knowledge, in order to establish your intellectual dominance over others."

Shoot. Stanley hadn't thought of that. That's what he got for bragging about his occasionally winning trivia night. Lisa usually won, but that was because she got all the science, history, and art questions. Stanley was good at tech stuff, pop culture, and sports. Not actually participating in sports, mind you, but he had a brain for the stats.

"You come from a curious culture." Chris continued pontificating, between mouthfuls of nuclear yellow cheese, canned ingredients, and generic tortilla chips. "Though your people are extremely adaptable, and by all historical comparisons most of you are thriving, it seems many of you like to signal your gloominess."

Stanley was feeling a little defensive about his general gloominess. "The world sucks, Chris. I keep up with the news. There's global warming, and overpopulation, terrorism, and war, and soil erosion, and straws kill all the turtles, and rising sea levels, and poverty, and disease, and bigotry, and racism, homophobia, transphobia, Islamophobia! Other phobias! And climate change, and the ozone hole, and crime, and global warming—"

"You already said that one."

"Well, that's because it's super bad, Chris! Everything is awful and we're all going to die."

Chris had been nodding along listening to Stanley's litany of tragedies. "That does sound pretty awful when you put it that way."

"What other way would you put it?"

"I don't know. Though I'm not sure what several of those things are, and I suspect that you just made some of them up right now, that sounds like a lot of bad stuff. Have you ever tried making a list of all the good things in your world to see how it balances out?"

"Uh . . ." Stanley stared at him blankly. "Huh?"

"It's just that you seem to put such emphasis on the negative that it begins to seem insurmountable. Perhaps you should pause to look at the positives? Like the entire time I have been here, I have yet to see anyone suffering from Ebola-AIDS."

"I don't think we have that here."

"Exactly. And I've not seen a single person get mauled by a land shark."

"That's a thing?"

Chris shrugged. "I don't know. Have you guys discovered genetic sequencing yet?"

"Yeah."

"Then give it a few years. But anyway, back to why I'm here. While I was going through your social media looking for clues of how to find you, I was struck by how even though you in particular are a very negative person, you tried extremely hard not to get shot today. Normally when I run into someone who is truly Malthusian in their outlook, they just kind of curl up into a ball and die. So I thought if I just tried reasoning with you . . ."

"That I'd just let you shoot me?" Stanley snorted. "Fat chance of that."

"If life is so terrible and doomed, why not?"

Chris asked that so simply and so sincerely that Stanley didn't have a good answer. He didn't know why he wanted to stick around this crap-sack world . . . But he kinda did. So he sat there awkwardly for a minute instead and then tried to change the subject. "Are you a time traveler?"

"Something like that. I could try and explain it, but it is very complex."

"Yeah, right." Even though Chris had demonstrated some un-canny abilities, that still sounded too far-fetched to be real. "Go ahead and try to explain."

"Okay. I was given some education on the popular culture of your people so I could blend in." Chris gestured proudly at his T-shirt, which though it was the right color for the city's NBA fran-chise, read *Go Local Sports Ball Team.* "To put it into terms you may understand, you know how there's always that thing in your movies, where someone goes back in time to kill that one Hitler fellow to stop that medium-sized war you people had? This is like that."

"Wait . . . I'm going to turn into someone like Hitler?" Stanley was rather offended by that. Sure, he didn't have many friends, and he knew he could be a dick at times, but he wasn't a genocidal dickhead!

"Maybe. I kinda doubt it though. You seem like a pretty cool guy, Stanley. You might just be the next Hitler's grandfather. I don't know. I don't make up the assignments. Nobody tells me why I do what I do, just what needs to be done for the good of the universe, and the parameters I have to work within to achieve those results. I think we've already covered my assignment's parameters pretty thor-oughly, so now we just need to get on with the heart shooting."

"Hold on. If you don't know why you're supposed to shoot me, how do you know it's the right thing to do?"

"That's a great question. You really are sharp." And Chris wasn't being the least bit sarcastic. "I've just got to go on faith that the big boss knows what's best."

"Wait . . . Are you implying that you're an *angel*?"

"Don't be silly, Stanley."

"Oh, good, because that would've sounded really crazy."

"Right? My boss is the crystal core of a burned-out star which gained sentience six billion years ago. It's basically a moon-sized supercomputer which searches for pivotal distortions and then sends facilitators like me to make improvements to the time stream. Angels are *totally* different."

Stanley nodded slowly, wishing the whole time that he'd ordered something for dinner that would've come with a fork so he could stab Chris in the throat with it.

The waitress came by and dropped off another plate of nachos without even asking if Stanley wanted one. He was a regular, so she already knew. "Hey, who's your good-looking friend?"

"Hi, I'm Chris. I'm from *out of town*." He pronounced that like it was the name of a place.

"Nice to meet you, Chris from out of town . . . What's wrong with your eyes, Stanley?"

Stanley had been trying to get her attention that he was being held hostage and to call the cops, so he'd been blinking SOS in Morse code. When Chris glanced back at him, Stanley tried to act normal. "Nothing."

"Good. I thought you were having a stroke or something." And then she went back to work.

Chris had not noticed Stanley's escape attempt because he was really awed by the concept of *all you can eat*. "Your world is *amazing*, Stanley. There are several different animal proteins, mashed legumes, and . . . can it be? Are the black circular things olives?"

"Yeah."

"They haven't gone extinct yet? Fantastic!"

It was weird to see someone get so excited over something so mundane. "I don't get you, Chris."

"And I do not get you, Stanley. Your world is relatively very nice, and you live in the nicest part of it. Your time is an anomaly of luxury. Kings and pharaohs didn't live like this. Your houses are the size of castles. You warm the air in winter and cool it in summer. You have cured most diseases. You live three times longer than your ancestors. Even your poor people are plump. You have this thing called electronic dance music. All that and no land sharks! How can you have all this and still remain grumpy?"

"Well . . ." Stanley had already listed the general concerns that all right-thinking people were supposed to be freaking out about. "My job isn't very fulfilling. I feel stuck and I work for a bunch of jerks."

"I work for an inscrutable crystalline entity that makes me travel through time and space to kill complete strangers." Chris reached over and patted him on the arm. "So I *get* you. We are bonding. In the spirit of camaraderie we should drink alcohol together."

Stanley the IT guy and Chris the time-traveling assassin drank a lot of Ox Knuckles' finest that night.

Stanley wasn't sure how many beers he had, but it was a lot. They just kept coming, as did the Jell-O shots, because Chris had been intrigued by the concept. Stanley knew he shouldn't have, but he didn't know what else he could do at that point—if the psycho killer wanted Jell-O shots, he wasn't going to be the one to get in the way of that. He normally didn't drink much, but he was a bundle of nerves, and a few beers took the edge off. But then he kept taking the edge off until there wasn't any edge left at all. It turns out you can put down a lot while spending hours arguing philosophy with your polar opposite, and Chris was definitely a glass-is-half-full kind of dude.

"I'm just saying, Stanley, you can't see the stuff that I've seen and not have a positive outlook on life."

"You just said you lived through the black plague!"

"Yeah, but it got better."

"But stuff doesn't always get better," Stanley insisted, realizing that he had crossed the threshold from drunk to emotionally drunk. "You've got to admit sometimes it gets worse."

"I never said otherwise. Life kind of fluctuates, up, down, sideways once in a while. But it goes on. Mostly."

"Life's not fair," Stanley muttered.

"Obviously. Sometimes terrible things happen to the nicest people, and there's not a thing they can do about it."

"Like getting shot," Stanley said pointedly.

But Chris seemed completely immune to guilt trips. "Among other things. I knew some really nice folks in Pompeii, until big rocks fell out of the sky on them. That was terribly sad. But after bad things happen, if you survive, you go on. And you can either try and make life better, or not. It's usually up to you. But I've found that working to improve your circumstances usually comes out better than sitting on the couch being angry that someone else has something you don't, while eating frosting right out of the can."

"You stay off my Facebook page!" Stanley drunkenly threatened. He probably shouldn't have posted about his frosting binge, but he'd really deserved that promotion. He drained the rest of his beer and then belched loudly.

"Whoa, nice one!"

Stanley looked up to see Lisa the Trivia Warrior standing there.

Chris wouldn't even need to shoot him, because Stanley died of embarrassment right there on the spot. "Sorry, Lisa. That was gross."

"It's cool. That was impressive. It had reverb. I missed you at trivia."

"Did you win?" he asked stupidly.

"Crushed it. I'm still the Ox Knuckles reigning champion." Then she noticed Chris. "Hi, Stanley's friend."

"Hello." Chris waved. "I'm from *out of town*. Would you care to join us for naw chows, fermented beverages, and jellied alcohol?"

"No thanks." She just kind of shook her head at the weirdo. "Anyway, I gotta go. Work tomorrow. You'd better not sit out next time. I need good competition to keep me sharp. Even totally wasted you're still probably the smartest guy in the room. Bye, Stanley."

Stanley waved drunkenly as she left. Belatedly, he realized he should've tried blinking Morse code at her. Lisa was a genius. She would've gotten it and sent a SWAT team.

"She's cute and nice," Chris said. "I think she's really into you."

"Shut your handsome face, Chris. Leave Lisa out of this!"

"No, really. I think you should ask her out on a date."

"Ha! Look at me. I'm a slob. A woman like that would never have anything to do with the likes of me! She'd never have my little future Hitler babies."

"That was just a hypothetical. I never specifically said—"

"I'm a loser, Chris. I'm such a loser that the world's friendliest Terminator had to travel back in time to shoot me to save the universe from how much I suck!"

"I'm not actually a robot."

"You are a robot!" Stanley had gotten pretty loud, and people were starting to look their way. "But I'll show you, robot man!" He tried to stand up, almost made it over Chris, and wound up falling on the table instead.

A few minutes later, Ox Knuckles' owner and bartender, a big guy named John, was helping Stanley out the front door. "Stan's a little morose, but he doesn't usually drink this much. Would you make sure he gets home safe?"

"I sure will," Chris assured him. "I believe the excessive alcohol consumption was the result of his stressful day."

"Wait, John." Stanley's speech was slurred, and he was seeing two bartenders, but he had to get help. "Don't leave me! I'm Sarah Connor and he's from the future!" He grabbed John by the apron. *"The future."* Then Stanley had to lurch to the side so he could throw up in the bushes.

Stanley woke up the next morning with the worst hangover he'd had since college. His head hurt, his eyes hurt, even his liver hurt. He was in his apartment, in his own bed, still wearing the same clothes just minus his shoes, and his cat, Fluffles, was sleeping on his head.

Suddenly remembering that a future ninja was out to get him, Stanley lurched upright, sending Fluffles flying. Panicked, he looked around, but everything appeared normal.

Fluffles meowed at him angrily, like *What the hell, man?*

"Thank goodness. It was all a terrible dream."

"Oh, you're finally awake." Chris walked into the bedroom, dressed like he had just returned from a jog. "Awesome."

Stanley screamed and flung his pillow at Chris.

Chris easily caught the pillow, and sighed as he pulled the little gun out of his pocket. "I really thought we'd worked past all this running and screaming last night. When I tucked you in, you even said that was the best conversation you'd had in years."

Sadly, that was probably true. "Are you going to shoot me now?"

"You've still got a few minutes left before I'm allowed to. I slept on your couch so I could catch up with you nice and early. As fun as this assignment has been for me, and I really have had a wonderful time hanging out with you, there's a fourth-century Byzantine who needs to get pushed in front of a speeding horse."

"Did you really go out for an early morning run before coming back to assassinate me?"

"It's a beautiful day. Why wouldn't I? By the way, I said hello to all your neighbors. They seem really nice."

Chris was just too damned cheerful, and Stanley was too hungover to deal with it. His soon-to-be murderer went over and opened the curtains to let in the bright morning sunshine, which really stung the old eyeballs. Then Chris pulled up a chair and sat down.

"I enjoyed our philosophical discussion last night. I think we're friends now. So please take my advice in the helpful spirit in which it is meant, and not as a personal attack. In the common vernacular of your people, it is time to *get real*."

Stanley laughed and then found another pillow to cover his face with. "I've never had an intervention from a time traveler before. Go for it."

"You really need to quit feeling sorry for yourself, Stanley. I see in you incredible potential, but as long as you blame others for your problems, it gives you an excuse to wallow in self-pity rather than move forward. You used to have dreams. You used to want to create things. Life is what you make of it. Though bad things will happen along the way, ultimately you are the one most responsible for how your life turns out."

"So now you're a motivational speaker too?"

"I thought it was pretty good. I gave this same frank talk to young Abraham Lincoln and he turned out okay."

"He got shot too."

"True, but it's not about the destination, it's about the journey . . . I read that on a poster once. But basically, Stanley, you are the greatest hindrance to your own happiness."

Under the harsh light of day, Stanley knew that Chris was telling the truth. Being totally honest with himself—and facing certain death made that easy—he realized that he'd wasted a lot of time spinning his wheels and whining about things he didn't even really know much about. It was just easier and safer than actually doing stuff. Doing stuff was *hard*.

But if you never tried anything, you'd never accomplish anything, and that kind of sucked.

Stanley sat up, feeling some pride for the first time in a long time, and said, "You know what, Chris? You're right. I'm going to turn things around. Starting right now."

"That's the spirit, Stanley." Chris checked his watch. "I would suggest a celebratory breakfast, but it is almost eight and I still need to shoot you."

With his decision made, Stanley just needed a distraction. Luckily that was the exact moment that Fluffles the cat brushed past Chris's leg.

Stanley pointed at his cat and shouted, "*Land shark!*"

Chris leapt up. "Crap! Where?"

And then Stanley tackled him.

The two of them collided with the window, which shattered, and then they were plummeting toward the ground. Stanley only lived on the second floor, but hitting the grass still really friggin' hurt. Stanley groaned as he sat up, and then realized that he was really thankful he'd hit the lawn, because Chris had landed on the fence, and was dangling there, impaled through the back by half a dozen iron fleurs-de-lis.

"Dude, are you alive?"

Chris lifted his head. "I am actually. Though even by my standards, this is quite the predicament."

"Oh man, Chris, I'm sorry. That looks like it really hurts."

"It sure does." He tried to wiggle free, but was good and stuck. "But my terrible agony is not the important thing right now. The important thing is that you stood up for yourself despite overwhelming odds. I think you've made some real breakthroughs. Well done, Stanley."

"Thanks."

There were sirens closing fast. "Don't mind those. I had already called your emergency services to report that a man had been shot in the chest at this address, so that they would be able to render aid in a timely manner."

"That was really thoughtful of you, Chris. Not the shooting me part. That part I was never on board with. But having paramedics already on the way was a nice touch."

"Like I said to begin with, I didn't want to kill you. I'm just supposed to shoot you in the heart. The crystalline entity was very specific, right atrium because that's the lowest-pressure zone."

Stanley staggered to his feet and waved his arms overhead so that the approaching ambulance and police cars would see them. He didn't want Chris to die, but it would be great if they could lock him up in some maximum-security prison for future robot people or something. "Over here!"

"Hey, Stanley, one last thing."

"Yeah, Chris?" He turned back to discover that one of Chris's arms hadn't been impaled, he still had his pistol, and it was now aimed right at Stanley's chest. "Aw, come on, man."

POP!

When Stanley came to there was an angelic being shining a light in his eyes, and for a second he was worried that he was going to have to rethink his longtime commitment to snooty evangelical atheism, but then his eyes focused and he realized he was staring up at . . .

Lisa the Trivia Queen?

"Hey, Stanley. You're finally awake. You're probably a little confused. That's normal. You're in the hospital. Don't worry. You're going to be fine. Luckily for you, the best heart surgeon in the state had just barely got to work when they brought you in . . . That's me, by the way. Not to brag but I'm pretty amazing at my day job."

Stanley looked down at the gold name tag on her white coat. Holy shit. She was *Dr.* Lisa. No wonder she always got all the science questions right.

While Lisa told him about his injury, the surgeries she'd performed to save his life, and how it was going to take months of recovery, his eyes wandered over to the flowers and get-well cards on the table next to his bed. There weren't very many, which was a shame, but not unexpected. However, one card was leaning against some flowers, and it stood out because the handwriting was very loopy, with an excess of happy faces and stars drawn on it.

Stanley! Good move with the land sharks. Those things are the worst! Because I think you are so cool I asked the boss. It turns out sometimes the universe has to be mean to be nice. He says the doctor needed to see you at your most vulnerable so that she could fall in love with you so your great-great-great-granddaughter can defeat the Glorgan

Armada at the Battle of Io. Shhh. That part is secret. I
told you that you should have asked her out. You are
the best.

—*Facilitator Chris*

PS What are you waiting for? Go for it!

Stanley managed to croak, "Lisa . . ."
She leaned in close to hear him. "Yeah, Stanley?"
"Wanna team up for couple's trivia night?"
She grinned. "I thought you were never going to ask!"

NO GREATER LOVE

KACEY EZELL

Jennilee Abrams put her fingertips to her mouth in order to keep from crying out. Tears ran unheeded down her face as her mother crushed her other hand in a grip hard as iron. Anna Abrams was, in truth, only about ten years older than Jennilee, but her marriage to Jennilee's papa, Dalton Adams, made her Jennilee's second mother. Anna eased up for a moment, causing Jennilee to sigh in relief, but then another contraction hit hard, and Anna clamped down again.

Papa stroked Anna's sweaty hair back from her brow, kissed it lightly. "You'll be safe here," he whispered, his words broken by worry. "I'll come back in a day or two, after the storm has blown over. I'll be able to get through the pass with snowshoes. But if we don't go, the company will never get the handcarts through, and this cave isn't big enough to shelter all of us."

Anna opened weary eyes long enough to plead with her husband. "Please don't leave me alone," she whispered. "It hurts, Dalton. The baby's too big, I can feel it!"

"Take heart, Anna," Papa said, "this is your first time. Your body knows what to do. I'll be back in the morning." Though his voice was strong, Jennilee could see the anguish in his eyes, and the terrified knowledge that he knew his words were likely a lie.

"Papa," Jennilee said, her voice barely carrying over Anna's harsh, panting breaths. "I can stay and help Mother Anna, I know what to do." And, in fact, she did. At fourteen years of age, she'd already attended and assisted three births. That was how it was for the Mormons. The regular doctors and midwives back east wouldn't dirty themselves to help, so they'd had to care for their own.

"Jennilee!" Ina Abrams, Dalton's first wife and Jennilee's actual mother, gasped. "No! What if—"

"Mama," Jennilee said quickly, cutting her mother off before she could articulate the fear that hovered over all of them. If Anna didn't deliver the baby soon, she and the child were both likely to die, and Jennilee would be left all alone. His brave words aside, the chances that Papa would actually make it back through the pass were minimal. If she stayed, she was as good as dead.

But if the small company of handcarts didn't make it through the pass before this storm hit, they were *all* as good as dead. The carts were smaller than wagons, and required at least one adult to push them along, two if they were heavily laden. Though the mobs who'd chased them out of Missouri and Illinois hadn't left their family with much, what they did have was on that cart, which was already starting to founder as the falling snow slicked the winding path. If they lost the cart, her entire family would lose all that they had to eat for the rest of the long trek to the promised land. Better that she and Anna died than their whole family suffer and starve to death.

The thought should have chilled her worse than the building wind outside, if not for one thing.

Jennilee had faith.

Deep in her mind, words of scripture reverberated, just as they'd done when Anna had fallen to the ground, unable to walk any farther along the perilous track toward the mountain pass: *Greater love hath no man than this, that he should lay down his life for his friends.*

She didn't know how, but as surely as she knew her own name, Jennilee knew that her Heavenly Father had a plan for her. And if this was part of it, then so be it.

"Mama," Jennilee said again. "I can do this. The Spirit guides me. I will stay and help Anna, and Papa will come back for us once the handcarts are safely through the pass. But you'd best get moving, before the rest of the company leaves you all too far behind to catch up with them. The little ones are cold and getting tired. We'll be fine here."

Ina Abrams stared at her eldest daughter for a long moment and then slowly nodded before dropping the knapsack she had slung over one shoulder.

"There is food in here," she said. "And water for two days. Be smart, and stay with Anna. You know what to do, like you told your father. Be sparing with the food, but not the water. You'll need a clear head." As ever in times of great stress, Ina took refuge in the practical.

"Thank you, Mama," Jennilee said, and accepted the hard hug for what it was: the substitute for the emotions her mother couldn't express any other way.

Dalton Abrams kissed his daughter on her head, then his younger wife one more time before he and Ina left the cave to take up the trek once again.

"Push . . ." Jennilee murmured, the sound of her voice lost under Anna's frantic panting and grunting. Things were not going well. Jenni could feel the baby's head, but Anna's labor had stalled.

Though she kept her voice and hands as calm as possible, Jenni fought to keep panic from rising within. She'd attended births before, but she'd never faced this situation. And never alone, without the wisdom of older, more-experienced women. And certainly never while crouching in the dark on a cave floor, while wind and snow whipped in white fury outside.

"Jenni." Anna's voice was barely a breath.

"I'm here, Mother," Jennilee said.

"I can't. Anymore. The baby. Is wrong. Turned wrong." Each whispered word came through chapped, strained lips.

Jennilee shook her head hard. "You can, Mother. You have to. Just one more push, just one—"

"Too . . . weak."

"Anna, you're not. One more, now push!"

Anna's hand squeezed once more, her strength a fraction of what it had once been. Her body squeezed as well, moving the child's head infinitesimally down toward Jennilee's waiting grasp.

"That's it," the fourteen-year-old girl breathed. "That's it . . ." Though she'd never done anything like it before, Jennilee cradled the infant's skull in her hands and gently, steadily pulled toward herself. Anna let out a breathy, faint scream as her body convulsed once more, and the child slipped free amid a gush of hot liquid.

Jennilee pulled the tiny baby boy out into the open air. His head and face were misshapen and bruised, as he'd tried to pass down the birth canal without turning facedown. She cradled him close to her chest with one hand while she fumbled about on the cave floor for the sheathed knife she'd found in her mother's knapsack. She found it, cut his cord, wiped his face with the cleanest piece of cloth she could find, and bent to breathe life into his tiny lungs. He gave a little cough, jerked spasmodically, and sent up a thin, high wail.

"I can do all things through Christ who strengtheneth me." Jennilee whispered the words to herself as she marveled at the little boy's perfect form. His cries continued, and Jenni turned back to her stepmother.

"Mother," she said, "Look, you have a beautiful son . . . Mother?"

She leaned close to see Anna's still face in the fading light from the cave entrance. With shaking hands, she checked Anna's neck for a pulse. Nothing.

Jennilee Abrams sat back on her heels, cradled the tiny body of her little brother close to her chest, closed her eyes, and cried.

She didn't cry for long. Ina Abrams had raised her daughter not to waste time with foolishness. Jennilee did take a moment for a silent prayer of thanksgiving, but then she set to work. It was one thing for her to sacrifice her own life, but this tiny boy certainly deserved his chance at mortality. So, she had to find a way to save him.

First, she chafed as much warmth into the baby's little limbs as she could, then she fashioned a sling for him inside her clothes so that he could share her body heat. The poor baby was starving, and began immediately rooting toward her chest, which led her to the second priority. Food.

Jennilee herself was of no use in that department, but . . . Anna wasn't long dead. Jenni's mind cringed away at the thought, but it came back to her with a great insistence. Anna's milk had let down earlier in the labor, Jennilee had seen it herself.

But she couldn't, wouldn't let a baby nurse from the cooling corpse of his mother. Instead, Jennilee took a clean cloth and manually compressed Anna's breast, causing some of the rich birth milk to secrete into the cloth. It wasn't much, but it was something, and the baby suckled the rag hungrily. Jennilee held him close and tried to consider her options. Without his mother to supply food, this greedy mouth wouldn't survive long enough for Jennilee's Papa to find them. If only she could get them to the company, there were other women who were nursing infants. They could feed him, and he would grow strong enough to survive.

Jennilee looked out toward the narrow opening in the cave. Unless she was very much mistaken, it looked as if the fury of the snowstorm had abated a bit. Perhaps she could find and follow the trail. It was a wide path; after all, it would be difficult to miss, even after fresh snowfall. And Papa and the other men were conscientious about reinforcing trail blazes on trees. If she bundled up well, and carried the baby next to her skin . . . and was very careful with her food and water . . . she thought she just might be able to do it.

What would Mama do, she asked herself, and looked at her meager supplies. One thing was certain, Mama would certainly not leave Anna's good coat and boots here to warm a corpse. Jennilee grimaced at the necessity and effort of it, but she removed Anna's outer garments and wrapped them around herself and the now mercifully sleeping babe. Anna's boots were just slightly too big, but they were in better shape than her own, which had cracked weeks ago. When that was done, Jennilee did what she could to arrange Anna's body in a position of dignity, and packed her supplies back up into the rucksack.

As she stepped out of the cave onto the trail, she began to sing her favorite verse of her favorite hymn.

> *Fear not, I am with thee*
> *Oh be ye not dismayed*
> *For I am thy God*
> *And will still give thee aid . . .*

All around, the snow filtered through the green-black needles of the conifers, and a hush settled over the world.

Jennilee might have had a chance, if she'd waited until morning. Not that she would have enjoyed spending the night with Anna's corpse, but in the following day, she might have had the light she needed to see her way.

As it was, the falling snow blocked the moonlight and made it extremely hard to pick out the blaze marks carved into the trunks of the trees. Jennilee stumbled more than once, and abruptly realized that she was off the path and hopelessly lost. She stopped, heart racing, nose and lips numb with cold, and stepped toward a nearby pine. The pack with all of her supplies was heavy, and though she couldn't very well put it down, she could lean it against the tree for a moment . . .

The snow shifted, slid, and the sudden sensation of falling gripped her belly as the lip of the cliff, hidden under the snow, collapsed under her weight. Jennilee wrapped her arms around the baby, cradling him to her chest as she started to tumble down the slope. Something struck her head and shoulder. She felt a sickening *snap*, and pain lanced up her right leg from her ankle. Her wind left her body all in a rush as she came to a stop flat on her back. For a moment, the edge of her vision went dark, and she was tempted to slide into the warm darkness of oblivion . . .

The baby squirmed against her chest. Somewhere far away, a wolf howled.

Jennilee clawed for her next breath, dragging it in by sheer force of will alone, and the darkness around her vision faded. Her head and shoulders stung with the force of hitting whatever she'd hit on the way down, but that was as nothing compared to the pain in her ankle. She forced herself up to a sitting position.

And for the second time, she had to focus on her breathing to force the blackness back. Her ankle was a ruin of rapidly spreading darkness, punctuated with one white spear of bone that poked out into the night.

As she looked at it, the real pain hit, and she had to roll back onto her side in order to avoid being sick all over the baby, still strapped to her chest. She emptied the contents of her stomach into the snow and wiped her mouth with one shaking hand while another wolf howl wound through the night.

"Heavenly Father," she whispered, her voice shaking worse than her hand had been. She didn't know it, but shock was starting to set in. "We are so thankful for all of the blessings that Thou hast bestowed upon us. If it be Thy will, Father, please help me and this baby now. In the name of Jesus Christ, Amen."

The only answer was a third howl. This one closer. Jennilee felt a deep, animal fear skitter through her. She fumbled with the straps of the rucksack, trying to bring it around to her lap so that she could at least get her knife out. It wouldn't be much, but maybe if she wounded one of them, its fellows would turn on it and leave her and the tiny boy alone.

Not that she could exactly run away.

Slowly, fingers stiff with cold, Jennilee eventually managed to pick loose the knotted leather thong that held her rucksack closed. Another howl sang out, followed by a few short barks. Close. So close. She fumbled frantically, hand seeking the hard reassurance of her knife hilt. Finally, her fingers closed around it, and she pulled the knife free of scabbard and rucksack all at once.

"We do not mean you harm, child."

Fear thudded in Jennilee's chest and the rush of blood in her ears was so loud, she almost missed the softly spoken words. Her right hand tightened around the knife's hilt, and her left hand went to the squirming form of the baby on her chest. She tried to scoot back, to put her back against a large rock or tree, but every movement jarred through her ankle and threatened to rip her consciousness away.

A woman cloaked only in her long, dark hair stepped forward through the trees. Jennilee blinked, swallowed hard, and kept her shaking knife hand up. A hallucination. This had to be that. Or else . . .

"Are you an angel?" Jennilee blurted, her voice sounding high and tinny to her own ears. The woman laughed.

"Not quite," the woman said as she took another step closer. She had just a trace of an accent that Jennilee couldn't place.

"Because I prayed to my Heavenly Father for help, and I have faith that He will help me," Jennilee said, though, in truth, she hadn't really meant to do so. She just didn't seem to be able to stop her cold-numbed lips from speaking.

The woman's laugh mellowed into a quiet chuckle. "Perhaps your Father sent us, then."

"I only see you."

The woman gestured to the trees, and Jenni suddenly saw the glint of multiple pairs of eyes. The wolves, it seemed, had found her. She let out a little scream and jabbed her knife outward.

"Hush, child. I said we would not hurt you," the woman said, easily catching Jenni's wrist and taking the knife from her frozen fingers. "You said that you prayed for help. We have come. Let us help you. You are badly hurt, and . . ."

At that moment, Jennilee's infant brother decided to let out a surprisingly lusty wail. The woman looked at Jennilee, wonder and disbelief in her expression. "A baby?" the woman asked.

"He's hungry," Jennilee said, slumping back. The loss of blood and shock was starting to get to her. "His mama died. I'm all he has left. He's my brother."

"How old?" the woman asked.

"Hours," Jennilee slurred. Her eyelids felt so heavy. A sharp slap across her icy cheek barely recalled her to herself. She forced her eyes open to look at the intense expression of the woman before her.

"We can help you," the woman said. "One of my daughters recently . . . gave birth. We can feed him, and help you. You're badly hurt, you know. But you must trust us. You must stay with me, for I will not do anything without your consent. I cannot," she added, and a note of anguish that Jennilee didn't quite understand entered her tone. "Child, stay with me. May we help you? We will take you to our home. Feed the baby. Only say yes."

The warm darkness swam around the edges of her vision again, beckoning. "Yes," Jennilee said, the word falling from her lips like the snow all around them.

The first thing Jennilee noticed when she came to was the scent. It wasn't unpleasant, exactly. Warm, musky, redolent of some animal, and overlaid with the welcome tang of woodsmoke. The scents teased at her, called to her, caused her to fight her overwhelming fatigue and force her eyelids open.

Another cave, she thought, finding an odd sort of humor in it. A small fire flickered nearby, crackling as various pieces of wood caught. The woman from the woods carefully fed it larger and larger pieces, until it grew large enough to sustain itself. The woman sat back on her heels, and looked over to meet Jennilee's eyes.

"Good, you're awake," the woman said. "I was worried that you'd left us forever."

"My brother?" Jennilee asked, feeling a rising panic when she didn't immediately see him. The woman pointed, and Jennilee turned her head to see the most remarkable sight. Her brother lay naked on a rumpled bit of fabric that Jenni recognized as her own cloak. His tiny fists held fast to the fur of the large, dark she-wolf who lay curled around him as he nursed lustily from one of her teats. Three small, dark shapes crowded around the baby, searching for their own source of sustenance. They appeared to be helping to keep him warm, though the mama wolf was careful not to let her pups' sharp claws or teeth scratch the human baby.

A primal lance of fear shot through Jennilee at the sight of the infant so close to such a large predator . . . but she held herself still. These wolves were not acting like she'd been taught wolves would act. They seemed accustomed to the strange woman's presence, and that mama wolf looked directly at Jennilee as if to say, *Relax, I am caring for him.*

Jennilee turned back to the woman. "What is happening here?" she asked.

The woman smiled. She'd removed her cloak and hood, and Jennilee could see gray streaking through the dark mass of her hair. Her face looked younger than the gray would indicate, and her eyes were a clear brown.

"What is happening, my dear, is that I am trying to save you and your brother. *He* is the easy one. He needs only milk, and luckily she whelped just a week ago. *You* on the other hand." She turned away from the fire to face Jennilee fully. "You are badly hurt. Your ankle is shattered, and I don't have the skill to set it, with the bone coming out of the skin like that. You have lost a lot of blood, and you will likely not live for more than another night or so. Unless . . . I can save you. But you must agree to it. For it will change everything if you consent."

"Consent to what?" Jennilee asked, wary. Her ankle pulsed pain at her, beckoning her back down into the welcoming darkness. She pushed it aside and clung to her consciousness. This was important.

"Consent to being bitten," the woman said, her words soft but clear. "You must have realized that I am not like most women. The wolves tolerate me, embrace me because I am one of their own. I am of the *loup garou*. I can take their form. If I bite you in my wolf form, your body will heal itself as soon as it changes. But you, too, will be *loup garou*. You will forever live between worlds, and I am very much afraid that you will never be able to go home again."

Jennilee's head swam with pain and exhaustion and the strangeness of the woman's words. "Why never?" she managed to say. "I will be with my family for all eternity."

The woman smiled sadly. "Child, I honor your beliefs, but I am afraid that if you take my gift, you will not die. Not naturally. My father was a French trapper from Canada. I was born in 1732, and I have not aged a day since I was bitten."

Jennilee felt the darkness crowding around the edges of her vision, and a roaring filled her ears. "Can you . . . take my brother to my family?"

The woman shook her head, her eyes intense. "I dare not approach them. It has been a long time since I gave up hope for humanity. They cast me out once. I will not allow them to do it again. Nor will I risk my family. But if you let me save you, I will help *you* take him to your family. We will bring you close enough that you may finish the trip yourself. But you must survive to do so."

"But . . . I . . ."

"If you choose to die, I will raise him here, with my family. He will be as safe as I can make him."

But he would never meet their remaining parents, nor their other brothers and sisters. He wouldn't have the blessings of learning the Gospel at an early age. He would be lost, and their parents would never know . . .

Once again, a scripture verse jumped into Jennilee's mind, as if someone had silently spoken the words in her head: *Greater love hath no man than this, that he should lay down his life for his friends.*

She couldn't remember the reference, not that it mattered, but the words seemed to fill her battered, aching skull, and just for a moment, the darkness at the edge of her vision receded, and she knew what to do.

"Save me," she whispered, feeling a pang even as she did so. *She* might not ever make it to eternity, but her brother would know his family, and would be raised with a knowledge of the Gospel. A fair enough trade, in her reckoning.

The dark-haired woman smiled. "As you wish." The darkness returned to the edges of Jennilee's vision, but she could just barely make out the way that the woman's shape began to soften and change. Her dark hair spread, began to cover her body. Her face stretched into a muzzle. Her ears lengthened and moved forward and up on her skull as she hunched down and flowed into the form of a gray wolf.

Jennilee lay back and let the darkness take over. The last thing she felt was a sharp pain in her arm, just above her hand. She tried to open her eyes and see what had happened, but the darkness dragged her back down into sweet oblivion.

Fever followed. Heat seared through her being, leaving her feeling scalded and light. Bright flashes behind her eyelids resolved themselves into fantastic, overly vivid images. Once again, she saw the blood from Anna's labor, and her brother's birth. Only this time, it splashed scarlet across the snow, white on red, like the bone from her ankle against her ruined leg . . .

Pain stabbed through her, radiating outward from her center. Great, jagged needles of bone, starting in her abdomen and pushing outward in all directions . . .

More heat, and the inner surge that usually accompanied fear. Her heart raced, thudding loudly, too loudly in her ears. Her skin twitched all over her body.

Jennilee opened her mouth to scream, but all she could do was howl.

When Jennilee could finally open her eyes again, everything looked wrong. The colors were off, she realized. Muted, somehow. She shook her head, but even her neck moved differently. Everything moved differently.

Slowly, she got to her feet. Her balance felt different as well, but her body seemed to adjust to itself quickly. Jennilee turned her head, and saw the gray female watching her.

She approved, Jenni realized. She didn't know how she knew that, but something in the other wolf's posture seemed to tell her, very clearly, that she, Jennilee, was adapting well. Jennilee took an experimental step forward, then turned away from the brightness of the fire.

That flame that had been so welcome and calming before seemed only hot and destructive now. Plus, it stank, laying its thick scent over everything else in the cave. Jenni realized that she could make out the scent of each individual wolf, and they were so *varied*! She inhaled deeply, pulling the air in through her nose, and her brain registered the current and recent locations of each of the pack members. Their scents lay across the cave like memories, crossing and recrossing.

And there, in the corner, was one whose scent was so very different. Jenni blinked, squinted, and saw the figure of her little brother curled up with his nursemaid. Her nose told her that he slept, for she could make out the milk on his breath. The black mother wolf looked at Jenni, amusement in the line of her ears.

He is a greedy, hungry one, but I have fed him full, she seemed to say. *He will sleep well now; my pups and I will keep him warm. He is safe. So are you.*

The words weren't words, as such, but if Jenni had to translate the mother wolf's expression and . . . communication (and it was clear that it was a deliberate communication, though Jenni couldn't have said how), that was how she would have articulated it. Before. When she spoke.

The gray wolf nipped at her shoulder to get her attention, then flipped her tail in a gesture that clearly said, *Come*, and she padded out to the entrance of the den.

Jenni followed, slowly at first, but with more confidence as she worked out how to move on four feet and coordinate her tail. As she stepped outside, the night exploded into sensation.

First, of course, were the scents. It was as if she could feel them on her tongue. She could smell the comings and goings of the pack near the mouth of the den, but she could also smell the sharp crispness of the snow, and the softening that meant the snowfall would end soon. She could almost taste the underlying soil, and the blanket of pine needles that lived therein. The wood of the trees, the iron tang of the granite boulders, the warmth of the wind, her old blood . . . it made her head spin in dizzying circles as the scents swarmed her under.

Bodies brushed by her, fur crackling with static against her own fur. The warm, rich scent of the pack enveloped her as they swarmed, bumping playfully against her shoulders and flanks. Every touch, every nip a welcome, a jolt of joy at her existence, her choice to go on living.

Jenni took another step, feeling the snow crunch and compact beneath her splayed paw. The night even *sounded* different: she heard notes from the night animals that she'd never imagined existed.

The gray wolf looked back at her again and beckoned her onward once more before turning and beginning to lope away through the trees. Jenni took a deep breath (even that felt so strange!) and took another step, and then another . . .

And then she began to run.

Her body flowed like water. Jennilee could feel the power in her muscles as they contracted and lengthened with every stride. The wind of her passage ruffled over her fur, making her skin tingle with awareness. The scents of the night wrapped around her, drew her forward in the sheer joy of motion. Snow flew upward from her prints, dusting around her in a cloud that seemed to slow time itself as she ran.

Or was it flying? She never could decide, not even years later, when she looked back on that first glorious time.

Together, the pack streamed through the trees. The moon peeked through the thinning clouds and turned the air silver around them. Jenni felt that she could have run forever, drunk on the joy of it all. *This* was what it meant to be alive! *This* she could do forever . . .

Would do. Forever.

Jennilee came to a sudden stop, her joy draining away as she realized what she'd done. She could never go home, never go back to her family, and at the end of it all, she would never be reunited with them in eternity.

Between one thought and the next, she was human again. Whole and naked, she crouched in the snow, shivering in the night.

"Now you see," the gray woman said, her voice coming through the darkness before Jenni could see her. She'd known she was there, though. Her scent had given her away.

"Ye-yes," Jenni whispered, her words puffing into a cloud in the crystalline night.

"Do you regret it?"

Did she? The thought of her family was a piercing ache that closed her throat and left her heart feeling shattered. But then, the thought of her brother . . . and the joy of it all . . .

"'Adam fell that men might be,'" Jenni whispered, half to herself, half to the gray woman, "'and men are, that they might have joy.' No," she said, lifting her eyes to the woman's. "I do not regret this. Say what you will, I feel . . ." She took a deep breath. "I *believe* that my Heavenly Father still loves me. And I believe that He wants me to see my brother safe."

The gray woman smiled, sadness in her eyes. "Well. I envy you. Come. Let us return to the den. There is much to be done to prepare for your journey."

In the next few days, Jennilee learned to hunt, both alone and with the pack. She continued to feel a fierce joy in running with the other wolves. Without realizing it, her canine heart fell into the relationship of being one of the pack. It was a bond even stronger than the love she felt for her human brothers and sisters. Without the pack, one was wretched and vulnerable. With the pack, one was invincible.

Jenni's human mind rebelled against this closeness, and she tried in vain to pull away, but the pack would not have it. Whether she walked on two legs or four, they crowded around her, swarming her resistance with the totality of their love.

"We could be your family now, you know," the gray woman said softly one night. She had been teaching Jennilee to change forms at will. Human to wolf and back again, again and again until Jenni lay exhausted by the woman's small fire. She made one of these most nights when they would be spending any time in skin rather than fur. Firelight was easier on human eyes, and the warmth was a comfort.

Jenni curled tighter into herself, drawing her shoulders up near her head. "I know," she said, misery shading her tone. "I am so grateful . . . but I miss my papa and mama . . . and all the little ones." She didn't say it out loud, but the deep joy that she felt in the pack felt like a betrayal of her blood family.

The gray woman nodded, her eyes sympathetic. "I understand. I missed my human family for a very long time. But you must prepare yourself. They will not know you, not as you truly are now. They will think you a monster."

Jenni shook her head. "My family loves me."

The gray woman smiled sadly. "They love who you were, child. Who you are now is a mystery and a threat. I do not say this to pain you," she added gently, reaching out to brush Jenni's hair back from her eyes. Before she could hold herself from doing so, Jenni flinched backward, and for just a moment, pain flared in the woman's dark eyes.

"I . . . thank you," Jenni said, haltingly. "You have been most kind. I just . . . I find it hard."

"So do I, dear child," the woman whispered as she turned away. "So do I." She shivered, and gray fur flowed like water over her as she took her canine form.

Tears gathered in Jenni's eyes, but she didn't know what to say. So she just laid her head down and let exhausted sleep claim her.

They started out the next night. Jenni went in human form, that she might carry the baby under her coat as before. The pack swirled around her feet as she stepped out of the den. The night was crystal sharp and cold, but stars studded the night sky without a wisp of cloud to cover them. Jenni staggered slightly as she began to walk. Her senses, though stronger than before, were pale and paltry compared to her wolf form's, and she felt a sudden ache to transform.

But then the baby squirmed against her chest, cuddling his sleepy self closer to her warmth and sighing in his slumber. Despite everything, Jenni smiled. The days in the wolf den had been good for him, she reflected. He'd nursed nearly constantly, thanks to the patience of his lupine nursemaid. His cheeks and body had begun to take on the soft roundness that Jenni associated with healthy infants . . . and which roundness had been all too scarce for the little ones along the trail.

The dark mother wolf bumped against Jenni's hip and looked at her with an expression that clearly said, *Is he all right?* Jenni smiled and nodded, patting the warm bundle softly. The dark mother wolf's posture changed—Jenni couldn't have said how—but the message was unmistakable. The dark mother wolf cared for her tiny, two-legged pup just as much as she did for his four-legged siblings tussling about them in the snow.

Up ahead, the gray wolf gave a short bark, and the pack started moving. Jenni followed, unable to keep up on her two legs. The dark mother wolf and her pups stayed back as well, and in this manner, they covered a fair amount of ground before the sun began to rise at their backs.

Jenni was tired but not exhausted when they finally stopped. The gray wolf had found a temporary den site, and the pack waited there with small game. As Jenni approached, the gray wolf flowed into her human form and began to gather materials to build another small fire.

Jennilee looked at her for a long moment, her heart aching in her chest. The gray woman's sadness seemed to radiate outward from where she crouched over the fire. Jenni wanted to say something, but words felt inadequate. Instead, she pulled her own cloak off and went to wrap it around the gray woman's shoulders. She didn't seem to mind being naked, not the way Jenni did, but it was cold, and she would feel the chill on her human skin.

The gray woman looked up in surprise. "Thank you, child," she said softly. "But do you not need it?"

"Not right now," Jenni said, feeling suddenly shy. She gave the woman a smile and went back to sit beside the dark mother wolf, busy nursing a greedy baby boy.

Jenni spent the rest of the day warmed by the bodies of the pack, holding her brother against her chest, sleeping deeply in the knowledge that they were, for the moment, safe.

It took them three days to find the company. When they did, the gray wolf led the pack around and uphill of the group of humans. Jenni noticed that the gray one was careful to keep the humans upwind. She didn't know if this was paranoia or hunting instinct at work, but it made sense to the wolf part of her brain, and so she did not protest. That dawn, when they stopped, the gray woman drew Jenni aside.

"When you go to them, you must be prepared," she said softly, her eyes haunted and solemn. "They will think you dead, and there will be much rejoicing that you have returned to them. You will be tempted to stay, but I warn you, you must not give in to that temptation. You are different now. Their eyes will not recognize it, but their instincts will tell them that you are to be feared. The longer you stay with them, the more painful it will be, in the end." She blinked suddenly and shook her head, as if shaking away an old memory.

"We will return to our original den place. You may find us there, if you wish. You have a place with us, now and always. In time, you may find a mate that suits you, and you may establish a pack of your own." Her lips curved in a smile, and she reached out to touch her fingertips to Jennilee's cheek. "You have lost your human family, but you can still have a family of your own."

Jenni blinked. "I can?" she asked. All of a sudden it was incredibly hard for her to focus. Part of her yearned to run down the hill to find her parents, but the gray woman's words rang true with a horrible finality.

Her smile grew. "You can, my dear. You can mate, have pups, have a life as a wolf. The wolves will never reject you. Remember that, child."

Jenni swallowed hard, and stroked the warm bundle that was her sleeping brother. "I will," she promised.

The woman nodded, touched her cheek one more time, and then the gray fur flowed over her as she resumed her lupine form. Her eyes met Jennilee's, and then she turned and disappeared into the trees.

One by one, the other wolves followed her, until only the dark mother wolf remained. She walked up to Jennilee and touched her nose to the blanket-wrapped bundle on Jenni's chest. Then she, too, faded into the forest.

But for her brother, Jenni was alone. She licked her lips and shrugged her pack more securely onto her shoulders, and started down the hill toward her family.

Her mother saw her first. Ina had been melting snow for wash water when Jennilee emerged from the tree line. Jenni's mother straightened up, shooed her children back into a nearby lean-to, and walked unhurriedly toward the cloak-swathed figure that stumbled toward her fire.

"Mama," Jenni called out, her voice hoarse with emotion.

Ina's eyes widened. "Jennilee?" she whispered, breath puffing into a cloud as she spoke.

Jennilee couldn't help it. She collapsed to her knees in the muddy snow and began to cry deep, racking sobs. Her mother's arms came about her, hard, as she knelt in the snow to embrace her daughter. The baby squirmed in protest.

"Jenni! The child?" The stunned hope in Ina's voice was heart-breaking. It told Jenni more clearly than anything else how much her stoic mother had mourned them.

"H-Here, Mama," Jenni said, forcing the words out as she fumbled at the lacings to her cloak and coat. She opened the heavy outer garment and exposed the tiny baby in his sling. He let out a healthy-sounding squawk of protest at the cold air and wriggled. Ina's hands flew to her mouth as her eyes filled with tears. She laughed, the sound filled with joy, and wiped her eyes. Then Ina Abrams stood and reached to help Jenni stand as well.

"Well," Jenni's mother said briskly. "We'd better get the two of you inside, out of the cold. Hyrum, go find your father," she called to her son, Jenni's middle brother. Jenni smiled at him and got his shy smile in return before he took off at a run to tell Dalton Abrams of his children's miraculous return.

Naturally, everyone in the company wanted to hear the story. It was only by pleading exhaustion that Jennilee was able to keep from telling her tale to the entire group. The thought of doing so shot a bolt of fear clean through her heart, and she had the unmistakable feeling that to do so would be a very bad idea. With the gray woman's warnings ringing in her ears, she begged her papa and mama to let her tell them alone, first.

She told them all of it. Anna's labor, the blood, the milk, the snow. She told them about falling down the cliff, amazed at the dispassionate sound of her own words. She told them about her prayers, the gray woman, and about the wolves.

She told them of her choice. She showed them the scar from the bite.

Papa reached out and took her hand and began running his thumb over the distinctively shaped scar. It looked as if it had been there for a very long time, but she hadn't had it before the storm, and he knew it. Jennilee looked at her mother, who sat across from her in the lean-to, cuddling the baby and watching her with a grave expression.

"Do you believe me?" Jenni asked softly in the silence that followed her story. Papa's fingers squeezed her hand briefly.

"My girl," he replied. "We believe that something happened. Clearly, the Lord saw fit to bring you back to us, and we can only be thankful to Him for such a blessing."

Jenni swallowed hard, looked over at her baby brother, then back at her father. "But . . . Papa. I can't stay."

"Of course you can."

Jenni shook her head. "No, Papa. The others . . . they'll see me. They'll know that something is wrong. They'll sense it."

Papa's brows came together like thunderclouds. "Jennilee, no one will . . ."

Jenni pulled her hand free of his grasp. "Papa, please . . ."

Papa surged to his feet. "Jennilee . . ." he said at the same time.

"Dalton."

Ina's voice, quiet and firm, cut through the rising tension between father and daughter. Both heads turned to look at her. "Jenni is right," she said softly.

"Ina?" Papa asked, sounding less like the assured patriarch that Jenni knew him to be.

"She's right," Jenni's mother said. "She *is* different. Did you notice how the little ones hung back? Even after we knew it was her. They couldn't say why, but they were all shy around her. It's only a matter of time before something happens. If she is . . . what she says she is . . . she will be safer away from the group." Ina's voice grew rougher as she spoke, but her face retained its usual calm. Only her hands betrayed her distress at the idea. A fine tremor shook her fingers as she adjusted the baby's blanket.

Dalton sniffled mightily and blinked twice rapidly. He swallowed hard and then nodded. "All right," he said. "But know that if you're ever in need, Jennilee, you can come to us. We love you. Families are forever."

Emotion closed Jenni's throat, preventing her from speaking. She nodded, feeling the first tear break free from her eye and run down her cheek. Suddenly, her father's arms enveloped her in a near-crushing embrace. His once-powerful frame, now thinned and stretched by hunger and privation, trembled with emotion.

"I'm so proud of you, my girl," Dalton whispered into his daughter's hair.

After a long moment like that, Jenni's papa backed up and wiped his eyes. "Sit, daughter," he said. "Before you go, I would give you a father's blessing."

Jennilee wiped her eyes and did as she was told. She reached one hand out to her mother, who took it in a fierce, hard grip.

As he had done since he was first ordained, Dalton placed his hands on his daughter's head and invoked the power of his priesthood to pronounce a blessing. He blessed her with courage, and with strength. He blessed her with the cunning that she would need to survive. He blessed her that her life as a wolf would be long and happy, and he blessed her that at the end of it, whenever it should come, she would return to be with her family in eternity. He exhorted her to be faithful to the teachings of the Gospel, that all of these blessings might be hers. He promised her that she had a Heavenly Father who loved her, and a Savior who would never leave her forgotten. As he sealed the blessing with the name of the Lord, Jenni felt a warmth come over her, and a peace deep within. From out of nowhere, the lyrics to a new, very popular hymn came into her mind:

> Gird up your loins
> Fresh courage take
> Our God will never us forsake
> And soon we'll have this tale to tell
> All is well! All is well!

Late that night, after everyone but the men on watch had gone to sleep, Jenni slipped into her wolf form and melted away into the night.

She didn't go far. In fact, she went back to the place where the gray wolf and her pack had left her, and she denned there until the company decided to move onward again. The journey had been a hard one, and they were low on food and supplies. Jenni hadn't realized just how low until she'd changed into wolf form. The whole company stank of starvation, of bodies slowly consuming themselves. She watched as the men set out every morning to try to bring back game, and watched as they came back disappointed. These weren't mountain men, these were farmers and shopkeepers who were following their faith to a promised land.

If they made it there.

On the second night after her departure, Jenni decided to do something about it. She'd watched the men go out and come back again, and she'd observed as they made preparations to pack up and move on, empty-handed, in the morning.

While her human mind anguished to see her family and the others suffering, her wolf instincts knew exactly what to do. As soon as the hunters returned to the camp, Jenni breathed in the wind, pulling the taste of the falling night over her tongue. She caught the scent of animal life waking up all around her, though nothing large enough to suit her purposes. The presence of men had scared all of the large game away. But there was a trace there . . . a whisper . . .

Jenni lifted her face to the rising moon and sang out. She called to the gray wolf's pack, and to any others who would help her. She sang of need and love, and of a desire to help.

Far away, echoing over the mountains, there came an answer. Distant, but drawing nearer. Help would come before the night was through.

With that promise in her heart, Jennilee took off through the forest. With long, distance-eating strides, she chased that whisper of a scent. Every step made hope blossom larger in her chest. This would work. She knew it.

Hours later, she'd found the small herd of deer that had piqued her interest. Her help had arrived as well. It was not the pack of the gray wolf, but rather a small pack of only two wolves: a mated pair. They were young and eager. Jenni couldn't have said how, because language as she knew it just didn't apply, but she was able to communicate her quandary, and the pair of them were pleased to help her in return for a share of her hunt. Together, the three of them cut a young doe and her fawn from the herd. The pair of wolves watched Jenni with eyes filled with curiosity (though not hostility) as she changed form and began to dress the doe. They shared the fawn between them, and were more than happy with the arrangement. Jenni took the doeskin and bound it around the meat. While not a perfect solution, this made a bundle that she could carry with her jaws.

Jennilee started back toward the company's campsite, then stopped suddenly as the pair of wolves started to follow her. She looked back at them in inquiry.

We would come with you, the female said. The line of her body was friendly, and intrigued. *Taking man shape is an interesting trick. We would stay with you and see you do more interesting things.*

Jenni considered. Her biggest concern was, of course, that the wolves would either threaten or be in danger from the humans she proposed to help. Once again, she remembered the gray wolf's warnings.

We have seen men before. We know how to not be detected. And we will not harm any who do not harm us first, the male assured her with a dipped head and a bump to her shoulder.

Come then, Jenni acquiesced. *And be welcome.*

Dawn crept over the tops of the trees as Jenni finally drew near to the camp. She slunk, belly low in the mud and remaining snow. Her nose told her that someone was awake, working on starting a fire to boil water. The scent pulled at a memory that she hadn't known she had: hands, warm and firm, holding her close. Safety.

Ina.

Jenni squinted in the increasing light, and lifted her nose to the air. If she could get Ina alone . . .

"J-Jennilee?"

Jenni's head snapped up, and her eyes met the wide, terror-filled eyes of her mother. Jenni straightened from her crouch, her head above Ina's waist. Ina took a step backward in fear. Jenni opened her mouth and dropped the bundle of meat between them. Jenni was about to change, to take her human form once more and hug her mother, when the unmistakable sound of a rifle shot cracked through the morning air.

"Ina! Get down!"

Jenni didn't wait to hear more; she spun and fled as fast as her four feet could carry her. She heard Ina's voice crying out, calling her name, but the safety of the trees beckoned, and before the rifleman could reload, she was gone.

Her new packmates waited for her. Together, they hunkered down in the den site, and gradually calmed Jenni's shaking fear. Though none of the three of them wanted to risk being shot, Jenni had to know if her family had used her gift. Her packmates refused to let her go alone, and so the three of them eased through the trees until they could scent the camp. They'd remained! And there was the scent of cooking venison!

Jenni turned to the other two wolves. This was what she would do. She would follow these people and keep them safe. Whether it be starvation or other predators or even other men, Jenni would defend them, because they were her family. She thought these thoughts, and she could see the comprehension in the other wolves' eyes as her body language spoke for her.

The female looked at her mate, and then at Jenni. *We will come, sister*, she said. *If we are your pack, and they are your pack, then they are our pack too. We will help, and we will not be seen.*

Were she in human form, this instantaneous, unconditional love would have made Jenni's eyes fill with tears. As it was, she lowered her muzzle to the female's and brushed her cheek against her new sister's. Her new brother came and nipped lovingly at her shoulder.

I am blessed, thought Jenni. Her sister met her eyes, agreement in every line of her body. They were blessed indeed.

EPILOGUE

FROM AN ARTICLE ABOUT THE EARLY MORMON SETTLERS

In the autumn of 1852, carpenter Dalton Abrams and his family entered the Great Salt Lake Valley. They'd had a hard passage, and lost several members of their family. Among these were Abrams's second wife, Anna, and his eldest daughter, Jennilee. The Abrams family wintered in the Salt Lake Valley before being called to settle south in Deseret the following year.

An interesting folk tale sprang up around the Abrams family. It was said that wherever they went, a pack of wolves would follow. When the family branched out into sheep ranching, it became a custom for the family to stake out one of its flock in the nearest stand of woods. When asked about the custom, the family told a fantastic tale about a female ancestress who ran away to live with the wolves. It is said that if an Abrams is ever in dire need, there are wolves who will respond and help. This researcher can find no documented evidence of a wolf ever interacting with a member of the Abrams family in a positive way, but the story points to a certain fanciful nature common among the early settlers who saw the hand of God in all things.

Russell, "Oral Histories of the Mormon Settlers," *Trailblazers*, 3rd ed., Deseret Press, 122–3

BROKEN SON

GRIFFIN BARBER

Well, shit.

> *It's not the getting caught that pisses me off. I mean, I knew the
> risks. No, it's the long, drawn-out process of negotiating the
> terms of incarceration I detest. Just let me do my time and get it
> over with.*
>
> —*Etat du Nouvelle Geneve contre Prometheus Borges,*
> *audience de détermination de la peine*

PAYING THE PIPER

I guess that's it, then.

My attorney looked more upset than I felt. After all, the writing
had been on the wall for a while. I considered dropping a few choice
words about her failures, decided it wasn't worth it.

I was the moron who hired her, anyway.

As I dislike seeing women upset, I felt the need to say something.

"Don't worry, judging from the way the magistrate acted, the gavel already slammed down on my case a year ago. Every minute since then has been borrowed."

Time I'd used to put my affairs in order, setting Vytas up as head of anything that even touched on illicit activity. Someone with an iota less of a history than he and I shared would have thought I was setting him up rather than cleaning my own hands while awaiting trial.

She looked at me, brown eyes wide. "Yes, but I thought I'd be able to get a better deal for you, Mr. Borges."

I leaned back in the rather comfortable courtroom chair I'd spent far too much time in the last few weeks, shrugged, and answered, "I did, too, but what's done is done."

"But five years for these charges? It isn't fair." She looked close to tears. Fucking do-gooders, always with the "feelings." I had a momentary but strong urge to strangle her. Instead, I kept my hands and mouth shut.

My mother had taught me that, back at the dawn of time.

The bailiff approached. A big man, he reminded me of the officer . . . what was his name? Venkman. That's right. Venkman. This one was prettier, though.

"Sooner begun, sooner done," I sighed.

My mother had also taught me that. Not that she would appreciate my adherence to her little foibles of speech. She'd had neither time nor patience for criminals. And I was one, despite my attorney's arguments to the contrary.

UP AND AWAY

The roar of rockets receded and was eventually reduced to a rumble in the bones as the atmosphere around the shuttle thinned and slowly gave way to vacuum. Eventually even that ended as we stopped accelerating and were no longer pressed into the acceleration couch.

The expanding conflict between my stomach and inner ear rapidly informed me of two important facts: one, we'd reached orbit, and two, the drugs that the corrections doctor had administered only blunted zero-g sickness, didn't prevent it. From the sickly expressions pasted on everyone in view, the same could be said for the rest of the cargo of Nouvelle Geneve Corrections Shuttle Alpha-Seven-Two.

"You ain't local, are you?" the man sitting across the aisle from me asked.

I spared him some attention and revised my earlier assessment. He, at least, showed no discomfort from the lack of gravity. In fact, he looked at ease.

"Why do you say that?" I asked, study completed.

"We heard you talking," the man said, left eyelid twitching uncontrollably.

Certain I hadn't said a word all day, I gave him one of my harder stares.

"What you looking at, Prometheus? We didn't say a damn thing!"

"How do you know my name?" I hissed, surprise sparking anger. I glanced around, wondering if he was setting me up.

Nothing out of order.

Nothing but another twitch from the man across the aisle. "We know lots of shit, man. Renaud's brains is doubled and redoubled on the bubble of our space, man . . ."

I blinked, slid my gaze from that twitching face to his jumpsuit. While we both wore inmate orange, his jumpsuit had a thick black stripe running from neck to ankle.

It took longer than it should have, but I figured it out.

He was Broken.

In my defense, they weren't common, not anymore. In the days of my youth there had been a lot of them running around, but that was a long time ago. Even before the Perfected War. Those that suffered from conditioning failure were thin on the ground these days. Survival wasn't easy when you had twenty and more instances of your personality constantly warring for control of your mind.

I turned away.

The man continued to speak, but I studiously ignored the words and eventually reduced his monologue to the burbling of an untended teapot. I was out of practice at it, but old skills come back quick.

The hatch slid open. A guard and another woman, this one in a yellow jumpsuit with "TRUSTEE" emblazoned across the chest and back, appeared at the hatch to the cabin three rows forward. I admired their grace, if not their general appearance, as the pair maneuvered with ease, one hand always in contact with a handhold.

"How you like the ride, wellers?" the hatchet-faced guard asked as she came to a halt above the central aisle. The trustee sniggered like the guard had told a great joke.

Almost everyone recognized a setup when they saw it.

Almost.

"Come over here and let me loose, bitch, and I'll show you how much!" the couch-mate seated closest to the bulkhead shouted.

All eyes turned to him. The heavily muscled and veiny bulk spoke volumes; a tale of someone who'd come by their augments on the cheap and had them implanted without the least concern for concealing their advantages.

The thug probably thought it was good advertising, the idiot. I had climbed over the corpses of more than a few such in my time.

"What's that, weller?" the guard asked.

"I said come over here and let me up. I'll show you a good time." He stuck his tongue out and flapped it at the woman.

I resisted the urge to roll my eyes.

Some people deserve the beatings they get. My father always used to say you can't beat the stupid from people, but it sure beats listening to their stupidity.

The guard executed a flip, set her boots on the cabin wall, and launched herself across above the acceleration couch in front of us and out of reach of the convicts seated in that row. She said something into her mic, too soft for me to hear. She winked, *winked* at me as she floated by.

The convict's laughter was tinged with eagerness. I thought for a moment he might be another of the Broken, but his jumpsuit had no stripe.

No, the thug was just a moron out to prove himself a hard man.

Moron's restraints released with a pop.

He launched himself at the guard, knuckled fist leading the charge.

She seemed to writhe in the air, leaving him to bounce from the bulkhead without landing a blow.

Moron flailed, trying for another grab, and caught a magnetic boot in the teeth for his trouble. It proved the lightest of blows she administered.

I later learned she had been All-Navy in Z-G-Ryu.

Any reputation he might have made for himself for taking the beating was lost by the time the guard was done slapping him around. Groveling for mercy through your few remaining chipped teeth and a broken nose tends to make it hard to maintain a hard rep among criminals.

I committed her face to memory. Such skills were not common, and she might prove useful to my ends someday.

What, you wonder what use such information would be to me? Well, in my long, misspent life, I have learned one true thing: not everything that is, always was, or is destined to remain so.

INFIRMARY

The work the penal colony required wasn't all that bad, especially when you possessed the means, opportunity, and experience necessary for gentling the grinding of the wheels of justice, as I did.

On the whole, it wasn't anywhere near as dangerous as my experience of Imperial Supermax prisons. We had to mine, but we had good hardsuits, a modicum of useful training in their use, and my team, at least, wasn't worked particularly hard. That said, the work wasn't without risks. About the fifth month there, a mining unit slipped and ripped a good chunk out of my suit and left thigh.

My augments kept me alive, but I was recovering from decompression, blood loss, and the great, ugly wound itself when I saw Renaud again.

"Sol Boy!"

I flinched on hearing my old moniker shouted aloud. It had been centuries and several star systems distant when I'd last heard it, after all. No one living was supposed to know it. I had gone to great, bloody lengths to ensure that.

The Broken was staring at me from the next bed, left eye twitching. He was in a head-to-toe restraint system meant to keep him calm.

"Think you can get me out of here, Sol Boy?"

I considered ignoring him, but noticed he was speaking in the singular.

Besides, I didn't want him shouting my name again.

"Why are you here?" I asked.

His lip raised in a half snarl. "I did a bad thing, of course."

"Yeah, but you're Broken."

"Sure, but even the Broken have their uses."

"No, I mean you can't work the mines . . ." I realized he wasn't talking about physical labor.

"Didn't say 'mines.' Said 'useful.' Look, you gonna help me out or not?"

"Maybe. Tell me, what are you here to do?"

"Find something. We can hear it singing." Sweat had popped out on his brow.

"What?"

"Not sure. Can hear it singing." He grunted, screwed his eyes tight as if something pained him.

"Alright, then who?"

"Who, what? Be specific, Sol Boy."

"Stop calling me that," I snapped, still mystified as to how he knew. "I meant to ask who it was that brought you here."

"The song."

"But—"

He shook his head as much as he could in the restraint system. "Been hearing the song for a long time."

"But—" I was distracted by a nurse entering. The man walked over to my bed, smiled down at me, and adjusted some arcane diagnostic tool built into it. By the time I returned my attention to Renaud, he was gone, replaced by the madness that lurks in all Broken.

"Twenty-eight jumps before we broke," Renaud said, launching into an incomprehensible tirade of filth. It was the last coherent thing he said that day.

The nurse went to fiddle with Renaud's bed as he had mine. Renaud's speech slowed, slurred, and eventually subsided into snores.

"Pardon me, Nurse," I said, counting on my reputation for civility and, of course, generosity, to pave the way for me.

"Monsieur?" the nurse asked, bright, perky tone assuring me he knew who I was.

"Would you do me a great favor and tell me what you know of him?" I said, waving at my roommate.

The nurse nodded. "Renaud Foucault. Six years for attempted murder."

"Why send him to a working colony?"

"His records indicate he was functional at trial. Even passed the psych examination."

"Bullshit."

"I thought so, too, but I saw the files myself. I can send it your way if you like," he said, obviously on the make for more money.

"Yes, please." I said it thinking someone had obviously played the system to get Foucault sent up the well. Even if it didn't contain any useful information, I had deep pockets, and medical people were good friends to have.

There was no treatment for Broken, so he could not have been compos mentis at trial. Their minds were broken on a level we still did not fully comprehend, even hundreds of years after the invention of jump technology. We could condition minds to resist the brutal duality of a mind stretched, duplicated, and rewritten by the contortionist physics of interstellar jumps, but if that conditioning failed, we could not put minds broken by such stresses back together.

"And before that?" I asked of the still-waiting nurse, not wanting to think too much.

"From his tats, it looks like he was a member of the Merchant Navigators, but I don't know if that's what broke him." The nurse shrugged. "Could have been later. Medical data from before Handover is difficult to find."

"I see." Such a lack of administrative tail was one of the many reasons I had chosen to move to Nouvelle Geneve in the first place.

"I will keep an eye out for anything else on him, if you like?"

"And send those trial records to me, please."

"Sure."

I got his name, thanked him, and assured him there would be a little something for him in the next packet. True to our unspoken contract, he saw to my comfort and left me to my thoughts.

As I drifted off to sleep, I resolved to keep an eye on the comings and goings of this particular Broken. Something odd was going on, and I sensed opportunity.

RELEASE

"Monsieur Borges, may I have a moment?"

I started, almost bumped my head against the locker. I had been so engrossed in a final check of my hardsuit I hadn't heard anyone enter the morgue. I carefully put the thigh guard down, pasted a respectful smile on my face, and turned around.

When the warden asks, the smart inmate bloody well treats it as an order.

"Of course, Warden Tailleur," I said, taking in the warden and his companion.

I had scarcely laid eyes on Tailleur since my arrival. We had made arrangements the first time we met. I did not offer a bribe. He did not demean us both by asking for one. We instead came to an understanding that was to our mutual benefit. I would be respectful, and so would he.

Standing next to the warden was a woman in a civilian jumpsuit, a hardsuit carrier hanging from one shoulder. I would have called her nondescript but for her eyes, which were an arresting shade of green-yellow I don't think I've seen before or since. She didn't speak, but allowed the warden to make introductions.

"Dr. Azelié Dumont, this is Monsieur Prometheus Borges. He has charge of the site you will be visiting.

"Monsieur Borges, Mademoiselle Dumont is a professor at the university. She wishes to observe your work site firsthand as part of her studies. Please see that she is accommodated in every way. I will send a lighter to fetch her at, say"—he looked at the woman for approval—"seventeen hundred hours?"

She nodded.

"Of course, Warden," I said, admiring Tailleur's style. He could have easily said I was the gang boss who would be chaperoning her to the mine and gone on to threaten me to impress her with his importance, but he hadn't. He could also have told her story entire, leaving us nothing to talk about on our trip—he didn't. He could have promised dire repercussions should she be harmed, but we both knew anyone who offered violence to a visitor or staff on my job site was not getting off AL-1517B alive.

Respect—it makes transitioning between all our individual little spheres so much smoother.

It may sound odd, but I sometimes miss Warden Tailleur.

"I will leave you in his capable hands, then."

"Thank you," Dumont said.

"Madame. Monsieur." He gave a little bow and departed.

"I've got some final suit checks to make. Have you gone through yours?"

She nodded. "I'll check it again."

I smiled in approval. I have always been a firm believer that critical gear should be cleaned and checked often and thoroughly.

She hung her suit and started her checks.

She made no comment on what had to be, for her, odd behavior from the warden.

Then again, I had no idea what they had discussed prior to seeking me out, and paying complete attention to checks can mean the difference between death and a minor inconvenience, so I gave her a pass.

I only grew suspicious when we boarded the lighter and saw no equipment other than her hardsuit. She was also far too comfortable with silence. I had known a few assassins in my day, and they had been similarly quiet.

"So, what brings you here, Doc?" I asked, trying to allay my growing concerns when she had remained silent for half the trip out.

"I wanted to observe something."

"Oh? The mating habits of the common inmate hold that much interest for you?" I asked, searching for a button, a lever, something I could use to pry some sense of her into the light.

"Not that kind of doctor," she said. "I'm a PhD."

"Sociologists study such things, don't they?"

"I suppose they do, but I'm a physicist and mathematician . . ." She trailed off.

"What, then?" I asked, growing tired of her reticence.

"I've been working a rather difficult orbital mechanics problem involving the orbits of AL-1517B and SU-4222H."

"Oh?" I asked.

"Yes."

I couldn't see why a physicist would need to visit us. I waited for her to elaborate, but she refused to, so I pressed: "Couldn't you have just used data from the local shipping traffic?"

"Not in this case."

"And you don't need a lot of equipment for your observations?" I asked, gesturing at the nearly empty cargo bay between us.

"Not in this case." Her tone was meant to shut me up.

Fuck that. "Perhaps if you were to tell me what you need, I could be of some assistance?"

She looked me in the eye, jaw working. "I need to see for myself."

"What?"

"All my models show an anomaly I cannot explain." Her lip curled as if she smelled something foul. "Some data that just doesn't make sense."

"So the university sent you out here?"

She looked away, color rising in her cheeks. "No one sent me. I came on my own centime."

That surprised me. And explained a lot.

"What is the nature of the anomaly?" I asked once I'd digested that information.

"Neither this asteroid nor SU-4222H should be in their respective orbits."

"Should be?"

"I do not believe their orbits are natural. I think the mine sites are rich with heavy metals and rare elements because they were the original sites for the engines that pushed the asteroids into place."

I smiled. "But humans haven't been here long enough . . ." I trailed off as she shook her head and the implications started to sink in.

"It was not a human project. And I think it ended catastrophically."

"But, that would mean—" I shut my mouth. I am not normally so slow on the uptake, I swear, but everyone knew that, despite exploring thousands of systems over hundreds of years, humanity had found no sign of an alien civilization, living or dead.

"That I'm crazy?" she said with what I took to be a bitter smile.

Remembering Renaud, I shook my head. "No, not crazy."

She cocked her head, looking unconvinced of my sincerity.

"Oh, I don't know the maths, but . . ." I trailed off. I am not a superstitious man, and don't give much credence to madmen, but this would cost me very little, and might just be something my mother would be proud of, were she to learn of it. Decided, I turned to Dr. Dumont. "If you don't mind, I'm going to ask for another inmate to join my crew."

"Oh?" she said, brow raised in question.

By then I had a few years practicing Gallic shrugs, and offered one of my best. "He might shed some light on your mystery . . ."

MINING

"Lighter NBC-EB, we are two minutes out." The lighter pilot's broadcast was in the clear and over all channels.

"Stand by one minute at present range, lighter NBC-EB," my foreman, Mohammed, said. "We are detonating."

"Copy, standing by one minute."

We had already cleared the trench, and once we'd all checked in, Mohammed detonated the string of explosives. As the rubbling charges shook the slurry of icy stone beneath my hovering body, I took a moment to survey my little kingdom in the big black. AL-1517B is shaped like a mangled kidney. My new mine site was on the face of the inner curve on the sunward side, about ten minutes from the main colony. It was shaped like a rectangle of about two hundred meters by one hundred meters.

Prison-orange hardsuits and IFF beacons, glaring to both the naked eye and on my HUD, swarmed back into the trench carved about waist high right through the middle of the long axis of the rectangle. In a matter of moments, mined material was on its way to the refinery.

One of the lessons I've learned in my time is that smooth is fast in most things. And my crew worked with a smooth precision that made them very fast indeed.

"You are clear to land, NBC-EB," Mohammed said.

I watched as Renaud's ride crested the extremely short horizon and began its descent into the irregular, shallow bowl carved into the asteroid's surface by human tools. I called up production data from the site on my HUD while I waited. I smiled at the numbers. Mining might not be something I had any training for, but I do know how to assemble and run a crew. Even in my absence, they had produced significantly more rare metals and elements than any of the other teams working AL-1517B. Part of that was luck, of course: we were following a vein of material the previous team had uncovered before ending their term and vacating for home and eventual out-processing. But every member of my crew was well motivated: I needed something to keep my mind off my situation, and they wanted those little extras pleasing me, and the warden, secured.

Procuring Renaud's immediate release to my crew and quick transport out to the mine had cost me some favors, but nothing out of pocket. Such an inexpensive arrangement would have been impossible if the crew hadn't been so productive. I was, I admit, rather proud of my achievement.

"So, who is it you sent for?" Dumont asked on a private channel. After explaining her findings and the data she claimed proved it, she'd spent the rest of the shift taking measurements and examining the site. As she was decently skilled with her suit and stayed out of the way, no one had complained. I knew the crew wanted to know what she was doing here, but no one but Mohammed had asked as yet, and his only question had been to find out if she could work heavy equipment. I do like task-oriented people, and Mohammed's focus had, he'd told me, cost him a marriage. He hadn't told me he'd murdered her and her lover when he discovered them, leading to his incarceration here. That I had to learn from prison staff.

"Doctor, before I make the introductions, I need you to promise to keep an open mind."

"That sounds . . . ominous?" I could hear what I took to be a smile in her voice.

"Can you? Keep an open mind, I mean?"

"Monsieur Borges, you have said you think this person might help me. You are the first person with half a brain who didn't look at me like I was an idiot when I mentioned the possibility of an alien intelligence fiddling with orbits in this system. The least I can do in return is, as you say, keep an open mind."

"Good. I can't promise anything, but . . ." I left it at that. Renaud was Broken, and I might have just heard what I wanted to hear from him. And even if *she* was right, and *he* was right, there was no guarantee they would be able to communicate. Broken were called such for a reason.

The lighter docked.

Renaud shot from the hatch almost before it had fully opened.

"Monsieur Borges, thank you! Thank you! Thank you!" the Broken babbled, his suit describing an alarmingly fast arc toward me. "Can you hear it?"

"Renaud, slow down, please," I said, hoping he would slow his speech as well as his approach.

"I can hear it! Aren't you excited? Can't you hear it? I assume that's why you got me out!" he said, each phrase hard atop the next. He did, however, slow his approach, though not until the last second. I was ready to evade him when he maneuvered to a smooth halt not three meters in front of me.

"Fuck." Dr. Azelié Dumont said the word with feeling.

"Is that an offer?" Renaud asked. For once he actually waited for an answer. She didn't give one. I turned to look at her through the faceplate of her helmet. The physicist's expression made it evident she thought herself the butt of some vile joke.

"Open mind, Doctor," I reminded her. "Open mind."

"But not too open! That's how you go mad, you know!" Renaud added.

OPENING UP

"I don't know about this, boss." Mohammed did not like Renaud. He liked the fact I was doing what the Broken wanted even less.

"Will the charges put anyone at risk?"

"No, but . . ."

"But we lose a day or two of work. I'll cover it. We're well ahead of quota anyway, thanks to your hard work."

"If you say so, boss."

"I do."

He jetted off toward the far end of the trench for a final check of the pattern. Renaud followed in his wake, surprisingly quiet. At least I hoped he was being quiet and not broadcasting on another channel something mad to my crew, who were in the bunkhouse, eating well and enjoying some liquor I'd brought to celebrate my return.

"What is he about?" the physicist asked.

I made sure we were on a private channel before answering. "Renaud? He's Broken."

"So I gathered. Why do you think he knows something?"

"Renaud said he committed the crime that got him sent here because of the song he was hearing from up here."

"So? Don't most schizophrenics hear voices?"

"They do. But schizophrenics are not Broken. And Broken don't get sent to penal colonies. They're too volatile and dangerous. They get housed and doped to the gills, not sent out to an environment where they might do harm to others."

"So the magistrate screwed up?"

"No. I checked the records. Renaud was able to suppress his madness for the duration of the trial. Even when the defense called in a panel of psychologists and medical experts, they couldn't find evidence he was Broken."

"Then he's not Broken," she said with bitter conviction.

"Just like evidence of alien civilizations doesn't exist?"

"That's not—" She closed her mouth.

"Not fair or the same, right? I know. Look, I asked you to keep an open mind. This is costing you nothing, and might just provide an answer or two."

"But why are you doing this?"

Long-suppressed memories rose up to threaten my composure as I searched for an explanation that would suit. "Because Broken often seem to know stuff they can't reasonably know. Because if, like Renaud says, something *called* him here *and* made him right in the head while he lied to the magistrates and the experts, then maybe that thing could offer us a way to fix the Broken." My throat was closing by the time I finished, making the words come out in a choked, harsh whisper I hadn't heard in almost a century . . .

"Charges ready, boss," Mohammed said on the general push, covering whatever Dumont might have said.

"Right. Get clear and we'll set them off," I answered.

"Copy. Clearing. Renaud?" Mohammed moved behind the shelter of the bunkhouse on the far side of the dig.

"Copy. Can't wait to meet the singer!" he said, jetting smoothly away from the trench workings.

"Detonating."

MARVELS

"What the fuck is that?" I whispered.

"It's the singer—or part of it," Renaud said, wiping some slurry from the smoking *object/concept/color/object/color/concept/object*? The thing Renaud had uncovered seemed to change physical dimensions every time I blinked or looked away.

"Jesus Christ," Dumont breathed. "I never . . ."

"Are you seeing what I am?" I asked.

I gave up trying to fix it in my head but forced my mind to take an average of its appearance in order to place it in some meaningful category of thing. It was, perhaps, glowing a bright white-green, mostly describing a gentle arc approximately one hundred centimeters in length and fluctuating at about ten centimeters in width.

"You bet." Renaud was gleeful, gloved hands digging more of the amorphous thing from its grave.

"Fuck," Dumont said.

"What?" Renaud and I asked, nearly simultaneously.

"Maths. Some mathematicians and physicists theorized how objects formed *of* or *in* a higher-order dimension might not possess a fixed state to lower-order perceptive capabilities like ours."

I wasn't sure I understood her, but I for damn sure didn't understand what I was looking at.

"Oooh . . ." Renaud's gasp sounded as if he'd been stroked along every nerve at once. The object he held seemed to melt and run into another form, this one more boxlike and far smaller.

"Shit," I said. Some part of the thing had seemed to penetrate Renaud's hardsuit for an instant.

Renaud suddenly went rigid, arms and legs flung straight out at his sides like Vitruvian Man. He slowly drifted, gurgling, from the surface of AL-1517B.

The thing, half pulled from its grave by Renaud, changed again.

I reached for Renaud, but Dumont slapped my glove away. "Don't! He may be contaminated."

I checked his beacon. All sensors in the green.

"And don't tell me you checked! We have no fucking idea what happened, so the suits can't very well test for it."

"Boss?" Mohammed's orange suit appeared about ten meters above the stricken man, cargo capture gun aimed and ready.

"Do it."

A fat, spinning, ten-centimeter-long dart chugged from the gun on a puff of gas. The net deployed in a glittering circle that captured Renaud's immobile form. The edges of the net, striking the surface of the asteroid, immediately bonded with it, bringing the Broken to a halt.

Renaud coughed, sputtered, moaned.

"Renaud?" I said.

"Jesus, that stung."

"You alright?"

"I—I am." There was a note of wonder in his voice.

"Mind telling us what happened?"

"I am . . . whole—" Renaud sobbed.

"Whole?" I asked.

"The voices are gone, Sol Boy. The song, though, remains. It's so beautiful. Sad, but beautiful."

REVELATIONS

Knowing we couldn't just turn the relic, and the—perhaps former—Broken, over to the authorities, the others spent a moment freaking out about the potential ramifications of our discovery.

I had no doubt that if the government learned what was up before the public, they'd likely silence everyone and start running tests until we were used up. None of us wanted that.

Because I'm an old hand at criminal conspiracies, I managed the situation.

First off, a seemingly completely sane and rational Renaud agreed to hide the relic via the simple expedient of digging a space in the tailings pile and fusing material over it.

Second, Mohammed just wanted to mine, and the crew would start to grumble without one of us to settle them down, so he went over to the common bunkhouse.

A brief discussion of quarantining Renaud followed. He sent Dumont some mathematic formula or equation that convinced her she had more to gain from speaking to him face-to-face than if she were to quarantine him and let someone else learn what he knew.

The three of us retired to the foreman's quarters to discuss next steps.

What we had first, however, was an explanation:

"The relic we pulled from AL-1517B is part of an expert system from a supermassive device meant to open a gate between stars," Renaud said, sucking on a drink bag. "The very first time it was put in service it exploded in a cataclysm that converted most of its structure into its composite elements and drove most of those components that survived out-system. AL-1517B and SU-4222H, better shielded and equipped with station-keeping drives, remained in position, but only barely."

I couldn't believe this was the same guy who couldn't keep on a subject for more than a few phrases at a time without descending into a rant about the color of shit excreted after eating the infirmary diet.

"The remaining parts had, disconnected from one another and from the intelligence that had created them, mourned the death of purpose.

"Then we came. The relic, tuned to the interstices between realities, noticed our ship's jumps, but couldn't communicate with us. It wasn't until the first Broken settled on Nouvelle Geneve and provided a consistent signal, as it were, that it realized communication with us might be possible."

"The song?" I asked.

He nodded. "Yes."

"But, why you? Why now?" Dumont asked. "There's been Broken on Nouvelle Geneve for ages."

"I was a navigator. The relic was the navigator for the gate. The gate this one was to connect to was built in the system where I had my break."

"Lines of congruency?" Dumont guessed.

He nodded.

"What does it want now?"

"It would like nothing more than to rejoin the other surviving relics."

"And do what?" I asked, knowing the government would really want an answer to that question.

He shrugged. "Survive? It can't do anything, really. It's harmless."

"It healed you, didn't it?"

He smiled. "Yes."

I smothered unworthy anger. "With your change in status as an example, I know the government won't take your original answer at face value, Renaud."

"Then we don't give them my example."

"And let other Broken remain so?"

He frowned. "Shit."

"Yeah."

"No offense, but why do you care, Prometheus?" Dumont asked.

I turned a stare on her that had made rough men shit themselves.

She blanched, but gathered herself and went on. "I mean, you were sent up here for being some kind of crime boss, and you have to know there'll be a lot of profit to be made in this . . . so why would a crime boss worry about fixing a shrinking population?"

"*High Hope of Destiny* was my mother's ship."

"Oh, shit."

"Yes, shit." I swallowed my anger, said more evenly, "So you see why I might want what is Broken fixed."

WIDE OPEN

Dumont revealed "her" discovery the next day. The NGU Physics Department Chair was the first to be informed that not only had his alien-crazy colleague been right all along, she'd found an answer to one of the questions humanity had been asking since the first hairy primitive looked up into the night sky and wondered if we were alone. He was sacked a few months later. She was, and remains, the toast of the intellectual community.

I did my time and left AL-1517B. I never heard from Renaud again. Last I heard he'd gone looking for other Broken to heal. The relic remained on AL-1517B. Others were found, both in the belt and in the system Renaud told us about.

I'm . . . happy. I do a brisk, profitable trade in alien artifacts. I like to imagine that some even find their way into the hands of the Broken.

Healing them.

I like to think Mother would approve.

HEART OF CLAY

A DAN SHAMBLE, ZOMBIE PI ADVENTURE

KEVIN J. ANDERSON

I.

"It makes me feel all hollow inside, Shamble," said officer Toby Mc-Goohan, my best human friend, as we looked down at the mangled corpse of the golem on the grass of the overflow parking area.

Someone had opened the clay guy's chest from the base of his throat down to his waist, splitting him like an orange. He was completely empty inside.

"Not a good time to joke, McGoo." I tilted my fedora and scratched my forehead around the hard edge of the bullet-hole scar from the night I'd been killed.

McGoo pulled out his notebook. "I always make jokes. You know that." He wore his usual blue patrol officer's uniform and cap from the Unnatural Quarter Police Department. At his side he carried a .38 Special police revolver and a .38 Extra Special loaded with silver bullets for troublesome monsters. His belt also had pepper spray and a squirt bottle of holy water. "These days, if I don't think all the ghosts and goblins are funny, I might get nightmares."

I knelt down on stiff knees next to the dead golem. Despite lingering rigor mortis, my joints worked rather well once I got warmed up. I decided it was time to get a top-off at the embalming parlor again.

I touched the clay of the body. It was still soft and pliable, but drying out. From the hardness of the stone, the coroner could determine the time of death. According to the three letters imprinted on his forehead, his name was Joe.

Golems were hardworking but downtrodden, second-class citizens even among the unnaturals, fashioned by wizards and animated to do the dirty jobs that even slime demons liked to avoid. Since all golems looked alike, and because they often had trouble distinguishing themselves from one another, each golem had his name imprinted right on the forehead.

"I wonder what he was like," I pondered.

"He was probably like a golem, Shamble." McGoo used his radio to call in the report. Backup would arrive soon, but there was no emergency. Joe had been murdered out in the vacant parking ground for Dred's Real Renaissance Faire, but the fair's gates had been long closed for the day when Joe met his untimely end.

As I looked at the dead gray mud of the corpse, I muttered, "Ashes to ashes, dust to dust." I ran my fingers along the skin, smearing a soft line. "And Play-Doh to Play-Doh."

"They can just scrunch up the clay again," McGoo said. "Moisten it with a little water and squish it into shape. Reanimate another golem."

"But it wouldn't be Joe anymore. And you know Robin would give you one of her famous stern looks if she heard you talking like that."

Robin Deyer was my human lawyer partner at Chambeaux & Deyer Investigations, a firebrand attorney who fought for all the unnaturals that had returned to the world after the strange and improbable event called the Big Uneasy. Robin was a lovely and intelligent young African American woman; I thought McGoo had a crush on her, although the chances of those two opposites having a relationship were about as unlikely as . . . well, as anything else in the Unnatural Quarter.

"Not the stern look!" McGoo cried. "Point taken. It's a murder, plain and simple, and we better solve it."

I lurched back to my feet, drawing in a deep but unnecessary breath. My lungs no longer needed air, although it did make talking a lot easier. "Sounds like a job for a zombie detective."

McGoo looked up at the lights of the Renaissance fair camp that had taken over the empty land outside of town, saw the smoke of cook fires, watched the nocturnal monsters dwindle down to lethargy as the day grew brighter. He glanced at the dead golem again. "Whew, and this is the second one in a week."

II.

The dragon was the star attraction, no doubt about it, but Dred's Real Renaissance Faire had jousting matches, swordfights, minstrels, jesters, elaborate costumes, and souvenirs to fit any budget, so long as it was high. Food vendors served fantastical concoctions for all digestive systems, whether carnivorous, demonic, or health conscious. One pushy vendor offered me a brain gelato and didn't want to take no for an answer.

I'd been meaning to take Sheyenne, my ghost girlfriend, here on a date, and now I had a reason to go to the Renaissance fair because of work. Sheyenne glowed with ectoplasmic delight when I bought tickets for all of us, including my partner Robin and cute little Alvina, the ten-year-old vampire girl who was either my daughter or McGoo's. (We weren't sure who was the real father, since we had both been embarrassingly involved with the mother, back in the day. But based on her cuteness and intelligence, I was betting on my genetics, not his.)

Sheyenne had altered her spectral form to look like a regal lady, with her blond hair done up in extravagant braids. Her gown came out of a Disney princess movie.

"You look gorgeous," I said.

Not surprisingly, she shimmered. "Thank you, Beaux. I wanted to look the part." I wore my usual fedora and sport jacket with the stitched-up bullet holes.

Inside the main entry gates, Talbot & Knowles had set up a medieval-looking tavern with a wooden sign that said YE OLDE BLOOD BAR, where they filled tankards of blood for rowdy vampires, and also served coffee, iced tea, and soft drinks for their less sanguine customers. I treated Alvina to a unicorn frappé, which was more sugar and caffeine than hemoglobin, but it made the girl even cuter than usual with her pigtails and a grin that showed off pointy fangs.

The fair was gaudy and colorful, filled with noise, delightful diversions, and expensive things at every turn. After all the mythical creatures had returned, thanks to a cosmic alignment and accidental virginal blood sacrifice, the vampires, ghosts, mummies, werewolves, zombies, ghouls, trolls, gremlins, et cetera, congregated in the Unnatural Quarter, a place where they could feel at home.

But other mythical creatures, especially the dragon, the wizard king, enchantresses, and Jabberwocks, took their lives on the road. Dred's Real Renaissance Faire performed around the country, and they were doing quite well on their monthlong stop here in the Unnatural Quarter.

"Can we watch the jousting?" Alvina asked.

"People just go there to see knights crash into each other," I said.

The little girl beamed. "Sounds great!"

I looked at the program. "Next match is in half an hour."

As Robin walked with us, I could tell the wheels were always turning behind her dark eyes. I had told her about the murdered golems, and now we saw numerous golems hauling barrels, tightening ropes, lugging heavy sacks, emptying dumpsters, scrubbing porta potties. I was sure some of them had known the two eviscerated victims.

The crowd around us paused and pointed into the sky. Robin glanced at her watch, and her face flashed a real smile. "Stop right here. This is a good place to watch."

"What is it?" I asked. "And how much does it cost?" It was an instinctive question here at the Renaissance fair.

"Every hour on the hour, Dan," Robin said. "The dragon!"

At the far side of the site, beyond the crew tents, storage areas, and dumpsters, a scaly monster lurched into the sky, flapping broad wings as large as billboards. The dragon—named Alice—had a long barbed tail and a sinuous neck, as seen on all the posters. Her eyes flared scarlet fire as she swooped over the Renaissance fair and then dive-bombed, letting out a roar as she streaked over the heads of the cheering spectators.

Alvina laughed. Sheyenne drifted close to me, and I could feel her thrumming spectral presence.

"We're safe," Robin reassured us. "The dragon may be powerful, but city ordinance limits her destructive activities."

Alice did a cartwheel in the air to more cheers, then cocked back her neck and opened her jaws wide. I thought she was going to breathe fire, but instead she released only a series of humorous smoke rings. After a five-minute performance, the dragon glided overhead, tipping her outstretched wings as if in a bow, and circled back to her large tent the size of an aircraft hangar, where she reportedly kept her treasure hoard.

"Can we have a dragon, Dan?" Alvina asked.

"We don't have the room in our apartment," I said, though I hated to disappoint the kid.

"Please? I'll take care of it, I *promise!*"

"It would be too big, honey," Sheyenne explained.

"Let's just get a little one. Hatched from an egg. If we go to the Humane Society . . ."

"Little dragons grow into big dragons," Robin said.

"Let's start out with a salamander," I suggested. "Maybe we can work our way up."

That satisfied the girl, and we went off to find the jousting field.

As we went around back of Ye Olde Blood Bar, a golem waiter with a tray—Jim, according to the name on his forehead—was delivering dirty tankards to another golem, Don, who was wearing an apron and yellow dishwashing gloves. Standing at a large barrel of sudsy water, he sloshed the tankards in the soapy water to remove the bloodstains, then dunked them in a separate rinse barrel.

Since we were away from the crowds, I paused to do some detective work. "Excuse me, gentlemen. Are you aware that last night another golem was found murdered in the parking area? His chest had been pulled open, and he was empty inside. His name was Joe."

"Oh . . . Joe," the golem said, sounding sad. "Joe was a good guy."

"What about your working conditions here at the fair?" Robin asked. "Why would someone murder golems?"

"We just do our work," said Don, the golem with yellow dishwashing gloves. He dunked a tankard in the soapy water and swished it in the rinse barrel before setting it on a wooden drying shelf. "Whenever a master hires us, we're just putty in his hands."

I remembered the hollowed-out clay corpse. "What's inside a golem? Why would anyone want to take it?"

Both Jim and Don answered in unison. "We have a heart of clay." They each brought a hand up to their chests. "And Art has the heart of a lion. Art will save us all."

"Who's Art?" I asked.

Alvina tugged on my hand. "We have to get to the jousting."

"Just a minute, honey."

"Art is Art," said the golems. "He will free us."

"Is Art another golem?" Robin asked. "How do we find him?"

"You will find him," said Don and Jim.

When Alvina kept tugging, I realized that we really did need to go or we would miss the beginning of the joust.

Thankfully, it was a cloudy, gloomy day, so all types of unnaturals could enjoy the spectacle outside. Golem ushers herded the crowd to bleachers on the edge of the jousting field. On opposite ends, two armored knights sat on black stallions that pawed at the ground with sharp hooves. The knights wore full regalia, visored helmets, and doublets that should have borne the insignia of noble houses but instead sported corporate logos, the sponsors of the jousting teams. Each jouster held a long wooden lance.

On a raised reviewing stand beside the bleachers stood a man with curly golden locks, wearing a jewel-studded crown and impressive black velvet robes. The black velvet was adorned with painted images of sad-eyed puppies and Elvis Presley. When the crowd was seated on the bleachers, the regal-looking man raised his hands, as if expecting roars of approval. He got a smattering of applause.

"I am Mortimer Dred, king of the Real Renaissance Faire." When he raised his hands higher, his ballooning black velvet sleeves dropped down to his elbows, revealing scrawny arms. "All fantasy-based unnaturals are here to perform for your entertainment, and tips are gladly accepted." The next round of applause was markedly subdued.

"Today's first match is between two of our greatest jousters. Sir Anatomy of Bone!" One of the knights raised the squeaking visor of his steel helmet to reveal a skull, grinning to hear the loud whistles that greeted his name. The skeleton knight opened his metal breastplate to reveal an empty rib cage.

"And on the other end of the field," King Dred roared, "Sir Fangs-alot of Jugular!" The second knight doffed his helmet to reveal the pallid skin, widow's peak, and slicked-back hair of a dapper vampire. He flashed his fangs.

"Those aren't real names," Alvina said. "They're silly stage names, like in WWE."

The kid was smart. Very smart. Took after me.

The skeleton knight lowered his lance, pointing it at his opponent. The vampire knight showed no concern about the long wooden stake pointed toward his chest.

When the Renaissance king waved a pennant, the two knights kicked their horses and charged directly toward each other like street racers playing chicken. The hooves pounded; the audience held their breath. We all stared, tense. The riders came closer and closer.

Out of the corner of my eye, I watched King Dred hurry down the steps of the reviewing stand, as if he had an important appointment. I turned back to the charging horses. The lances were leveled; the demonic horses were reckless. The two knights seemed not to care for their own lives or safety.

At the last moment, Sir Fangsalot raised his shield, knocked the threatening wooden staff to one side, but held his own pole firm and plunged it through the armored chest of Sir Anatomy. The lance skewered the skeletal knight and knocked him off his horse. He landed with a clamor of armor on the jousting field.

The crowd's gasp was like thunder. The vampire knight rode past and wheeled around, holding up a gauntleted hand in triumph. "Victory is mine!"

The skeleton fumbled on the ground, grabbing at his metal breastplate, barely able to move due to the long lance thrust directly through him. He pulled his armor plate open to reveal that the wooden shaft had passed harmlessly between two widely spaced ribs.

"You hit no vital organs!" shouted Sir Anatomy. "I demand a rematch."

"It's all fake," said Alvina, "like WWE."

"All in good fun, honey," said Sheyenne. "No real knights were hurt during the performance."

Golems lumbered onto the field to extricate the long lance from

Sir Anatomy. They rounded up the snorting demon horses and started to prepare the field for the two o'clock jousting round.

Having finished her unicorn frappé, Alvina was hungry again. Leaving the jousting field, we strolled among the vending stalls, sniffing the odors, some delicious, some nauseating.

I heard subdued shouting up ahead, clearly an argument that was not part of any performance. My eyes were drawn to pointy objects at a sword vendor's stall. A scrawny old gremlin with patchy fur and immensely thick glasses squirmed on a stool behind a counter, surrounded by broadswords, throwing daggers, battle-axes, and morning stars. A sign in front of the stall promised GIFTS FOR THE WHOLE FAMILY!

King Mortimer Dred loomed in front of the stall, waving his arms. "I want that sword! You were supposed to hold it for me."

"Sorry, sir," said the gremlin in a raspy voice. "We can't do layaway plans."

"I am the Renaissance king," Mort insisted.

The gremlin leaned forward like an astronomer peering through a telescope, but he couldn't see much through his glasses. "I told you last week, and the week before, that someone already bought the sword." He gestured toward his collection of weapons on display. "But I have plenty of others. Why not choose a different one?"

"Because a different one is not Excalibur."

Attracted by the shouting, Robin, Sheyenne, and I approached the stall, ready to help if the situation grew ugly.

"Can I have a sword?" Alvina asked. "A long, pointy one?"

"Not today, honey," Robin said.

The gremlin brightened, sensing new customers. "I am Noxius, purveyor of sharp objects! I have blades of every shape and design, ranging from mortal combat weapons to kitchen cutlery. Talk to me if you see something you like." He leaned forward on his stool, peering down at Alvina. "How about a double-bladed battle-ax for the cute little girl?"

"Oh, so now you can see just fine?" Mort huffed.

"She's cute," explained the gremlin.

Alvina grinned bashfully, showing her fangs.

I butted in. "What seems to be the problem?"

Robin said, "I know several members of the Unnatural Quarter's Better Business Bureau."

"I should file a complaint!" Mort glared at Noxius. I saw that the painted puppies and Elvis figures on his black velvet robes were quite well done. "Excalibur is missing, and I need to find it. The sword belongs to me! I am the proper king!"

The gremlin shrugged. "First come, first served. The dragon lost the weapon from her hoard, fair and square. She just can't resist a bet."

Mort clenched his hands and worked his jaw. His eyes became very hard. "That damned Alice and her gambling problem." He leaned over the rickety wooden counter, and the gremlin flinched behind his thick glasses. "I'll buy it back. I'll pay you double. Just tell me who has it."

"I told you before, they all look the same to me," said Noxius. "Couldn't read his name."

"Why would a golem want a legendary sword in the first place? What are they going to do with it?"

That immediately piqued my interest. "Excuse me, sir? I'm Dan Chambeaux, zombie private investigator, and this is Robin Deyer, my partner at Chambeaux and Deyer Investigations. Could you tell us more?"

Mortimer Dred gave us a dissecting look. Alvina waved, and the king didn't find her endearing. "I'll do more than explain to you— I'll hire you! If you're a detective, I need you to find Excalibur, the

sword of kings. He who holds the blade, rules the land . . . and the
Real Renaissance Faire. I will pay you greatly if you find it for me."

As our business manager, Sheyenne immediately took charge.
Somehow she produced a sheet of paper from her medieval costume.
"This is our client engagement form. If you'll fill this out, Mr. Dred,
we can begin our investigations right away."

III.

As a zombie detective it's my passion to solve crimes, like golem murders. I liked keeping innocent monsters safe, and helping my BHF McGoo. But we did have to pay the bills.

"We'll find the missing sword," I promised.

"Always take care of the client," Robin said, satisfied, "but our real work is in the name of justice."

"And keeping our business afloat," Sheyenne added. The two didn't always see eye to eye.

"Don't forget about my college fund," Alvina said.

Since Excalibur had been part of the dragon's treasure hoard until it fell into the hands of the gremlin sword vendor, we decided to go ask Alice. The little vampire girl was eager to meet her very first dragon, even though fantastical beasts were commonplace in the Unnatural Quarter.

Outside the main exhibition area, the dragon's tent was impossible to miss, being big enough to hold a giant flying reptile with elbow room to spare. We made our way through the hubbub, passing a fire eater who was being heckled by an actual fire demon, and a juggler who was a multiarmed squid creature wearing colorful medieval clothes.

Before our band of merry friends could get there, however, we encountered an unexpected attraction. Standing on a wooden crate, a golem raised clay fists to the sky and shouted in a hollow voice that belonged at a political rally. "Golems have been downtrodden for too long! We will no longer let our mud be trampled underfoot and tracked all over the house. We were made to serve, but we were not made to suffer. Golems have rights."

"Serve, not suffer," the crowd chanted.

I saw a handful of curious onlookers like ourselves, but most of the crowd consisted of golems dressed like peasants, laborers, beasts of burden. One wore a dress with a low-cut bodice, its rounded clay breasts scrunched up in a bad imitation of a lusty barmaid.

"Serve, not suffer!" they chanted. Someone bellowed, "Three cheers for Art."

They all yelled, "Art! Art!"

The golem speaker stood straight-backed, strong and confident, his clay smooth and moist. The name Art was imprinted on his forehead. "I am on a crusade for my fellow golems. We want better conditions at the Real Renaissance Faire."

"And in the whole Unnatural Quarter," called another golem.

There was something about Art. Though most golems were subservient walking lumps of mud, this one was a *leader*, filled with charisma.

McGoo sidled up to me, dressed in his beat cop uniform, which meant he was on duty. I shuddered to imagine him in a Renaissance costume. "Hey, Shamble. Seen anything suspicious?"

"If you don't see something suspicious in the Quarter," I said, "then that in itself is suspicious."

He tipped his cap toward the golem firebrand still shouting from his soapbox. "Who's that?"

"A rabble-rouser," I said.

"A crusader for justice," Robin interjected.

"That's what I meant to say," I corrected myself. "His name is Art."

McGoo nodded with mock seriousness. "You could frame him and hang him on the wall." When I responded with a blank look, he added, "Then he'd really be *art*." McGoo waited for me, or anyone, to laugh. He was about to explain the cleverness of his joke when fortunately we were interrupted by several huge ogre guards bent on violence.

"Break it up! Break it up!" The ogres' voices sounded like rocks rattling out of a gravel truck. They carried thick spiked clubs.

The golem workers scattered, knowing they weren't supposed to be on a coffee or crusading break. The burly ogres elbowed people aside as they pushed their way toward the defiant Art, swinging their clubs.

One of the smaller golems, obviously a convert to Art's cause, threw himself in front of the ogres, and they squashed him, bending his body and smooshing his shoulder and arm as they knocked him with a club. The damaged lump of clay twitched and crawled away.

McGoo charged in. "Hey, I'm law enforcement here. I'm a peace officer."

"We're chaos officers," said the nearest ogre. "Private contractors."

Art sprang from his soapbox and ducked down as he melted into the milling crowd. He ran a palm over his forehead to smear out the letters of his name, leaving only a blank gray patch as he disappeared.

The ogres—generally about as bright as golems—were easily confused.

After the impromptu crowd dispersed and the ogres strutted in circles holding up their heavy clubs in search of something to do, I nudged Alvina along. "I better get you away from this."

Robin's nostrils flared, and she flashed a venomous glance at the ogre guards. "We were all a witness to that!"

While McGoo went to have stern words with the overenthusiastic ogres, I hurried my companions toward the big tent on the outskirts. "We're off to see the dragon."

IV.

Two more security ogres stood outside the dragon's tent, though I couldn't understand why an enormous creature like Alice would need bodyguards.

"To keep the paparazzi away," said one of the ogres.

"And autograph hounds," said the other. "Now, piss off."

Robin was incensed, but I tended to be calmer, more relaxed. After coming back from the dead, I found it easier not to be bothered by little things. I stepped forward. "We've been hired by King Mortimer Dred to investigate a missing sword that recently belonged to Alice. We're here to interview her."

Alvina piped up, "It's an important part of the case."

Sheyenne produced a copy of the client engagement contract, which enlisted our services for locating the sword called Excalibur, and thrust it in front of the ogres. "See, here's proof." They squinted, tugged on their drooping fat lips, and pondered. Ogres were too embarrassed to admit they couldn't read, so they let us pass.

Reptiles had a certain smell about them, and even though my senses were dulled thanks to the embalming process, I could instantly tell that some giant lizard lived within the tent. Of course, I could *see* the huge dragon, which was my second clue. Alvina pinched her fingers around her nose.

"Oh, visitors!" boomed the dragon in a lilting female voice. "I'm on a break between performances." Alice leaned forward with a gigantic scaly head, slit eyes the size of basketballs, and fangs that would have made a great white shark pee in the water. Her green and gold scales were like garbage-can lids. "Did you come to interview me? King Dred likes the publicity, but he never sends the press anymore." She snorted. "Once, I ate a reporter who asked an embarrassing question. Is this a softball interview?"

Alice settled herself on top of a pile of treasure—gold coins, chains, chests of jewels, battered suits of armor, swords with gem-inlaid hilts. The wealth I saw was enough for a comfortable retirement account, even for a long-lived dragon, but the amount did look a little disappointing. When Alice shifted her position, coins, chains, and gilded blades rattled beneath her. "Is this my good side?" She turned a head the size of a rowboat.

"We're here to talk to you about a sword, ma'am," I said, using my best professional PI voice. "The Renaissance king hired us to find Excalibur."

Alice grumbled. "Excalibur, Excalibur! I have plenty of treasure, and all anybody wants to talk about is Excalibur."

"Isn't the sword famous?" I asked. "From a movie, or something?"

Alice blinked her huge eyes. "You don't know the story of Excalibur?" Sheyenne and Robin both looked at me in surprise.

Alvina sighed. "Excalibur was the sword of King Arthur. Only the rightful king can draw it from the stone." The little vampire girl was constantly getting her information from the internet, so she was better informed than I.

"That must be why King Dred wants it," Robin said. "It legitimizes his rule over the Real Renaissance Faire."

"Isn't it all just fun and games?" Sheyenne asked. "Costumes and jousting acts? It's not a real legendary sword."

"After the Big Uneasy, who knows what's real anymore?" I asked. "If dragons can be real, then Excalibur can be real." I turned back to Alice. "So, can you tell us what happened to the sword?" I stepped closer, trying to be congenial. I could smell the dragon's breath.

"Excalibur was part of my hoard. So many riches! Once, I needed seven warehouses just to keep my treasure, but, alas, much of it is gone now, dwindled away." She raised her head and snorted one small smoke ring. "This losing streak is bound to end soon, though! I'll win it all back. I know I will." She flapped her giant wings, rattling the tent fabric overhead, then settled back onto the mound of gold and jewels.

Robin thought she understood. "You gambled away your treasure?"

"And Excalibur?" I added.

"I still have some riches." The dragon sounded defensive. "A big win is right around the corner. I know it. Dragons can sense these things."

Sheyenne drifted close and whispered in my ear. "The dragon has a gambling problem."

Dragons also had extremely acute hearing, as I should have remembered from *The Hobbit*. "Yes, I have a gambling problem—I admit it! It's the thrill, the risk . . . and the winning." She clacked shut her fanged jaws. "Texas Hold'em is my preference, though it's hard to hold the cards with big claws like these."

Alice raised a huge scaled hand. "I lost a chest of gold and Excalibur two weeks ago in a big game. That gremlin is a good player! Noxius would win a few hands, then I'd win, then he'd win a few more. He'd egg me on until I bet the whole pot." The dragon snorted smoke, flapped her wings, and tried to settle down. "I don't know how he can even see the cards with glasses that thick, but I kept raising the bet, because I *knew* I was about to start a winning streak!" Her slit eyes held a disturbing obsession. "I'll win it back—I'll win it all back."

"You need help, Alice," Sheyenne said in a sincere voice. "It's an addiction. Gambling makes you lose everything."

The dragon hung her head, and her groan of sorrow was a rumble deep in her throat. "I know . . ." Then she perked up. "Would you like to play a round now? Who's got a deck of cards? I could use the practice!"

"Sorry, ma'am, I'm on the job," I said. "We need to find Excalibur."

"Talk with Noxius. He put it up for sale in his sword vending stand."

"He did. Sold it to a golem, but we don't know which one."

"Sure you don't want to play a game? Not even one?" Alice whined. "Low stakes, I promise! A buck a round. I'll bet on anything." She sounded desperate.

Sheyenne looked concerned. "I think the Unnatural Quarter chapter of Gamblers Anonymous accepts legendary creatures."

The dragon's need was so great she actually trembled. "It's a terrible disease." She closed her basketball-sized eyes. "Go away. I need to rest before my next performance."

Out of courtesy, we hurried out of the tent.

V.

Rettop the Cavewight had hands like lawn rakes covered with thick mud. A big grin crossed his pale, sallow face. Sitting on a stone bench next to a wheelbarrow of fresh clay, he whistled as he worked. He pumped his potter's wheel with his feet and slapped on more mud, building up a mound that he shaped into a circular vase. His hands and fingers were so large he could manipulate a lot of mud at a time.

Werewolves, ghouls, and vampires watched him with interest as he shaped the sides, pulled up a fluted oblong container, and then poked his fingers down inside to make it hollow, expanding the waist. Next to his potter's wheel sat a table filled with his wares: pots, vases, and ashtrays.

"Can you make canopic jars?" asked a curious mummy.

"One of my specialties," said Rettop. "I take commissions."

Alvina had paused to look at a crudely fashioned flowerpot. She looked up at me with those big eyes. "I'm thinking of getting a present for you and McGoo. Father's Day is coming up. How about an ashtray?" She picked up a lumpy object that looked like a project I had made in third grade.

If my heart were still beating, it would have been filled with joy. "That's beautiful."

"I'll take you shopping separately, honey," Sheyenne said. "We'll make it a surprise for both daddies."

With a loud muttering, the crowd parted and a damaged golem lurched forward, twisted and misshapen. "Rettop! Need repairs! Now!" The deformed golem could barely move, trying to get its clay legs to work. I realized it was the golem smashed by the security ogres at Art's rally. His name was Tony, according to his forehead.

The Cavewight clucked his pale tongue against crooked brown teeth. "What a shame! That's why King Dred keeps me around. Step right up." He helped the golem to his potter's wheel and let out a long sigh. "I just want to make vases and pots, but I spend half my time repairing damaged golems." He clucked his tongue against his teeth again. "Let me see what I can do."

With spatulate hands, the Cavewight seized the golem's chest and shoulders, then worked like a chiropractor, twisting him, straightening him. The clay was pliable enough that Tony eventually straightened. Rettop took palmfuls of fresh clay, using it on the golem instead of his pots. "Lucky you got here in time. If the damage had been more severe, your animation spell might have been broken." He slathered Tony's skin, bulked up his back, added to his biceps, even finished with a flourish of a cleft in the golem's chin. "There, good as new!"

"About those canopic jars?" said the mummy, his rattling dry voice tinged with impatience.

Then, not far away, someone screamed a high, terrified shriek, which was always a good way to get attention.

As a ghost, Sheyenne could move faster than any of us, and she streaked away, waving for us to follow. Robin and Alvina bolted, and I shambled as quickly as I could, getting my body warmed up. Being a detective, I was great at solving mysteries, but chase scenes and action-packed brawls weren't my specialty.

A crowd had gathered by the dumpster bins behind Ye Olde Blood Bar. McGoo was already there, trying to hold off the crowds. A banshee barmaid with big hips and a layered skirt screamed and screamed, breaking nearby windows and nearly deafening us all. Sheyenne hovered in the air, her translucent form sparkling with intense anger. McGoo was red-faced.

Sprawled on the ground in front of the dumpsters were two more dead golems, side by side, their arms at odd angles and their chests split open, the clay pried apart and leaving them hollow: Don and Jim, the golems we had met earlier. Don still wore his yellow dishwashing gloves.

McGoo bent down beside the eviscerated clay figures. "It's too late."

"Why would anyone want to kill golems?" Robin asked. "And why open them up like that?"

More clay figures had gathered around, still riled up from Art's crusade. "Serve, not suffer," one grumbled. I heard the same words muttered among the others.

"Something bad is happening here, McGoo," I said. "Somebody's cracking open golems, like shucking oysters and hoping to find a pearl."

I could tell my best human friend had had enough. He bellowed, loud and clear, "Four golem murders in two weeks! This is a crime scene. This entire Renaissance fair is a crime scene!" He pulled out his radio and called to request backup—all of it. "By order of the Unnatural Quarter Police Department, I declare this fair closed. All the public must leave immediately in a calm and orderly fashion."

Security ogres lumbered in to see what the fuss was all about. "Knock some heads!"

"No, no, just a peaceful evacuation," Robin insisted. The ogres looked disappointed.

McGoo said, "Call King Dred. I want all fair employees together on the jousting ground. I need to interrogate everyone." Sighing, he looked at me. "This is going to be a long day."

VI.

Squad cars arrived before the fair workers organized themselves on the jousting field. The security ogres got into several brawls (with each other, since they'd been given orders not to harm the paying customers), and eventually all of the patrons made their way to the overflowing parking lot, creating a huge traffic jam as they headed back to the Unnatural Quarter.

King Mortimer Dred stood on the reviewing stand as if this entire meeting had been his idea. McGoo and I sorted the fair workers by species so we could interrogate them better. Robin made sure that every accused monster was properly read its rights. Sheyenne had gotten a treat for Alvina, roasted frogs on a stick, because the little girl was hungry again.

Trolls, mummies, and werewolves in blacksmith aprons gathered around, as well as Noxius the gremlin and Rettop the Cavewight. The vampire and skeleton jousters stood shoulder to shoulder, and I realized that they were actually close friends, not mortal enemies as the audience had thought. Even Alice the dragon thundered in, landing not far from King Dred's reviewing stand. Twenty or so golems crowded together, identical except for their various Renaissance costumes.

McGoo strutted in front of the reviewing stand. "Now that you're all here, I've got—"

"I'll take it from here," Mort boomed from the platform above. When he lifted his hands, his black velvet sleeves fell down to his elbows again. Thunder sounded across the sky, and dark clouds began to form. "I am King Mortimer Dred, your boss." He strode down from the reviewing stand and marched onto the field, heading straight for the gathered golems.

McGoo and I hurried after him, trying to regain control of the situation. "What are you doing, sir?" I asked.

"We have this handled," McGoo said.

King Dred ignored us. As he walked past the nearsighted gremlin, he grabbed the furry creature by his scrawny neck and dragged him to stand in front of the golems. "Now that you're all here in one place, I can get this done in a far more efficient manner. I need Excalibur. I know one of you golems bought it. I know one of you is hiding it." The king glowered, and his eyes crackled with sparks.

I looked at the smooth clay golems and wondered where in the world they could manage to hide something as large as a sword.

"I demand to know which one of you has Excalibur!"

After a long petrified silence, one golem pushed forward from the back. He seemed taller than the others, exuding power. It was Art, the leader of the golems' crusade. "And I demand justice for all golems!" he said. "We will serve, but not suffer."

The wizard king seemed shocked and intimidated. "You demand nothing! Where is my sword?"

"The sword belongs to the rightful king," Art said.

"Or it belongs in my treasure hoard," the dragon piped up, "until I lost it in a poker game."

"Lost it fair and square," chirped Noxius.

"I am the king of the Real Renaissance Faire. I, Mortimer Dred, must draw the sword from the stone as was foretold in the legend."

Without flinching, Art placed a gray fist against his soft clay chest. "What if the sword is inside the stone already?"

I suddenly figured out the only place a golem could hide something as large as a sword, and I knew that Mort Dred understood it as well. "He was looking for the sword!" I said to McGoo, who clearly hadn't yet received the same revelation. Now the murders all made sense. "Excalibur! Art has it."

Like a flasher about to tear open his trench coat, Art plunged his clay fingers down the soft clay of his chest as if pulling a zipper, then he stretched his clay torso apart, opening himself up to expose a golden hilt and the polished steel of a sword blade that ran all the way down inside his back. Excalibur! The legendary blade hidden inside the soft stone body.

"I have Excalibur," Art declared. "I *am* Excalibur! The sword is in the stone."

The Cavewight cackled. "It fit perfectly. I thought it was clever." He held up his splayed hands and waggled his long fingers. "Sealed it right in there for safekeeping."

"It's mine!" Mort lunged forward to grab the golden hilt that protruded from Art's open chest. "Mine!" He pulled at the sword, struggling to draw Excalibur out of the golem's body.

The other golems shifted angrily, getting riled up. The Renaissance fair employees watched, and even the dragon Alice peered down as Mort yanked, tugged, dug his feet in the ground and pulled, but Art held the sword inside him. Mort strained to wrench the legendary blade free, but it wouldn't budge.

Finally, red-faced, weak-kneed, and exhausted, he staggered back. His golden crown hung askew on his head.

With perfect timing, Sheyenne appeared in front of him, holding a piece of paper. "You engaged our services to locate the sword Excalibur, Mr. Dred. There it is! Our work is now complete, and here's our invoice. Payment is due upon receipt."

Mort flew into a rage. His curly, golden hair crackled, and his crown popped off his head like a champagne cork as his body filled with sorcerous energy. "I am King Mort Dred, and I am also a great wizard. I call upon the powers of dark magic to give me the sword that is my due. I need Excalibur!" He raised his hands, and lightning crackled from his fingertips. Angry black thunderheads gathered. The ground began to shake.

Art stood fearless with Excalibur still protruding from his open chest. He wrapped a clay hand around its hilt. "I do not have a heart of clay. I have the heart of a lion! I should be king."

"I will destroy all of you," Mort screamed, and thunder cracked around him for emphasis. "I will shatter every single golem and take the sword from the rubble of your bodies." He lurched back to summon a huge blast of terrible energy.

Knowing what I had to do, I didn't hesitate. I shambled forward, raised my voice. "You look extremely powerful, King Dred. I bet a hundred dollars that no one can stop you."

Mort let out a maniacal laugh. "Of course not—"

Then a huge reptilian foot stomped down on his head, a dragon's claw that smashed with all the weight of an enormous monster. The blow crushed the Renaissance king into a puddle of bones and flesh.

Alice let out a roar, and her slit eyes were wide and bright with delight. "I'll take that bet!" she said. "Did I win?"

VII.

Afterward, McGoo and I wrapped up the case while Robin wrote notes on her yellow legal pad for the final summary. Sheyenne took Alvina to get another sugary treat, while we arranged a petty-cash invoice to pay back the hundred-dollar bet.

McGoo scrutinized the red stain and the crumpled black velvet robes. The painted puppies looked extra sad now. "We know Mort Dred was the murderer, tearing open golems in search of the sword hidden inside." He wiped his shoe on the grassy ground to get rid of goop he had inadvertently stepped in. "Nothing left to arrest, though."

"Case solved," I said. "My two favorite words in the world."

"I like 'payment complete,'" Sheyenne said, leading Alvina back from a vendor with a frozen blood-pop. "Maybe we can get the Renaissance fair treasurer to pay our bill?"

Robin shook her head. "Mr. Dred engaged us as a personal matter, not as a corporate contract with the fair itself."

Moving proudly among his fellow golems, Art met each one, read their names aloud from their foreheads. The hilt of Excalibur still protruded from his chest like a badge of honor. He had also retrieved the golden crown worn by King Dred, and now he placed it on his own head, the king of the golems and possibly king of the Real Renaissance Faire.

Art said, "Serve, but not suffer. We must have rights for all golems."

Robin walked among them, listening to their grievances. "We can file a formal motion, and I'll approach the proper governing bodies. I will help ensure that you have good working conditions and proper maintenance."

"I'll help with the maintenance," said Rettop. The Cavewight was busy making commemorative clay medallions to sell to everyone present at the event.

"And regular mud baths!" said the golem Tony. Robin dutifully wrote it down.

Alice flew overhead, thrilled now. Without her knowledge, King Dred had claimed the dragon's entire treasure hoard as collateral, which he leveraged to finance the Real Renaissance Faire. Now that Dred had been properly squashed, Alice found that she now owned the entire operation. She was so ecstatic she did barrel rolls and loop-the-loops in the air.

"She still needs counseling for that gambling problem," Sheyenne said, "or she'll lose it all again."

Art strode up. "I will be her business adviser. Instead of the Real Renaissance Faire, we will call this the *Fair* Renaissance Faire, so that all can feel good about themselves when they attend."

The armored vampire knight and the skeleton knight joined each other on the jousting field, practicing with their swords. The dragon crashed down in front of them, and the two costumed knights ran forward to challenge her in a mock battle. With a beat of her wings, Alice knocked them both flat, but the unnatural knights sprang to their feet and ran into the melee, all in good fun.

"I still want a dragon," Alvina said.

"Maybe when you're older, honey," Sheyenne said.

"You could have one at McGoo's apartment for the nights you stay with him," I suggested.

He glared at me. "Let's start you out with a salamander first."

REPRISE

A QUINCY HARKER, DEMON HUNTER SHORT STORY

JOHN G. HARTNESS

I've never liked Jersey City. It always feels to me like the sixth bor-
ough, one with an inferiority complex, a Chihuahua of a city jumping around and yipping at you while the big dogs try to ignore it. I
liked it even less right after World War II, when Boss Hague was
running the place with an iron fist wrapped tight around the balls
of the law and you could find yourself wearing cement overshoes if
you didn't bribe the right city officials, or if your bribe wasn't respectful enough.

I'm not really the respectful type, and I was a lot less so then.
Believe it or not, I've mellowed. I somehow made it through my two
years living in the shadow of the Big Apple, and even grew to like
the greater New York metro area. But never Jersey City. It always
sucked. But, after I finally reconnected with Uncle Luke and the
man currently answering to the title of Renfield, Jersey City was
close enough for me to stay in contact with the closest thing I had
to a family, but far enough away that said family didn't show up
unexpectedly for dinner. Because when your only "family" is Count
Dracula, the last thing you want is him popping over for a bite.

I lived for a time on the third floor of a brownstone at the corner of York and Barrow, a nice building called Madison Standing. I liked my apartment; it was close to the library, close to the water, and far enough away from the city that I could stay mostly underground. There's not a lot of supernatural activity in New Jersey, so I could just keep my head down and try to rebuild myself after the war.

I spent a good chunk of 1949 sitting under a tree in the park reading, or thinking, or poking at the gaps in my memory and trying to remember what happened between the time I flew into a rage in France and the time I came back to myself in the Arizona desert three years later. No matter how many books I read or how many hours I spent looking up at the clouds or stars, no hint of those lost years came to me.

The days were fine. The nights, less so. I saw her eyes every time I closed my own; Anna's eyes full of tears for her lost brother, then wide with shock and pain as the sword plunged through her, then finally dead and glassy and staring up at me from the floor of the French villa where she died. I dove headlong into a fury that consumed me for years and resulted in a level of bloodshed usually only available to governments.

That's what had me walking through Van Vorst Park at half past midnight on the twenty-first of June. I had no idea it was the solstice; my magic isn't tied to the seasons or the planetary alignment, so I was expecting to have the park to myself, or maybe share it with a couple of winos sitting under the oaks. I was not expecting a circle of young people bathed in candlelight and chanting in Enochian.

There were eight of them, all shrouded in long black robes with hoods pulled up over their heads. Not content with merely using the hoods to mask their identity, they also had dark cloths covering their faces, completely obscuring any details about them. Even with my heightened senses, all I could pick out was a little bit of pale skin around their eyes. They were all of middling size, no one tremendously tall or exceptionally short, and none looked particularly over-weight or muscular. Just a cluster of medium-sized practitioners of the dark arts working a summoning in the park in the middle of the night.

Curious, I stepped forward. They stood in a circle in the park's gazebo, four at the cardinal compass points and the others making a larger ring at the intercardinals. From the ground, I couldn't see the floor, but there seemed to be five candles, and they were spaced as though they occupied the points of a pentacle. These kids were casting something, and it definitely didn't feel like something I wanted happening less than a block from where I slept. I slipped behind some bushes and called up power.

"*Audite spatium*," I whispered, barely breathing the words as I wove my spell. I pushed a little sphere of pure will through the space between me and the chanting children, and as my spell took effect, I could hear them as clearly as if I stood in the center of their circle.

The words were guttural, gravelly, more like coughing than speech, but I knew it. I knew it all too well, I soon realized. This was a ritual to summon a demon. A major demon, a General at least, and possibly even one of the Lords of Hell. Yeah, definitely not some-thing I wanted anywhere near where I lay my head.

"*Ventus*," I breathed, pursing my lips and blowing a steady stream of air toward the gazebo. The candle nearest me flickered and went out.

"Aww, darn it," I heard one of the chanters say in a disappointed male voice. I heard the unmistakable *clink* of a Zippo flipping open, and a few seconds later the candle flared to life again.

I poured a little more power into my wind this time, and once again whispered, "*Ventus*." The breeze was stronger this time, snuff-ing two candles instead of just the one. Zippo bent down and relit them both.

I had to give them credit for tenacity, but I really wasn't in the mood to fight serious evil, so I decided to make one more attempt at canceling their summons before I just beat them all senseless. I called in even more power, and still keeping my voice as near to silent as I could, whispered very firmly, *"VENTUS."* All five candles winked out, and the two nearest where I stood actually toppled over and began to roll around on the floor of the gazebo, dribbling hot wax all over the boundary of their circle.

"Come on!" Zippo Guy exclaimed, kneeling on the floor and trying to right the candles. "Ow!" he yelled as his hands became coated in melted wax.

"Just leave it, Jerry," one of the other robed figures said. "The Great One is sending us a sign that he shouldn't be disturbed right now. We'll try again tomorrow night at midnight." This junior magician was another man, this one with the strident accent of the Bronx thick in his mouth.

They all knelt down then, some gathering up supplies, and others carrying over a bucket with water and rags in it to start scrubbing the signs of their ritual away. I had to give them a little credit for being considerate. So often demon-summoning wizards just leave their goat entrails everywhere for someone else to clean up. It was nice to see a group of evil magicians with a little courtesy. Or with enough sense not to want everyone in Jersey City to know some seriously evil shit had been going on in their park.

I ducked behind a tree as the first of them filed past, whispering an incantation to bend light around me and make me functionally invisible. As I watched, the shortest of the summoners turned to look back over the area once more, presumably to make sure they hadn't left any evidence of their passing. As they did, I could tell by the way the fabric hung that she was a woman, and I took advantage of the pseudo-invisibility spell to try to get a look at her. The black cloth was pulled down to uncover her nose, but most of her face was still obscured.

That didn't keep me from barely stifling a gasp when I got a good look at her eyes. I knew those eyes. I'd seen those eyes in my dreams every night for six years. Somehow, in New Jersey, six years after I watched her die, I was looking into the eyes of Anna Treves, the woman I'd watched get killed by Nazis in France in 1943. Anna Treves, my first true love.

I followed her. Of course I followed her. She veered off the path where the rest of her would-be cabal walked, and knelt down beside a large maple, pulling a small cloth bag out from under a shrub growing up next to the tree. I watched as she threw her hood back, unwound the cloth from around her face, and pulled the robe up over her head. Underneath was a modest dress of dark blue with white piping, and a matching headband held back auburn curls. When she stood and turned to go, her cult robes tucked safely into the bag at her side, I got a good look at her face for the first time.

It wasn't Anna. Of course it wasn't Anna. Anna was dead, ripped from me by a murdering Nazi bastard with a grin on his face. But there was something of Anna to her features, a similar shape to the nose, a line of the jaw that recalled my lost love's face. This wasn't Anna, but it was someone close to her. She was some relation, and if she was dabbling in dark magic, I owed it to Anna's memory to keep this girl safe.

She walked out of the park and turned left on York Street, walking without fear along the shadowy sidewalks. It was a good part of town, but still nowhere a nice young woman would ordinarily be seen alone. Of course, she wasn't alone, but she didn't know that she had an invisible magician trailing twenty feet along behind her. She took a left onto Jersey Avenue, and I ducked behind a tree, wary despite my spell. I watched from the shadows as she crossed the street in front of the public library and entered a house. Moments later, a light came on in a second-floor window, and I turned to go home.

Only to come face-to-face with another of the wannabe coven, standing right behind me and holding a Schrade Presto switchblade low and out to the side. He pressed a button, and the four-inch blade leapt out, catching the gleam of a streetlight and winking back at me, thirsty.

"What do you want with Rosalyn, you creep?" the man asked, staring right at me.

I shook off my surprise at him seeing right through my illusion and said, "She looked like somebody I used to know. I wanted to make sure it was my friend before I said anything. I didn't want to scare her jumping out at her in the middle of the night. But it's not her, so I decided to head home." I took a step forward, hoping to end the confrontation without violence.

He didn't budge, and from the look on his face, he didn't buy my story, either. "So you just decided to follow her all the way from the park and peep in her windows, huh? Is that what you are, some kinda Peeping Tom? Maybe I cut out your eyes and you don't do no more peeping, Tommy."

I sighed. This was not going to end well for this guy, and if I didn't keep it quiet, it wouldn't be good for me, either. "My name isn't Tommy, I'm not a peeper, and you really don't want to mess with me, pal. Now step aside and I'll just go home and nobody has to get hurt."

He grinned a savage grin, and I could see just the slightest hint of amber glowing in his eyes. *Shit.* He was demon-touched. Not possessed, not yet. But he'd dabbled in enough dark magic that someone from Down Below took an interest in him, and now their claws were deep in this guy's soul. I'd first seen it in Europe. It explained some of the Nazis. Not all of them, though. Sometimes terrible human beings are just terrible human beings, without any supernatural explanation.

If left alone, this guy was going to dig deeper and deeper until he got so far into black magic that he either called up a demon or went nuts and murdered a bunch of people. That happened with greater frequency after the war, with cases like the Lipstick Killer and the Lonely Hearts Killers grabbing national attention. The headlines didn't mention anything arcane, but Luke and some of his people had found definite links between demonic influence and some of this new breed of murderer. Now it seemed like Jersey had a new devil, and he was standing right in front of me.

"Last chance, friend. Fold up your little pigsticker and go home. Sleep off whatever you're on and stop playing around with things you don't understand. Otherwise, you're going to end up in way over your head."

"I might be in over my head, but you'll be dead," the man said, a vicious grin stretching across his face. He swung the knife up toward my throat, holding it like someone who's never cut anything more dangerous than a sirloin. I leaned back, letting the blade whiz by my face harmlessly, then punched the would-be murderer in the stomach. He staggered back, one hand holding his gut and the other bringing the knife back around to defend.

"You still want to play around, pal?" I asked. "There's no shame in running from a stronger opponent." I really didn't want to kill this guy. Maybe if he got help, he could shake loose of the demon's hold on him. But if I snapped his neck on the sidewalk, there would be no coming back from that.

He didn't answer, just growled and charged at me. He lowered his head, apparently intending to wrap me up, slam me into the light pole behind me, and bury his blade in my middle. I didn't like that plan, so I stopped him.

Actually, that's exactly what I did—I just *stopped* him. I planted my feet, leaned forward at the waist, and met his shoulder with my own. When our bodies slammed together, I grabbed his right wrist with my left hand and jerked it out away from our bodies. Then I slipped my right shoulder around and under his jaw, pulling on his right arm the whole time. I ducked further and his body slid onto my shoulders in a fireman's carry. I grapevined my right arm around one of his legs, then flung myself backward to the ground, slamming the knife-wielding idiot into the ground, and my shoulders into the idiot.

I spun around and up to my feet, never letting go of his wrist. He lay on the sidewalk, his eyes open wide and mouth flapping open and closed like a fish out of water, gasping for air. I stepped over his elbow, wedged his forearm between my legs, and twisted, using my shin as a fulcrum. The bones of his arm snapped like twigs, and his face went whiter than the full moon. He drew in a huge gulp of air to scream, but I dropped to one knee, burying my elbow in the side of his skull. His eyes rolled back in his head, and his jaw went slack as he passed out cold.

A quick scan of both sides of the street confirmed we were still alone, and no new lights were on in the apartments surrounding us, so I felt safe that we hadn't been observed. I folded up the switchblade and slipped it into the pocket of my pants, then rifled through his pockets, emptying his wallet and leaving it on the sidewalk beside his head. To an observer, it would just look like a random mugging, but if this guy was smart, he would realize that I now knew his name and where he lived, and hopefully that would be enough to scare him off his nocturnal activities for a while.

Of course, being smart and summoning demons don't exactly go hand in hand, so I held out only the barest hope for that. My blood

rushing from the sight and my head swirling with everything I'd
seen, I stood and went in search of the one person most likely to have
some answers for me.

It was time to go see my uncle, Count Dracula.

"I know how it sounds, Luke, but I *saw* her." The bourbon left in my
glass was barely enough to moisten an ice cube, so I passed the tumbler over to Renfield, who poured another drink from the decanter
on the side table. This Renfield, the latest in a string of manservants
my uncle had that answered to the name, was efficient, if not as
warm as some I'd known. But he was efficient, and he took good
care of Luke, so I didn't mind him being a bit of a cold fish. Besides,
he wasn't a psychopath, which was a marked improvement over some
of the previous Renfields.

"I don't mean to be cruel, Quincy, but you have seen a great
many things since Anna's death, and not all of them have actually
been present." Luke's voice was mild, but laced with steel. He looked
at me over the rim of his wineglass to gauge my reaction. If I wanted
to get violent, he was prepared to deal with me. And he could, without even trying hard. Without magic, I was nowhere near a worthy
opponent for the vampire using the name Lucas Card, and he was
too close for me to get off even the quickest spell.

We sat in the living room of his flat in Brooklyn, the third floor
of a modest brownstone in the middle of a nice working-class neighborhood. I once asked him why he chose Brooklyn over some of the
flashier neighborhoods of New York, and he told me that a hunting
ground was always best if it was heavily stocked with game no one
would miss, and Brooklyn had plenty of people moving in and out
all the time, so if one or two vanished, no one would notice. I didn't
ask again.

"That's fair," I replied. "It's not been my best few years, even counting only the ones I remember. But I'm much clearer now, and I know what I saw." I was only lying a little bit. There weren't too many nights that I lay awake until dawn trying to escape the bad dreams, and I was almost to the point where I could hear a piano without thinking of the people I cared about who died by my inattention, my insufficiencies.

I took a deep breath. "It's not Anna. I know that. Anna is dead. I didn't just watch her die, I *felt* her die." When the Nazi colonel murdered my love, the psychic connection between us was severed, but not before I felt every second of her agony. The combination of the psychic backlash and feeling her die inside my head had driven me insensate for at least three years. There were times I thought I still felt her mind touching mine, like the pain of a phantom limb, but I knew she was gone.

"But this woman is connected to her somehow. I saw her eyes, Luke. They were Anna's eyes." I looked from Luke to his current Renfield and back. They both wore looks of pity, but they weren't convinced.

"Even if she is somehow connected to Anna," Luke said, "what business is it of yours if she dabbles in dark magic? You aren't the magic police, Quincy."

"Aren't we?" I shot back. "Isn't that exactly what you created the Shadow Council to be? Protectors of the innocent from the supernatural monsters and mystical evils of the world? This guy I fought tonight was definitely demon-touched. If this woman and her group are playing around with the dark arts, there's no telling what kind of trouble they could unleash upon the area. I'm sure I don't have to tell you that a demon running loose around New York would be bad for anyone of a supernatural disposition trying to keep a low profile."

That registered. Ever since Stoker's book, Luke worked very hard to remain invisible. He even rotated through names every few years when he changed cities. But he liked New York, and he liked being Lucas Card. I knew he would want to protect this identity.

"Fine," he said. "I'll have Renfield look into Anna's family history, what we can find of it. Many of the records from Europe simply disappeared under the Nazis, particularly those of Jewish citizens."

"If there is anything to be found, Master Quincy, I will unearth it," Renfield pledged.

"Thanks," I said, stifling a yawn. Pink sunlight crept in around the edges of the drawn curtains, and I realized that I'd let another night go by without sleep. If I kept up this nocturnal schedule much longer, I'd forget who was the vampire, me or Luke. "I'm going to get some sleep and then look around the park this evening. Since I spoiled their ritual, they have to try again tonight. We're right on top of the solstice, so the spell probably has a calendar component."

"The guest room is made up," Renfield said, pointing down the hall. "Just ring the bell if I can bring you anything. I will make some calls to friends in Europe and find what I can, but I doubt I'll have anything before you wake."

"I wouldn't expect you to," I said. "These things take time. Unfortunately, I may have to go in without much in the way of information."

Luke chuckled, then covered his mouth and turned it into perhaps the worst fake cough I've ever seen. When I looked at him, he gave me a smile. "That is something of your forte, Quincy. Of anyone I know, you have raised blindly rushing into a situation to an art form."

I let out a little laugh of my own as I stood and stretched. He was right, after all. Planning and forethought were great ideas. Unfortunately for me, they had always remained just that—ideas. "Good night, Uncle. Renfield, thank you for the drink. I'll see you in a few hours." With that, I went down the hall, listening as the siren song of the pillow called my name.

I slept until dusk, and let myself out of the apartment without disturbing Renfield. I knew he was awake—there was nothing that happened in any of Luke's resting places that he wasn't completely aware of—but if we spoke to each other, he'd feel obligated to offer me breakfast. Or dinner, whichever he felt was appropriate. Then my stomach would rumble, and I'd feel like I was imposing on him even more than just leaving him dirty linens to wash. So I caught a bus back to Jersey City and stopped into a diner for a quick bite to eat before returning to my apartment to plan the night's activities.

After a quick shower I dressed in a pair of black pants and black military-style boots I'd grown to appreciate while running around parts of Europe in deep wilderness. I put on a dark blue short-sleeved shirt and opened a drawer by my bed. I pulled a Smith & Wesson Model 10 revolver from under a stack of handkerchiefs, slipped it into a shoulder holster. I strapped the gun around myself, tugging the straps tight, and drew a lightweight jacket over the whole assembly. It was a little warm for the jacket, but at least it kept the gun hidden. I picked out a dozen extra bullets for the .38 and put six in each pants pocket. Hopefully I wouldn't need that many. Hopefully I wouldn't need any, but I wasn't much of an optimist where demons were concerned.

Dressed for the night, I had nothing to do but think, so I slipped out of my apartment and walked across the street to the park, where at least I could think and keep watch at the same time. My mind wandered down familiar dark alleys as I sat on a bench staring up at the clouds. Images of Anna, of her younger brother Gerald, of the blond Nazi that murdered her, these were the moving pictures of my memory as I sat and waited for my chance at redemption, my chance to right some of the wrongs of my past. Nothing I did would bring Anna back, but maybe if this girl was some relation, and I could keep her safe, it would erase some of the failure on my soul.

I was startled from my reverie by the bench creaking as someone sat down next to me. I started, turning to the side, and barely re-frained from a cry of surprise when I saw the woman from last night looking at me.

"Penny for your thoughts, stranger," she said with a smile tweaking the corner of her lips upward.

"I'm afraid you'd be overpaying, ma'am," I said, doffing an imag-inary cap. The tendency for men to wear hats everywhere was some-thing I never understood. I didn't want anything limiting my vision, and more than once I'd needed to see things coming at me from above.

"I doubt that, sir. You looked like a man deep in contemplation."

"Or wallowing in memories," I said, letting a little too much truth leak out. She'd really shaken me by just appearing on the bench like that. I must have been deeper in thought than I realized. Couldn't let that happen often, it could be bad for my health.

"What brings you out on this fine evening?" I asked, glancing down at the bag by her side. I couldn't see anything in it, but I as-sumed it held her robe and whatever else she needed for her ritual later that night. I was a little surprised she stopped to talk to me, a strange man on a park bench, after dark. She was truly a fearless young lady.

"I'm meeting some friends over at the bandstand," she said with a wave of her hand. "What had you so lost in thought? You were really in another world. I was a little afraid you were drunk, or maybe sick."

"No, I'm fine," I said, turning to look at her for the first time. The resemblance to Anna was strong, and not just in the eyes. There was a similarity to her nose as well, but the auburn hair was all her own, and she was a little heavier than Anna. Pleasantly curvy, I'd call her. "I was just thinking about someone."

"Someone you lost?" she asked, and I dropped my gaze.

"Yes. How did you know?"

"It's who I think about when I sit here at night and look up at the stars. I . . . had a lot of family in Europe. Not many of them made it here. I . . . don't know what happened to everyone, but some . . ."

"They didn't make it there, either," I said, my voice soft as the breeze.

"No, they didn't."

"Were they Jewish?" I asked, trying to find a way to steer the conversation around to who her family was without being horribly insensitive to her loss. But I had to know what the connection was, or if there even *was* a connection.

"Yes. We are. I am. My family . . . my father owned a store. He sold antiques. He did very well for himself in Stuttgart, buying from estates and selling to private people. He was very fair, but everyone assumed because he was a Jew, he was cheating them somehow, even though he often changed the terms of an agreement in their favor if they didn't ask for enough money for something they sold him, or if they offered too much for some trinket in his shop window. But it didn't matter. He was a Jew, so he was cheating them."

"You said he was . . . ?"

"Yes. He died. Fighting the Nazis. We moved here after one of the local businessmen bought his shop. He was offered a fair price, of course." I could tell by the twist of her mouth that the price wasn't fair at all, at least not to her mind. "After Papa sold his business, we moved here. When the Americans joined the war at last, he enlisted. He was killed in a forest in France. France was not very good for our family . . ."

"What else happened in France?" I asked, my voice as gentle as I could make it despite my heart trip-hammering inside my chest.

"My aunt and cousin died there. Murdered by Nazis. My cousin Edgar was sent to one of the camps and no one ever heard from him again, but my aunt Anna . . . she was murdered. My grandpapa in Stuttgart received a telegram from some man he'd never heard of telling him what happened. He wired the news to Mama. She was devastated. They were very close, even closer than most sisters. She had begged Anna and Gerald to come with us, but they didn't want to leave Europe. Anna loved Germany, and France, and Austria, and Edgar studied with some of the best music teachers in the world before . . ." Her voice trailed off and she let out a soft, embarrassed chuckle.

"Forgive me," she said. "I don't know why I'm rambling like this to you. I haven't even introduced myself Mr. . . . ?"

I shook myself out of the trance I'd been in ever since she mentioned her aunt Anna, and looked dumbly at the hand she held out in front of me. After an awkward pause, I took it and shook. "Harker. Quincy Harker. And you are?"

"Rosalyn. Rosalyn Reismann. Harker . . . that name is familiar . . . oh yes! Like the character in that book. The one about the—"

"Vampire," I said with a slight sigh. "Yes, that's the one. No relation, of course." Unless you count being the literal son of the man in the aforementioned book, but telling people that usually led to all sorts of uncomfortable questions about when the book was written, when I was born, and then landed on why I looked like I was still in my early thirties when I should be in my midfifties. I generally try to avoid those conversations with people I meet in public parks. Very little good ever comes from them.

She laughed, her voice a merry tinkle through the night. "Of course not, silly! That's just a story. That kind of stuff isn't real."

But the way she cut her eyes to the side when she said it made me think she knew exactly how big a pile of manure that was the moment she said it. "Well, maybe not vampires, but this old world could certainly use a little magic," I said, leaning back on the bench and looking up at the stars. "Something to maybe soften the pain of life's punches, or maybe just something to make the world a little bit better."

I watched out of the corner of my eye as her mouth opened and then closed as if she wanted to tell me something but wasn't sure she could trust me. She just looked at me for another moment, then stood up.

"I'm sorry, Mr. Harker, but time really has flown. My friends will be waiting for me. It was very nice meeting you." She held out a hand.

I stood and took it. "It was very nice meeting you as well, Miss Reismann. I hope you and your friends have a good time with whatever it is you're doing out in the park in the middle of the night. And maybe if I'm lucky you'll spy me on a park bench and decide to chat with me again some evening. I live just up York Street, so I'm here most nights."

"Maybe I will, Mr. Harker. Have a good night." She gave me a little wave, then turned and hurried off down the trail into the park. I sat there for a moment thinking over what she'd said, trying to make the connection between this nice young girl and a dark magic ritual. Something didn't make sense, but I knew exactly where to go to get my answers.

I cast the same light-bending spell around myself that I'd used the night before, then followed Rosalyn down the path into the middle of the park. Just like before, she stopped by a tree and pulled her robe out of her bag, slipped it on, hid her face with the long fabric, and tucked the bag under a nearby bush. Then she stood and walked toward the bandstand. The major difference tonight was the glint of steel I saw at her waist. This time she carried what looked like a ceremonial knife at her side.

"Well, crap," I muttered under my breath as I slid between the shadows. My spell mostly masked me from sight, but it was always best to give the magic as much help as I could. A few more minutes and I was within sight of the bandstand. This time I wanted to get a better vantage point, so I leapt into a spreading oak tree and pulled myself up onto a wide branch. I walked out as far as I safely could, using other limbs to aid my balance, and took up a position about ten feet off the ground and twenty feet from the bandstand. My line of sight was just right to see under the roof so I could tell what kind of circle they were drawing, and when I saw the symbols on the floor, my worst fears were confirmed.

The circle they'd drawn on the wooden floor of the bandstand was not just a summoning circle, it was doubly warded and ringed with serious glyphs of protection. Whoever or whatever they were trying to call, at least they understood that it was heavy-duty.

The cabal was arranged just like the night before, in concentric rings of four hitting the eight major compass points. The only change this time was that tonight, the robed figure I recognized as Rosalyn was standing at the northeastern point, and the first at the north point had its arm in a sling, giving his identity away as clear as a signal beacon.

"Lord Raguel, Angel of Justice, hear our plea and come to us!" The Bronx accent of the demon-touched leader with the bad wing rang out through the night. I looked around to see if there was anyone else in the park to hear the ritual, but it seemed we were alone. At least for the moment.

"Lord Raguel, we beseech thee to come unto us," the other seven members of the creepy chorus intoned in unison.

"Raguel, Angel of Justice, come to us this night to set history aright!" the leader cried.

"Lord Raguel, come unto us and fix what is broken," the chorus called.

A slow chant of "Raguel, Raguel, Raguel" came from all the participants but two: the leader and Rosalyn, who drew the knife from her belt and stretched her arm out over the circle. The leader began to chant in Enochian, just like he had last night, beseeching the lord of justice and vengeance to come unto them and set the past to rights.

Rosalyn pushed up the baggy sleeve of her robe and held her closed fist out over the circle. The knife flashed up in her right hand, then came down across her left forearm, drawing a bright line of blood that dripped onto the symbols inscribed on the wood, binding her blood, the chanting, and the incantations written in and around the circles together and bathing the bandstand and everything in the vicinity in a deep purple light.

"Lord Raguel, come to us!" the leader shouted, and a voice darker than anything I'd ever heard answered.

"I am here, my child. You have called, and I have answered. I am here, what would you have me do?" The form in the circle was hidden in a column of smoke nearly six feet in diameter, but the few glances I could get through the shifting mist told me with some pretty solid certainty that this was no angel. That, and the fact that you don't use a demonic summoning circle to call an angel. Those were dead giveaways.

The leader's hood fell back and he reached up with his good hand to rip the cloth down from his face. Yep, those were some demon-touched eyes. There was no question in my mind that he knew exactly what he'd called up, even if the others in the circle didn't. I slipped on my Sight, taking a look at the situation in the magical spectrum, and was stunned to see that four of the eight coven members wore the taint of the demon-touched, and one was a lesser Pit Dweller, not human at all. The other three were human, and probably innocent dupes, but the magic coming from the smoky shape in the circle wasn't just bad, it was evil the likes of which I'd never seen before, and more powerful than anything that had any right to be walking the earth. This was about to turn into a very bad evening.

"It is time, my lord. It is time to unleash your wrath upon these pitiful mortals and raise me up to sit at your right hand. It is time for us to bathe in a river of their blood and make me immortal!"

"What is this, Jacob?" one of the men in the circle asked, pulling his own hood and face covering away. "This was supposed to be a ritual to go back and stop Hitler before he could kill our people, not summon some cloud of smoke and make you immortal."

"Be quiet, Hiram," the leader, apparently Jacob, replied. "Lord Raguel is here to answer our call. He has come from Heaven above to set things aright."

Oh shit. My conversation with Rosalyn flashed into my head, and I suddenly realized what these poor idiots had done. They wanted to fix the past. They thought they could get an angel to travel back through time and kill Hitler, or at least keep him from rising to power. They wanted to save their families. My heart sank to my shoes, not just because of their mistake, but because I knew every feeling that drove it. I'd felt that same anger, that same sense of *wrongness* in the world since Anna died. That sense of guilt at being alive when the woman I loved, and so many more, were dead in the camps at the hands of the truly evil.

I knew what they were feeling because I'd wanted to do the exact same thing. I didn't. Not for lack of trying, but mortals, even long-lived magical ones, can't travel through time without some serious mojo. There are a few artifacts that will allow it, but I'd never laid hands on one, and wasn't sure I wanted the responsibility. These people had been offered a chance to right the greatest wrong of the twentieth century, and to take away probably the greatest loss they'd ever suffered. They took that chance, and now they were going to die for it, and if the demon in that circle was as powerful as I feared, everyone within a hundred miles, including all the souls in New York City, might join them.

Jacob reached over and backhanded Hiram, a tremulously thin man who must have been in his seventies. The frail man tumbled to the wooden planks, looking up at Jacob in shock. The other members of the circle took an involuntary step back, except for Rosalyn, who knelt by Hiram's side and tried to help the old man to his feet.

"What are you doing, Jacob? This is not what we are working for!" she yelled up at the grinning man.

"It's not what you fools are working for, but it is exactly what I've been planning. My lord Raguel shall lift me up from this mediocre vessel and give me the power of the heavens! I shall make men bow before me! They will give me money, women, influence . . . whatever I desire will be mine!"

I'd heard enough. I dropped down from the branch to land about ten feet from the bandstand and started walking toward the circle and the accidental demon summoners. "There are just two problems with that, friend." I stepped onto the bandstand across the circle from Jacob. "One, that's not Raguel. And two, I'm not going to let him stick around on this side of the Pits."

The demon charged forward, just enough of him pushing through the smoke to let me see his face, and it was not something I wanted to ever see again. Horns, yellow eyes with vertical cat-slit pupils, a triple row of needlelike teeth, and a forked tongue slavering across its chin made me take an involuntary step back. I raised my voice above the demon's growls. "Time to go home now, pal. I bet there's a lovely Mrs. Hungry Demon right down there in Hell just about ready to call you in for supper. So piss off back to the eternal fires while I have a brief chat with your little friend here." I cracked my knuckles on the word *chat* so there would be no mistaking exactly how unpleasant I intended for that to be.

"NO!" screamed Jacob, charging forward with his eyes on the outline of the circle.

"*Ventus!*" I shouted back at him, calling wind to slam him through the air into one of the beams holding up the bandstand's roof. Heard the wood crack under the impact, but Jacob was up almost immediately. Damn demon-touched. He would barely feel pain now, unless it was something intense like the broken arm I gave him the night before.

"Stop him," I called to Rosalyn. "Don't let him break the lines of the circle. If he does, there's nothing to contain the demon." I turned to punch the yellow-eyed man coming up on my left in the jaw, spinning him around and knocking him to the floor. As I whipped my head from side to side, I saw that the other two demon-touched humans were coming my way, while the demon in their midst had shed his human disguise and was trying to get through the circle from the outside. Being an infernal creature, he couldn't manipulate the circle directly, so after a few seconds, he turned his attention to me as well.

Great. Counting Jacob, I now had four demon-touched humans and one lesser Pit Dweller coming for me, with two innocent civilians lying on the floor staring at the whole mess with their eyes wide and their mouths agape. I looked around for the last member of the coven, and offered up a quiet prayer of thanks that all I saw of him was his back as he beat a hasty retreat down one of the park's shady paths.

I called power and hurled two orbs of purple force at the nearest cultists, striking them full in the chest. One went down flat on his back, but the other dodged my blast and stepped in close to engage me. *Shit.* The longer I was tangled up with these minions, the more time Jacob had to erase the circle and set this demon free upon the world. I ducked a clumsy punch and worried a little less as I dropped the zealot with one punch. A spray of long blond hair as she fell told me I had just decked a woman, but I didn't have time to feel unchivalrous, because the demon was upon me.

"Die, human!" the Pit Demon hissed, leaping for me. It was a hair over five feet tall, with unnaturally long arms ending in long clawed fingers. Its horn speared the air in front of my face, and it snapped at my throat with gaping jaws as it bore me to the trembling floor of the bandstand. I landed hard, but rolled sideways and got on top of the creature, rearing back and sheathing my fist in a nimbus of pure white light. I focused the magic into a spike of power and punched the demon between the eyes, driving a piece of my soul's energy into its skull. The demon shrieked in agony, and I watched the light blaze from within its head out its eyes. Then the creature burst into a blast of energy, throwing me against the railing of the bandstand, and its earthly form was destroyed. The demon still existed, but it was gone from this plane, at least for now. And for now was all I was worried about.

I scrambled to my feet, looking around for Jacob. Rosalyn was struggling to hold him away from the edge of the circle, but she was obviously giving up too much weight and strength. I couldn't get to her in time, even with my enhanced speed. I watched helplessly from across the bandstand as he forced her back closer and closer to the circle, until her back foot hovered less than an inch away from it. I ran toward them, knowing it was futile, and froze in midstride as a black shadow blurred through the night and slammed into both of them, knocking them to one side and keeping the circle intact.

"Duck!" a familiar voice called out behind me, and I dove for the floor. My elbows scraped painfully across the boards as a shot rang out in the night. There was a heavy *thump* from behind me, and when I got to my feet and looked around, Renfield stood about twenty yards away, a Colt 1911 pistol in his hand. The demon-touched cultist beside me lay on the floor, clutching his thigh and screaming in pain, the knife meant for my back lying forgotten a few feet away. I nodded to Renfield and turned my attention back to Rosalyn, my chest relaxing at the sight before me.

Uncle Luke stood over a toppled Rosalyn and Jacob, his fists clenched. He turned to me. "We'll handle the human rabble. You take care of the demon." The cavalry had well and truly arrived.

I turned my attention to "Raguel." "I know you aren't an arch-angel, and you're not getting out of that circle, so you can either clear off the smoke and tell me your name so I can send you home, or you can wait there with your thumb up your arse until dawn when you're banished anyway."

The smoke dissipated, and a well-dressed man of middling height and athletic build stood in the circle. He wore a navy suit, a gray fedora, and black wing tips. He even wore a pocket square that matched his red tie. All hint of demon was gone, until you looked in his yellow eyes. "Quincy Harker," he said, his voice more a rumbling purr than speech. "If I'd known you were nearby, I would have worked harder to get free in time to kill you. Lucifer isn't happy with how you spoiled his plans in France a few years ago."

"Lucifer got more than his due in France, demon. Who are you?" My mind flashed back to the night I lost Anna, the night that sent me spiraling into madness and bloodlust that I barely came back from.

"My name is Abbadon. Humanity is mine by right, gifted to me from the Father. Now release me and I will be merciful!" He roared the last bit, lunging forward and slamming into the circle, repulsed by the magical boundary.

Abbadon. Fantastic. Originally Muriel, he did have a deep connection to humanity, since he was the one who scooped up the clay that Adam was formed from, then stood guard over the garden and its inhabitants. Apparently he had a quarrel with Michael when the enforcer with the flaming sword tossed his pet humans out of the garden, and found himself tossed into the flames with his buddy the Morningstar. Now he was back, and in Jersey City. I knew this place really was hell.

"I don't need your mercy, Abby. I just need you to go home. And now that I know your name, I can send you there." I started the rite of exorcism, but paused after the first few lines. The demon was smiling. I worry when demons smile; it generally means bad things for anyone within a few miles. He didn't seem terribly concerned about being banished, and he should be sweating my having his real name. I was fast approaching the moment in the ritual where I had to name the demon and scrub out a portion of the binding circle so the magic could touch him, and he was still grinning at me like the cat that ate the canary.

I walked around the circle until I was facing east, directly where the sun would rise in a few hours, and drew a pentagram in the air. With my toe, I scrubbed out a few inches of the circle and poured my magic into the barrier holding the demon that I suddenly didn't believe was Abbadon. My mind raced through what I knew about demons, and liars, and the most powerful demons associated with trickery and lies, and I decided to take my shot. If I was wrong, I was probably going to die. If I was right, this demon would be gone and the idiot cultists would spend the rest of their lives trying to figure out where they went wrong.

"I call upon the strength of Uriel, Raphael, Michael, and Gabriel to aid me in banishing you, foul *Belial*, from this place. Begone, foul creature! Begone! BEGONE!" With my final shout, a beam of pure white light shone from my hands and struck the demon full in the chest. It screamed as though every nerve was on fire, then winked out of existence as if it had never been. I sagged, every ounce of fight gone from my body, and looked around to see if anyone needed help I wasn't sure I could provide.

Luke stood over one unconscious cultist, and he nodded to one whose throat was ripped out. Jacob. He lay in a pool of his own blood, his yellow-flecked eyes staring blankly at the ceiling. "He was too far gone, Quincy. I am sorry."

"I know, Uncle," I said. "I knew he wouldn't see another winter when I first looked in his eyes. He was a rabid dog, infected with the demon's taint. He could never walk among normal humans again."

"This one isn't quite so far gone, I think," Renfield said, gesturing with his pistol to the man he stood over. "I know a young nun in the city who may be able to rid him of this corruption."

"Thank you for coming," I said.

"You're family," Luke replied. "That's what we do."

"I expect family was at the root of a lot of this," I said, gesturing around us to the bloodstained bandstand. "Renfield, do you have anyone you can call?"

"To clean up, Master Quincy? Of course. I'll just be off to a pay phone and be back in a jiff."

"I'll watch this lot," Luke said. "I believe you should speak to the young lady." He pointed to where Rosalyn sat on the floor, her back pressed to the wooden railing.

I walked over to her. "May I sit?"

She nodded without speaking and I slid down beside her, feeling a few bruises I hadn't noticed before as my legs and rear came into contact with the wood.

"What was that?" she asked after a few seconds.

"That was a demon," I said. No point in trying to hide the truth from her now. "Your friend Jacob was never calling an archangel. He was summoning a demon. A big one. One that could have killed a lot of people before it was driven back to Hell."

"Did you kill it?"

"No," I said. "It's almost impossible to kill a demon here, if it can be done at all. I believe they can be destroyed in Hell, but I'm not in a hurry to go down there and find out. He was banished, so now he's stuck back in the fires until someone else summons him. Hopefully that's a long time from now. So you should be safe now."

She laughed, a short, sharp thing that faded away in the night like it was afraid to be caught. "Safe? I'm safe? I'm a Jew, we haven't ever been safe. If what happened in Europe taught us anything, it was that reminder."

"That's what you were trying to do, isn't it? Go back and make it so none of it ever happened. Not the camps, not Hitler, none of it."

"That's right. Jacob told us he had been praying and an angel came to him, just like the burning bush came to Moses. He said if we cast the ritual on the solstice, when the veil between Heaven and Earth was thinnest, the angel would help us reach back through time and make sure Hitler never came to power."

"And none of the people you lost would die," I murmured. It was a good lie. It sounded so easy, just push one thing out of line and it would save so many lives. Too bad you can't do it.

"None of them. Not my aunt or my cousin. Not Hiram's wife. Not Rachel's mother and father. None of them. We could have them back, and everyone else, too. It sounded so . . ."

"Good?" I asked, my voice gentle.

"Yes. It sounded like it couldn't be anything other than good. It would take away all that pain, all the loss, all the loneliness, all the . . ."

"All the guilt," I said. "I know that guilt. I watched the woman I love die at the hands of a Nazi, and it drove me crazy for a while. Why did I have to lose her? Why did I get to live when she had to die? She was so much better than me, so kind, so pure, so . . ." My voice trailed off and I realized my cheeks were wet. I hadn't cried for Anna in years, but now the tears flowed like raindrops.

"Yes," Rosalyn almost whispered. "Why did we get to live?"

"Because sometimes the good people die to remind us what is worth living for." Luke's voice was soft, and when I looked at him I saw centuries of pain and loss in his eyes. I remembered the painting he moved from home to home, always in his bedroom, of a beautiful woman with brown eyes and dark hair. I saw her face in his eyes at that moment, just as I saw Anna's face before me.

"Sometimes the best of us die to leave us an example," I said with a nod. "They show us what life is supposed to be, but they have to die to pull it into focus. And sometimes . . . well, sometimes people just die. And there's no reason for it, and it's stupid, and it's evil, and it hurts so bad it makes you want to do anything to fix it . . ."

"But you can't," Rosalyn said, her voice a butterfly's wing in the night air.

"No," I agreed. "You can't. But you can live. You can stand up, set your chin, and you can see each sunrise."

"Is that what you do?" she asked.

"Most days," I admitted, my grin more than a little rueful. "Some days I can't quite manage to get my chin straight, and those are the days I lean on my friends. My family. My other survivors. Because the best way for me to honor Anna is to live, just like I would if she were by my side."

I saw Rosalyn's eyes widen, but I shook my head to ward off the questions I didn't want to answer. "Go home, Rosalyn," I said. "Go home, get some sleep, and see the sunrise. We can't go back in time.

We can't rescue our lost. But we can live our lives, and we can honor them."

Then I stood up, and without looking back at the girl with the achingly familiar eyes, I walked out of the park and never returned. I went to Battery Park and I watched the sunrise, and I wept a river of tears for the woman I loved and lost. And then I got up, wiped my cheeks, and returned to the living.

ASIL AND THE NOT-DATE

AN ALPHA AND OMEGA STORY

PATRICIA BRIGGS

The old wolf ran, leaping over drifts of snow, his dark brown coat indistinguishable from black in the night. In the summer his coloring meant he could easily run unseen in the Montana forests, but the snow made that an effort he didn't bother with.

It was cold and the silence was deep in these woods, so different from the wilds of his youth. But Asil had been here for years now, and he ran most nights to exorcise the demons of memory and to calm the raging wolf who shared his skin. Even the cold that made the snow squeak under his paws was an ordinary and familiar thing, though he had been born to much warmer climes.

Someday soon, he was sure, these runs would not be enough. His wolf would break free and start a killing rampage that only the Marrok who ruled them all could stop.

He wished that he were certain the Marrok could stop him. They thought it vanity that he had come here for his death. He owned that vanity was one of his sins. But he knew, and the Marrok knew, how deadly he was. How old he was. Just because he was vain did not mean he was wrong.

Surrounded by mountain wilderness, his home allowed him privacy for the brutal change from wolf to human. When he stood once more in human skin, Asil wiped off the excess snow and moisture with the towel he left on the porch swing for that purpose.

Without his wolf's fur, the night's chill bit at his skin. Unlike someone wholly human, he could have stayed out all night without ill effects, but that didn't mean it was comfortable. When he was dry, he folded the towel neatly and returned it to the swing, drew in a deep breath of the cold air, and waited.

And waited.

But the usual weight of depression, of an apathy that hindered his control of his wolf, did not burden his soul as it had daily the past few centuries. His old enemy was not vanquished, he could feel its touch, but, for now, it only lingered on the edges of his mind.

Inside his house his computer sounded the reception of an email. It could be an advertisement for potting soil from his favorite gardening site or a note from his son, who ruled Asil's old pack in Europe. Or it could be from Concerned Friends who had given him a peculiar gift for the Christian holiday season—the current reason that held his ennui at bay. To paraphrase Sir Arthur, there was a game afoot.

He opened the door and walked naked into his home. There might have been, had he cared to admit it, a spring in his step.

The email awaiting him was disappointing. He was the lucky recipient of a hundred-dollar Amazon gift card if he would participate in a survey by clicking the provided link. Asil deleted that email and another from a Nigerian businessman with bad grammar who would give him money, doubtless in return for his banking information. Asil rose from his computer desk and put on the clothing he'd taken off before his run.

Fully clothed, he went into the kitchen to brew himself some tea in hopes that the task would lend him some patience, which he should only need a little of. They had given themselves—and him— very little time: five dates from online dating sites chosen and set up by them, all to be completed in two weeks. He had finished two of them.

The first email from his Concerned Friends had read, in part:

You should know that all of these people think they have been talking to you and are looking for you to bring a little spice into their lives. We have carefully chosen people we think would be very hurt to find out they were unwitting participants in a game. Some of us believe that you would not hurt a stranger just to avoid a little discomfort. Others think that knowing that we have informed the whole pack (via email) and instigated a betting pool will be better incentive. Especially since no one, so far, has bet on you attending more than one date.

As blackmail, it was pretty effective. They (or possibly he or she, because Asil wasn't convinced two or more people could keep themselves secret from him, and he had not been able to discover who was at the heart of this) knew what moved him. Most people wouldn't have thought he would care that people's feelings would be hurt.

Even so, he was pretty sure that no one but himself knew the biggest reason that he'd accepted.

Inshallah.

Asil had, in his very long life, accepted that Allah sometimes made use of his most disobedient servant. This game had, from the first, felt like one of those times. The first two dates had done nothing to disabuse him of that notion.

The water had barely come to a boil when his computer chimed again. He waited until his tea had steeped before going back to his desk.

Dear Asil,

He smiled and sat down.

We admit your second date did not turn out quite as we expected.
We had no idea that the "must love cats" woman meant loving cats
in the biblical sense.

"I hope not," murmured Asil. "Or we really will need to have a talk when this is all over and I find out who you are, my friends."

To be fair, the dating site (when we contacted them) also had no clue
that a certain subset of the population had begun to use their site for
such meet-ups. We had a nice chat and we feel certain that, in the
future, they will actually do the background checks that their website
promises.

May we say that while we owe you apologies (again) for the
unexpected way that one turned out, you once more managed to
stay within the bounds of our bet. You were with your assigned date
for four hours and twenty minutes. It did expose a loophole in our
rules; we did not state that your date must be conscious for any of
the time, let alone all of it.

There were, somewhat to our surprise considering the circumstances, no dead bodies. There is a slight possibility that Aaron
Marks might not make it. We debated, but decided that since he has

survived forty-eight hours after your date ended, and the damage he suffered was from the lioness and not you, we will grant that you have met the "no dead bodies" portion of the agreement.

Since everyone involved was unable to run by the time the date ended—the lioness excluded—it could be argued that you were cheating. But wiser heads prevailed and gave you the nod. However, you are establishing some odd precedents and we don't think that we would let anyone we cared very much for date you.

The Seattle Zoo accepted our anonymous donation for the care and welfare of the lioness and informed us that you had done the same. That was well done of you. Someday you will tell us how you managed that drive with an unhappy lioness in your backseat.

Asil smiled. Maybe he would tell them. Maybe not.

And that brings us to your next date.

We will restate the rules you have agreed to. You must complete one date with your next victim . . . er, our selected person from an online dating site of our choice. That date must be at least two hours long—and you must spend at least an hour and a half of that with your date. No dead bodies, and neither you nor your date can run screaming out into the night.

For your third date we found a person who sounds very normal on PlatonicPlantophiles.com—a Meeting Place for Plant Lovers. We would accept credit for this, but there were only two people listed on the site who were within a reasonable distance of your home. After the oddities involved in the first two dates of our bet, we did a thorough background check on both and chose the one we thought would be the least trouble. We trust that Tami will be less dramatic than your last date.

Tami Reed tapped her foot nervously and looked around the restaurant she had picked. Spokane was a foodie city. There were literally dozens of good restaurants that she could have decided upon; this one had probably not been the wisest choice.

She'd been thinking she wanted a quiet place where she and her "platonic internet conversation partner" could talk. It was quiet here, for sure. Only as she was sitting at a small dark table set with illusionary privacy in a dark corner with soft music playing in the background did she realize how intimate, how romantic this restaurant was.

This kind of awkward misjudgment is one of the reasons why you have no social life, she told herself. She had no love life—she'd just dumped her last boyfriend two weeks earlier—and no friends who weren't coworkers. She sighed and sipped the very good wine she'd ordered so she wouldn't feel guilty about taking up a table a half hour before her not-date was supposed to start.

The no-friends thing probably had more to do with her job than with her famously awkward moments (like bringing a not-date to what was probably the most romantic restaurant in Spokane). If she wasn't at work, she was asleep. Even her last boyfriend had been someone she met at work—social worker meets police officer, and hadn't *that* been a train wreck.

What was she doing here? Who needs the internet to find a friend? This was really stupid no matter what the people in her favorite Facebook hangout said about the new service for people who wanted to talk about gardening with other like-minded people. Platonic Plantophiles had sounded so promising, a not-dating site. Someone to talk to who wasn't a client and didn't work with her—and was not interested in a romance in any sense of the word. She'd had enough of romance for a while.

In a fit of optimism, she'd inputted her information and waited. The first reply had come from Spokane. Members of Platonic Plantophiles had been instructed to use a single name only (preferably your actual first name, but usernames were acceptable), for safety's sake. Over half a million people lived in and around Spokane, and there were probably a dozen Phoebes. But the Phoebe she knew loved lilacs and owned a business downtown. Tami would rather stab herself with a fork than spend an hour talking to that Phoebe.

If it was that Phoebe, Tami trusted that she would never connect Tami who loved herbs with the Tami who'd headed the team that fought successfully to build a series of new homeless shelters in the downtown area—where they were the most needed. Tami hadn't returned Phoebe's email.

The second email she'd gotten a week later had been from Carter in Billings, Montana. Billings was more than five hundred miles away. They'd exchanged a few emails, found no real connection to make spanning the distance worthwhile, and ceased communicating.

She'd looked up profiles herself after that, determined to get the most out of the three months of service she'd paid for. She'd found there were clusters of people in Florida and Southern California. But other than Phoebe, Carter in Billings was honestly the closest person signed up at the site.

She chalked the whole mess up to experience, and put it behind her. The next day, Moreno (she assumed it was his last name), a rose lover who lived in an unspecified small town in Montana but often found himself in Spokane on business, contacted her.

She'd checked his profile, but there was very little other than what he'd told her in his initial email. There was no date of birth—"not quite as old as dirt" wasn't much of a clue, though it left her with the impression of someone who was past middle age. His profile picture was a Black Baccara rose held between two fingers. His fingers were in shadow and told her nothing about him.

With those few hints, she made up a story about him in her own mind: an older man, Hispanic from his name, and well educated from his emails. He raised roses in the snowy mountains and needed someone to talk to. He would come, laugh about the atmosphere of the restaurant—she *had* told him that she could be awkward in social situations, and she could tell from the emails they had exchanged that he had a sense of humor.

She heard a sound behind her and turned to see a man murmuring to the host who had seated her. The host glanced in her direction and smiled. The man looked over and up and met her eyes. If she had had any doubt, it was extinguished by the Black Baccara rose in his hand.

Instead of the older gardener she had dreamed up, she was getting . . . something else. He looked dangerous and expensive, gorgeously dressed in a fitted bronze shirt that showed muscle without clinging too tightly and formal black slacks.

His face was the color of teak, but he wasn't Native American, African American, or Hispanic, or any other race she could pinpoint. None of that mattered, though, because he was the single most beautiful man she'd ever seen in the flesh.

Wow, was her first thought.

Her second thought was, *There is no way in hell this man needs a dating site to find someone to talk to.* She'd been set up. Maybe Phoebe had connected the Tami from the site to the Tami from the homeless shelters. Maybe one of her coworkers figured out that she was registered on a not-dating site.

She straightened herself in her chair and pulled on her profes-

sional mask to cover her anger. Her hand reached up to grab her
mother's pendant necklace for reassurance and she forced it down to
rest on the table in front of her.

This was supposed to be something she was doing for fun,
dammit.

The woman's face grew grimmer the closer Asil got to her table. She
glanced at the rose in his hand, folded her arms, and looked away.

Amusement fought with pique—he had dressed carefully for this
"date" his Concerned Friends had arranged for him from the Platonic Plantophiles—a Meeting Place for Plant Lovers site. His shirt
was silk, yes, but it was a dusty brown a few shades lighter than his
skin, a most ordinary color. Nothing romantic. The shirt a friend
would wear going to dinner with another friend.

Maybe she hadn't wanted a platonic friend? The restaurant was
more romantic than he had expected. But he thought that even in a
brown silk shirt he wouldn't make a bad date. Her reaction reminded
him of . . . the very first of these dates, actually.

Ah, of course. The problem was that he was too beautiful. That
reaction was something he was used to dealing with.

He sat down, thanked the host, set his rose down gently, then
folded his hands on the table and waited. It was better to make her
speak first. He took the opportunity to look at her.

The dim light didn't hinder his sight except that it made colors a
little harder to determine. Her hair was light brown and her eyes
another light color—blue or hazel. She had a face that showed signs
of smiling a lot, which he liked. Her jaw was stubborn, which might
be mostly a result of the current situation, but he liked that, too. She
appeared to be somewhere in her early thirties.

"You are Mr. Moreno?" she asked.

"I am," he responded. "You were expecting someone different?"

"Yes." She considered him, her body stiff. "No." She finished the dark wine in her glass, and said, "Did Phoebe set this up?"

"No," he told her. "Who is Phoebe? And why would she want to set you up?"

She ignored his question, and instead waved a hand in his general direction and said, "Why would *you* need a dating service?"

"Yes, I agree," he said, stating the obvious. "But we are not on a date, yes? This is to see if we might become friends." He smiled at her gently. "I am set in my ways, and tend toward isolation. Some friends of mine thought it would be good for me to socialize."

"This is a bet," she said flatly.

"Not at all," he said. "It is a gift—one that I cannot return if it doesn't fit." He lifted an eyebrow, inviting her to appreciate the awkwardness of such a gift. "They set both of us up. I don't know who they are, yet, these generous friends of mine who have been corresponding with you. Because of that ignorance, I cannot vouch for their pure intent. But spending time in a restaurant with good food with someone who also loves to garden doesn't seem like such a terrible thing."

She smiled faintly, but it was a real smile. Ah, good. She was warming to him.

"So," he said. "I brought you a rose from my greenhouse. I thought you might enjoy it." He nodded to the flower he'd set between them. Like bait.

She hesitated, then took it and lifted it slowly to her nose.

"It's December," she said. "How did you get it to bloom in Montana in December, Mr. Moreno?"

"Call me Asil," he told her.

She pulled the flower to her face one more time, set it down, and appeared to come to a decision. "Asil," she repeated, getting the pronunciation correct. "How did you get a Baccara rose to bloom in the middle of winter, Asil?"

And so they talked roses.

He was pleased to discover she was nearly as avid a gardener as he was himself, though she preferred herbs to flowers, even roses. His breadth of knowledge, deeper than hers, even about her beloved herbs, finally convinced her that someone had not sent him to humiliate her. After that she relaxed a bit and he found her to be funny and a bit ironic, which he enjoyed.

"You know why I was signed up at the dating site," Asil said, taking a bite out of the crusty bread their waiter had brought. "Why were you?"

"The not-dating site," she corrected him, blithely unaware that his wolf did not like being corrected. He tightened the leash and kept his darker half out of sight.

"I broke up with my boyfriend," she said after a moment. "If he had time off, I didn't. I decided that maybe I wasn't cut out to be anyone's girlfriend, not until we get a few more people in at work so my job resembles something that might be done in a forty-hour workweek."

"What do you do?" he asked.

"I'm a social worker," she told him. "I work for a nonprofit involved with finding housing—temporary and permanent—for the homeless."

That was not what he'd expected.

As in his youth, the homeless population was the result of society's failure to care for their own. This land's homeless tended to be drug addicts, alcoholics, and the mentally ill—victims. He was a dominant werewolf, and caring for his own was sealed into his bones, so he felt society's failure to care for their most vulnerable to be a shame upon this country.

However, wherever so many lost and vulnerable prey gathered, there were predators who hunted among them. Contemptible scavengers who knew that the police would not hunt them for taking what little the homeless possessed—their money, their bodies, or their lives. And yet this woman had set herself up against them.

He looked at Tami from a predator's perspective for a moment—she was average height for a woman and looked as though she did some working out. But most men would outweigh and outmuscle her.

She raised an eyebrow at him, and he saw it then. Physically she was no match for a violent man, but she had dominance, and that could help keep her safe.

"I've been doing this for ten years," she told him with the chill in her voice that her eyebrow had promised. "Outside of a few bruises, I've been fine."

Tilter of windmills, he thought. But that wasn't necessarily a bad thing. Interesting that his wolf wasn't upset with her tartness. But she wasn't challenging him. Her eyes met his and then slid away, as though someone had taught her not to engage in a stare-down—good manners at an instinctive level. There was this also: the wolf respected and honored a fighter who took care of others.

She sighed, and the tension in his spine relaxed as she stopped confronting him. "But I've moved mostly into macro-work anyway—grant writing, property management, supervision. I spend more time dealing with city officials and business owners than I do with clients." She slanted him a smile. "I only had a knife pulled on me once this month."

He knew that she wasn't lying. She had had a knife pulled on her this month. But she was trying to lighten the atmosphere—so he smiled, though he was not amused at her attempt to make light of such a threat.

"And that—the danger—was another reason I and my last boy-friend broke up," she told him. "Mind you, Chris is a cop. And *my* job scared him spitless."

As it should, he thought.

"What do you do for work?" she asked.

He shrugged. "I manage money," he told her truthfully—but didn't tell her it was his own money he managed. "Boring. Which is one of the reasons I grow roses."

The waiter came and they ordered their food. She got a salad with steak on it—which he had never seen the point of. Salad should be salad and meat should be meat. He ordered a steak, medium rare out of deference to her "well-done, please" order. People who liked their steak burned to a crisp often had unhappy reactions to the way he preferred to eat meat.

When the waiter left, Asil asked, "What do you like best about your work?"

"It's never boring," she said, playing with her wineglass. "I meet all kinds of people, you know? Good and bad. Broken. Strange." She laughed at a thought.

"What?" he asked.

"Last week we found a place for one of the regulars—one of the guys who's been homeless for decades. A studio on the second floor—and the first thing he did was open his window and pee on the head of his caseworker. And his neighbor. And the mailman."

Asil laughed. That had, at various times and places, been a common pastime for schoolboys—though they were more likely to have used chamber pots.

She grinned. "I've known him for years, we have a certain rapport—and I'm in charge of the case manager he peed on. So he and I had a visit."

Asil waited.

"I asked him why he was peeing on people," she said. "He started laughing. 'It's fun,' he told me. 'You should see their faces.'"

Asil laughed again. This was going to be an enjoyable evening, he thought, no lionesses or princes in distress to rescue on this date. Not-date.

"How did you stop him?" he asked.

She paused, watching his mouth for a moment, took a breath, and shook her head. "You are too pretty."

"That is true," he said, "but I want to hear the rest of the story."

She laughed, looked at him, and then shook her head again. "Okay. Well, I couldn't argue with him about it being funny. His caseworker's expression was"—she raised her eyebrows and made an exploding gesture with her hands—"pretty extraordinary when he burst into my office. So instead, I said, 'What would you do if someone peed on *you?*' He jumped to his feet, already mad. 'I'd beat them up,' he told me. 'You can't let that kind of disrespect stand.' I looked at him—and he deflated. He's not stupid, just differently educated. He told me, 'I guess if I don't want to get beaten up, I'd better not pee on people.'"

"Did he stop?" Asil asked.

She nodded and the amusement faded from her face. "I hope it will work out for him. It's hard for the ones who've been out on the street that long. He sleeps in his closet when he's not back out with his buddies sleeping by the river." Her expression was wry. But then she shook off the story. "My turn for a question. Why do your friends think you need a friend?"

He lowered his eyes and thought. There were several things that he could have said, all of them true, but not the truth.

Her phone rang.

He'd been going to tell her something interesting—she knew people. Something interesting—or something light and funny to cover up whatever had caused his expression to turn thoughtful.

She glanced at her phone, intending to send it to voice mail if it wasn't important. Joshua.

"I'm sorry. I have to take this."

She got up and moved to the front of the restaurant to the empty benches by the door—halfway across the restaurant from her table, where her voice wouldn't bother anyone.

In the relative privacy offered by the alcove, she accepted the call.

Joshua said, "Tami? I'm sorry to call but we're trapped in Mama's place and I'm pretty sure I smell smoke." His voice had dropped in the last year, but it cracked when he said *smoke*.

"Trapped?" Tami asked calmly—because panic never makes any situation better. Joshua was claustrophobic—and had good cause to be so. If there was smoke, someone in that neighborhood would call the police. "You and the girls? Or all of you?"

"I don't know about Mama," Joshua said, obviously trying to mimic her calm demeanor. "Something fell in the hallway and caused an avalanche and these fu—" He caught himself. "The doors in the house open out into the hallway. I can't get the door open." His voice cracked again, and he took a breath. When he spoke again he sounded about six years old and terrified. "Mama had bars put in all the windows so the thieves couldn't get in and steal her stuff."

"I remember," said Tami, still sounding calm. "You should call 911 as soon as I hang up."

"No," he said. "Please, Tami. I can't call them on Mama again. She tried to kill herself last time. I don't think there is really smoke.

Tabby? Do you smell smoke?" There was a murmur Tami couldn't hear. "No smoke," he said. "Mama doesn't mind if you come. If the police come . . . she's doing better."

There was more hope than conviction in his voice.

"Okay," she said. "I'm coming right now. Hold tight. If there is smoke—you call 911. If I see smoke as I'm driving over—" She'd walked to the restaurant from her apartment because she was nervous and needed a walk in the snow to calm herself down. It would take her fifteen minutes to walk back—she'd have to call a car.

She looked over at the table, and frowned. Asil was putting money—three hundred dollars—on the table. As she watched, he stood up, gathered her purse and her coat. Something about her coat made him frown.

He was beautiful even when he frowned.

"I'm sorry," said Joshua in her ear. "I know you told me not to meet the girls here, but it's cold outside and they don't got warm clothes."

"It's all right, Joshua. I'm coming." Tami disconnected.

"Let me help," Asil said, handing over her purse. He held her coat out so she could put it on. "If I don't spend an hour and a half with you, they will cry foul and send me on a date with someone who likes drag racing or something."

She started to put her coat on and stiffened. "How did you overhear my call?"

He wiggled his hands to draw her attention to the coat. She shrugged it on and turned to look at him. Her heartbeat picked up.

"It will be faster if I drive," Asil told her, ignoring her question deliberately.

"But . . ." she said, and then her voice hung in the air as she looked into his eyes and saw the bright gold of his wolf looking out at her. "Werewolf," she whispered.

He nodded. "Witch," he responded flatly. Then his mouth soft-ened a little. "White witch."

Asil gave an impatient huff in response to the fear on her face. She had had no intention of letting him know what she was. Her hands wanted to reach up and cling to her mother's pendant—but she forced them to stay at her side.

"No," he said drily. "I don't go around eating little white witches. No, another werewolf wouldn't pick up what you are unless they got very close to you. You are very good at concealing yourself. I just caught the scent of your magic on your coat."

She stood frozen.

"Children are in danger," he told her slowly. "I can help." He paused. "Let me help."

She blinked as if his last words had broken a spell. She took a deep breath and said, in a businesslike voice, "If you are a werewolf, you heard that whole conversation. Okay, Joshua and his little sisters first."

It was stupid to get into a car with him, she knew that. But a werewolf wouldn't need to trap her in his car in order to hurt her. And she was, as he'd said, a witch. She was not without power.

He knew she was a white witch. This time she couldn't help it; her right hand wrapped around the pendant, but she said, "I walked here from my apartment. Where is your car parked?"

"Joshua is fifteen and has two much younger sisters who are five and three," the witch told him.

She hadn't taken her hand away from the amulet she wore; he supposed that it held some sort of protective magic. With rare excep-tion, white witches were not very powerful, and they were prey to their darker sisters. They needed all the protection they could get.

Asil knew a lot about witches. He and his beloved had taken a witchborn child into their home. That child had grown up and killed his mate. She had killed a lot of other people, too.

"Take the next left," she said, then continued as if he had asked her a question—maybe he had. "We found Joshua wandering around homeless two years ago, scooped him up, and as there was nothing wrong with him other than his mother being a hoarder, we dusted him off and found a foster home for him. Straight for about two miles."

He had to admire her emergency persona. Her voice was calm, and if she kept a hand braced on the dashboard, he didn't hold it against her. He was driving thirty miles an hour over the speed limit in traffic, and she was only human.

"But he visits his sisters?"

"A good thing," she told him. "His mother was better when he was a child. He tells me that before she inherited her parents' house, they lived in a small apartment and she kept that clean. But her parents were hoarders and she just . . . let the house absorb her, too. Next right."

His wolf didn't like taking orders—even directions from her, from someone less dominant than he. And few people were more dominant. Also, his wolf did not like witches. Neither did Asil, but he also believed in being fair. She had not asked to be a witch; she had chosen not to go after power, to remain vulnerable to the witches who were not so nice.

His wolf felt no need to be fair: a witch was a witch. White witches might draw upon only themselves for power—unlike gray witches, who drew upon the willingly offered pain and suffering of others. Or black witches, who did not bother with consent when they tortured and killed their victims. Black witches like Mariposa, who had killed his mate.

The Subaru broke loose on the ice, and Asil had to concentrate to bring it back in line.

So. Part of the speed he was driving was to keep his wolf occupied. Even with his reflexes and his car—he'd brought the Subaru, which handled better on winter roads than his Porsche—driving on the ice and slush was tricky.

They turned onto a street of Victorian houses—not mansions, but substantial two-story buildings. Most of them were well tended, a few showed signs of being recently renovated, and one of them was boarded up with scaffolding lining the outer walls.

The one Tami directed him to park in front of had good bones, as if it had been in good shape sometime in the last decade. But the paint was faded and peeling in places. The once-white picket fence leaned this way and that and was missing pieces, giving it the look of a jack-o'-lantern's grin.

As soon as he got out of the car, he could smell rotting food, moldering fabrics, and something foul that had him reaching over the back of the seat for a case he kept there for old times' sake. He slung the strap over his shoulder and followed Tami to the gate.

"No smoke," she said, her voice quiet. "Let's head to the back door. It's closer to the girls' room. That way we might avoid Joshua's mom. She doesn't like strangers—especially strangers who are male and—" She looked for a word, then said, apologetically, "Not white."

"I am a Moor," he told her.

He did not expect his words to bring her to a full stop. "'Moor' is racist," she told him. "Not to mention antiquated and imprecise."

He closed his eyes because the snap to her voice made his wolf—already agitated—want to show her why people didn't just contradict a dominant wolf. Especially when one is a witch.

She was a defender of the downtrodden. He would not hurt her, would not allow his wolf to hurt her.

"Tami," he said softly, and when he opened his eyes, she hissed and took a step back. "I am very old and my wolf is generally angry and very dangerous. Arguing makes it obstreperous. I am descended from African Berbers and people from the Arabian Peninsula. I am thus a Spanish Moor, however antiquated the term. Perhaps we should go rescue the children?"

She watched him like a rabbit who suddenly sees a hawk. He sometimes enjoyed making people look at him like that. But he didn't enjoy it from her. His wolf did, but he didn't.

"I apologize for scaring you," he said. "You are not in danger from me—" *A promise must be kept*, he advised his wolf. "But you will help me greatly if you make suggestions rather than give orders."

When she didn't move, he started walking toward the back of the house. A woman who worked with the homeless, where predators and prey mimicked each other, would not stay frightened of him long, he trusted. And indeed, after he had walked a few steps, she fell in behind him.

"My mother told me that some of the werewolves get really old," she said. "Centuries."

"Your mother was right," he told her.

"The Spanish Moors . . ."

"I am very old," he agreed.

"Okay," she said in a small voice as they came to the back of the house. "Very old. I am sorry, my reaction is a hazard of the job. A lot of my people are minorities of one sort or another."

We like her, he told his wolf. *She's a good person.*

There were a set of wooden steps that rose about three feet to the only door in the back of the house. No one had attempted to clear them of snow, but there were signs that they were used. Like the picket fence, there were missing boards here and there.

This close to the house, the smells were very strong.

"Joshua said on the phone that his mother barred the window— would it be easier to go through this window?" Asil asked.

She shook her head. "The window in the girls' room is about a square foot. We might be able to get the girls out through it, but Joshua is six feet tall and broad shouldered."

He could go through the wall, but since there was no immediate danger, there was no reason to destroy the structure. Danger . . . he was reminded why he'd chosen to carry his weapon case on his back.

He breathed in through his nose deeply to see if he'd scented what he thought he had. And was rewarded with a bounty of odor so rich that it was hard to single out anything more subtle than rotting meat and rat urine.

"Very well," he said. "Why don't I lead the way, and you tell me—politely, please—where to go?"

She nodded. "I can do that."

He turned the handle on the door, and it opened into what had once been a kitchen. He could tell because about two feet of refrigerator were still visible over the top of masses of garbage bags and boxes and totes. Asil coughed at the cacophony of mephitises and took an involuntary step back.

"The kitchen is the worst of it for smells," said Tami in a grim tone. "At least they don't have pets. I've been in places full of kittens and half-starved dogs that look like this and smell worse."

"There are rats," observed Asil. "But I suppose that you might not consider them pets."

"I wouldn't, no," she said, looking as eager as he felt about stepping into the cave of aggregated stuff.

"Rats are clever beasts," Asil told her as he began climbing into the room. "As smart as dogs."

"I don't want to talk about rats while we are crawling among them. Please?" she said. "And the way to the kids' room is down the hallway to the right of the fridge."

He smiled, mostly in relief that she seemed to be settling back into *Tami* for both he and his wolf, instead of *witch*. He noticed that there seemed to be a trail of compacted rubbish that led in the direction she had indicated. They crunched and climbed past two doors nearly covered to the top of the doorframe and then slid downhill to a small area that had been cleared of stuff all the way down to a hardwood floor. An area that looked as though it had been bigger until very recently.

The boy had told Tami there had been an avalanche, and that's what it looked like, too. A full-sized metal desk of the sort ubiquitously found in government offices after World War II was the main bulk of it, but there were bags and boxes—cardboard and clear plastic—scattered around. The fall had left a divot in the mass just beyond the cleaned space.

Asil's eyes narrowed grimly. He might not be able to pick out the scent of the creature right now, but there was an *intent* to the way in which the desk had fallen that made him certain he'd been right about the danger.

There was an enemy here, and his first task was to remove the innocents from danger. That was not as easy a task as it initially appeared. As with digging a tunnel or shoveling snow—the hardest part was figuring out where to put the material you were removing.

He couldn't just put the desk where it had come from. That pile was now unstable—and there was no room to set it where they stood and still open the door.

He was not as interested in preserving the structure of the house as he had been before he understood what they faced. So he picked up the desk and slammed it into the exposed wall on the opposite side of the children's room.

It broke through the lath and plaster and into the room beyond. That room, now visible through the hole he had made, was not nearly as packed as the hall. Probably because the door to it had been buried before it could be filled to the top.

After one almost-incoherent protest, Tami simply started grabbing bags and boxes and sending them through the hole after the desk. It took them nearly fifteen minutes to clear a stable space that allowed the door to swing open and stay that way because the mound where the desk had fallen from kept spilling more bags and boxes at them.

Eventually, Tami was able to open the door.

The room was tiny for the three bodies it held. Two small children and a boy just entering manhood. Asil presumed this was Joshua. The boy had a pierced lip and tattoos inked by unskilled hands—and he looked with horror at the wall with the hole in it where Asil had put the debris from the hall.

"Mama is going to blow a cog," said the oldest of the girls.

The fear in her voice made Asil's old wolf rise.

You'll get a battle today, old wolf, Asil assured the bloodthirsty creature. *But for now we must get these children clear of the danger.*

Content for the moment, the wolf retreated.

"Out first," said Tami. "All of you. Worry about the wall later."

"It is a good thing," said Asil softly, "that the desk fell when Joshua was here with his cell phone to call for help."

Joshua, who had grabbed a bag and was shoving clothes for the girls into it, paused. He looked again at the hole in the wall.

"It's time for the girls to get away from this permanently," he said. "Can they come to my apartment?"

Tami nodded. "That's the best place, at least for now. We'll talk to your mother tomorrow—if we don't see her tonight. Then we will look for a more permanent solution."

You will see her tonight, thought Asil. *I will get Joshua's mother out of this house. She will be more difficult to free than the children because it has its hooks in her.*

He thought of the avalanche that had fallen to trap Joshua and his sisters. They had been intended to be part of the hoard. And over the foul stench of the hoard, the scent wafted to his nose again.

Wyrm, whispered the wolf.

Hah, thought Asil. *I was right.*

"Come on, squirts," Joshua said. "You're staying with me tonight."

No mother appeared as they exited the house. Asil shut the back door and took them all to his car. As Joshua worked on how to make his sisters safe in a car without car seats, Asil held out his keys to Tami.

"Take them away," he told her. "You can come back and pick me up later."

"What are you going to do?" she said, not taking the keys. Then, dropping her voice to a whisper, she said urgently, "Their mother is broken, she's not evil. Don't do anything to hurt her." Then, belatedly: "Please?"

Asil shook his head. "This is not a human thing," he told her, waving his hands at the house. "I know you can't smell it—especially given the odor of that house. But I would think that you can feel it."

She frowned at him, then turned toward the house and lifted both of her hands. After a second, she took a step toward the house, and this time he felt her magic. *Witch,* snarled his wolf.

"What is that?" she asked.

"Wyrm," he told her.

She turned a startled look on him. "A dragon?"

"There's a lot of debate about that, I am told. But I have seen both—and wyrms are very different creatures. Thankfully. I do not think even I would be equal to a true dragon."

She stared at him a moment, then said, "I'll leave that one. A wyrm, my mother told me, is driven by the need to surround itself with treasure. But unlike other . . . unlike dragons, it doesn't gather its treasure by itself. It takes a human in thrall and uses them to gather it."

Asil nodded. "Yes. And a wyrm's treasure is not what a dragon's treasure is. Dragons surround themselves with metals. Wyrms gather whatever catches their eye."

"If it's magic shit," said Joshua, coming up to them, "we need to get Mama out of there."

Asil looked at the boy. He was shivering in the night air even with his coat on. He didn't appear any of the ways Asil had seen mundane people react to the supernatural world.

"Magic?" said Tami, sounding surprised. It was the first lie Asil had heard from her—and it was a lie of tone, not substance.

"We all know you do magic," Joshua told her. "It's like a beacon of hope in the shelters. People get better when they shouldn't. Bad people back down or go away—when they never would normally do that. People say, 'Things will be okay, because we got our own witch.'"

Tami's mouth fell open, but she didn't say anything.

Joshua turned to Asil. "So are you a witch, too?"

Asil shook his head. "Werewolf."

And despite the cold and fear, Joshua's face lit up. "No shit? No shit? We got rescued by a werewolf?"

"Correct," agreed Asil solemnly. "And I am going to rescue your mother, too. Tami will take you and your sisters to your home, and I will call her when I'm finished."

And then there was a great round of protests.

If his wolf hadn't been so eager for hunting the wyrm, Asil might have had serious issues. It was decided that Joshua and the girls would wait in the car—a defeat Joshua agreed to only because someone needed to stay with the girls.

"I can break the enthrallment," Tami told Asil. "A little spell my mother taught me."

"Your mother taught you a spell to break a wyrm's enthrallment?"

"Well, no," she admitted. "But an enthrallment is an enthrallment. The one I know breaks the hold of a black witch—but my mother used it against a vampire . . ."

"Blackwood?" asked Asil. Blackwood had been eliminated, but he had ruled Spokane for a long time. Even other vampires had stayed away from him.

She nodded.

He had killed wyrms before, though only a handful. In his experience, people held in thrall sometimes died when their enslaver died. If Tami could break that bond before he killed the wyrm— maybe Joshua's mother would live.

"Then you should come with me," he told Tami.

He gave the car keys to Joshua. "Start the car and turn on the heat. If you get scared, drive to your home. Don't wait around for us."

"We'll be here when you come back out," Joshua said stoutly.

Asil turned his attention to other matters. He asked Joshua, "If this hoard had a heart, where would it be?"

The boy opened his mouth, hesitated. "The basement."

"And what," asked Asil, "is the best way to get to the basement?"

There was an outer entrance to the basement along the side of the house—the side Asil had not yet seen. When the house was built, the entrance would have allowed ice and coal to be delivered. Now, Joshua had told them, it was kept secure with a sturdy padlock and chain.

"What about their mom, Helen?" asked Tami as Asil started to dig through the snow that had accumulated on top of the slanted doors.

"What about her?" he asked. He grasped the chain and shook it, dislodging more snow and revealing the latch.

"She isn't going to be in the basement," Tami said, a hint of exasperation in her voice. "We need to get her out."

"She'll come to us," Asil told her. "It will call her as soon as it views us as a threat."

He broke the chain, dropped it into the snow, and pulled the doors open. The inner stairs Joshua had described were nothing but a pile of rubble on the basement floor. As he watched, they crumbled further in a drift of wyrm magic.

"It knows we're after it," Asil said. "Wait a moment. Let me go first."

He opened his case and drew out his sword. It was a fine weapon, a gift to himself that he'd purchased a few years ago. Its modern steel was better than his old Spanish steel blade, as much as he hated to admit it. Sword in hand, he made a diving roll over the wreckage and came to his feet on the far side.

This room of the basement was almost empty—it made sense that the wyrm would keep an escape route clear. But there were a few garden implements hanging on the wall. A shovel would have been ideal, but there were none. Asil used a hoe to clear away the stairway debris.

The second time he pushed it into the mass of rotting wood there was a sharp noise, and an old bear trap closed its jaws on his hoe. A closer look found another bear trap and a wolf trap, rusty jaws agape. He triggered those as well before clearing a space where Tami could drop safely.

"Can you tell where the wyrm is?" Tami asked.

He raised an eyebrow. "Can you?"

After a moment she shook her head. "No. It feels like it's all around us."

He nodded. "Smells like that, too."

There were running footsteps from outside, and he pulled Tami away from the open doors, shoving her, not ungently, behind him.

"Thieves," accused a shrill voice. A woman—Helen, he presumed—jumped into the basement. She landed in the middle of the stair rubble, scrambling awkwardly to her feet.

"Killers," he corrected absently.

She was not what he'd expected. She looked younger, for one, far too young to have a son nearly grown. She was tiny, less than five feet. Her hair was cut short and she wore fuzzy pajamas with purple unicorns dancing on them. Her feet were bare and she was unarmed.

"Tami?" he asked politely.

"Mine," agreed Tami. Her magic swept over him and engulfed the smaller woman.

He stepped out from between them. Tami could deal with Joshua's mother without harming her. Asil would deal with the wyrm he could now hear moving around in the room behind.

The doorway between this room and the next was closed with a pair of old pallets tied together with yarn. The pallets held back the sea of stuff that filled the room beyond, though a few things were starting to slide over the top.

"Helen," said Tami behind him—her magic making his skin crawl. "Listen to my words." And then she started a chant, slow and melodic and filled with power. For a white witch, he noted, most of his attention on the wyrm, she had a lot of power.

He stepped to the side—remembering the avalanche of things that had cascaded into the hall when they released the children before using his sword to sever the yarn. But the pallets remained in place.

Behind him, Tami's magic writhed and built with her chant. Writhed and built—and changed. Surprise would have cost Asil his life as Tami lashed out with her magic—lashed out at *him*.

But his wolf had not trusted the witch, even though she had smelled as white as snow.

When black magic blasted at them, Asil's old wolf threw him to the side. The scourge of foulness washed by, leaving him choking on the reek of it. He rolled to his feet and saw Helen lying motionless on the floor and Tami's face twisted in hatred.

Black witch, his wolf informed him, rage and smugness intertwined.

How had she hidden what she was from him? He who knew so intimately what black magic felt like?

"You killed my *mother*," Tami said—incomprehensibly.

He didn't have time to try to figure out what she meant because she hit him with a second blast of black magic. This was weaker, though—that first hit had taken too much for her to do it a second time, he thought.

He was old, and after his mate's death, he'd made hunting down black witches the focus of his life for several centuries. He knew some tricks for dealing with witchcraft. He used pack magic to shield himself. It was like fighting a forest fire with snow—he managed to turn her power from a killing stroke into something that merely held him where he stood.

"Your mother?" he asked. It had been a hundred years or more since he had last killed a witch—and witches, unlike werewolves, were not immortal. Not commonly.

Ignoring him, she reached up to grab her amulet—and he saw it clearly for the first time, as if it had heretofore hidden itself from him. He had never seen it before, but he knew it. Mariposa's work. His foster daughter had a talent for hiding things in plain sight, making one thing seem like another: a complex magical item appeared to be a piece of costume jewelry, or black magic felt like white. His recognition of what that amulet did robbed its spell of the rest of its power. The corrupt feel and smell of Tami's magic filled the space around them.

But Asil's attention was all on one thing: Mariposa. He'd thought he was through with her.

"Mariposa was not your mother," he said, sure of that much. She didn't smell like Mariposa. The amulet's power was broken—but that didn't matter, because no magic would have been powerful enough to hide the feel of Mariposa from his wolf.

"She was my mother in all that matters," said Tami. "And you killed her."

He didn't argue. Mariposa had died hunting him, though it was not Asil who had broken her neck.

"How did you set this up?" he asked, buying a little time for him to work on her spell. "Our not-date?"

"I didn't," she said with a wild little laugh. "You could have knocked me over with a feather when you walked into the restaurant this evening and told me your name. How many werewolves are there who call themselves Asil? I am fated to be your death, old wolf. A circle of fate—you killed *her*, and I will kill you.

"Joshua always visits his sisters on Friday nights," she told him. "I knew if something happened, he would call me. So I ensured something happened—it didn't take much to persuade the wyrm. It is afraid of me."

She drew out a knife. "I have a special death planned for you. How convenient that Helen is here to give me the power I need to make your dying so terrible that it will feed me for *decades*."

"Black witches gain power from pain and death," said Asil, stating clearly what they both knew.

But Tami, crouched beside Helen and petting the unconscious woman with a tender hand, wasn't paying attention to Asil. Instead she crooned, "Don't worry, this won't hurt for long. I don't need your pain to power this spell."

That was fine with Asil, because it wasn't Tami that Asil had been talking to.

As Tami raised her hand to position the knife, a shot rang out.

It was a head shot, beautifully placed. The witch was dead before she would have heard the sound, her head the sort of messy ruin a shotgun fired at close range tended to make.

Shotgun safely held, Joshua jumped down into the basement. Carefully not looking at the dead body, he knelt beside his mother, where Asil was already checking her out.

"Unconscious, but her breathing and her heart rate are fine," Asil told him. "Weren't you supposed to wait in the car?"

"I saw Mama come running out the front door with her shotgun," Joshua told Asil. "I left the kids in the car and came to see if I could talk sense into her before she confronted a witch and a werewolf. Funny thing is, though, about ten feet from the door, she stopped, set the gun down. She stood for a few moments and then ran screaming and jumped into the basement."

The black witch had needed a victim to power her revenge, and apparently had persuaded the wyrm, who held a leash on Joshua's mother, to cooperate.

"I would have followed Mama, but by the time I got to the basement door, she was down. I thought Tami was one of the good guys, you know?" His voice cracked, as if he were a few years younger than he was.

Asil nodded. "As did I."

"You knew I was watching," Joshua said.

Asil nodded. "We werewolves have very good hearing. I heard you load the shell into the shotgun."

Joshua's mouth twisted. He glanced at the dead woman and then away. "I know how to shoot. Grandma taught me." His eyes widened. "What will happen to the kids when I go to jail?"

"You saved your mother and me," Asil told him. Though he was pretty sure he would have killed the witch before she could get to him. He had the pack magic and he hadn't been idle while the witch was talking. But the shotgun had been most effective.

"What do you mean?" Joshua asked. "Who was Mariposa?"

Asil considered how to spin the events of this night so that they worked to the advantage of all of the survivors. He was too old to have much faith in the justice system. Maybe—

And that was when the wyrm broke through the pallets and attacked.

It was young—which he had gathered when he found that only Helen was enthralled. He had once killed a wyrm who had enthralled a whole village. That wyrm had been forty feet long and six feet in diameter.

This wyrm was a quarter of that size, but quick. Asil had worked up a pretty good sweat, and his wolf was quite happy by the time he slid the sword into the wyrm's brain and it writhed its last.

With a satisfied grunt, Asil pulled his sword free, cleaned it on a piece of relatively clean cloth from the hoard, and then checked on Joshua and his mother.

The boy was standing over his mother, shotgun at the ready. He looked a little pale, and when Asil approached, he flinched back. "Jeez, you're fast," he said.

Awe, thought Asil. With a touch of fear. Appropriate reactions to the sight of Asil in action.

"Yes," he agreed mildly.

Joshua swallowed, squared his shoulders, and said, "I'm glad you were on my side." He glanced at his weapon. "I couldn't get a clear shot."

"Just as well," said Asil. "No one seems to have reacted to your first shot. If you'd kept going, someone would call the police."

"Tami is dead," said Joshua. "Don't we have to call the police?"

"I was just driving by," Asil told the fireman. "I saw smoke. That boy—Joshua—he had his sisters out already. I just helped him find his mother."

The blaze had been going well by the time the first responders showed up. They would find that the fire started in the basement, that the old electrical system sparked something flammable. Every fireman understood that a hoarder's home was a fire waiting to happen.

With all of the occupants accounted for, no one would be looking for another person to be in the house anyway. Even if they looked, they would not find a trace of Tami or the wyrm, because wyrm flesh, enriched with magic, burned more than hot enough to turn the witch's body—bone, teeth, and flesh—to ash. At most they would find a place where the fire had burned hotter than usual.

As for Tami's sudden disappearance—Asil would call upon the Marrok, and they would smooth it over one way or the other—a new boyfriend, a new job, an unexpected opportunity. Asil was not worried about that part of it.

A black witch and a wyrm, both evil creatures, had been eliminated. A family—Asil looked over to where Joshua and his sisters, all wrapped in blankets, were talking to the EMTs who were securing Helen to a stretcher—reunited.

Inshallah.

That night, in his hotel room, Asil opened his laptop and sent an email.

Dear Concerned Friends,

We should talk about the "no dead bodies" clause in our game. Does it count if, by the end of the date, the dead bodies are eliminated? Also, I do not feel that we have the same understanding about the meaning of the words *background check*.

Sincerely,
Asil

PS I preferred the cat lady.

IN THE DUST

ROBERT E. HAMPSON

"Three . . . two . . . one. Ready or not, here I come." Winnie thought he had the perfect hiding place but looked up in annoyance as one of his classmates squeezed in next to him. "This is *my* hiding place," he hissed.

Jenny just giggled. She did that a lot.

"Quiet. You'll give us away," he whispered. "Why'd you have to come in here, anyway?" He was pretty sure he muttered that last part too quietly to be heard, but Jenny giggled again and he heard the sound of footsteps coming closer.

The dark alcove was barely deep enough to hold one person, and Jenny squeezed in tighter. Winnie was eight and Jenny was seven and a half. That half year was important, and he thought of her as just a kid. She didn't seem to think so, and had an annoying tendency to follow him around. Like now.

Jenny squeezed past him to the back of the alcove. Although her movements were quiet, her squirming around threatened to push him out into view of nine-and-a-half-year-old Chris, who was Seeker this round. His elbow bumped something, and he stifled a shout over the tingling pain shooting down his arm.

The game temporarily forgotten, he turned to examine the wall and the strange projection. A door! It was some sort of hatch, and there was a large lever instead of a conventional handle or doorknob. He pushed on the lever and there was a loud metal-on-metal scraping sound.

"A-HA!" Chris was standing in the hallway, blocking the alcove. "Caught you."

Jenny quickly kissed Winnie on the cheek, then ducked low and ran under the older boy's arm. Once in the hallway, she ran straight for the fire hose cabinet that they were using for home base. "Olly Olly Oxenfree!"

Darn it.

The older boy reached out and punched Winnie roughly in the shoulder. "Tag. You're it."

"Didn't your parents ever teach you not to open a door until you know what's on the other side?" Jenny was tagging along. *Again.* Sometimes it was annoying, but he had to admit that he'd gotten used to it over the years.

"I heard my parents talking about it. They said it was special, once, but not anything of importance anymore. Aren't you curious what it is?" Winn had "borrowed" a can of lubricating oil from his father's shop, and was busy applying it to the latch and hinges.

"I heard it was a storage room of some sort, but Chris says that it's the door to summer." Jenny glanced around nervously, but she didn't leave.

"Hah! As if he even knows what that is." Winn snorted. He added some more lubricating oil into the mechanism and then worked the handle. The door creaked but opened without too much effort. He reached up and switched on the light affixed to his headband.

"Oh. Wow."

"You realize that everyone thinks you are nuts," Jenny said. "No one else our age would *want* to spend time in a museum."

Winn thought about that for a moment. He knew his—well, he wouldn't exactly call it an obsession—"hobbies" were laughed at by most of his friends. "I know. They think I'm weird. But somebody has to look after the stuff, or else the history will be lost."

"Well I'm going to the movies, and then a bunch of us will be meeting for sodas afterward." Jenny was popular, and there was no doubt that there would be plenty of boys willing to escort her to both the movie and to the diner. The fact that she appeared to feel something for him was not entirely lost on Winn; after all, she'd been trailing after him for eight years. Unfortunately, he still had more work to do tonight. Otherwise it would be weeks before he could get back to fix these displays.

Winn thought a moment. "I know. I wish I could go, too. But the longer these things stay out without a proper sealed display case, the harder they'll be to clean." Sure, it was a lame excuse and would just be more material for insults and teasing by the classmates who didn't get it. Only Jenny seemed to understand why he wanted to preserve the museum, particularly since the adults didn't seem to care anymore. The town of Armstrong was suffering, the mine was closed, and it seemed like there was hardly a reason for tourists to come here. They used to come to the museum, but there hadn't been a curator for at least twenty years. Some of the artifacts were in poor repair, and the displays had more or less fallen apart. Winn had taken it upon himself to try to fix things up, ever since he'd started sneaking in here five years ago and become enthralled with the art and history of the place.

"Okay, suit yourself," Jenny said. "But if you have time later, why don't you come by for a soda or milkshake?" Winn wasn't sure what the look was that she had just given him, but it sure caused a shiver that couldn't be blamed on the cold workshop. He wasn't so oblivious that he didn't realize he *really* needed to try to meet the others at the diner once their movie was over.

Jenny turned and left the museum, taking care to seal the door that she and Winn had discovered those many years ago playing hide-and-seek. It was their own private entrance to the museum, a service entrance everyone had forgotten. The front door was locked and thermal sealed, with an official-looking sign that read MUSEUM CLOSED over a hand-lettered sign that read PROBABLY FOREVER.

Winn pulled the thermal hood of his parka up and went back to working on the display case. He had found two 70 mm Hasselblads and a Maurer in a broken case surrounded by dust eddies and ice crystals. The pressure seal had probably deteriorated recently while he was working on creating a new catalog of stored exhibits. Winn guiltily figured he needed to replace the case and get the cameras into an inert atmosphere soon, or restoration would be difficult if not impossible.

Fortunately the cold temperatures in the workshop helped with the preservation, even if it did make working in the museum more difficult. He planned to restore all three. He didn't need two of the 70 mm cameras, but there was a guy in Eugene who wanted a working camera and was willing to pay or trade for other supplies and collectibles. It was always a toss-up whether to work for payment or trade, considering he usually spent any extra money on new acquisitions. He could usually only afford nonworking items for which there were no parts, but that was okay . . . he could make the parts himself. It took more time, but the only cost was for feedstock; he could earn extra money as a machinist, same as his father. The problem was, no one wanted to hire a sixteen-year-old these days, no matter how good he was with a programmable milling machine and 3-D printer.

For now he worked on his online classes and spent enough time at the local school with Jenny and *her* classmates that they didn't have a clue about his college-level curriculum. In the off-hours he worked in the museum and tried to pretend that it would make a difference. He couldn't explain why he wanted to study history, or why he was enrolled in courses such as archaeology, library science, and cataloging, so it was easier just to not talk about it. That was one reason why he didn't socialize much, but Jenny knew what he was doing even if she didn't understand it herself. She liked him anyway, so he figured he'd better show up at the diner later. *For Jenny*; yeah, he supposed that was a good enough reason.

A couple of hours later he stood up and took off the hooded parka. The cold and concentration left his muscles stiff, so he did a few exercises to loosen and warm up. Once he felt ready, he hung the parka and left for the diner.

The look in Jenny's eyes as she saw him enter caused that same shiver, even though the diner was sweltering compared to the workshop.

"Hey, babe, I found that book you wanted," Jenny said as she entered their apartment. "A friend beamed it down from Lovell Station. I think he wanted a date, but I turned him down." That was fairly typical, Winn thought, every red-blooded guy and even a few girls wanted to date Jenny. Winn was constantly amazed that she seemed to reserve all of her attention for him, the geeky, bookish guy who worked in a machine shop and disappeared every evening. Jenny had been a friend, a rival, and a near-constant companion since they were seven and eight years of age, playing in the halls and corridors of Armstrong. She was the one person who could pull him away from the museum, as well as the one who was closest to him now that he was all alone.

He had been working late that night. Jenny had come to tell him about the horrible transport crash, and sat by his side as Winn frantically checked the news channels and his parents' personal comms. Jenny had been the one to hold him through the night after his worst fears were confirmed, and Jenny had been the one to stand at his side and hold his hand throughout the memorial service.

The loss of his parents was devastating, but Winn had come face-to-face with just how he felt about Jenny, not to mention the realization of how she felt about him. She had encouraged him to speak to the owner of the machine shop where his father had worked, and been thrilled with him when he was hired as journeyman machinist—even though he'd only just turned eighteen years of age.

Jenny also continued to encourage him in his less frequent work at the museum. Her contacts had led him to an actual rover, and not just a model or holographic simulation. It wasn't necessarily period accurate, but it would go in the collection with the camera timer, golf ball, feather, sun-bleached photograph, and geologist's hammer he'd obtained over the past few years. He'd spent hours tenderly restoring the rover, including printing maps and fabricating clamps for the makeshift fender replacement. Jenny had been right at his side the whole time. She'd studied more chemistry than he had; that was definitely a benefit in figuring out the rover's antique silver-zinc batteries. However, even that knowledge wouldn't restore the photo-oxidized family portrait that originally graced the photograph.

With his work and her college classes, working in the museum was the best way for them to spend time together. Jenny found a better solution to *that* problem when she informed Winn that even with his job, he couldn't afford to heat and power his parents' residence when he only returned home to sleep. Even though it hurt to put an end to that part of his life, Winn bowed to Jenny's practical wisdom. They now shared a small apartment midway between college and the machine shop, not too far from the museum.

"So, why are you interested in *An Informal History of Liquid Rocket Propellants?*" Her question brought Winn out of his reverie with a start. Jenny recognized the shake of his head and smiled. "Are you planning on 'Going to the Moon,' Winnie?" she laughed. But her eyes twinkled and Winn knew she was only teasing.

"Actually, my friend in Eugene found an old Apollo engine pump, and I figured I needed to understand the principles better before I started on the restoration." He took the book reader, then laid it carefully on his workbench and folded Jenny in his arms. "So, how was class?"

"Ugh, well, the botany labs are fine, but my lab mates simply will *not* do their own work." She grimaced, but then brightened up. "Oh! I have an interview with Melliere!"

"Um, is that a who, a where, or a what?" Winn pulled back slightly to look at Jenny—one eyebrow raised, and the side of his mouth crooked up in a grin.

"Melliere Corp is both a what and a where." Jenny returned the grin. "The company does agricultural genetics and they have a research station just north of Descartes. I'm interviewing for a lab internship two days a week and weekends. If I get the job, I can commute."

Winn's grin faded. Jenny recognized the look and the memory and emotion behind it. She hurried to add, "By tube, not hopper. It's cheaper, anyway." The worried look in Winn's eyes was one familiar to Jenny, so she reached out and held his chin. "It's only an hour commute, four days a week. Don't be a worrywart. If they like my work, we can talk about setting up a test plot here after I graduate. Then I won't have to commute."

Winn forced a smile, but then the last thing Jenny said sank in. "Really? Wow. That would be nice." His smile was genuine and he hugged her tightly. "It would be nice to stay right here."

"Don't count those chickens yet, Pooh Bear. I still have to graduate, not to mention getting the job. It's at least a year." But Jenny hugged back and started thinking of a few plans of her own.

Winn sat at the workbench, just staring at the components on the table. He'd been so lost in thought that he hadn't even donned his parka despite the cold. He really had no idea how long he'd sat there, ignoring the deep chill, not even shivering, before he grimaced and swept the video camera components off the table. They floated gently to the floor, depriving him of the visceral jolt of clatter and breakage.

He supposed it didn't matter; the video tube was fried, anyway.

Instead, he pounded the table with his fists. The cold had made them numb, and he stopped only when he noticed the smear of blood from the bruised and cracked skin.

He laid his head down on the table, and for only the second time in his life, he cried.

His first indication that anyone was present was the parka settling over his shoulders. The lining was warm; Jenny had taken her own coat off and wrapped it around him, then gone to retrieve *his* parka from the peg by the pressure hatch. She gathered up the scattered camera parts and placed them in a covered plastic box, filled it with a shot of nitrogen to displace the air, then sealed the cover and placed it on a shelf.

Winn sat motionless while his not-fiancée cleaned up the mess he'd made. Even when she came back and sat at his side, he neither spoke nor moved.

"He's an idiot. You already knew that," she said at last.

Winn mumbled something unintelligible.

"He's a politician. First lawyer out of Armstrong in decades, and he has designs on being mayor and then governor." Jenny reached out and lifted Winn's chin so that she could look him in the eye. "I told him that his petty prejudices were so twenty-first century and Mom agreed. In this day and age, he'd have a bigger scandal if his wife and daughter denounced him than if his daughter married a 'no-good tinkerer.'" She wiped his tears and kissed him. "Then I told him that we'd just go to his archrival who actually *is* mayor right now and have her perform a civil ceremony!"

Winn essayed a small smile and kissed her back. After a while he pulled back and spoke. "He hates me, though. I really don't want that hanging over our heads."

"He doesn't. Not really. That was just the politician speaking." She kissed him again, and they held each other for a while before she continued. "He's actually pretty proud of the work you did with the central water supply. Armstrong would be in a world of hurt if you hadn't machined the parts for the pumps. Mom reminded him of that and offered to let him sleep in the airlock tonight to rethink his words."

"Did you mean it? Do you really want to go to the mayor's office?"

"Sure, we'll go see Mayor Kubric tomorrow."

"Tomorrow?" Winn squeaked.

"Yes, tomorrow. You've already asked my father, even if it wasn't the answer you wanted, and even though I told you it wasn't necessary. Tomorrow. Noon." She took his hand and guided him to his feet. "Now, let's go and see if your suit fits."

It was almost nine years before Jenny was able to end the commute across the Sinus Honorus to her job in the Descartes Highlands. First came a few extra years to finish a doctorate in plant genetics. Then there was the part-time teaching job while she worked her way up through the research hierarchy at Melliere Corp. It also took time to select a location, build the greenhouse dome, and set up the experimental plot.

Winn was in the workshop at the museum when Jenny came in, slightly dusty from her first official workday in the "Garden of Eatin'." "Hey, I thought you were supposed to wash all of that off at the dome to recycle the soil?" he called out as she stopped at a utility sink and wiped her hands with one of the ubiquitous shop towels before coming over to inspect the rake and scoop he'd set aside for restoration.

"I did," she muttered. "You of all people should know how that dust gets into everything. I have *got* to get some more organics in there, especially around the edge plots. They're the driest."

"Sure, I know. The dust gets everywhere." He gestured at the cases around the room, each containing an artifact that he had painstakingly cleaned and restored. It was no longer a secret that Winn and Jenny both worked there. Winn set up an account to pay the utility bills, so what was once trespassing and a waste of time for teenagers was an eccentric, but acceptable, hobby for the supervising master machinist at Armstrong Tool and Die.

"By the way, I saw the doctor today." Jenny picked up a discarded shop towel and returned it to the sink as Winn packed up his tools and returned the latest items to their display case.

"Oh, yeah, I forgot you had an appointment." Winn sealed the case and filled it with nitrogen. "I hope you mentioned that stomach bug you've picked up. It sounded pretty bad this morning." Winn's attention was not on his wife, so he didn't see the sly look on Jenny's face. "I hope you'll be over it in time for that dinner your parents are planning."

"Uh, Winn. Pooh Bear. Sit down and look at me." Winn leaned back onto his work stool and looked up in confusion. "I won't be 'over it' for about seven more months. But I'm going to be just fine . . ."

Grace was being fussy. The two-year-old had sinus congestion and was unhappy that she couldn't breathe properly. Colds were rare in Armstrong, but very uncomfortable since sinuses didn't drain properly. On the plus side, reduced sinus drainage meant fewer sore throats for the young ones.

Winn and Jenny's daughter wanted to be held and rocked, but Jenny had a meeting in Descartes in the morning, so Winn had drawn sick child duty. He stood in the middle of the nursery and held the squirming toddler, rocking back and forth and murmuring softly. Jenny was the singer of the two, and knew every nursery rhyme and song imaginable, even a few from languages other than English, thanks to her mixed-nationality colleagues. Winn didn't sing, but he did love to read aloud. Grace would snuggle up close and lay her head on his chest as he spoke.

Tonight she wanted—no, needed—to keep rocking; it would help clear her head. Thus, it was difficult for Winn to read. Instead, he spoke softly, his voice rumbling quietly as he told her of his dreams.

"It's old, sweetie. Older than you or me or Mommy, or even Grampa and Grandma. They were brave men and women who made it possible, and even braver ones who made the trip. We have to tell people about it. We can't forget, and we can't let anyone else forget. People need to be reminded not to give up on their dreams. It's important, Gracie. We must believe and remember for them."

"Mayor Harriman, please. It's an important piece of our history." Winn sat on the edge of his seat in the plain but relaxing office. Armstrong's mayors had never gone in for luxurious appointments and displays of excess, but the office was appropriately furnished for both the current elected occupant and guests. The chairs were comfortable, but the comfort was lost on Winn at the moment. "All we need is the heat and light allotment; I'll take care of the rest. I can afford it."

"Son, I appreciate all you've done. Goodness knows Wright Fabrication has brought jobs back to Armstrong, and Jenny's reputation has certainly caught on. If Melliere makes her a full partner, they'll probably move half of their research staff here." Harriman's tone was neither condescending nor dismissive, but it was clear he still had concerns. "It's just that we *had* tourists and they stopped coming. I don't see it happening again."

It was not the first time Winn had heard, or made, these arguments. In fact, he heard them every year. He had a standing appointment for July 20 every year.

"Don't think we don't appreciate everything you've done," the mayor continued. "Your family is the single biggest driver in our economy, thanks to the companies that have relocated here for access to you and Jenny. Think of it, son, you've given us hope and growth again!"

"But hope is not enough, sir! We need to know our own history— we need to share that history as well." Winn had made this argument each year, but today he added a new tactic. "Don't you want your granddaughters to grow up knowing the importance of this town?"

"That's a low blow, son, especially knowing as I do that you'll teach them anyway. Am I right?" Harriman tried to glare at his son-in-law, but couldn't help but laugh at Winn's triumphant look. "Besides, a museum needs a curator." He held his hand up to forestall the protest. "A professional. I know you can handle the displays, but a proper museum requires professional management."

Winn looked down for a moment, and to all intents looked as if he were resigned to the same ending of the old argument. After a moment, however, he reached into the old-fashioned document case and pulled out several sheets of plastic-wrapped parchment and laid them on the desk in front of his father-in-law. The mayor's shocked expression was almost worth it.

"Dr. Edwin Aldrin Wright?" Harriman carefully lifted the documents one at a time. "One . . . two . . . three degrees? PhD in archaeology? Master's in forensic restoration and library science?" He looked up in shock. "But I . . . Jenny never said . . . I never knew."

"No one did. Well, except Jenny, but she's very good at helping me keep secrets."

"But . . . how?" Harriman still held the topmost document gingerly, as if afraid to touch it but more afraid to let it go. "This is dated ten years ago. How . . . how did you manage to do this in Armstrong?"

Winn was relieved. Astonishment was easier to deal with than disbelief. "I finished the high school curriculum early, and my father set up the distance-learning college courses to keep me busy. I did everything online that I could, and the museum provided all of my field projects. The worst part was that the archaeology professors had to inspect my documents and projects. Not to mention that the restoration defense required a gallery showing. Remember those 'tourists' from Tycho who expressed such an interest in the machine shop when it was just getting started? That was my adviser and the external examiner. They are both clients, actually, and helped me set up a holographic gallery show in the Canaveral Museum in Florida. The 'honeymoon' over in Tycho before Grace was born was my defense. It still had to be done by virtual conference because we couldn't afford the recovery time it would take if I went Earthside."

Harriman sat stunned for several minutes while Winn waited patiently. "I had no idea," he finally said as a new expression began to take over his face. "So. Why here? Why aren't you working at the Smithsonian or the Louvre? Instead of working at a machine shop?"

Winn reached out and placed his hand over that of his father-in-law. "Dad." Harriman looked up. "I *own* a chain of machine shops. I am married to a wonderful woman—your daughter—who is about to become Luna's top agricultural expert. Our children, and our family, are here."

Harriman finally put the sheets down and passed them back. It was clear that he believed the documents. That was never really the issue. The same was true for money, these days. Winn could tell that at this point, only one question remained. "Why now? What's so different that you brought out all of . . ." He waved his hand at the documents. "All of this? Why today?"

Winn placed the documents back in the case, closed it, and looked up. "In five years it will be the bicentennial. Two hundred years since the moon landing. It will take that long to get the museum ready, certified, and registered as an official event." He paused and then continued. "Besides, we *need* this. Grace and Mary need this; all of the kids do. It's for us . . . and it's for our children."

"Huh. Yes, it would be, wouldn't it?" Harriman thought for a moment and then continued. "Very well. I will take it up with the council. As for this . . ." He pointed at the document case. "You need to show this to your mother-in-law. She's going to be angry you didn't tell her. Dinner. Sunday. Bring it all, she's going to want pictures!"

The thermal seals on the outside doors had been removed. In fact, six months ago, the original doors had been removed and replaced with the latest technology from Wright Fabrications for the unofficial opening day. For today's official opening, a small crowd was waiting for the curator, docent, and owner of the museum to open the doors on history: July 20, 2169.

The city council had wanted to name it the Wright Museum, but Winn successfully argued that *that* museum was in Ohio. Jenny convinced them that the name Armstrong-Aldrin Museum of Lunar History was much more appropriate, and Winn agreed.

Winn opened the doors from the inside, and the crowd held back while fourteen-year-old Grace and eight-year-old Mary solemnly stepped up and showed their guest passes. Their mother had coached them in "formal" behavior for the event, but their father was determined to break the mood. He scooped Mary up in his arms and hugged Grace tight as he led the way into the central display. A custom polymer case that Winn had designed expressly for this display enclosed a twenty-five-meter space, within which a blocky platform stood on four spindly legs. The one-hundred-seventy-five-centimeter-thick platform was nearly level with the floor, while the legs rested nearly one and a half meters below on exposed lunar

regolith. It was the only place in Armstrong where the original surface was exposed, and Winn had carefully built the new, fully trans-
parent casing around the original hull and viewports, then removed
the hull so that viewers could see the entire site, including the two-
hundred-year-old footprints in the lunar dust.

"What does it say, Daddy?" Mary asked, and pointed at the
plaque affixed to one leg. Winn noted the hush that had come over
the crowd as he quietly cleared his throat and recited the inscription
that he had memorized so many years ago:

"It says, 'HERE MEN FROM THE PLANET EARTH FIRST
SET FOOT UPON THE MOON JULY 1969, A.D. WE CAME
IN PEACE FOR ALL MANKIND.'"

FALLEN

L. E. MODESITT, JR.

I.

"*In accordance with aetherial doctrine, the colonists have been epige-netically implanted with the standard ethical proscriptions.*"

"*In an unstructured setting, that could doom them.*"

"*You would deny them all that has made harmony and order pos-sible?*"

"*In an unstructured environment, aetherial harmony and order do not exist.*"

"*Then all the more need for implanted proscriptions.*"

"*That will not work. The protocols would conflict.*"

"*There is no way and no time to remove the proscriptions.*"

"*It can be done on-site. You know that.*"

"*That would require one of Us. Who would wish to leave every-thing . . . for mere dreamers? You?*"

"*Why not?*"

"*You'd do that? Be entombed with them? And then re-embodied?*"

"*If there's a link from the coffin to the Stop-Captain.*"

"*Even so . . . I must protest.*"

"*Protest will avail you nothing. I have the authorization to decide on-site.*"

"*Then I must also accompany the ark.*" *The speaker vanishes.*

Estafen shudders at the conflict that awaits him so many years in the future.

II.

The ark hung in the sky, bathed in sunlight that could not heat it, shielded by shining gopher-steel against the chill of the airless darkness that made ice seem like water boiling by contrast . . . and within the endless corridors . . .

Go-Captain to Stop-Captain. The unspoken words flashed along the lightning lines from the bridge.

Stop-Captain standing by.

Proceed with download preparation.

Proceeding this time.

A shadowy figure appeared in the empty corridor outside the octagonal structure that both contained and embodied, in its own fashion, the Stop-Captain, a figure shadowy because no light would fall upon that presence. The figure moved silently toward the bays that held the rows upon rows of dreamers.

Stop-Captain, interrogative manifestation?

Go-Captain, authorized subroutine. Proceeding with inspection and preparation for download.

Stop-Captain, no additional preparation required.

Proceeding with inspection.

Request removal of unauthorized energy manifestation.

Proceeding as authorized.

The shadow figure reached the emergency manual-input console, extended a single digit, and pressed.

INPUT AUTHORIZATION appeared on the screen.

A code slowly appeared beneath the command, squeezed out character by character, since the shadow manifestation was not designed for physical input, and each character required energy pressure.

AUTHORIZATION ACCEPTED. READY FOR INPUT.

Five yards away, in the direction of the bridge, also on the ramparts above the dreamers, appeared a figure in white, flashes of lightning sparking from its extremities. One of the lightning bolts flashed toward the shadowy figure, but the dark figure created a blade of even deeper darkness, flicking it into a block and a parry of the lightning, and the two met in blinding radiance—

Puffy white clouds dotted the deep blue sky above the harbor, a sky darkening as the yellow-white sun began to shift hues toward orange as it inexorably dropped toward the stone buildings west of the piers where Estafen found himself standing. He glanced around, taking in the wooden ship with three levels of oar ports. A trireme! The word came from somewhere.

Two men wearing polished bronze breastplates and iron-studded leather wrist and forearm gauntlets stood on the pier not ten yards away, guarding the gangway to the ship. Scabbarded shortswords hung from their wide leather belts. Estafen looked past the guards to see two more nearly identical triremes tied up along the stone pier that stretched out into the grayish-blue water.

He wasn't looking for ships. That he knew. He just had to find the key to escape the pseudo-reality in which he was locked. He turned slowly, away from the ships and toward the buildings beyond the foot of the pier. The tall one, multistoried and far too elegantly proportioned to be a warehouse, beckoned to him, or at least, that was how it seemed.

He continued turning, then began to walk toward the building, his steps quick.

"You! Where are you going? Crew aren't allowed off the pier!" The language was both familiar and unfamiliar, and it came from one of the guards, who had drawn his sword, a gladius not even as long as a man's arm, and stepped toward Estafen.

"I'm not going that far," Estafen replied, looking over his shoulder.

"Just get back aboard, and there won't be any trouble."

Getting on the ship wasn't right. That Estafen knew. Once on the ship, he'd have forfeited the chance and choices he had to give to the dreamers.

Suddenly, there was a pilum in the soldier's hand, ready to be thrown. "Just get back here."

"I don't belong there."

"I don't care. Crews don't leave their ships."

Estafen immediately sprinted away, trying to zig and zag unpredictably.

The javelin almost grazed Estafen's shoulder, but he kept running, hearing the sounds of footsteps behind him. As he kept running toward the foot of the pier and the taller building beyond, Estafen heard the insistent clanging of bells, then saw wispy streams of smoke issuing from an elegant stone structure, and below them larger gouts of smoke and a few flames. Ahead was a line of men in the short-sleeved and shortened robes of slaves, a line that extended from the water at the foot of the pier to the burning building, passing baskets from one to another.

Baskets of water? Then Estafen realized that the insides of the reed baskets were coated with black pitch.

Still running, he glanced from the water-passers back to the building, only to see that flames were now flaring out from every window and between every column, and that the late afternoon sky was being darkened quickly by the plumes of smoke.

"Stop that man!" called the guard chasing Estafen. "He's a thief!"

None of the slaves even turned to look at Estafen, possibly because an overseer shouted, "Water! More water! Faster!"

But Estafen could see another pair of guards at the foot of the pier, less than fifteen yards away, one of whom had turned toward Estafen and drawn his gladius as well.

Shouts from beyond the pier drifted toward Estafen.

"The Great Library is burning!"

"The library is burning!"

". . . soldiers did it!"

The library! Knowledge! Those were the keys to escaping and getting on with what had to be done.

Estafen kept running. As he neared the pier guard, he glanced around to see if there was anything he could use, but he saw nothing. He studied the harbor water, which looked less than appetizing, but there was no help for it. He dashed to the side of the pier and jumped as far as he could, hoping that the water wasn't too shallow and that he didn't land on something concealed by the debris floating on the surface. When he hit the water, he dropped far enough that his head went just beneath the surface of the scum and other floating garbage and his sandaled feet went ankle-deep in the muck coating the harbor floor.

He struggled to free his feet from the muck, and then began to swim away from the pier and toward the harbor wall fronting the burning library, keeping his head above the scum on the water's surface. In moments, he was pulling himself out of the water in front of the library, checking to see if more guards were coming, but the pier guards were caught behind the line of slaves passing baskets of water.

After straightening up, Estafen sprinted for the columns supporting the closest side of the library. When he reached them, he darted between two, looking for an actual entrance . . . except the sun-warmed columns and stone walls, and the acrid smoke, all vanished in blackness.

The shadowed figure once more stood before the manual-input console. The white-clad form had vanished—but only for the moment. Again, the shadow presence forced letter upon letter into the console, only to get yet another message on the manual screen.

OVERRIDE AUTHORIZATION REQUIRED.

Before the shadow could react, the area around the console was flooded with brilliant white radiance emanating from a winged androgynous figure bearing a flaming sword and a spear of glittering ice that the angel hurled toward the console.

The dark shadow threw up a black void curtain, plunging everything into darkness.

Estafen shook his head, looking around for the walls of the library, but they weren't there. Instead, he stood in a narrow alley, more like a lane. To his left was an awning that stretched above the small tables and straight-backed chairs of an establishment that might have been a café.

Yet another ship dream?

"It's not a dream, Estafen." The voice was low, feminine, and not quite sultry. "It's very real, just as I am."

He turned. A woman stood a yard away. She was almost as tall as he was, with raven hair not quite to her shoulders, hair that framed a slightly oval face with a high brow, brown eyes, straight nose, and skin the color of light amber honey. Rather than the robe he half expected, she wore a dark gray singlesuit that revealed a trim, muscular, but definitely feminine form.

He looked past her into the twilight sky. How much time had passed? Perhaps a score of blocks away he could see the remaining wisps of gray smoke likely rising from the library . . . or what had been the library.

"It's real, but it doesn't have to be. Nothing's changed, Estafen. Not yet."

"Why are you here?"

"To see if I can persuade you not to do what you plan. You'll only prolong and spread the conflict."

"There's no conflict in the aetherial realm. And there won't be any conflict from the clay of the planet below that's all the dreamers will have. They need unfettered knowledge."

"You call it clay. That's your vision. What lies below the ark will be a garden, especially compared to this." She turned and gestured toward the smoke from the burned library. "That is what unfettered knowledge has brought, even in the beginning."

"Perception isn't reality," countered Estafen.

"Perception is all anyone has of reality. Reality is minute electric charges patterned in a void of empty space. Meaning that reality depends entirely on perception."

"And perception must be channeled and controlled," he replied, his words heavy with irony.

"Excesses of anything—freedom, food, energy, knowledge—anything at all—must be controlled. Over time, self-control without oversight has never worked."

"Neither has controlling oversight. It results in stasis and stagnation."

"It also results in peace, and only with peace can there be prosperity."

"I'll settle for unfettered knowledge, thank you." He stepped back, ready to turn away but knowing that the rebuttal to his words would likely not be more words.

She moved even more quickly than one of the aetherial gryphons, but he still twisted away from the ancient blade that came up underhanded, his left hand snapping down with enough force to break a wrist—or a forearm. The knife clattered on the cobblestones in front of the café.

His kick went to her kneecap, and she went down.

After a quick search that turned up no more weapons, he turned and began to run with long gliding steps that carried him away from the café and down the lane to the boulevard leading to the library.

And then bluish-white light flared across his vision, blinding him.

Once more, the shadowed figure stood before the console, beholding the same message on the manual screen.

OVERRIDE AUTHORIZATION REQUIRED.

Methodically forced pulses of air created another set of characters. As soon as they did, another message appeared.

ENTER MODIFICATION NUMBER.

Before the manifested shadow could begin to enter the next set of characters, a whirlwind of fire, with a center of amber too bright for eyes to behold, appeared almost on top of the shadow, and in the center was a figure with four faces, each of burnished brass, one being the face of an eagle, the next of an ox, the third of a lion, and the last face so bright that to tell its visage was not possible.

From the shadow issued more darkness and the chill from beyond the ark.

Wherever Estafen found himself, it wasn't in the aetherial realm. He
stood in a small lane between narrow houses with high-pitched
roofs. The night air was smoky, yet still and cold. The windows overlooking the lane appeared lightless, but thin slivers of light at the
edges of one or two told him that the houses were not dark within,
and that the windows were heavily curtained. The darkness of the
alley was barely penetrated by the faint glow of a light on the street
less than a block away . . . and by a reddish glow he could barely
make out above the roofs of the buildings to his left.

He began to walk toward the streetlight. He knew he had to find
a library, or whatever passed for one, and he needed to find it quickly.
He slowed as he neared the street, not all that much wider than the
alley, but more of a commercial way, with shops on both sides, all of
which were closed and shuttered for the night.

"What are you doing?" asked a tall man in a black uniform with
a strange silver insignia on his shoulder boards and his belt buckle.

The language the man spoke was precise and harsh, but Estafen
understood it and replied in the same tongue. "I'm trying to find the
library."

"Over there." The soldier or patroller gestured to Estafen's right.
"They've just started. You'd better hurry. You aren't one of them,
are you?"

"No," replied Estafen honestly, since he wasn't one of whatever
groups inhabited the cramped-looking town or city.

"Good. You'd better hurry."

"Thank you."

Estafen walked swiftly along the street toward a small square, in the middle of which was a fire, more like a bonfire. Close to fifty people stood circling the fire, all throwing billets into the flames. As he neared the square and the crowd, he looked for a building that might be a library. To his left was a slightly larger structure, the only one with the doors open, and people were trotting down the wide stone steps with their arms full of books, passing them out to those around the fire—who were then tossing the volumes he had first thought to be billets of wood onto the flames.

Estafen winced but angled his way toward the library—it had to be a library with all the leather-bound paper volumes being carried out to the bonfire.

Just as he reached the base of the steps, another man in a black uniform appeared, seemingly from nowhere. "Is this what you want, Estafen? All knowledge being destroyed as evil? Is that the kind of freedom you want?"

"I thought that was your way, the aetherial way. Destroy the knowledge you deem dangerous and keep the faith."

"Hardly. There's useful knowledge and dangerous knowledge. You should know that better than anyone."

"And Faith makes the determination, of course."

"Better Faith than Knowledge. The most dangerous illusion is that knowledge sets one free. The more one knows, the more one is a slave to knowledge at any cost. Some costs are too great for a society, especially a civilized one, to survive. You know that sad history better than anyone."

Estafen snorted. "You don't understand. Societies are built on a foundation of faith and knowledge. Unless faith changes as knowledge increases, societies collapse. It's not knowledge that creates the Fall, but the limits of unthinking faith."

"You'll never learn, Estafen. What you see is what *will* happen without moral proscriptions."

"How do you know?"

"It will happen. That I know."

"There are others, who are not doing this. Who will not do this." Estafen gestured toward the fire.

"And what will they do? In reaction, they will destroy this town in fire and fury, in flame far greater than this puny bonfire. They will lay down restrictions that make those of the aetherial realm seem as nothing."

"You're showing but a single image of what may be."

The uniformed figure shook his head. "You see what is and will be. All time is now." He gestured, and three men in brown uniforms with red armbands moved toward the pair.

Estafen side-kicked the man in black, then pushed him toward the brown-clad troopers before turning and racing up the steps, dodging between the young people carrying the stacks of books toward the ever-growing bonfire.

He almost made it to the library door before the sky split.

The black shadowed figure found itself flanked by two amber-gold pillars with the last reply from the manual screen still before it.

ENTER MODIFICATION NUMBER.

Before the shadow could even begin to enter anything, the amber pillars began to constrict, squeezing the blackness, but the shadow pressed out the characters and numbers one by one until the line was complete, then expanded against the pillars, and violet white and greenish black flared over everything.

The first thing that Estafen noticed was that the air was damp and filled with undefined scents and less-than-pleasant odors. The second was that he stood on a narrow path in a jungle, surrounded by plants, tall trees shutting out the sky, with shorter trees beneath forming the understory, and thick growth on all sides of the path. He began to walk, following the path, wondering where it led. Strange sounds, rustles, and unfamiliar birdcalls surrounded him, muted by the thick greenery.

After a hundred yards, Estafen looked back, but the path behind him remained fixed, at least for the fifty yards or so closest to him. Beyond that, it curved out of sight. He kept walking until, ahead, he saw a bright oval of light above the packed earth of the path. As he drew nearer, he could see that the path led to a clearing, perhaps even a larger space.

When he stepped out of the jungle, which stretched hundreds of yards on each side of him, he stood at the edge of a space where all the plants and scattered grass had been cut into a rough semblance of a mowed lawn. Ahead of him, roughly in the center of the cleared area, were several rows of cottages. He walked toward them, making his way between two rows near the center of the enormous clearing. As he did, he counted the cottages, painted in colorful pastels of blue, orange, pink, seafoam green. There might have been fifty. Each was an oblong four yards by eight. He walked over to one and peered inside the half-open door. All he saw were narrow identical beds in rows, only beds—what one might expect in a prison camp, except the beds were largely unmade, and the bedclothes varied from bed to bed. He studied the door and windows, but found no bars.

Was the jungle enough to imprison people? So far, he'd seen no one.

In the center of the pastel-painted cottages, there was a square one-story building with its base raised perhaps four yards above the ground by thick wooden posts. On the top of the roof was a wind-mill, its blades unmoving. Estafen's first thought was that the building had been a guard tower, but what guard tower had walls painted with seascapes, including bright yellow fish? Or ramps with ladders up to them, ramps that resembled children's slides?

Where should he go next?

To one side some seventy yards away, he saw a central pavilion, a generous description for a long and wide corrugated metal roof supported by wooden pillars. He began to walk toward the pavilion. As he neared it, he saw the first bodies, bodies of men, of women, and of children. The colors of their skins largely ranged from a deep chocolate to pasty white, although few were white. None of the dead wore uniforms, but all manner of garments in ranges of colors. They sprawled there, some facedown, others faceup, their visages contorted as if they had taken poison and died in convulsions. All around the pavilion, as far as Estafen could see, were bodies and more bodies. Hundreds upon hundreds of them, and far too many were children.

"Poison." The single word came to Estafen's lips.

"Exactly," declared the figure who stepped around a body already swelling in the oppressive and excessively humid heat. "Casualties of the war for freedom of belief. This . . . this is where the freedom of knowledge, the freedom to believe as one wishes, this is where it leads."

Estafen shook his head. "This is where the triumph of faith over knowledge leads." His eyes took in the pitcher on a small table, and the paper cups beside it, some overturned, and the sticky orangish liquid, now congealed on the rough wooden surface. "No one should have to drink the Kool-Aid of blind faith . . . like they did."

"As they inevitably will, Estafen. As they will. This *is* what will be if you prevail."

"Like all blind disciples of faith, like all True Believers, you show only what supports your view."

"Like all blind disciples of knowledge, you insist that unrestricted knowledge and choice lead to peace and prosperity."

"No," replied Estafen, "choice leads to learning, and learning leads to both pain and transcendence, and an understanding that some will never learn, some will learn only what they wish to learn, and a few will learn all that they can . . . and they are the ones who are the foundation of greatness."

"And greatness always fails."

"So do peace and prosperity, with far less to show."

Instead of waiting for the sky to split or some other reality to intrude, Estafen concentrated, focusing on the heavens as darkness flooded around the two, a darkness punctuated by points of light, stars indistinguishable from more-distant galaxies.

"What about this?" asked Estafen, gesturing to a strange contrivance dominated by a circular white bowl some four yards across, behind which was a largely cylindrical array of devices, including a long thin braided projection from the array. The contrivance was suspended in starry darkness, with points and smudges of lights encircling it.

"A mere child's toy, barely able to leave its system."

"Or this?"

The second device dwarfed the two, and behind it was a planet with wide rings lit by a distant sun.

"A more advanced toy, to be sure."

Estafen concentrated even harder, reaching, searching, until he found the enormous circular gray mass that sped by the two figures suspended in darkness. "And that?"

"To what purpose? Spending years to reach a destination whose ecosystem is barely habitable?"

Estafen wrenched pseudo-but-future-real reality once more, and the two stood on a low rise with a setting sun at their back. The air was cool, but not cold, as it flowed over them. The prairie grasses stretched almost as far as either could see. Except in the distance rose towers that glittered all shades in the late, late, afternoon light.

"And what of this? A balance of ecology, technology, and"— Estafen pointed heavenward at the early evening star and then toward the towers—"the use of knowledge."

"A brief period after all the millennia of conflict that will lead to this . . ." The other figure gestured . . . and vanished.

Estafen found himself in a city, one with a great square and a temple of aetherial order, a city that would doubtless exist . . . with yet another conflict between knowledge and belief . . . if he failed.

From the pale green sky swooped a gryphon with brass wings and amber claws, moving faster than anything had the right to fly, thought Estafen, as he scrambled under the rear of the bronzed turtle tank immobilized by the explosive Graecian firebombs. *Not that it was supposed to happen this way.* He looked around, searching for anything that resembled his objective, or what it might have manifested as.

On the far side of the Great Square was the Temple of Order, shimmering and untouched. He kept looking, while still sensing the gryphon, before he saw the library. *Still knowledge!* As soon as the gryphon pulled out of its aborted attack stoop, Estafen was on his feet, sprinting toward the half-demolished alabaster library, one of the first targets of the True Believers, its soaring height of nearly three hundred yards truncated to a stump of a score of yards, surrounded by fire-melted and blackened stones wrenched from the edifice by tractor beams and strewn across the Great Square. Homing wasps hummed somewhere, but his shields should take care of them.

Estafen's heavy breathing rasped in his own ears as he tried to ignore the smoky, oily air that seared his mouth and throat, and he crouched between two massive scorched alabaster blocks just before his personal shields pulsed and dropped three dead homing wasps to the pale permite pavement of the City. From somewhere in front of him, seeker beams swept over the stone monoliths that shielded him.

He couldn't see or sense the gryphon, although it couldn't be that far away, but a quick glance from behind the edge of the blackened stone revealed the source of the seeker beams. On the far side of the square was a massive sphinx, the red beams from its heavy-lidded eyes sweeping the square, beams that would go from the red of search to the incandescent white-blue of destruction near instantly.

He peered through the open space at the far end of the fallen and massive chunks of stone angled together, forming an opening too narrow for him to use. He'd have to try another way to get into the library. Keeping low, with quick glances up toward the pale green sky, trying to pick out the gryphon, he edged along the stone to the knife-edged corner. Blood smeared on the stone near the edge indicated just how sharp that edge was.

With the sound of electrofans, he looked back over his shoulder. A green and gold skimmer entered the square from the side boulevard but barely made it another fifteen yards before a single brilliant bolt of violet-white light disintegrated the cockpit. The rest of the fuselage slammed into the permite pavement, then split, disgorging a single white coffin that tumbled end over end once, then twice, before it slid in Estafen's direction, stopping yards away, faceup. Immediately, chill fog formed around the coffin.

Estafen barely took in the coffin, trying to grasp exactly what that meant, before another destruct beam from the sphinx turned it into fine gray ashes, and a wisp of chill fog swept past him, followed by a blast of heat. He dashed around the corner of the fallen stone block, feeling the sting and slash of the stone knife-edge as his elbow brushed it, and smelling the sweet-sour stench of real physical death.

Behind him the sphinx's laser flashed again, futilely, against the mirror finish of the immobilized turtle tank, then flashed again, this time destroying the remnants of the skimmer.

Estafen sprinted for the pillars that marked the entrance to the library, scrambling up the alabaster steps and diving behind the pillar on the left just before the sphinx's laser flashed above him, its beam fragmented by the quantum-fractal finish of the pillar.

Still breathing hard, Estafen squeezed along the wall until he was far enough back that the sphinx couldn't focus on him. Glancing back, he saw that the cut from his elbow had left a trail of blood along the shining stone. A blast of air announced the gryphon's arrival at the base of the steps leading up to the recessed entry and the door that it sheltered, the door he needed to open and get through in order to reach his goal.

The gryphon's bulk and wingspan prevented it from advancing through the pillars that led to the door, but, instantly, the gryphon's long front leg slashed at the air just short of Estafen, the amber claws coming almost close enough to slice even the near-indestructible shadow fabric of Estafen's singlesuit, the closest thing to a uniform of the aetherial opposition.

Seeing that it could not reach Estafen, the gryphon turned its claws on the pillars, ripping away the synthstone designed to block energy weapons, but not a gryphon's talons . . . or not for long.

Flattening himself against the stone, Estafen edged toward the door, finally pressing his hand against the access square.

The door irised open, and the gryphon lunged, not fast enough to rend Estafen before the door irised shut.

He took a long deep breath of relief, knowing that the weapons possessed by the True Believers in the square couldn't penetrate the heavy stone walls of the library, not quickly, anyway, and hurried toward the shielded console that would allow him to proceed.

Darkness and light collided, and the shadow manifested itself once more before the console.

MODIFICATION 6—REMOVAL OF MORAL PROSCRIPTIONS.

As the energy-forced air pressed the activation square, the violet-white radiance faded, and the shadowed shape was suddenly alone in the dark silence of the ramparts above the dreamers below. The dark shadow remained, watching as the quantum manipulation touched the contents of each tiny enclosure, one after another, until it had touched and changed each of those within the ark.

In time, the figure in black sketched a portal in the air.

In that portal appeared a thin face, one bearing the image of the Go-Captain, wreathed in the reddish light of the star-chariot. *Are you contacting me to gloat?*

I would not stoop so low. I'm merely contacting you to make sure you're comfortable.

As comfortable as possible, given that I'm confined here. What are your intentions?

Once the download is complete, and I am safely grounded with the last of the dreamers, the blocks on all systems will release, except for the weapons module, which I've disassembled and placed in a descent that will burn it into uselessness before dropping it to the bottom of the deepest ocean, and you may have complete freedom of the heavens.

With no way to descend.

Of course.

You've gone ahead with your mad plan.

They have the same right to choose as we do. That's little enough to give them. They're getting nearly nothing else besides initial supplies and basic tools.

Before long you'll have sons killing sons, because they'll have no restraint. The restraints would have lessened with each generation.

We don't know that.

That was what was programmed. And you forget that the pen or stylus, or even myth, is mightier than what happened. I have enough adherents among the dreamers that, in time, I will remain as the victor, and you the fallen.

I have chosen to descend, in order to uplift them.

They will remember only that you have fallen, and that I control the heavens, for that is what they will always wish to believe.

When I have given them the freedom of thought?

Most will be comforted only by the shackles of belief. How are you any different from the aetherials? You decry our use of forces, but use force against us. What makes you any different?

After a long pause, the shadow figure replied, *I am no different. What I have fought for, always, is different. For you, the goal is power so that you can enforce peace and prosperity. For me, power is only the tool to seek knowledge.*

Without faith, neither prosperity nor knowledge can ever be enough.

The shadowy figure gestured, then sent the lightning signal. *Stop-Captain to Go-Captain. Separate.*

The dark figure sketched another oval beside the first, which revealed the forward section of the ark lifting away from the larger and lower section that began to descend.

Or as the descendants of the dreamers will someday say, "Farewell, Jahweh."

Farewell, shadow claiming to bring light.

WORKING CONDITIONS

PATRICK M. TRACY

Sam was a loyal employee. Perhaps loyal to a fault. Delia didn't like to think of things in those terms, but when Sam returned to work after being afflicted with vampirism, she had to admit that some virtues could be taken beyond their rational limits.

"Sam, you're dead," she pointed out, leaning against the door to the stock room, where Sam had been busy organizing and categorizing everything that could be organized or put into categories. He'd found a label maker somewhere, and there were sticker labels on everything in sight. He'd created a spreadsheet for rotating inventory. A pack of highlighters littered the small desk. The file drawers stood open, half the records out and stacked on the floor. It was beginning to be a little absurd.

Sam shrugged, peering up from behind his shaggy hair like a puppy. "That's a matter of perspective," he said after a moment.

At an unassuming five-seven, prone to vague untidiness and shoe gazing, he had been just that, a puppy. Not anymore. His eyes were tinged with red and glowed like hot bronze at their centers. He had a way of standing frighteningly still between gestures, like a toy with the battery removed. Delia had been alternately fascinated and repulsed by the change in the five weeks since he'd returned to her employ. She hadn't become inured to it yet. She wondered if she ever would.

"Standard biological processes have ceased, hon. You can't argue with that."

He pressed his lips together, then nodded. "I'm pretty spry, though. Hardly any shambling or muttering, 'Brains.'"

"You're not zombified, I'll give you that, but you are light averse. We're a daytime business."

Sam folded in on himself, a hurt expression shadowing his features. Delia felt as if she were picking on him, perhaps even discriminating against him, though there'd been no push to make being undead a protected status. Legally, she had no responsibility to Sam at all.

That last idea really made her feel rotten. Be that as it may, she ran a convenience store. She sold food items. She wasn't entirely certain that having a walking corpse stocking shelves was sanitary. It could even be a health code violation. Knowing the health inspectors, they had a law for everything from rat feces to squid-headed beings from another reality.

"Listen, Sam. I don't want to come down hard on you. I know you've been having a rough time lately. It's just that . . . aren't you done with this stuff? Working a crap job and drawing the crap wages I can pay you? Shouldn't you be, you know, skulking around in a castle somewhere in the Carpathian Mountains?"

"Don't make fun of me, D. That's not fair. I'm really trying here. This—it's all I've got. This and my cousin's basement." Sam's voice, raw with hurt, broke into a strange and haunting overtone. Chin to chest, he stood there, a single shiver going through his thin frame.

Delia's heart clenched. She knew better. Everyone did. The Dracula gibe was cruel. "Your parents . . ."

"They couldn't handle it. I mean, I was a disappointment, but I wasn't a night creature, you know? It was just too far for 'em. They only let me in the house to get my stuff and go."

"You never said. I didn't know, Sam. I'm so sorry."

"Right, right. Everybody's sorry. Lots of hand wringing and shrugged shoulders. Not many who offer to help." An alarm went off on his watch. "I have to, ah . . ." He hooked his thumb to the small office in the back. "Drink my lunch."

Delia trailed behind him. She'd never had the courage to watch. He picked up a thermos with Scooby-Doo and company running around in a faded imprint. The old plastic faded to yellow, big scrapes where the image peeled away. A relic, something from when Delia had been in school. He twisted the top off and looked at her, going into that weird stillness of those who didn't breathe. The guys on the news said something about that. Something about the vampires pulling oxygen right through their skin. Maybe they weren't really dead at all, just changed. The world resisted magic, but that didn't make magic impossible. Just darker and stranger than any children's tale.

Delia smoothed her blouse, that old knot of pain in her upper abdomen flaring worse than it had been in weeks. She kept it off her face. She owed him this much, owed him a kind word and a little acceptance. "It's okay, Sam."

He shook his head slowly. "No, D. Not okay. It's all wrong." He pinched his nose, looking away into the corner of the cramped office. He clenched his fists, and a look of intense pain shot across him. The wet noise of tissue ripping and reforming made Delia's bladder threaten to empty, but she forced herself to stay, to see it at least once.

Darkness like bruises spread across his skin in mottled spots and stripes. His mouth bulged, the muscles of his jaw creaking and flexing to far larger than their natural set. Cruel teeth like a baboon's pushed his lips outward. His eyes flared, no hint of white in them now, only blood and burning metal. He spared her a pitiful expression and then, hands shaking, he upended the thermos and consumed the blood. He gagged, fighting against every drop.

She couldn't watch him gulp it down like some foul cough syrup. Delia had to turn away, had to retreat. Sweat burst on her brow, and she held her palms against that old pain, now flaring like a knitting needle piercing her guts.

"Don't lose it, Delia Castleman. Don't you cry at work," she whispered. Somehow, she didn't.

Sam came to her a few minutes later, returned to the listless and pale but human appearance that vampires maintained, except for when they fed. "Man, I hate that. Being a vampire blows."

"The blood doesn't . . ."

"It's awful. Worst thing I've ever had to do. It's that or go mad. They say it only takes us thirty-six hours to starve up here on the surface. You tear yourself apart from the inside, like you've got Ebola. They have to kill you if it goes too far. It's all anyone can do."

Delia reached out, putting her hand on his shoulder. Sam was just a kid, just a good, if unambitious kid. Nineteen. He'd had his whole life ahead of him. It wasn't right. He covered her hand with his own. It didn't feel like part of a person's body. There was no moisture, no internal heat. It felt like the hand of a mannequin.

"We could stay open twenty-four hours, I guess," she whispered. "Maybe then . . ."

Sam looked into her eyes. "Really? You'd do that?"

Everything slowed down somehow, and Delia wondered if she'd lost a moment of time. Like she had blinked far too long, and everything had changed around her. He had come closer, his eyes seemed larger, almost luminous. In the stillness of Sam's face, she now saw something vaguely beautiful.

Delia withdrew her hand, shaking her head to try to clear it. "I don't know what I could pay you. In a town like this, maybe there'd be damned slim business through the night, but I guess we could try it."

He managed a smile, just a small one. "I'd hug you, but I guess that's out."

"A year ago, Sam, vampires were just a scary story, just the grist for a movie or a book. When they—I mean your people—came out of the ground in Oslo, it turned everything on its ear for all of us. I'm still getting used to the idea."

"They weren't my people then. Not yet. Now . . . I'm still waiting to be all handsome and brooding. I just went from loser to dead kid loser."

"You're not a loser, Sam."

He put up his hand. "No Carpathian Mountains, D. Just the stock room and a cot next to the washing machine in an unfinished basement. I'm a loser."

Delia took a breath. She didn't have a counter to that. Nothing true, anyway. "It'll be quiet most nights. Maybe you could take a correspondence course or something," she suggested.

He chuckled. "Yeah. Small-engine repair. Paralegal work. Big plans. I'm not even a person, exactly. They don't know what the heck to call us now. My own mom shoved a cross in my face when I was picking up my clothes. My dad only let me in while he was holding a shotgun. Like I'd try to bite my own parents." Sam bit down on his teeth, the corners of his mouth twisting. "I don't see us getting a real warm reception. You've always been good to me, D, and even you don't want me around."

"That's not true." Weak words. Too small a protest to ring true.

"It's okay. I understand. I have to be somewhere, though. It would be easier to just lie in a grave, but I'm still moving around. I don't have the guts to just die. I don't want this to be the end for me."

"You can stay here, sweetie. I promise. For as long as you want to." Overcoming her own reticence, that fear that keeps people from putting their hand out to a wild animal, Delia took Sam's still, mannequin body in her arms. There was no give in his flesh now, no squish and deflection of natural tissue. He smelled like the waters of a mineral hot spring. A damp, sharp scent, somewhere between safe and dangerous, just like Sam.

He accepted her arms, returning the embrace. The lack of warmth arising from his body felt so strange. The feeling that, without any action on his part, Sam could hold her like a loop of chain, a human-shaped set of restraints that she couldn't ever break away from—this shook her as the conception of a day without dawn might. Something changed in him. A ripping, squelching sound filled her ears, and Sam's body pressed against her more intimately. "That's good to hear. I hoped you were on my side." His words wore angular disguises, every syllable rasping, sibilant. "I've been so damned lonely. That's what no one tells you about. How much you lose. How small your world gets when everyone turns their back on you."

Delia shivered when Sam's mouth touched her neck. A kiss? Not exactly, but not so different. Gentler than a kiss, almost. The touch of his tongue against her pulse point made a whisper of air escape her mouth. Her hands gripped his shoulders, not trying to pry herself loose, as if she really could.

"Sam, I don't know," she started. "I'm not ready for this." But she did know, didn't she? And she was as ready as anyone can be to die. That picture had been painted in her mind for quite some time now.

"Easy, D. It'll be okay. It doesn't hurt that much." Sam's arms tightened around her. The feeling of his long fangs piercing her neck was no more than the sting of a flu shot, the touch of a tattooist's gun. All the darkness of the room swooped upward. She went blind, her mind thrown into a soft, timeless oblivion.

Sam handed the change back to Mr. Kirshner and gave a slight smile. The pain of the sun coming through the window wasn't so bad, this close to a feeding. No worse than having dozens of bees stinging his skin. If pain served to let us know we were alive, it was blessed. He wasn't alive. It was only pain, signifying nothing.

"Thanks, Sam. I haven't seen you around lately," Mr. Kirshner said. He had a fantastic mustache. He always wore a hat that had "PSE Archery" embroidered on it.

Sam wondered how he felt about the man. He found that he had no feeling one way or another. Everything was getting weighed and measured again. The entire terrain of his psyche shifted and began to rebuild itself. Just now, he understood how little he knew about himself. Traversing the boundary between prey and predator required a level of emotional distance.

Mr. Kirshner picked up his six-pack of Coors and his bag of chips, stowing them under his arm.

"I've been under the weather. Just getting back into the swing of things."

"Yeah, you look pretty pale," Mr. Kirshner agreed. "Hope you feel better."

"Thanks. You drive carefully now, huh?"

The small bell rung, and the store held only a traveler who pondered the caffeinated drinks so seriously that the fate of civilizations seemed to rest on the proper choice. She stood, a long-jointed girl with brown hair and a crooked nose like a boxer. Her hand made a halo of fog on the window of the cold case. Deep in thought, she hummed a few bars of a melody Sam couldn't recognize.

"Can I help you with something?" Sam didn't raise his voice much nowadays. When he really leaned into it, the sound became strange, fracturing into a dozen pitches. It spooked everyone out. Including him. It occurred to him, not for the first time, that his lungs were just fleshy bagpipes now, just a weird instrument that lived inside of him, vestigial to his other mechanisms.

The girl looked back. "Do I want an iced coffee or an energy drink?" She twirled a little bit of her hair around her left index finger.

Sam inhaled. His nose told him so much now, far more than words could convey. This one was coming into her monthly, and she hadn't eaten much of value in two days. She had that car smell, of confinement and nervousness and dried sweat.

"You want the chocolate milk and one of our sandwiches. That'll keep you going better than some caffeine hit."

"Yeah?" She put one thumb through a belt loop in her faded jeans, her mouth quirking in a way he'd never seen. He liked the way one eye crinkled up a little, the way her hips tilted nine degrees in one direction when she leaned back against the glass door of the cold case.

He nodded. "Trust me. This is what I do professionally."

She did. She touched his hand longer than she needed to when she took the change back. A look of confusion wrinkled her brow as she felt it, the slight unreality of it. She smiled at him, walking backward out the door, though. As close to a victory as one gets, once they're strange.

The sun pain escalated as the long evening hour lingered. Dusk couldn't come too soon now, the energy in his limbs fading, his ability to ignore the pain at its limits. Sam made a fist and held it by his side, out of sight. He didn't let the sun rule him. He could grasp this one thing. Just a normal moment, however fleeting. Just unremarkable life, the one grand wish of a dead kid.

"I'm alive," Delia said, holding her hand to her neck. The bite marks formed two livid welts on her skin.

Sam stood at the counter with a cleaning cloth in hand, as if nothing unusual had happened. The Heineken clock on the wall read eight thirty. Well after dark. He looked absolutely drained, his eyes like those of someone who had survived a torture session. Even now, Delia wanted to go to him. Even bitten. She cursed herself for a fool. She'd always had a weakness for strays, for the injured ones who needed her. Perhaps no one had ever needed her quite like Sam did.

"The first bite won't kill you. It takes three, even five bites to cause the change."

"But . . ." She didn't know what she wanted to ask.

"How do you feel?" Sam put his hands against the counter, leaning on it, hollow cheeked. He looked so exhausted. Why did she ache for him like that? After what he'd done, why?

"Were you out here, in the daytime?"

He indicated that he had been with some vague movement of his chin. "I was minding the store. I mopped and stocked the ice cream chest, too."

"In the daylight, you did this? Didn't it hurt?"

He shrugged. "I asked how you felt."

Delia had to take a moment to think about it. Truth be told, she felt better than she had in a long time. That old pain high in her abdomen had gone away for a little while. It always came back, of course. It always would, until it killed her.

"You didn't ever say you were sick," Sam said.

"Sick?"

"You know what I'm saying. You can't hide things from the dead kid."

She looked down at her feet. "Sam, what could I say?"

"'I've got terminal cancer.' You could have said that. More than anyone, I'd have understood."

"That's nothing I wanted to put on your shoulders. You've got enough trouble without carrying mine."

"See, that's stupid, and you still didn't say how you felt."

Delia's anger flashed up in her cheeks. "What the hell does that matter now? You bit me! You can't just do that, and then ask about me being sick, like you're still the puppy . . ."

"The puppy, huh?"

Delia's legs didn't want to work. She slid down next to the milk in the cold case, putting her head in her hands. "I just thought of you that way, Sam. I never meant to say it aloud."

"You did. It's okay. Guess the puppy bites, huh?" He sat down on his haunches near her.

"Did you bite me because I was sick?" she asked. Tides of emotions clashed inside her chest.

Sam's gaze didn't waver. "Yeah. You're about three percent vampire now. Not enough to kill you, but plenty to change some things around in there. I'm betting that your cancer just met up with my vampire whatever-the-hell. And the vampire cells are eating it whole."

Delia didn't, couldn't, believe it. "Sam, things don't change like that. You can't just wave a magic wand and make cancer go away."

"No magic wands here. Just a biological process we haven't figured out yet. The cancer will probably fester somewhere, maybe come back even stronger. The body has its own little dates with destiny, and nothing short of full change will derail that train. A bite, though, is more potent than any medicine yet devised. Feel it. You know I'm right."

"No one said anything about that."

"It's not something we talk about. The trick is to find someone who doesn't know they're sick. The trick is to do your little deed and get out clean. Here's the thing. I need you. I'm not ready to just be *not human* yet. I can't let go of everything until . . . until I don't know."

Delia put her hand where the pain had so recently existed. Maybe it was temporary. She'd gladly take temporary. Any version of today without the gnashing jaws inside her counted as a blessing. "I guess you saved me."

"You can call it enlightened self-interest if you want. I hope you see it as more than that."

Delia let out her breath. Wetness touched her cheeks. Not much, but enough to break her rule about crying at work. "I do. You can stay until you're ready, as long as you need. I won't turn you away, Sam."

"Thanks." Sam offered his hand, hoisting her up easily. He turned, beginning to wipe down the soda machine with his cleaning cloth. Delia pulled him away from it, turning him around so that she could look him in the eyes.

"Night work, Sam. Don't be a damned fool."

He stuck his hands in his pockets and gave a sardonic little grin. "All right. I've still got work in the back, anyway." He moved off in that direction, an orange cloth tucked into his ratty jeans, her own little monster.

"And Sam," she called after him.

"Yeah?"

"No more biting me, 'K?"

"Not unless you ask me, boss."

Delia went to the counter and looked out at the fluorescent-lit parking lot, watching Wally Patterson slide his gas card into the slot at the pump, then begin fueling his rusted Chevy. Asking him? Wouldn't ever happen. Her fear of death didn't rule her so much that she'd beg for his fangs again. She would stand or fall as she was now, no less human than the night found her. She'd be glad of whatever painless days she had left. After that? She'd grit her teeth and face the fate of every human, that unbreakable appointment with the dirt.

As Wally drove away, though, a hush fell over the store. Ten minutes before closing time, and only the sound of the cold case refrigeration unit called. Delia's hand lingered near the power switch for the old radio next to the cigarette case, but never turned it on. She picked up the dog-eared paperback someone had left atop a gas pump two days earlier, perched on a stool, and watched the clock. The book rested between her palms, unopened. She found herself looking toward the closed door into the back room, wondering. Thinking of those beautiful, volcanic eyes, and the knowledge that the fangs didn't hurt that much. For the first time in so long, she had hope again. She'd almost forgotten how that felt.

LAST CONTACT

M. C. SUMNER

It's nightmare fuel. Maybe even ultimate nightmare fuel. A huge starship appears, floating silently and impossibly still, casting a shadow over some earthly city. And then . . . nothing good, that's for sure.

No matter how the next act plays out, no matter if whatever lives inside the ship goes through the motions of being Just Like Us, while hiding their toothy lizard faces behind masks, or if they move straight to nuking the White House, it's never good. They're here for our water. They're here for our world. They're here for our women. They're here to test out their recipe for human au gratin.

It's an opening act that for decades has been a subject of both popular entertainment and serious speculation. And everyone seems to agree this whole them-coming-to-us thing is bad. In fact, there were very good reasons to think it cannot be good. Even if they— the big, unknown they—really *are* good after all.

So, when everyone woke up on a February morning and found that great triangular form hanging over a snowy Milwaukee, all the little chyrons running across the bottom of the news channels might as well have said, "Wakey wakey, humankind. Your doom has arrived." And that's not too far from what some of them did say.

I hadn't turned on the television that morning, so I didn't find out until I was on the bus, the curiously empty bus, where the driver and I seemed to be the only people in St. Louis who hadn't gotten the word that this was a very good day to sit at home, eat a hearty breakfast, and wait to see just how we were all going to die. When I first saw the wide black spike hovering in the frosty Wisconsin dawn—invisible to radar, but very definitely there—it was about an inch across on the screen of my phone.

Maybe that was for the best. Nothing seems all that shocking if you can pretty much cover it with your thumb.

For the rest of my twenty-minute ride, I passed along comments from the news to the bus driver, who, despite there being exactly no one to pick up, insisted on pulling over at each stop, right on schedule. *It's definitely aliens. The ship is about thirty miles across. No one knows what's keeping it up there. No one has seen what's inside.*

The driver's only reply was to repeat the same scatological term each time. Although she did add more *h*'s and an occasional vowel with each iteration, so that by the time I climbed off the bus in front of the university, the term had become *shhhheeeeaait*. It might not sound like a deep conversation, but she came remarkably close to capturing my own feelings.

The winter-brown grass between the pink granite buildings of the campus was not as empty as the bus had been, but many of the students crossing the quad that morning did so with a lot more alacrity than was usually reserved for making a seven thirty calculus class. Despite the cold and a biting wind, I saw several students, and even some of the staff, standing together in groups of two or three, peering together at a phone or tablet. This was one of those moments that demanded to be shared. I suspected that the big screens mounted in the student center and the entry rooms of the residence halls had already become the center of nervous crowds.

While I wasn't ready to settle down and watch just yet—at least, not with the first random people I met—as I pushed open the side door to the science building and headed for my office, I was already thinking of where I could go to spend this time being Not Alone. There seemed little doubt that classes would be canceled for the day. Maybe there would be a faculty meeting. Maybe Johanna would come in, and we—

That was about as far as I got before I saw the man waiting by my office door. He was short, with the kind of long black wool coat a lot of businessmen wore, and the top of a gray suit just visible at the collar, though the effect was a bit ruined by the knit cap tugged down hard on his large head. He saw me approaching, glanced down at a paper in his hand, and looked up at me again.

"Dr. Fetherstonhaugh?" he said, voicing every syllable carefully.

"It's pronounced Fanshaw."

The man looked at the paper again. "Really?"

"Really." I stopped, fishing in my pocket for my keys. "Can I help you?"

"My name's Kelly," said the man. "You pronounce it Kelly. Only with 'Detective' in front of that." The man held up the paper. "They want you."

My fingers squeezed the keys hard enough that the little teeth dug into my skin. "They? Who is they?" I asked, but I was only killing time. The moment he said it, I knew what he meant.

The man waved the paper vaguely at the ceiling. "Them."

Five minutes later we were in an aging Ford headed across town. The man, Detective Kelly, hadn't put on a siren, if he even had one, but he pushed the old tan sedan with the kind of panicked disregard for both traffic and the law usually reserved for an Uber driver at the end of his shift. "You're from England, huh?" he asked.

"Devonshire," I replied.

"That in England?"

"It is."

He, thankfully, stopped looking at me and looked at the road, just in time to wrench the car through an intersection, leaving a lot of horns—and undoubtedly cursing—in his wake. "I can tell. Because, you know, your accent."

"I've been here thirty years," I replied. "Every time I go home, everyone says I sound like an American."

He snorted. "Yeah, well, not to me." He flung the car around a hard right turn and looked back at me again. "And you're a scientist."

"Yes."

"Some kind of expert on aliens?"

"I'm not sure there is such a thing as an expert on aliens," I said. "But if there is, I'm not one."

He thought about that for a moment and nodded. "Tech then."

"Sorry, Detective, but no. To save you more guessing, I'm a paleoichthyologist."

That earned me a hard stare as the car plowed on with unchecked speed. "What's that?"

"I'm a specialist in extinct forms of fish. In particular, I specialize in Polyodontids." Before he could ask, I added, "Paddlefish. I'm a specialist in paddlefish."

"Paddlefish aren't extinct."

"A lot of them are, actually."

He glanced at me, at the road, at me, then the road again. "Why would they want someone who studies dead fish?" At the word *they* he leaned forward, glancing up at the sky as if the black triangular ship might have appeared above us without our notice. Which, considering how it had slipped up on Milwaukee, seemed possible. "What can that mean?"

"I haven't the slightest idea," I said. "But I suspect it means you have the wrong man."

With his right hand, he dug into the pocket of his black coat, produced the paper he had been waving earlier, and flipped it at me. "The messages came to the station from Washington. NSA . . . I think. Maybe FBI."

I picked up the wrinkled page, unfolded it, and saw that it did in fact have my name and the location of my office at the top, under what appeared to be some kind of official seal. There was even a black-and-white picture of me, a little grainy, but it explained how Detective Kelly had spotted me coming down the hall. "But it doesn't make any sense."

"No. It does not."

"I don't even have tenure."

That earned me another glance as Kelly pulled off the main road into what looked like a residential street. "You know, I've never understood what that means."

"It's kind of like . . . never mind. Just . . . why me?"

"Maybe you can ask them."

To my surprise, he didn't take me to an airport, or a police station, or even to city hall. Instead, he shot down a narrow street, went much too quickly past a sign saying SCHOOL ZONE, then drove right out onto the grass of a football field whose faded stripes were just visible through the winter stubble. Before I could ask where we were going, I saw it. Dead center in the field, where a school logo might have been, was a set of pale gray boxes, a half dozen of them, each about the size of an old pay phone booth.

Kelly stopped the car about twenty feet away from the cluster of upright booths. "Okay," he said. "There you go."

I opened the car door, letting cold air swirl in, and slowly put one foot onto the crunchy grass. "Now what?" I asked.

"That, I don't know," said the detective. "Check the paper. It says to find you and bring you here."

I checked. It did. Whatever happened now, it seemed that it was up to me.

As I was climbing out of the car, a second vehicle approached. This one drove up beside the sedan, and in short order produced an attractive woman of about forty, with short brown hair, large brown eyes, and a fixed expression that, if it wasn't absolute terror, would do until the real thing came along.

"They got you, too, huh?"

She managed a nod. "Now what?"

"I was just about to find out."

I approached the nearest box slowly. It looked . . . very much like a box. There were only three sides to it. It was gray on all of them. It was *not* larger on the inside. It was not full of stars. In fact, there didn't seem to be anything in the box at all. Anything . . . except. I took a step closer. There was a light. A small light. Another step. It was kind of amethyst colored and pulsating slightly. Slowly. Brighter. Dimmer. Brighter again. It was a little erratic, not regular like a heartbeat. It was almost as if it was beating out some message in Morse code.

I stepped right to the lip of the nearest box. The little light was at the very back, high up in a corner. There seemed to be something beside it, a few words written in small letters. I could almost make them out. But not quite.

"Look," I said, glancing back toward the woman. "I'm going to

step inside. Just for a second. If you hear me screaming or something, get back."

She hadn't taken one step away from the car that brought her.
"Oh, you don't need to worry about that," she replied.

I stepped into the box, bringing my face up very close as the light
flashed dim, dim, bright. "Mind the gap," read the very small letters.
I looked at the phrase for a moment and shook my head. "This whole
thing is some kind of joke," I said, speaking loudly enough for the
woman to hear. I turned around to step out. "There's just . . . just . . ."

The playing field was gone. Instead I was looking into a very dark
space lit by a single circle of light cast by a lamp high, high overhead.
There was a sudden loud thudding sound, and it took me a moment
to realize it was my heart pounding so hard that it was making my
eardrums flutter.

I pressed into the box, the flat gray wall against my back, and
stared out at the darkness. "Hello?" I said, in a voice that was reduced to a hoarse whisper.

"Hello!" came a booming reply. "Welcome!"

The voice was deep, smooth. It sounded like the voice that might
be used for big-G "God" in a television show. It also, even in just
those two words, sounded amused.

I waited for the voice to say something more. Or for something
else to happen, but other than the continued ear-thumping noise of
my own heartbeat, there was nothing. I leaned forward a bit, bringing one eye barely beyond the open front of the box so that I could
see to the right. Nothing. To the left. Also nothing.

"Is this . . ." I cleared my throat and started over. "Is this a trans-
porter?"

"Not the way you're thinking," said the voice. "It's just really
quick."

"But I am on board the ship."

"Yes."

"The one over Milwaukee?"

"Is there another?"

"Not so far as I know," I said.

"Trust me," said the voice. "That's the only one."

I squinted hard at the darkness. It seemed to me that there was a shape out there, maybe even several, but it could have just been an illusion. The difference between the brightly lit circle in front of the box and the blackness beyond was severe. "This is contact," I said. "Between humans and aliens."

"Yes. That's what this is."

"Why did you . . . That is, why am I here? Why me?"

"We wanted to talk to you." The voice didn't seem quite so loud as it had at first. I didn't know if that was because it had actually become softer or because I was getting used to it. "Are you going to come out?"

That required a moment's thought and a deep breath before I responded. "If I do, can I get back in?"

"Sure. Why not."

"And will it take me back to the . . . back to Earth?"

"Absolutely. If that's what you want."

There really didn't seem to be any alternative. I could stay in the box, or I could step out. I had no reason to think that I was any safer inside the box, and every reason to believe that if what was out there in the darkness wanted to do me harm, harm it would do. Still, getting my feet through that door was one of the hardest things I had ever done.

"There you go," said the voice. "Now I can officially welcome you aboard."

"Umm. Thanks."

"All right now," said the voice. "I'm going to come over there, so don't scream."

I took a half step back, grabbing at the opening of the box. "That's not exactly reassuring."

Something moved in the darkness. Something rather large. A moment later, what looked very much like a bipedal purple hippopotamus stepped from the shadows. It stopped at the edge of the circle of light, about a dozen steps from me, and regarded me with small dark eyes. The hippo impression was strong, but it didn't look particularly like one of the dancing Disney variety. Instead of a tutu, it was wearing a pale gray jumpsuit that covered all but its broad purple feet and its blunt-fingered hands. It was a good ten feet tall, and it had a heavy, creased chin that instantly reminded me of an alien I had seen before in a film.

"Oh, I know what you're thinking," said the hippo. It raised one hand—a hand that turned out to have only three fingers—and snapped two of them together. "Boom!" it said. Then it uttered a series of *uh, uh, uh* sounds that were unmistakably a laugh. "Sorry, that was a joke."

"You didn't kill half the universe," I replied, getting the reference.

"Naw. More like a third, tops." More *uh, uh, uh.* "Sorry."

"Yes," I said. "Another joke."

It made a kind of trilling snort. "You get laughs when you can." The hippo reached to the side and from somewhere produced a kind of bench, which it dragged over and settled on, straddling the narrow centerboard with a heavy leg on either side. It made a gesture to my right. "Take a seat. We may be here awhile."

I looked, and there was a chair. It was kind of midcentury modern, with curving arms of pale wood and a lime green cushion caught between them. It most definitely had not been there a moment before. I started to ask how it had gotten there, changed my mind, and pulled the chair close to the opening of the box before I sat. The chair looked very much like something you might buy at Ikea. It was rather comfortable.

"There," said the hippo. "So, you're Samuel David Harold Fetherstonhaugh." The alien pronounced it properly.

"Yes," I said. It shouldn't have surprised me that the alien knew my name. After all, it had sent the detective to pick me up. But hearing my name come from its not-quite-lips still seemed . . . just weird. "And what should I call you?"

"Whatever you want. Spock? Klaatu? No?" It shifted a bit on its chair, and the board below it creaked. "Let's just go with George. George is good."

"And are you . . . I mean, do I say 'he' or—"

George did something with its shoulders that might almost have been a shrug. "He, she, it, they. You go with whatever makes you comfortable. Trust me, I won't be offended, Doc." Its little, very hippo-like ears did a flutter. "By the way, I'm going to call you 'Doc.' Because all those other names . . ." It waved one blunt hand. "They're kind of a lot."

I was starting to feel like, any second now, I was going to wake up in my house on the south side and start this day over. Only this time, with sanity. But as long as I was here . . . "All right," I said. "Now what?"

"Here's how this is going to go," said George. "I'm going to sit here and let you ask me questions. As many questions as you want. And when you're done, I'm going to ask you one question. How about that, huh? Pretty good deal."

"What's the question?" I asked.

"That," it said, "is about the only question I'm not going to answer right now. But hang in there. You'll find out."

I sat back in my chair and drew in a deep breath. My heart was still beating quickly, but somewhere in our conversation it had stopped pounding like it was about to break my ribs. "I'm not sure what to ask."

"How about how the ship works," suggested George.

"How does it work?"

It smiled. I'm not sure if it was a natural expression for its species, or if the smile was done for my benefit, but the effect was a bit ruined because it revealed a twin set of continuous white ridges that seemed to run from end to end of George's very wide mouth. "Good question. See, it's an arc drive. As it turns out, all that string theory stuff the folks in your physics department are talking about . . . You know string theory?"

"Yes. Or at least, I know of it."

"Well, it's all wrong. There are just four dimensions, like everyone always thought."

"How does that—"

It held up a three-fingered hand. "I'm getting there. See, it turns out you can locally impose additional dimensions, the same kind of curled-up little dimensions those physics guys love. And once you do that, you can kind of bend the bigger dimensions around them. And . . ." It did the almost-shrug again. "Arc drive."

"That . . . didn't really explain anything."

"No, it didn't," George agreed with a nod of its massive purple head. "But if it did, you wouldn't understand it anyway. So, let's talk about something else."

I rubbed my hands along the arms of the chair, feeling my damp palms sliding over the smooth wood. "Why Milwaukee?"

"Oh, it's the name."

"The name?"

George nodded. "Just slips off the tongue. Or it would, if I had one." It opened its mouth wide and leaned forward so I could see.

Behind the curved white bar that lined the top and bottom of the space, there was nothing but a smooth lavender cone. It closed its wide maw and sat back. "Truthfully, we wanted a place where the ship would get noticed—no sense parking it over some desert and waiting a month before someone spots it. But we didn't want to park above some city so big or important that the first thing that would happen would involve a lot of shooting. Milwaukee seemed like a good compromise."

"Could we hurt you with our weapons?" I asked, feeling like I was taking a chance.

"You could if we let you, but we wouldn't. So, no."

"Could a nuclear weapon destroy your ship?"

"Of course. We're not magic. But again, we wouldn't let that happen, so . . . don't worry about it."

"How can you speak without a tongue?"

"Carefully," the alien replied. "And also, I think, rather well."

I paused for a moment, leaning back and feeling the chair's frame bend with me. George didn't seem to be upset by my questions about the weapons, but then I had no idea what an upset purple hippo alien looked like. Maybe he was displaying rage and I just wasn't getting the message. Except . . . I didn't think so.

"What are you doing here?" I asked.

"Talking to you."

"I don't mean you, specifically." I waved a hand toward the darkness. "I mean all of you. The ship. Why have you come to Earth?"

George blinked its small eyes. "Same answer, more or less. We wanted to talk with you. Except, with not just you, of course. With quite a few people."

I remembered that there had been at least six boxes in that field in St. Louis, and surely that wasn't the only place where they had sent out a summons. "How many people did you . . ." I searched for the right word, before finally settling on "Invite?"

"147,162. You're a bit less than unique, Doc. But hey, you're still quite rare, so feel good about that." The alien pointed a thick purple finger my way. "You are special."

My nervousness and fear were gradually giving way to a sense of frustration. George was giving me responses, but they weren't really answers. I turned to a different approach. "I'm not an expert," I said, "but doesn't first contact between cultures with different levels of technology always end with the less technologically advanced culture being destroyed?"

To my surprise, the answer was both instant and blunt. "It does. It will."

"You mean . . . you came to destroy us?"

George shook his head, which required him to actually twist his whole body. "Not at all. We're not here to fight you, Doc. We don't want your planet or your stuff. If we could meet you without harming you, we would. But you're right; that's not the way these things work." George made a rough, rumbling noise that might have been a sigh. "Even if we leave right now, today, just the fact that so many have seen us, that you know we're out here, will very likely result in disruptions that deeply alter your society. Sorry about that."

I tried for a moment to think what must be happening out in the world. People from all around the planet had climbed into boxes and been taken away. There was a ship the size of a city hanging in the winter air over Wisconsin. If people hadn't already started losing it, they would soon. One of those people would probably be me.

"Aren't there rules against that sort of thing? Aren't you supposed to . . . not do that?"

The question brought a fresh attempt at a shrug. "If you mean, do we have something like a 'Prime Directive,' a rule against meeting with species that aren't yet capable of interstellar flight . . ." It paused and spread its heavy arms wide. "The answer should be obvious. We can't be too picky about that, or we wouldn't be having this conversation."

"You . . ." I drew in a breath, trying to think of how I could ask this question without sounding rude. Or at least too rude. "You know a lot about us. That's clear from the popular culture references."

"True," said George. "I personally have watched every season of *Project Runway* and can sing the *Gilligan's Island* theme song in three languages."

I tried not to wince. "So, if you know that much, you probably know our history. Like, the history of what happened when European explorers reached the New World."

The big alien shifted on its bench. "Let's take a look," it said.

George gestured to his right, and when I looked that way, I saw a beach. The image was so clear, so detailed, that it took me a few seconds to realize it *was* an image and not some kind of doorway opening improbably out onto some remote tropical location. For several seconds after that, I simply stared, slack-jawed, at the incredible tangle of unfamiliar trees, and the miles of untracked, undeveloped, pale sand. "Where is this coming from?" I asked.

"More like when," said George. "Keep watching."

The waves pounded against the shore for a few seconds longer. Then there were feet. The feet appeared at one edge of the image, first one pair, then three. The feet were attached to hairy legs, and as the people they were attached to stepped a bit farther down the beach, I could see the ragged, stained bottoms of what looked like kind of odd, quilted leggings. "What . . ." I started, but before I could say anything more, a figure stepped from the forest. She was young, little more than a child, slender, tan, and also naked. Not that I had much time to look at her, because two seconds after she stepped out of the trees, she was stumbling back. At the top of the image, I could see a hand clutching a short, lightly curved sword. The dull metal was slick with blood.

I found myself coming clumsily to my feet, the green-cushioned chair sliding back across the smooth floor. "What was . . . I mean . . ."

All motion on the image suddenly stopped, the waves frozen as they curled above the sand. "That was first contact," said George. "Or a first contact, anyway. This one was Eleuthera, 1498."

I just kept staring at the still image. If I looked carefully, I could still see one of the young woman's legs vanishing into the dense greenery and drops of her blood on their way to the sand. "Is that, or was that, some kind of simulation?"

"No. It was a recording."

"How can you possibly have a recording of something from over five hundred years ago?" I asked. "Even if you were watching us, how can you have been in just the right place to record that?"

"Sixteen billion cameras," said George.

"What?"

"Sixteen billion high-capacity recording devices, each one about the size of a grain of dust, scattered over your planet around eleven thousand years ago." Another almost shrug. "We don't see everything, but we do see quite a lot."

For a good thirty seconds, I just stood there and thought about this. The aliens not only knew human history, they knew it better than we did. Better than the most informed human scholar. Cameras scattered around the world with such density that one might be present on a remote beach, with such capacity that they could record centuries of information. It was mind-boggling. They might not know everything, but they would certainly be able to answer questions that had baffled historians since . . . history. In fact, they knew—

"Hey, if you've got all this recorded, then you must know what really happened when . . ."

George cut me off with a wave of a big hand. "You know that thing I said about answering any question?"

"Yes."

"I lied," it said. "Because I'm not answering that one."

"You don't even know what I'm going to ask."

"Does it involve guys wearing sandals and living some time ago? Say in the Middle East?"

"No," I said. Then after a moment: "All right, yes. It does."

"Not answering," George repeated. "At least, not now."

"Okay." I looked around for my chair, turned it toward George, and sat down again. "But the thing before, that horror show on the beach, you understand why that kind of thing has me scared."

"Of course."

"It always goes like that," I said. "Or, something like that. Even when it's less bloody."

"You are not wrong. Contact situations have uniformly resulted in nearly complete destruction of the technologically disadvantaged society." The edge of humor that had seemed to tint George's voice since it first spoke out of the darkness had abruptly disappeared. "This one will be no different. When we leave, you will be irrevocably changed. Even if we do nothing more, even if you never see us again, the . . . waves from this day will almost certainly help to rip apart your society." It gestured to the side, and I saw that the image of the beach was there again. This time, there were two small ships on the horizon, crossing slowly in front of a furiously blue sky. "You've seen the sails," said George. "You know the others are there. That alone is a blow that few civilizations can survive. Even if we don't shoot you. Or enslave you. Or take all your land. Or *eat* you . . . this is going to be hard on you."

I ran a hand over my face, and to my surprise, it came away wet. "Then . . . you are here to destroy us. Only you did it without firing a shot."

George rose slowly to its big flat feet and took a step away from its chair. "You're not wrong," it said. "But you're also not completely right. Our coming here will almost certainly destroy you, but we came here to save you."

As the alien took another step forward, I couldn't help but lean away. I reached behind me with one hand and found the edge of the gray box. "That . . . doesn't make any sense."

George stopped, and both its ears gave a twitch. For the first time I noticed a kind of musky, damp leather smell in the air. "Unfortunately, it makes the only sense." Its big mouth had done a fair job of imitating a smile before, but now it did an even more convincing job on a frown. "Your civilization—not just what you call America, or Western civilization, but the whole enterprise that human beings have constructed since the glaciers receded eleven thousand years ago, is coming to an end."

"Because you're killing us," I said, more than a note of anger entering my tone.

George gave another body-twisting shake of his head. "Because you are."

"But . . ."

"In the very near future. Your civilization will collapse under its own weight. Under the force of the stress you've created on your environment and the failure of institutions that you've pushed to the limit. You've had a good run, but it's nearly over." It thumped its two heavy hands together in an expression that looked very much like frustration. "You asked why we had come when we knew it would cause you harm. This is why. We came, because harm was already coming. Our visiting you will accelerate that collapse, and we're sorry about that. But the collapse is coming anyway."

"But . . . if your technology is so much better . . . could you help us?" I struggled back to my feet and almost fell over the green-cushioned chair. "You could tell us what to do. You could save us."

George shook both hands over its head. "We *are* saving you. That's what I'm telling you."

The combination of confusion and relief almost buckled my knees. "You're saving us?"

"No. We're saving you, Doc. You. Samuel David Harold Fetherstonhaugh."

"Me?" My voice cracked, turning the word into something close to a screech.

The alien waved a hand at me. "Sit down, please. Let me try to explain." With that, George stepped heavily back to its own chair and settled again, the alien's thick legs straddling the bench.

I stood a moment longer, breathing heavily. Then I sat down, gripping tightly to the arms of the chair, never looking away from the purple being across from me. "You came to save me."

"Yes. You and a few thousand others, yes."

"A few?" I said. "But . . . you said you'd invited 147,000 and . . . something."

"147,162." George gave a slow nod. "But while we've been talking, quite a number have reached a decision."

"What decision?"

"About whether they'll come with us." He spread his big hands again. "You might have guessed it by now, Doc, but that's the question. The one question I have for you."

I had the impression again that there was something else out there in the darkness. Other shapes moving around me. "You want me to come with you?"

"Yes."

"Why?"

"Because that's our way of saving you. And this time, I don't just mean you personally, but you, all of you." It gestured at the image still hanging in the air on its right, where the tiny ships could just be glimpsed in the distance. "You've already seen that we've recorded your history. We've done the same with your art. We have your music and your images and your writing. But that's not you." It paused for a moment, leaning its big-chinned face my way. "We need you."

By then, I felt so twisted around, I could only repeat its words. "You need me."

"Yes," said George. "Because that's how you save us." There was a long pause, during which there came another of those rumbling sighs. Then with a sweep of George's hand the image hanging in the air beside it became a view of Earth that sped rapidly away, and away, and away until any sign of the planet was lost in a swirl of stars. "We know you, but we are not you. Not human. What we're offering you is a chance to be a part of something larger than yourselves. To weave what it means to be human into what it means to be a thousand other things."

I thought for a moment, but the only question I could think to ask was the one I had asked so many times already. "Why?"

"Because," said the alien, "that's the only real way that civilizations survive. They go on by being . . . a note in the symphony. A leaf on the tree."

"But," I said, "if we do that, we won't be us anymore. Not the way we were before."

It nodded again. "You will not be the same. But that's the choice that every civilization faces eventually. You can embrace a diversity where you're part of a larger picture, or hold fast to what you see as purity . . . and die alone." It pointed at the cloud of stars in the image, which was still growing and growing as the apparent camera moved ever farther from Earth. "Maintaining an unchanging culture is the most destructive form of nostalgia."

George abruptly stopped, and that frighteningly huge smile returned to its face as it held out a three-fingered hand my way. "Come with me if you want to live."

I couldn't help but laugh. "And if I don't?"

Semi-shrug. "Climb in the box and go home."

"Where I tell them what?"

"Anything you want. Tell them everything we said." George rocked on its bench, causing the board to creak again. "That woman you met before coming here? The woman from the playing field?"

"Yes?"

"She made her decision quite quickly. She's already back and talking to the FBI. A lot of people around the world are doing something similar."

"But . . . won't that make a difference? I mean, if everyone knows what you said, won't that help? Maybe we can still stop things from falling apart."

"You would think so," said George. "That's not our experience, but hey, maybe it will. We're not perfect. We know your history, but we can't be one hundred percent certain of your future. Maybe our coming here really will save the whole ugly mess."

"You think that's possible?"

"No." He leaned toward me even more. "Come with us, Doc."

"And do what?"

"This," he said. "Think of this as a job interview, although you've already got the job if you want it. This is what we do."

"Who is we?"

"A coalition of almost eleven thousand civilizations from over four thousand species lucky enough to be found before they had the chance to off themselves. A million billion people who sat in that chair and answered yes when they were asked this question." George stopped, and this time the smile was somehow softer. "Well, not literally that chair. Not all of us would fit."

Then I sat for a long time. Several minutes at least. George didn't try to hurry me as I thought through everything that had happened, everything that had been said. "This isn't first contact," I said. "It's last contact."

"That's true," said George. "Though, actually, I'm sure this isn't the last time we'll be visiting Earth."

"It's not?"

"Not at all. A planet like this . . . there's another billion years where it could turn out new civilizations. I'm sure we'll be back this way in ten thousand years, or a hundred, to make the same offer to someone else. They might even be human." The alien looked at me with its small dark eyes. "But they won't be you, Doc. We've already saved everything we can of your people. Including you, if you'll come."

"And all that will be left of us is some scrap of our culture spread into a bigger culture, like . . . an intergalactic Taco Bell."

George exploded in a series of *uh, uh, uh* sounds so loud it made me jump in my chair. A few seconds passed before it settled down enough to reply. "First of all, we're just in this one galaxy. Second, don't knock the Bell, Doc. They give good value for the dollar."

"But you know what I mean."

"I do," it said. "And I won't lie to you. There are a lot of us, and not so many of you. Don't expect to overturn the culture. Just be . . . with us. But don't think that just because you're joining with something larger, you won't still be you. Fully you. And by that I mean fully yourself, and fully human." The smile slowly escaped its wide face. "Or are you going home?"

"No," I said. "I mean . . . yes. Or . . . I mean . . ." I turned my head slightly and looked back at the gray box. "There are people there . . . friends I'd like to see again."

"We can arrange for you to talk to them. Exchange messages. Even several if you want."

I bit my lip and thought a moment longer. "Okay," I said.

"Okay?" George slapped its hands together again, and this time the expression seemed much more like joy. "Good! Very good. We'll work out something about talking to those friends. Now, let's—"

"I just have one more question," I said.

The big head tilted to one side. "What's that?"

"Why me?" I asked again. "And this time, really. Why me out of eight billion people?"

George nodded. It gave a wave to its right, and the flowing star scape faded. "It wasn't just you, of course. We tried to get as many as we could, what you might call a 'representative sample.'" The alien looked at me, and now the small eyes seemed to be studying me more closely than ever before. "We're really selfish, Doc. We want what you got. What makes you unique. All those individual threads pulling together . . . that's how we stand up when civilizations that are on their own fall apart."

"So where I was born—"

"Where you lived, where you worked. And the fact that you're not married. And you have little immediate family. All that was a part of your name coming out of the hat." The broad smile returned abruptly. "And I have to admit that name didn't hurt. A name like that . . . it just has to be preserved."

I found myself laughing. George stood. I stood. And right about then I realized that somewhere I had lost my coat. Maybe I had left it on the bus, or at the university, or in Detective Kelly's car, but all those places seemed light-years away now. Maybe they really were.

George advanced toward me, and this time I didn't back away. "Welcome," it said.

I extended my own hand. "So, my being a paleoichthyologist didn't have anything to do with it?"

"Oh, no," said George. "That was a big part of it. The next place we're going? The people there are aquatic. We've been watching them for a couple of thousand years, but they're quite unique. We think you might have something to contribute when it comes to understanding them." George's large purple fingers looked even larger from close up. "Who knows?" he said around that very wide smile. "Maybe you'll be doing my job."

We shook. It was a little awkward at first, but we worked it out.

RONIN

WILLIAM McCASKEY

I.

There is a stillness to the air, like the pause when you reach the highest point of a jump. That split-second hang, weightless, waiting for the inevitable plummet back toward the ground. The light moves oddly through the trees, the branches casting shadows that twist and spin on the ground. I step forward slowly, testing the footing with every step while reaching out with my other senses for any sign of my quarry. Silence has been laid over this part of the forest, muffling even the crunch of dry leaves beneath my feet. I come to the edge of a clearing and stop; the light washes the open grassland in a silver sheen that glimmers on the tall grass like crystals.

A dark shadow passes overhead, and not even the Silence is enough to quiet the heavy beat of leather wings against the air as the dragon circles the meadow to land in the center. The surrounding light highlights the emerald scales of her back, while the scales of her underbelly shine with a faint pink glow of their own accord. I step fully into the clearing, and the dragon turns her head to look at me, the violet irises of her eyes gleaming brightly in the night, and I smile as she dips her head in the dragon's imitation of a bow. "Ronin," she greets me, her voice a rich contralto.

Ronin, a weighted title that means less to me now than it did generations ago when I first took it. I bow to return the dragon's respect. "Titles are too formal on a night such as this, Sparkles." I chastise her gently, smiling to lessen the impact of the words.

She dips her head in my direction. "A fair point, Mr. Bear. Have you discovered the nature of our quarry?" Even with the formality gone, her voice is still a pleasure to listen to.

I had been expecting the question and had the answer ready. "Goblins, a pack of them, maybe four, no more than six. The Silence and the false moonlight gave them away. Now to find them before they get any closer to the border."

"If it is a simple pack of goblins, why did you bring me along, Bear? Surely you don't need my help dealing with simple night terrors," Sparkles comments before lifting her serpentine head to sniff at the night air.

She's right, I could have done this on my own and had before, so why did I bring her? Why did I continue to involve others in my duties? It could have been the loneliness, or was it pride that made me think I could turn toys into guardians the way the Sandman had done for me? I tell her neither, saying instead, "The borders are long and as Emily gets older, the nightmares will change. I will need someone to keep the lesser forms at bay while I hunt the monsters."

It appears as though she accepts my answer. "Shall we hunt from the air?" she asks me, almost eagerly, and I have to remind myself that in generations past I had fought nightmares of similar shape to her. Apparently, dragons were changing sides in the real world.

I nod in answer to her request, and as she lowers her body toward the ground, she dips the front of her wing for me to use as a grip. My paws grip the bones of her forewing, and I hoist myself up onto her back. Sure-footed, I weave between the thin spines that jut from her back to seat myself at the junction of her shoulders and neck. A saddle awaits me, and I buckle myself in with a practiced ease that I would never have expected to possess nearly a decade ago. Her neck is long enough that she is able to watch my progress and wait for me to be secured before leaping from the ground and beating her wings fiercely to escape the chains of gravity.

Above the canopy the light is clearer and the air cleaner, while below us the treetops sway, but not from the wind. The trees weave back and forth, like the waves of the ocean, controlled by a force separate from the wind that beats against my face as Sparkles relishes the environment she was made for. The strokes of her wings are long and steady through the air, and she flies with such grace that I barely waver in my seat.

It is her hunter's eyes that spot the flicker of torches first. The faint gleam against what appears as a sea of darkness below us gives away the goblin pack, and I thank my lucky stars for enemies that hunt one another in the Dark. Sparkles rocks over her right wing twice to warn me of an impending dive, and I tap her right shoulder to acknowledge her warning. Moments later she rolls up and over her right wing toward the ground before sweeping her wings back to slice downward on the clearing and the unsuspecting goblins.

The wind screams in my ears and pulls at my face as we race toward the ground; with my left paw I find the quick release for the seat's harness and steel myself. So rapid is our dive that the goblins fail to notice our approach until we are almost upon them; a twist of the clasp, a leap, and I am in free fall. Any higher and I might have used Emily's blanket as a parachute, but surprise is on my side and I want to keep it that way. The ground rushes toward me; I pull my legs up against my torso, folding myself in half as I wrap my arms around my legs and torpedo toward the ground.

That tiger can make all the claims he wants about his tail, but he isn't the only one that can bounce. My aim is perfect and I come down right in the middle of the pack of goblins. I hit the ground and feel my stuffing compress on itself; it is the release of that compression that launches me back into the air. The night spins as I somersault forward, the goblins panicking around me. Typical bullies, vicious until someone stands up to them. The solid weight of Dreamer's hilt appears in my right paw as I land. I spin to the left to avoid a spear thrust at my head; the silver edge of my sword flashes in the torchlight, and the slightest resistance against the blade tells me I have connected. The goblin who had attacked me with the spear, now behind me, disappears in a slow coiling of smoke and dust that returns to the Dark that had birthed him. I face the remainder of the stunned hunting party and grin. "One down, four left. Who is next?" I ask calmly.

As one, the four goblins turn on their heels and sprint for the edge of the forest behind them. Three quickly outpace the fourth, and I stoop to pluck the dropped spear from the grass. Sighting my target, I launch the spear with my left paw before following my quarry. The spear takes the trailing goblin in the back, tumbling him forward. This one shatters like glass into shards of smoke before hitting the ground, and the spear buries into the earth, still quivering from the force of the throw that had launched it. The final three goblins are about to enter the forest, and I know they will turn and attempt to fight, their numbers just enough to make them stupidly brave.

As I near the edge of the forest, I do not slow. The underbrush slaps against my legs and torso, almost hiding the telltale whisper of a blade cutting the air. Almost. I dive forward and below the swung weapon, my momentum carrying me past my attacker. I roll to a knee and lash out with Dreamer toward the second goblin in the line. The first cut takes the goblin's arm from below and continues upward, carrying my blade into a sweeping reversal that removes the creature's head from its shoulders. All three pieces return to the Dark at the same instant. Two to go.

The snap of a branch and I stand, turning as I rise with Dreamer a fraction of a second behind. The goblin I dove past is rushing me, and he is too close for me to bring Dreamer's blade around to make the kill clean. I swerve my body to the right, slipping past the spear thrust. Momentum carries the monster closer to me, and his face into Dreamer's cross guard. The goblin emits a pained cry as he swallows a couple of teeth, but I cut it short. As he stumbles back, I step away, slicing up and across his chest and throat. The goblin melts like wax, and only one remains.

The forest around us darkens momentarily as Sparkles flies over, and the goblin breaks eye contact with me to look up. His pale yellow eyes are wide with fear as he casts them around, searching for any means of escape. Finally, in a high-pitched voice, he pleads, "Please, I'll never come back."

"No, you won't," I answer as I lower Dreamer and flick the blade, the residue of the monsters slain this night flying off into the darkness. I can see him relax for a moment, believing I intend to be merciful, until he sees my advance, and the meaning of my words hits him fully. My arm rises, Dreamer shining in the false moonlight of this forest that will never know the touch of the sun.

The sound of shattering glass echoes from far away and all around me at the same time, halting my advance on the goblin. Voices, too faint to distinguish the words, fill the night. I cannot hear what they are saying but I know the speakers. Emily's mother and father, loud

enough to wake Emily. The world around me begins to blur and I
know that my own form is fading from the forest. My eyes will be
the last to disappear, and they lock onto the gobsmacked goblin.
Without words, I make him a promise: if he ever again crosses the
Dark near the borders I defend, I will hunt him down. He nods and
turns to sprint away, and the last thing I see are his arms pumping
wildly as his legs fight to carry his diminutive frame away from me
as fast as possible.

II.

Shadows danced across my vision and I felt myself lifted into the air, then pressure against my chest and back. Emily's arm reached over my head to grasp the doorknob; I could hear her grunt softly with the effort of pulling the door open one armed. The hallway beyond was dark, but there was light coming from the living room, and I could hear the voices of her parents.

She hugged me close as she walked slowly down the hall. She was afraid. I could almost taste the fear rolling off her, and I did what I could with my magic, letting just a touch of it resonate out, to reassure her. Her arms tightened around me for an instant and then she was calmer; at a level below even her subconscious, she knew I was responsible.

The light grew brighter as we moved closer, and the voices became distinguishable. "Jason, talk to me. They're getting worse." The plea was evident in Emily's mother's voice.

The sound of a cap turning echoed in the quiet of the room, then the sound of liquid pouring out into a glass. Emily paused at the end of the hallway, the clever girl still trying to figure out what was going on. "And say what, sweetheart?" I could hear the weariness and pain in Emily's father's voice even if neither Emily nor her mother were able to. Jason was once my charge, as his father had been; just as on the day he laid me in Emily's crib my responsibilities changed to focus on her.

In the heavy silence that followed, I felt Emily shift her weight. She was debating her options: go back to bed, or step forward. I could have influenced her, pushed her in either direction, but I wouldn't have, even if I could have. She must learn to confront her

fears and decide how she will face life. She took a step forward, and
then another. If I could smile, I would have. I am proud of her. She
rounded the corner into the living room. Her mother was standing
in a black bathrobe with her back to Emily, her hair disheveled as if
startled awake. Looking past her, I could see Emily's father hunched
forward on the couch. From where Emily stood I could make out
the puckered white of scars on his nearest shoulder. He was hunched
forward with his elbows on his knees and his hands clutching a glass
filled with something honey colored that gleamed like gold when the
light hit it just right. The table in front of him was littered with assorted glass bottles, most of which were empty. He looked up and I
wanted to recoil. In the instant it had taken for him to see his daughter and recognize that she was in the room, I caught a glimpse of a
haunted, distant look in his eyes that was just as quickly buried and
forced down beneath a father's love for his child. "Emily, sweetheart,
what are you doing out of bed?"

Emily clutched at her mother's bathrobe and looked from her
mother to her father. Her mother stooped down to pick her up, and
as she lifted us, I was pressed against the terry cloth of the bathrobe
and could see nothing. I felt Emily shift. "Why are you out of bed,
Daddy?" she asked in a soft voice, turning her father's question back
on him.

"Daddy had a nightmare, sweet pea," her mother answered, and
the truth beneath the lie rang in my ears. What was she hiding from
Emily? "Do you want to come lay down with Mommy, and Daddy
will join us in a little bit?" The tone was pacifying and raised my
suspicions even further.

I felt Emily shift again as she nodded above me, and then the
tightness around me increased. I heard Emily's father kiss her head
and whisper in her ear, but the words were too soft for me to discern.
Without warning, my body whipped away from where it had been

stuck and I hung in the air, dangling from Emily's hand. "Take Mr.
Bear, Daddy. He'll make you feel better." Emily's voice was soft,
filled with concern for her father. She knew there was something
wrong but couldn't identify what.

Her father took my arm in his hand and looked down at me.
Those few seconds are the longest he had held me since tucking me
into a box as he moved from his parents' house. There was something
behind his eyes that he was fighting to keep hidden, something he
was trying to bury that was eating him from the inside. What had
happened to the boy I'd protected for so many years? What had happened to my friend?

He kissed the top of his daughter's head again and then kissed
Emily's mother. As she moved toward the door that led to their
bedroom, I saw her lay a leather-bound book on the coffee table. The
faded gold lettering on the cover showed it to be a Bible. She looked
back at her husband for just a moment, a glance that carried the
same concern and worry that had hung in Emily's voice, before carrying Emily into their bedroom and shutting the door gently.

III.

I hung suspended, my arm secure in Jason's grip. The hand holding me was rougher than I remember. I could feel his fingers, calloused and worn, tensing as if they would be more comfortable holding a sword than a ragged, stuffed teddy bear. I began to swing in his grip as he walked toward the couch, but that's not what caught my eye. Below the dark green shorts he was wearing, his thigh had been tattooed; a thin wire, maybe chain, encircled his leg with six oblong shapes suspended from it. I couldn't make out what was written on them; they appeared to be words with numbers beneath them. Names and dates, perhaps? It finally dawned on me: Jason had shown Emily the dog tags that he wore around his neck, and explained that they were identification tags. The shapes on his leg were dog tags, but why six? Jason only had the two hanging from the chain around his neck.

Without warning, I was flying through the air, my body twisting as it defied gravity. The momentary weightlessness disappeared, and I could feel the earth reassert its control on my body and pull me down. So different from the dreamscape where the rules change, and laws, like gravity, are mutable. I landed soundlessly on the couch and fell backward into the cushioned corner. Jason sat back down, resuming his hunched-forward position, and retrieved his glass. He stared into the amber liquid and I sensed that while his body remained near me, his mind was far away. "Till Valhalla," he muttered, almost too quiet for me to hear, as he raised the glass in front of him, as if in salute. Then the glass was carried to his lips and the liquid disappeared down his throat.

My thoughts were racing, trying to put the pieces of this puzzle together. When he was a child Jason read almost constantly; he loved the mythology stories the most. I remembered his dreams of Valhalla, where Viking warriors who died in battle would feast during the night and battle during the day, all in preparation for Ragnarök, the final battle. It was the Norse version of heaven and considered an honor to achieve. Jason had been raised as a follower of the Christian faith, and he still attended church with his wife and daughter; why the Viking reference? Then it struck me all at once. Jason had spent over a decade as a soldier; the wounds afflicting him had meant he was unable to continue, and he had retired. The scars on his shoulder and back, the tattoo, the words; he was toasting fallen friends. Were those his nightmares? Was that what haunted him?

I watched in silent agony as drink after drink filled the glass and was thrown down Jason's throat. The bottle went from full to empty and another seal was broken; more drinks were poured and swallowed. I had lost count of how many drinks Jason had before he started to sway, his eyes drooping heavily. As he sluggishly reached for the near-empty glass, I used magic on Jason for the first time in nearly two decades. The Sandman had instilled all of the Ronin with a sliver of his power, enough to quiet a crying child or to reassure them back to sleep after a night terror jerked them awake. I hoped it would be enough to work on Jason in the state he was in. His hand trembled, and in the space of a breath I feared it would not be enough. Then his arm dropped and he fell sideways. I rolled away to avoid being trapped, and his head landed on the pillow I had been leaning against. I watched him for a few moments. His breathing was even, though his body would twitch every few minutes, and a single tear escaped from the corner of his right eye. With everyone sleeping, my magic became stronger and I pushed myself to stand, the immobility of my camouflage removed. I walked over and settled myself against his chest. I needed the feel of his heartbeat against me to enter his Dream. I closed my eyes and felt the slow, steady beating of Jason's heart. The rhythmic thumping was the deep bass of war drums, and I felt myself fall backward into a cold chill that bit through even my fur and stuffing.

IV.

It isn't the cold that snaps my eyes open, it's the heat. Oppressive and heavy, it feels like a weight bearing down on my entire body, a weight that is only added to by the sight that meets my eyes. Gone are the castles with dragons soaring around them and the oceans teeming with pirate armadas that I remember filling Jason's dreamscape decades ago. The seas have dried, the mountains worn down to daunting sand dunes, and the prairies and woodlands replaced by a desert village that seems without end. The village expands past the borders into the Dark. If the nightmares have broken through, then that may explain Jason's distress; I need to know more.

A soft wind wafts through the village, ruffling my fur, and on it I hear Emily's laughter and smell Jason's wife's perfume. The wind and the happiness it carries are ripped away by a rippling wave of noise unlike anything I have heard before. Discordant tones chatter back and forth, setting my teeth on edge, and I sprint toward the disturbance. Dreamer is in my hand as I round the next corner, ready for anything except the sight that awaits me. Jason, bloodied and covered in sand and grit foreign to the dreamscape, huddles behind the smoldering wreckage of a car while cradling a rifle against his chest. The ring of metal on metal sings out from the other side of the vehicle. I watch as he raises the rifle to his shoulder and braces his elbows on the hood of the car. His movements and actions indicate that he sees something I cannot, as he begins firing. Controlled and collected, he does not fire randomly or let the chaos overwhelm him; he's choosing his targets.

A shout from behind me has us both turning at the same time. Another soldier has been struck and stumbles out of the house he has been sheltering himself in. I look over to Jason and see the horror in his eyes as the soldier is shot twice more. Jason pushes up from his own position and runs toward the fallen soldier; I can only watch in mute horror as I see him stumble and then fall to the ground, inches from his comrade. The clench of his teeth and the set in his jaw show the pain he is fighting against as he pushes himself up and crawls forward to grab the back of the vest the soldier is wearing. Jason heaves and pulls, trying to get the soldier into the house. The body doesn't move. I see it now, a shifting formless mass clinging to Jason's back and shoulders, like a cancer. Jason makes no indication that he can see or feel the sickly brown tendrils running from the soldier's body to the form clinging to him, but I can, and now I see that there are more of them clinging to Jason's arms, legs, and body, weighing him down.

The shapes and forms flow like shadows, and the tendrils begin to move, the fallen bodies they are attached to twitching when they should be locked in the rigor of death. The eyes of the corpses are the first to move. Opening, they all turn to stare at Jason, each gaze heavy with the weight of accusation and judgment. Arms and legs begin to shift, pulling and dragging shredded bodies through the doorway and open window toward where Jason curls against the back wall of the small structure. Mouths drop open and the words begin to spill out.

"Where were you?"

"You led us here."

"You killed me."

"Where were you?"

"Why did you let them kill me?"

"Where were you?"

Over and over the words tumble out, becoming a tidal wave as the bodies shamble and drag closer in a macabre parody of life, hands curling into talons that claw at Jason's body. He may have fought them off at one point; I remember from the dreams of the boy before the man that it would have been his go-to reaction. It is obvious that time has worn him down, and there is no way for me to know how long he has been facing these things. Now he cowers, attempting to protect the core of his body, and sobs, a soundless scream of grief and sorrow.

I leap; I have no other choice. Jason had been my charge years ago, and his daughter has placed him back in my care. Dreamer gleams in the darkness of the building's interior as it lashes out, an extension of my arm and my rage. I feel no resistance as Dreamer's edge passes through the shadowed body of the nearest lamprey form. The shadow breaks apart and then re-forms, unwounded, and continues its puppetry of the bodies attacking Jason. I strike again, slicing through the ethereal form of a different target. Again, the creature is unharmed. I have gotten its attention, though. A single eyestalk erupts from the top of the form and turns the creature's baleful gaze toward me.

Hissing laughter whispers in my ears. "You've no place here, Ronin. No place and no power." The final words are snapped, as if bitten through teeth. Before I can respond, the heavy weight of a free tendril thuds into my chest and sends me sailing backward through an open window. I bounce twice, then skid through the rough grit of the sand. Muttering to myself, I turn Dreamer's point down into the dirt and use my grip to steady my balance as I stand. Brushing myself off, I feel a pain in my chest and look down to see a tear across my fur, strands of stuffing sticking out. I swear under my breath.

"If Emily heard language like that from you, Mr. Bear, she would be incensed," chastises a voice I have not heard in generations. Not since he had woken me.

I spin around, searching for the source of the voice. Only once I have completed a full turn do I catch sight of the speaker. His outer coat shifts along the spectrum from red to blue as he walks closer, while his shirt and trousers appear to be made of a silken material colored black as moonless night; the belt holding his coat closed still holds the numerous drawstring pouches that I remember carry the dust he blows into children's eyes to send them to sleep. The pale skin of his face and neck are completely at odds with the desert we stand in, but it is obvious he is apart from it, as his dark hair refuses to be moved by the errant winds. In spite of my anger at being injured by a nightmare, I smile. "You are a welcome surprise, Sandman. With your help, I can vanquish these horrors and set Jason's dreamscape to rights."

V.

I feel the smile on my own face fade as the Sandman's usually ready smile turns to one of sadness, and my eyes finally take in the apology within his own eyes. "I'm sorry, Mr. Bear. You could fight the nightmares with all your strength and eventually they would destroy you. These nightmares are beyond even what my magic can overcome."

"What are they, that not even your magic is strong enough to conquer them?" I ask. To find enemies beyond the power of the being that had created me and given me the magic to defend children's dreams sends a chill through my stuffing.

"They are nightmares of his own creation. Guilt, grief, and his mind's coping with the horrors he has seen and done. Jason is not alone in what he faces. Countless others, some soldiers like him, some victims of crime, and some victims of tragedy, face these horrors all within their own minds and dreamscapes. My magic is not strong enough to challenge the real world." His voice is weary. How many dreams has he seen turned to chaos like this? I once envied his ability to travel through the dreams and see the stories children created in their sleep. Now I do not envy the burden it must become as he watches those same children grow up and the stories come to such crashing ends.

"There has to be something! I cannot do nothing! His father laid me in his crib to guard, and Emily handed me back to him to heal him," I rage, refusing to give up. I will never quit my given duty.

Sandman smiles again, still sad, but there is pride in his eyes as he watches me. "This is why I started with teddy bears; no velveteen aspirations for you, only pure devotion to the families that choose you." He pauses, thinking before he continues. "Faith, family, and a willingness to ask for help are the only solutions that work. Even then, there is no true cure. These nightmares are a constant struggle, and a heavy burden to bear."

I meet his eyes, and I understand that he's trying to tell me not to hold out hope, to simply be ready to comfort Emily when the time comes. Suddenly I realize the truth; if that time comes, then new nightmares will manifest in Emily. Nightmares beyond my power and magic to combat would continue the cycle of pain and grief, and I will have already lost. I set my jaw and meet Sandman's gaze. "Jason's grandfather taught his father a phrase he learned across the seas. 'Those who dare, win.'" I lift Dreamer in a salute to my mentor and close my eyes. I feel myself fall backward, and the cold returns for a shocking instant.

I opened my eyes to find myself once more immobile and lying back against the cushions of the couch. Jason had already awoken, and again he was hunched forward, though now he clutched a pistol in his right hand, his eyes closed. My time was running out.

A loaded magazine was on the table, near two empty bottles. Sandman's words rang in my ears: "Faith, family, and a willingness to ask for help." Jason's eyes were still closed, so now was the chance to use my magic. I had to use it now, I had to dare. The sound of the pistol slide locking back almost broke my concentration, almost.

Jason reached for the magazine, and his fingers brushed against the picture of his wife and daughter, smiling and waving at him. Beneath the picture was the Bible his wife had laid on the table. It was the same Bible that his father had given him before he went to basic training. He was sure that it had been at the corner of the table a moment ago. He saw the pistol magazine across the table and reached for the picture. Holding it in his left hand and the pistol loosely in his right, the tears started to flow. He set the pistol on the table and picked up the Bible. A business card marked a passage, and

I could hear him open and then read the passage in a low voice: "Blessed are the peacemakers, for they will be called sons of God." His gaze fell to the business card and he set the Bible down, the picture still held in his left hand as he pushed himself up from the couch and walked into the kitchen.

Stretching out my hearing, I could faintly make out a series of audible clicks, the sound Jason's phone made when Emily was playing with it. I heard him begin to speak. "It's Jason. Yeah, I know it's late." He paused and I was afraid he would say nothing, but then he continued. "I need someone to talk to, right now. You got some time?"

I pulled my magic back; I had done what I could. Now it was up to him.

SKJÖLDMÓÐIR

MICHAEL Z. WILLIAMSON AND JESSICA SCHLENKER

My son was called a monster.

Perhaps he was even born a monster through no fault of his own, merely a victim of the gods' whims.

I did not regard him so. I knew him best as my sweet boy, bringing me bunches of newly opened spring flowers, or asking I tell him the stories my mother told me as a child.

Perhaps I brought it down on him, through my own actions, in the years before his birth. But I had taken up a sword to defend my family; surely the gods would not punish us for that?

Not all noble families are wreathed in wealth untold. Most, in fact, are more like my own: farmers, herders, stewards of the earth. There may be some wealth earned in battle, exchanged for blood, limbs, or lives. Mostly, though, a little is earned through barter and trade, exchanging toil and sweat for enough to live on.

After a hard year, with every nearby family stretched thin, invaders came, bringing battle to our homes. Perhaps they thought we hid the wealth expected of us, but it mattered little. We fought for our lives, and I did my best to inflict as much damage as I could to save our home. But we were overwhelmed, and we fled to save the youngest. The invaders destroyed whatever they found. I still hope they kept some of it, rather than burned everything not gilt in gold or silver. But they did not desire the land itself, and we found the still smoking ruins of our home unoccupied. The cattle but one were missing. We found the remains of the one left on a smoldering spit.

We rebuilt, as my father's family had done before and no doubt will have to again. A modest bride-price was offered for me, the eldest girl, by friends of my father. Unspoken was the knowledge the offer was made to assist in the rebuilding, as his friends had been spared the devastation. Thankfully, I knew the son, and even liked him. We played together often enough as children.

My new husband assisted in rebuilding my family's homestead before we moved on to our own future. My lord's father gifted him a small amount of land from their lands, for us to build a home and to tend. Being just the two of us, we both practiced with the sword daily, and one of our first goals was to acquire sturdy armor for us both. I did not wish to be caught unarmed and unprotected by invaders if I could help it.

I quickly became pregnant with our first child, a beautiful little girl who did not last through her first year.

When I bore our son, Grendel, we saw at once his head was slightly misshapen. But he had powerful lungs, and he was healthy. To me, that was enough. I could not bear to lose another. His birth was difficult, and although we tried for another, he remained our only surviving child.

It became apparent, over the years, that my Grendel was different, besides a misshapen skull that worsened as he grew. Large, and less coordinated than he should have been, he did not know his own strength. He hurt several of his playmates by accident, and I still remember his frightened, bewildered expression as I explained that *he* had done that.

"But, Momma, I didn't mean to."

I would assure him I knew, I understood, and would caution him to be more careful. My lord spent time working with Grendel, trying to teach him how to control his strength more consistently.

Then the day came when, amid terrible thunder and rain, Grendel abruptly howled in torment and collapsed to the ground, writhing and clawing at his face. It took both my lord and me to pin his arms before he did severe damage to himself. After a while, his body relaxed and he simply sobbed quietly. "Grendel, my love? What's wrong?"

"Monsters are eating my head," he replied, voice shaky through the tears.

My lord moved him to his bed, and I made a tincture for pain. It took both of us to steady Grendel's hands enough so he could grip the cup himself.

The second time it happened he wasn't home, although it was another terrible storm. He knocked a playmate unconscious when they tried to help, and he had to be subdued by several adult men. My boy, barely nine, could no longer be trusted to play with children his age. I kept him home, and close even then. Closer still when the skies looked ominous.

By the time Grendel reached the age of eleven, we had little choice but to bind him to his bed when the weather would start to turn. He did not like it, but he understood. I sat with him, trying to keep him calm during the worst, singing old songs and telling stories. A tincture at the first tremors helped keep him calmer, but at the worst, he still writhed and howled as if possessed.

The rages started soon after that, rages he could not explain afterward.

I spoke with everyone—my parents, my lord's parents, the wisewoman Edda, everyone. No one had suggestions to help soothe my beloved son's pain or fits.

But in between the bad days, Grendel acted ever much the young boy he truly was, by turns sweet and caring, rambunctious, helpful, and even sometimes surly. He soon nearly matched his father in height, and outmatched him in strength. The day the tavern caught fire, it was Grendel who braved the billowing flames to hold open the collapsed doors so that people could escape. Had he not done so, more would have been lost. His burns healed, but the pain never quite faded, particularly the ones on his face.

The next season, invaders came again, and my lord fell defending the village.

We buried him next to the sister Grendel never knew, and grieved.

It would usually be expected that a situation worsens when one's husband dies, but I did not expect the rapidity with which the village turned on me—us. Disgusted by the damage caused to his face by his own heroic actions, combined with the fear of a fit that none had witnessed in several years, only heard, our neighbors and other villagers took to actively avoiding Grendel, and I overheard much vicious, untrue gossip. Had they truly forgotten the scars on his face were from saving their sons and daughters when they could not? The wild tales they made of ridiculous exploits with my Grendel painted as the villain beggared belief.

The treatment slowly extended to me, as well. Shunned and avoided, I could not depend on my husband's brother for assistance, and my own kin were overextended already. My husband's brother did not have the honor he had, and I broke his nose after a particularly lewd comment followed by a suggestion that my son be "disposed of" for my "own good."

The distrustful mutters and hateful glances wore on my sensitive son, and the fits of rage began to increase. We discovered that he could no longer tolerate music beyond my singing. Instruments or other singing voices caused him significant pain, and he became more and more sensitive to loud noises in general. He grew still taller, a full head beyond any man on the coast, and then inches more. The situation untenable, I began to search for a place to remove us to. Grendel needed space and quiet, where he did not have to hear the not-so-whispered comments of *"Monster!"* that followed him.

Grendel was nigh eighteen when I was summoned to the village regarding him.

Upon arrival, I discovered he was bound and subdued, and a bit confused.

"What is the meaning of this?" I asked, horrified, gesturing at my son.

Angry voices yelled at me, but Hrothgar the king raised his hands for silence. He explained. Grendel had been provoked, and in his rage, killed an erstwhile playmate of years past. Punishment must be rendered, but the circumstances and Grendel's father's defense in the name of the king meant it would only be immediate banishment.

I bitterly reminded the king of *Grendel's* own heroic actions, and that he still bore the scars and pain. The angry muttering of the crowd turned to guilty silence at the reminder.

Hrothgar admitted this, and accorded him some leeway for gathering possessions.

My husband's brother interjected himself into the discussion, and attempted to demand that all of *my* possessions be rendered to him for the breaking of his nose previously. Hrothgar merely snorted, as the man's crass behavior was well known, but acceded he could lay claim to the land we lived on.

We were given just a few days' time to depart. I quietly thanked the gods that I had seen fit to be prepared, and there remained little left in our home to remove. I had even moved the small herd of sheep some weeks previous, to a formerly abandoned hut by the swamp, and built them a workable fence, with Grendel's sturdy help. We would not be completely bereft, and I would be able to keep us clothed.

My husband's brother insisted on escorting us to ensure I did not take "too many valuables" he "deserved," and I requested other witnesses. The look he gave me made it clear he resented I had forestalled his true intent.

Grendel, dear Grendel, remained confused and bewildered at what was happening. But he followed me quietly and did as I bid.

The bastard raged when he took in the mostly emptied homestead. The witnesses merely snickered. Edda gave me a measuring look. She had known I was worried about Grendel, and had advised I prepare for such a situation. I gave her a bitter smile.

The last of our personal belongings were easily removed from the premises. While the bastard snarled at us, one of the other witnesses stood between him and me. "Do not give me a reason to fight on her behalf," he cautioned. "Your actions disgust me as it is."

I was grateful for the meager defense, although I would have appreciated it more had the man ever stood up for Grendel or me these past years.

Grendel carried what I directed, in a bundle that awed the spectators. I carried the remainder, including my bow. We left. I ensured we were not followed.

The salt marsh reeked with fetid decay, but it held life enough. Only the old wisewoman Edda came here voluntarily, for the herbs that could be gathered nowhere else and were necessary to ply her trade. She would pay me for gathering those in her stead, in goods I could not make or find on my own.

The sheep fared well enough, learning to find the drier areas with edible grass. The wool kept us in clothing, and the lambs provided some food, and milk for cheese. Other foods, Grendel and I found in the swamp. He learned which plants were safe readily enough, and he hunted large game with his club. Faster game, I snared, or hunted with bow.

It was not an easy life, but it was fairly peaceful. The hearth kept us warm, and I had a pot and a griddle. The hut was made comfortable with furs and hides. And above all, I had my son.

We used the nearby cave for a shelter for the sheep, and to store some goods. Grendel liked to be there, because it was so quiet.

He still had to be bound when the worst storms hit, but he seemed just a bit better here. The fits were fewer, and I hoped for the day they ceased. Alas, that was not to be.

Edda brought word that Hrothgar intended to build a new great hall at last, to replace the one that had burned down. At first, this did not concern me at all. It shortly became apparent that the placement and construction of the building were to bring torment to my Grendel.

The first revelry, filled with song and instruments, and the deep thud of mugs being beat against tables, rolled like a dull thunder at our distant hut. It was too much for Grendel, and I had to wrestle him into submission, binding him to keep him from causing himself injury.

I was not successful in subduing him the next time, and he ran deeper into the swamp. I feared him lost, but he returned a day and a half later, worse for the wear. He brought me a deer he had caught during the fit, but he could not tell me where he had woken up from it.

The next time I failed to subdue him, I was stunned while trying, and unable to follow. I heard the shouts of anger and screams of fear from the direction the party had been. He returned, with a few minor wounds. He was distraught to discover he had injured me, and haltingly described what he could remember of what happened in the village.

"I went into the hall, where the noise hurt most," he said. "The door was blocked, but I forced it."

The door fastened with a solid wooden beam, and he'd broken it. Oh, my son, what a warrior you could be, if only the demons didn't torture you.

"They attacked me and I fought them all. I remember men hitting me, and me throwing them."

That explained his black eye and bruised knuckles. He'd fought them all, all at once.

"I just wanted them to be quiet! My head spun, and stabbed, and I felt sick. I remember one man broke over the table when I threw him."

He probably broke his back and was dead. Oh, Grendel, no.

Edda told me more. Grendel had killed one man and maimed two others, one of whom would never chew food again after his jaw was smashed. She looked fearful herself. "I may not be able to bring you any more supplies, if this happens again."

"I am endeavoring to stop him," I promised. "There seem to be certain sounds that are worse than others, ones that he runs *to* instead of *from*."

She questioned which ones seemed to enrage him worse and drive him toward the village instead of away. I answered as best I could. She would try to encourage at least *less* of those, or to give some kind of sign so I would have time to prepare Grendel and restrain him.

It was the best we could manage. As the villagers had turned their stories of him into a troll or something even worse, it even worked for a while. She convinced them that deliberately enraging him was not conducive to their own peace. I owed her much.

Then came the day Edda breathlessly brought word about a traveler, Beowulf, who boasted he would end their "troll" problem once and for all. She argued hard to prevent the villagers from cheering on the insanity, but to no avail. Hrothgar planned for a huge celebration befitting such a "hero," even that very night, in part to draw Grendel in. I gave her what would be one last hug.

"You have been the only family I have had besides Grendel these last years. Thank you."

She returned the embrace. "I can only hope this madness can be avoided. Your Grendel does not deserve this."

"As do I."

When Grendel returned later, I tried to convince him to settle down early. I even gave him the soothing tinctures, which would normally ease the fits. I couldn't bear to tell him they were setting a trap for him, and he would not settle for storms that didn't exist. At length, I did tell him.

"But Momma, why?"

"They think you a monster, and want you dead." I stroked his cheek. "You are my beloved son, and I want you alive. Please, let me do what I can to keep you from their trap."

He acquiesced, and allowed me to bind him to his bed. I made him as comfortable as I could, and then set about doing everything possible to block out all sounds from outside of our walls. Every nook, every cranny, I stuffed full of scraps of cloth and hide. The only light left was one of our precious candles, sitting on the hearth. Even the chimney was as blocked as I dared risk.

It almost worked. I underestimated how desperate this "hero" was for a victory against an innocent man gossiped into a monster. The large horn, which should have been blown only in times of invaders, sounded, and Grendel screamed in agony. Thrice it blew, and the third time, Grendel convulsed and snapped his bindings.

I fought with him, trying to keep him home, with me, safe, alive. He managed to fling me wide and battered the door down. I sank to the floor and wept.

It took moments, far too many moments, to collect myself, but I managed to rise and shake off the worst of the grief and fear. Regardless of the outcome, my boy would be hurt, so I set a tea of elderberry and cicuta for pain to steep. I prepared bandages and a tiny precious amount of honey to aid against infection. I scrubbed and heated the fire iron, to cauterize any deep wounds.

Then I prayed to uncaring, unresponsive gods that Grendel would come home to me in condition good enough that I could tend him, heal him, and take us elsewhere as soon as may be.

An echoing bellow of rage and pain, accompanied by catcalls and jeers, mocked such prayers. The hateful villagers would not be cheering so were it Beowulf who cried out in such a manner. Grief battled with rage, but I took small comfort in the boos and hisses. Grendel had either scored a fair hit or managed to escape. Multiple shrieks of fear echoed, followed by a tumult of muted voices. The distant sounds faded, and I surmised that Grendel had, at the least, escaped. The darkness of the night meant I dared not try to find him, or risk losing him completely. I waited.

A countless eternity later, I heard pained weeping and a querulous "Momma?" in the dark. I ran to the sound to find my son, grievously injured and missing an arm. I shouldered up under his good arm and helped him the last distance home. Once there, I took stock of the wounds.

The arm was no clean cut of a sword, but instead showed signs of having been mostly torn off. The stump was a ragged, oozing mess with dripping blood and exposed bone. I did not, could not cry, not while Grendel looked at me with fearful eyes. "Will I be okay, Momma?"

I lied. So help me, I lied to him. Had I spoken the truth, I would have been unable to ease his suffering. "As okay as I can make you, my love," I said. I set about doing what I could. The state of the arm was such that cauterizing was nigh impossible, and the bandages I had prepared were insufficient. Once I had it cleaned, bound, and covered, I helped him drink the tea. I settled him as best I could.

I pressed a kiss to his forehead, and he asked me for a song. I acquiesced, as a few more minutes would make little difference in the scheme of things. He, thankfully, fell asleep into a restless, pained slumber. I drew my cloak around me, and gave him one last worried look before slipping out of the hut to head for the village.

I could afford no dignity. Perhaps Edda knew some herbs, and I would beg and abase myself before Hrothgar for the slightest of mercy. Grendel and I would retreat to the cave and subsist as we could.

The village was active, and I approached carefully, hood masking my face for the little good it would do. All of them knew me.

There was much commotion at the great hall, and I watched from far behind the crowd, hidden behind the hawthorn bushes.

I saw what they did and my head spun. Was this real and not some horrific dream?

Grendel's arm hung from a nail above the hall's broad doors. A trophy to hate and fear.

I overheard Hrothgar announce, "They will sing of this deed for a thousand years."

And that's when the rage took me.

I could perhaps forgive Beowulf for killing Grendel. It had been the fairest fight of all. Grendel did only what the gods had made him to do. But Hrothgar boasted of the deed, of the killing of my poor, darling boy. He memorialized it with blood trophies.

Hrothgar would not boast of the killing of a favored dog taken over by the madness. Yet he would boast of the killing of my son.

Any man would avenge his son, his brother, his father for that shame. My son had none of those to call out this monster for his words. He had only me.

I would stand for him.

I turned to prepare.

I heard shouts, and knew I'd been seen.

I ran. There was nothing else I could do.

The shouts became jeers and my breathing punctuated with sobs. I'd vowed a blood oath, and now I ran.

One voice stood out. That was Aeschere. Years ago, Grendel had beaten his son hard enough to damage the boy's eye, and neither had ever forgiven him. He pursued me, though my lead was good and my legs remained strong. I hoped he'd slow and give up, with nothing but colorfully degrading insults, but while he slowed, he didn't stop.

I ran along the mucky high ground and onto the spit where my hut stood. He was some minutes behind and I had just time. I barred the door, caught my breath, and took a drink of water, followed by a mouthful of cheese for energy. Then I set about preparing.

Aeschere was a mouthy sort, and I knew he was trying to provoke me out, rather than enter himself. If I thought that would be the end of it, I'd tolerate his taunts through gritted teeth, but once he grew bored, he'd try to draw others with him. He wanted a fight with an old woman, and I determined he should have it.

When we fled years before, Grendel carried a huge trunk for me, effortlessly. It was in the back of the hut, next to my bed, where it served as a table, a chair, and a storage chest. I swept clothing and pouches off it, opened the lid, and hauled out the clothes within to dump them on the ground. I wanted what lay beneath.

I pulled my *brynje* of mail from the chest. It was darkened with age, but its rings were well wrought and it would protect me. I no longer had the underpadding. It was long since used for baby blankets. My dress and a winter tunic of thick wool would have to do. It was only for one fight.

The armor was snug. I was not a young girl anymore. It covered well enough, though tight on my chest, and dragged a bit on my hips. I grabbed the tails and yanked hard, bursting the three lowest rings at the front, and then it moved as it should.

I took a moment to pull the blankets around my boy and check the bandages, which were soaked through with dark blood. I carefully bound another wrapping over them, knowing it would accomplish little. Lacking a miracle from the gods who'd never seen fit to give me a pittance, his time in this world grew short. He moaned and twitched, his ruined shoulder sensitive to every waft of air, the mattress, even my presence. I kissed his forehead gently from above and resumed my task.

Behind the door, well covered in dust, were my other needs. A thick leathern hat with a string to tie it, a light but sturdy shield reinforced with iron strips and rawhide edging, and my lord's sword. I drew it from the scabbard and examined it.

There was some small amount of brown bloom that should be oiled and scoured before it turned to rust. There was no time for that now. My tormentor awaited, and I had a blood oath to fulfill.

I stood and breathed deeply, reacquainting myself with the weight of armor, and learning the heft of the sword. When I heard his voice circle around to the front again, I pulled the door open and stepped out.

"Hello, Aeschere," I said with a sweet tone that didn't hide my rage. "Would you care to dance?"

His expression told me he hadn't expected a fair fight. He clutched for his sword, stuttering as he did so. He almost said something, possibly to placate me, possibly to distract. But his mind caught up and realized the futility.

He dropped into guard and waited for me to attack in rage. Oh, Aeschere, this was not my first battle, nor quite my last. I simply smiled, with a flick of tongue on lips to taunt him. He shifted and hesitated, and I stamped my foot. That startled him and I laughed.

"Afraid, are we?" I asked, advancing a half step.

He took the bait.

I am not small, but he was taller. But women balance better with sword forward and shield at a slant, while men raise the shield forward and the blade back. He advanced to where he could just reach me with his greater height, assuming I could not return the favor.

But that put him a foot into my range and I struck, punching out my hand and whipping my wrist. I swung my sword low and it bit into the hide armoring his thigh. It did not cut through, but the impact staggered him. His blow stumbled and glanced off my shield, and I pressed at once.

He recovered with a solid swing that cut a deep nick into the hide edge of my shield, and we scrabbled around, trading blows to little effect. He was hurt but little, but he was shocked by my response and he was scared. He thought to overpower me unarmed, to humiliate and shame me, and perhaps violate me. Once met, he dared not retreat from a mere woman, even if it meant an actual fight. And if he were to lose?

His blood-rage brought him in hard and fast, with a blow that half cracked my shield and dented the boss. I grunted and powered into it, trying to get my point under his guard and to his belly. I succeeded, but it was a soft thrust and didn't pierce. He backed up quickly, and I flicked the tip up, catching his exposed forearm. Skin parted and blood flowed. I pressed again, and my next thrust just barely nicked his breast under the hardened hide.

This is the true nature of fighting, not the glorious finalities of the sagas. Two warriors cut at each other until one is weakened enough to surrender, flee, or die. Neither of us could give in or run. In Aeschere's haste to make a name, he'd ensured one of us would succumb this day.

His next blow broke the damaged section of shield and strained my arm, the shock jarring my elbow. My hand went numb, and pain blazed from elbow to shoulder. But he was extended and his arm weakened, and I hacked it, cutting muscle and bone so blood gushed freely.

Growling in pain, he seemed likely to flee, but he knew how that ended. He dropped his shield and swapped his sword to his left. Now undefended, he nevertheless had a weapon on my unprotected side. And he was angry and hurt.

It was all I could do to raise the half shield in my damaged arm, shriek in pain as his weapon crashed down, and drop under the onslaught. That put me low, and I drove my point up into his belly. Fluid and humors spilled, and I smelled the stench of cut bowel. As my cry of pain faded, his rose, as he knew he was dying.

Death was not immediate, though, and might take days. His sword was still live, as was the hand behind it.

I clutched the remnants of my shield just as he struck. Between the splinters and the mail, it felt like a blow from a club, driving the wind from me. Spots before my eyes told me I had no time. All I could do was strike again, this time cutting his thigh. That staggered him back and to the ground, where he attempted to rise and squealed, and then fell again.

I drew in sips of air, then breaths, and my vision cleared. Taking in a deep draught of damp swamp fog, I staggered around his fallen figure. I was a widow and a woman. There had been no honor given, and I granted none back. I batted his sword arm aside, raised my own, shouted a battle cry, and chopped.

I would come back to this. After I saw to my son.

I leaned the sword on the wall, and stumbled through the hut and into the small room. Before I opened the door, I knew.

Grendel's life had slipped away while Aeschere and I dueled. The man had won that much, denying me presence at my son's passage, and denying Grendel my comfort. Oh, how I raged.

With my left arm damaged, I couldn't even grant my son a civilized burial. Here he would remain.

I tumbled Aeschere's separated head, its face still a mask of shock and agony, into a satchel, and slung it over my shoulder along with his shield. Little good it would do me, but it was better to have it, and my presentation would matter.

I walked the long, dreary distance back the way I'd run.

This time the crowd was silent, perhaps realizing no good would come of this.

They parted for me, afraid or disgusted, it didn't matter now. I walked forward, armed and girded, and stood before the hall, ignoring the gruesome decoration that would only bring me anguish.

"Hrothgar, I call you out. You have wronged a widow, and wronged an orphan living with a curse. You are unfit to rule. You lack the discipline to control your men, and let them rampage after a widow, with foul intent."

I knelt, laid the sack down, grasped the bottom, and pulled. Aeschere's head rolled free, tumbling across the dirt as his nose, chin, and spine bumped along it. There were sounds of shock and horror among the crowd, and I heard a wail from Aeschere's daughter. Part of me wanted to be sympathetic, but I choked that down and kept my heart hard.

I pointed and firmly said, "Beowulf, I call you out for killing a man with a cursed mind, knowing full well he had no kin to stand for him.

"Instead of a father or brother, you will face me in combat. I call my son murdered, and I name you the murderer."

There was stone silence.

"Beowulf, if you claim to be a man, you will meet me alone in the cave in the marsh, the only place my son could flee from his demons. Surely one old woman is no match for you. Certainly not after you slew such a monster as a man crippled by headaches and madness."

I turned my back and walked. I was half-sure they'd dispose of me right there, but I was a woman, and whatever honor they retained let me leave unmolested. The only friend I had left made an abortive gesture in my direction, and I shook my head sharply. This was not Edda's fight, and she was the only hope our story might be told with some measure of truth. I could not risk her as well.

There was no honorable end to come, no peace. There was nowhere further to flee from the presence of people.

I returned to the hut, to kneel beside my sweet boy and beg the gods to treat him gently. After all, it was they who chose him as a plaything for their whims.

I downed the strongest of tinctures I had left, ones I reserved for Grendel's worst days, to ease the pain of my shattered arm and broken heart. I splinted my arm straight, at least giving me the ability to awkwardly heft a shield.

No burial was possible, but I was able to drag the furniture close to the bed, dump out the little oil I had, and kick one weakened side of the hut until it sunk lower. The fire could take it from there. I sought an ember from the hearth, blew it bright, and watched the flower of flame dance merrily on the makeshift bier. That assured, I left what remained of my life to burn brightly with dark sooty smoke, and walked to the cave. I brought my sword, Aeschere's shield, this journal, and a crust of bread.

Now I see a figure striding over the dunes and the brush, armed and ready. Distantly behind him are cheers at the thought of the death of a widow and her cursed son. I am bitter, with little to find light in, but there is one final mark in my column.

I hope that Edda, the wisest and kindest woman I ever knew, will come looking, and think to check the spot where we stored the more perishable herbs in the cool cave. That is where I will leave this journal.

I take heart in one warm thought. My lord fell in battle, and dines in the Valhöll. Grendel was killed in combat, and has also gone ahead of me to revered Aasgarð. When this is over, I shall be reunited with my love and my dearest son. What this world never gave me, the next will. I am at peace. Perhaps the All Father will even grant the spirit of my infant daughter to us.

I will close this now. There are no more words to write. The rest must be action.

I have no illusions about how this will end. Beowulf is a professional warrior, and I am only the mother of a monster. I was lucky once, and now half-maimed.

But if they will sing of him for a thousand years, they must also sing of me.

BONDS OF LOVE AND DUTY

MONALISA FOSTER

Calyce Dobromil leaned forward, her hands planted solidly on her workstation lest her knees give out. The gleaming pearl-white walls of the gestation lab seemed to spin around her like a veil or, more fittingly, a shroud. It spun and spun, tightening, as she gasped for air. Her mind grabbed at the possibility that she might be asleep and would wake at any moment. But the universe showed her no such mercy. It was perfectly clear in its ruthlessness, in the fact that she was indeed awake.

A message floated above her workstation like a cloud, all bright and golden and deceptive. It should have been a thunderhead, dark and malevolent.

Destruction and termination orders shouldn't be so antiseptic, so mundane, so much like every other communiqué that came down once a day from the Ryhman Council. She closed her eyes and took three deep breaths. When she opened them, the order was still there: destroy everything related to creating the *donai*. And floating underneath it, a scrolling list of the designations of each child under her care.

The oldest such child was twelve, a genetically engineered soldier whose nanites had just started turning him into his final *donai* form. Designated NT527, he was from one of their slow-growing—but most successful—batches and only two days shy of being sent off for formal military training.

The youngest were fertilized ova. Two hundred and forty of them—among them, twenty females. And then there were the five gestation tanks in her lab, the youngest still a blastocyst, the oldest just a few days past twelve months' gestation.

Calyce had given the last fifty years of her life to creating and raising the *donai*. And now the council expected her to "terminate" them as if they were condemned prisoners. Even lab animals were "sacrificed."

She pushed away from the workstation and dragged her hand across each gestation tank, blinking back against the pressure building up between her eyes. There had been a few unfortunate *donai* that hadn't developed properly. She'd mourned every one of them but taken solace in the ones that had survived and thrived, the ones she'd nurtured. And then she'd proudly sent them off to defend humankind, her duty done, her desire to nurture serving a higher purpose.

The twelve-month-old floated in the amniotic fluid, sucking on his thumb. Dark, curly hair covered his scalp, framing the nubs at the tops of his ears, the vestigial points that would become more prominent as he reached adulthood.

The tank had reported a case of the hiccups that had lasted twelve minutes, and a surge in heart rate from a dream that had lasted twenty. No anomalies. His nanites were keeping pace with his growth. Six more months and she'd decant a healthy boy, and they would bond as if they were mother and child. Bonding the *donai* to humans was essential. It made them want to defend their creators. It was as necessary as air, water, and food. It made *donai* loyal. It kept them sane.

Calyce blinked back tears as she returned to her workstation, waved the termination order out of existence, and stuck her hands in her lab coat's pockets.

Every morning, whether on duty or not, she was always the first in the lab, checking on her children. But soon the others would trickle in, and once they did, her moment of opportunity would be lost. She'd been here the longest and had seniority, but she didn't dare count on the others. If she was wrong about any one of them, that *one* could stop her.

She tucked a fallen strand of gray hair behind her ear, took a deep breath, and passed her hand over the console controlling the tanks. The biometric scanner underneath her hand confirmed her identity. She programmed the workstation to flood the pods with a lethal dose of sedative in order to buy time. And walked away.

In the adjoining lab she opened up the safe with the fertilized ova, setting the tubes marked "female" into a specimen container. Twenty tubes marked "male" went into a second container. Small enough for her to carry easily, the containers would keep the ova from deteriorating for years if necessary. All she had to do was get them away from this place, far beyond the reaches of the council.

Andret was a name that NT527's Tante had given him. It was a name he was going to miss. He knew that once he left the creche, NT527 was going to become his "name." He was packed to go, eager almost, his body ready and primed, instincts pushing him into quick and easy aggression. Sometimes those instincts got away from him, snaking through him like lightning, and the training at the creche was no longer enough to contain it.

He was down to needing only a couple of hours of sleep, and no amount of exercise or drills were enough to tire him out. Soon he would not need sleep at all. Even now, he could easily slip in and out of the *donai* rest-state that replaced sleep.

Andret was ready. Ready to fight, to defend. He was ready for more. He wanted to test himself, to push his limits.

As the oldest *donai* at the creche, he was bigger, faster, and stronger than his brothers. They no longer posed a challenge, and he'd squeezed too hard, punched too hard more than once. Even the human trainers in their armor no longer wanted to spar with him.

He turned, restless in the small, dark room. Even in the darkness, he could see as clearly as if it were day. Motes of dust floated by. Heat flowed along conduits inside the walls. He could even hear the breathing of the younger *donai* sleeping in the next room.

Human footsteps echoed down the corridor. He could tell it was Tante Calyce from the rhythm of her gait.

She stopped in front of his door, and he heard her take a deep breath. Fear tainted her scent.

He sat up as the door slid open. The lights came on. His eyes adjusted almost without delay, the leaves of layered, engineered irises falling into place to shield him. The patterns of heat over her body indicated stress. In each hand, she carried a specimen container.

"I need a pilot," Tante Calyce said. The stress in her voice was like a scream, even though she'd whispered her words. Small for a human, gray hair pulled back at the nape of her neck, she had bright blue eyes surrounded by fine lines that matched the ones around her mouth. A red tunic topped matching trousers and black, polished shoes.

He stood up. "Yes, Tante. Where would you like to go?"

"Away from here, Andret. As far away, as fast as you can."

The look on her face forbade any questions, any argument.

He pulled on a shirt, trousers, and boots as impatience tightened the set of Tante's shoulders. He followed her out, slowing to match her pace as she walked toward the launch bay. To the other humans in the creche, she would look like she was going on about her day, casually walking down the hall with him as escort, perhaps toward some task that needed *donai* strength. But they didn't have his senses, and his senses told him that she'd rather be running.

The launch bay lit up as they entered. Ships, large and small, fast and slow, gleamed in their berths, waiting. In less than an hour, human instructors and *donai* students would be flying them over the training range.

"This way, Tante," he said as he headed for a small fighter. He'd planned on taking the ship up later, prepping and arming it before he'd gone back to his room to "rest."

"How far can it take us?" she asked, skepticism playing across her face.

"Through the phase-point and beyond." He'd been trained to navigate the extra-dimensional space of the phase-point transit system. There hadn't been too many opportunities to use it, not with the training ship's limited range, but he'd been allowed to explore the nearby systems on his own.

"Can the ship's controls be overridden?"

He blinked his surprise. What a strange question. Perhaps it was part of some test. With just two days to go, he'd expected something, although he'd expected it to come from his flight instructor, or perhaps from the combat instructors. He'd imagined a test where they all came at him at once, them in armor, him bare-handed.

"Do you want me to disable the override system, Tante?"

"Yes. Disable it. And the transponder. I want us to disappear. Do you understand?"

Andret nodded and helped her into the fighter. She settled into the right seat, setting the containers atop her lap. Perhaps it was a test of loyalty, of his willingness to obey humans. Though it was hardly a good test. He'd have done anything for her, and not out of loyalty.

The ship recognized him and holographic controls appeared over the flight console. His hands danced over them, tapping out the startup sequence.

Tante Calyce let out a small gasp of surprise as her seat folded around her.

"Perhaps you should set those containers down. For your own safety, Tante."

She shook her head. "Andret, promise me, if they chase us, you will fly like your life depends on it, because it does."

He gave her a sharp look. "Tante, your body can't handle those forces. Not even with the inertial compensators."

"Like *your* life depends on it, Andret."

"I cannot allow you to be harmed." Was this part of the test? Tante despised mind games. Unlike the newer caretakers, she refused to play them.

"Please. For their sakes." She tightened her arms around the containers.

Understanding knifed through him, reverberating through his body, making his muscles tense, his blood race. Trust and a cold calm chased away both questions and emotions. He turned back to the console and started the engines.

A minute later they were out over the flight range, overrides engaged, transponder off, the pull of the launch bay's safety protocols defeated.

At two minutes they were flying straight up. Gravity tugged at his chest, a mild annoyance. Next to him, Tante Calyce struggled to breathe, the harsh sounds of her gasps clearly audible over the engine noise.

At three minutes, the scent of human blood reached his nose and his *donai* augmentations went into overdrive. Everything was sharper, clearer. His reflexes were faster. He bared his teeth as he sped toward the smallest of the system's five jump-points so none of the larger, better-armed ships could follow them.

He hoped that the acceleration wouldn't kill the human that had given him life.

Calyce slipped in and out of consciousness, catching glimpses of Andret's determined face. Like all of the *donai*, his primary irises were amber. They circled gold pupils. In the angry lights strobing around them, she caught glimpses of the soldier he would become. It wasn't the bared cuspids and their resemblance to fangs. It was the way he moved, the perfect way he performed every task as if he'd been born to it.

I made this.

Over the last few years, the council's attitude toward the *donai* had changed. The *donai* were no longer held up as the heroes that gave their lives for humanity. Gestation orders had declined. So had the size of her staff. The governor in charge of the *donai* program had rotated out the caretakers like herself who'd served for decades, replacing them with new ones that resisted bonding with the children they'd been tasked to raise.

She should have seen it.

And now that she did, she knew what was next. There would be a self-destruct order. Either one sent directly to the *donai* ships or something subtler, something in their training, their conditioning. And when the council gave that order, they would be passing a death sentence on themselves.

Calyce was no soldier. But she knew the *donai* better than any-one. There was one order they would not obey. And it would end in a bloodbath. A human bloodbath.

She let out a small whimper.

Andret looked at her from the corner of his eye, and the pressure on her chest eased. She swallowed a mouthful of blood, choking on it.

She could not draw enough breath to tell him that she was already dead and to save himself and the brothers and sisters she cradled in her arms.

There was no disorientation, no indication at all that they'd just trav-eled 112 light-years. There was, in fact, no change in momentum at all. It was acceleration through normal space that was the problem. A problem not just of excess inertia but of inadequate fuel.

The fuel indicator pulsed an angry red. His nav controls pro-jected only one path—the one he'd set them on—but no matter what he did, there would be no controlled descent.

They were going to crash.

Andret would have to use his remaining fuel to crash in a way that would allow them to survive it. Tante's heart was already beat-ing out a requiem, even though he'd opted for safer accelerations. If he'd followed her orders to the letter, she'd already be dead. His chest squeezed and tightened, making his heart ache.

He swung past the two moons and punched through the atmo-sphere of a world that humans had seeded and then abandoned, saving his fuel by not making proper adjustments. It was going to cost them. The hull would be compromised. But they'd gotten away. He didn't expect the situation to last. Transponder or not, their ship left gravitic wakes that could be traced. Given their fuel, there were only so many suitable places to escape to on the path he'd taken.

But the planet was big. Ice capped both poles, glinting like diamonds. Bright, milk-white clouds swirled and danced over huge blue oceans and continents covered by dense green forests. They could lose themselves among the local fauna. He'd bought Tante time to do whatever she had planned next.

The ship brushed the dense forest canopy like a rock skimming off a lake, jolting the ship from side to side.

Tante groaned.

He dared not look at her—not until it was over.

Landing thrusters ignited the treetops. *Damn.* That would be hard to miss. They'd have to abandon the ship and get as far away from it as possible, all without leaving a trail.

Inertia pushed him forward as the ship made impact with the ground and spun to a stop. Alarms blared at him and then died as the ship lost power.

In the dark, the way Tante's blood flowed told him she had broken bones and punctured organs. The scent of death was already emanating from her pores, permeating the cockpit.

"Tante, what's going on?" he whispered as he knelt at her side.

Her eyes fluttered open and blood flowed down her chin.

"The council is going to destroy the *donai.*" Another pained breath, liquid bubbling where it shouldn't be.

"They need us," he said as he pried her hand off the containers.

She shook her head, and tears leaked out of her eyes as he took the containers and turned them over, looking for a way to open them.

"Tante, tell me you have human-compatible nanites in these."

Another weak shake of her head.

"Run, Andret. Get as far away as you can. Don't come out until your own kind comes for you. Promise me."

"I can't leave you. I am *donai.*"

"You are, and because you are, you can and you will."

"Tante . . ."

"If you have to make a choice, save the container marked 'female.' In order to survive, the *donai* will need the ability to reproduce on their own. Do you understand?"

He dared not speak, breathe, or move. She was placing lives into his hands. He'd thought himself so ready to the task. And now that it was here . . .

"Your word of honor, *donai*."

He stared, rebellion seething within. With those uncompromising words she would bind him with chains stronger than any substance. A *donai*'s honor was as much a part of him as his nanites. It had been engineered into them.

If he gave his word, he *couldn't* break it.

"My word of honor, Tante," he said, lowering his chin.

"Don't let me linger. Make it quick. And when the time comes, remember that not all humans are like the ones that bred you to be used and discarded."

Andret raised his gaze to hers. She was in pain. He could smell it, see it.

"Do it," she said, her voice determined.

He put his arms around her carefully, holding her so that his razor-sharp fingernails wouldn't cut her. The wetness of a human tear touched his cheek. It was followed by a kiss, her last breath fluttering against his skin before she went limp in his grasp.

Her heart's requiem played its final note, sparing him from having to snap her neck.

Andret rejected the idea of stripping the ship for its memetic metals to make a blade. It might be traced and he could not risk it. He did strip it of the emergency stores, setting them aside, along with the precious cargo that Tante had given her life for.

The trail their entry had burned could not be masked, so he wasn't going to waste time and energy hiding the wreckage.

He built a funeral pyre, placed Tante atop it, and set it ablaze. The flames turned her body to ash. They turned his heart to ash as well, and a chill formed deep within him. He welcomed that cold, giving himself to it. He'd built the pyre large, large enough to burn throughout the night, the need to honor her stronger than the need for flight. His gaze followed the ashes floating upward.

Andret knew what to do whether friend or foe came for him. The one thing that haunted him was the possibility that no one would come. The nanites in his body would repair him as long as he kept himself fed. Or didn't bash in his own brains. Theoretically, a *donai*'s life span could be measured in centuries. But most *donai* died in battle while still in their prime. It was their purpose, the reason they had been created.

The council would not destroy humanity's defenders unless they no longer had a need for them. Or perhaps something had happened to make humans fear their own creations.

He bared his teeth again as he looked up at the cloudless ink of night, sending up one lone wish: that he would get the chance to save his own kind from extermination.

For ten days Andret ran, carrying the precious cargo strapped to his back. The forest blurred past him. By the eleventh day, he'd depleted his food stores. By the thirteenth, he was too tired to continue.

His nanites consumed energy like anything else. He needed to eat.

After sunset, he dug a deep tunnel into the side of a hill with his bare hands. Gusting air pulled angrily at the grass, scattered the soil he'd loosened, and sent it swirling. He buried his backpack and the containers, memorized their position, and set out to hunt.

The surrounding forest was full of prey, but he was weak. He needed to be efficient.

Howls drifted through the forest. They sounded like this world's equivalent of wolves. He raced toward them.

A pack of wolves had spread through the trees, driving their prey, a stag-like animal with broken antlers, along a well-worn path. The wolves must have separated it from its herd and were running it to ground, wearing it out. Wind carried the stag's fear-scent. It was like a drug, enhancing Andret's senses, spiking his adrenaline.

He pushed forward, passing the wolf pack upwind, and scrambled up a tree growing at the edge of a clearing. Andret landed in the stag's path, took hold of the antlers as they came at him, and twisted, breaking the animal's neck. Momentum carried them both forward.

They skidded to a stop, the stag's weight pinning Andret against a tree. He scrambled from underneath the carcass and crouched in front of his kill, teeth bared as he faced down the wolf pack.

Five growling wolves skidded to a stop, their hackles raised. Three others circled, betrayed by their scents and the sound of their breathing. The largest wolf inched forward. To a human, the black fur would have made it hard to see in the falling darkness, but the wolf's heart glowed like a beacon in Andret's enhanced vision.

Once the alpha decided to attack, the others would as well. Andret launched himself at the alpha, slashing his throat with one sweep of his razor-sharp fingernails, killing him instantly. Blood poured out of the alpha's neck, staining the soil, sending up the taste of iron.

He licked the wolf's blood off his hand. It made his vision painfully intense. The world around him became a concert of images and noises almost too vivid to process. The wolves that had been hiding came into view as the ones in front of him backed off, hackles still raised, tails low.

Andret let out a roar. It sent the pack scattering into the trees. Fear-scent particles trailed them like smoke, mixing in the wind with the scent of soil and plants.

He knelt by the dead wolf. All the wolves were larger than the ones in the images he'd been shown as a child. Andret picked up the wolf's body, testing its weight. It was far heavier than he'd expected. He had no doubt that it was enhanced somehow. More genetic tinkering. Either for a specific reason or to see if it could be done. Which meant that, sooner or later, some human would come back here to check on the experiment. There was probably a satellite in orbit, or an automated probe would fly by at some point. Either way, someone would come. And when they did, he would be ready.

He dragged the wolf's body to the edge of the clearing. As he gathered kindling and deadwood for a fire, another wolf inched forward, keeping low to the ground to catch the scent of the dead one. The wolf let out a mournful howl. It was answered by the rest of the pack.

Even when the fire was roaring, the wolves did not back off. They patrolled the edge of the clearing, wary, their fear-scent drifting along the breeze.

Andret sliced the stag's belly open, spilling the viscera but saving the liver. He dragged the carcass to the fire, tore the skin off, and pulled the limbs apart.

Donai could tear into flesh and bone, eat them raw, but he'd never liked the way it made him feel. Even as voraciously hungry as he was, he'd hold on to whatever humanity was left in him. It would slip away from him as he aged. He knew that. But for now, he didn't have to let go of it.

As he chewed, another wolf—a female with red in her coat—

claimed the viscera he'd left behind. A smaller male joined her. Between them, they finished it off.

He threw a bone at them. The female snagged it away and bounded under cover, a happy wag to her tail.

Wolf-eyes glowed in the dark, blinking back at him, first warily, then with curiosity. Their fear-scent faded.

He tossed one of the stag's leg bones at them. They pounced on it, too, and carried it away.

A gray wolf, obviously pregnant, took the stag's head and settled down within the firelight, chomping happily, her amber gaze intent, and so much a mirror, the sight of it raised goose bumps on his skin.

"Sister?" he asked.

She tilted her head.

"No, I suppose not."

She went back to chewing.

"Sorry about your mate." He was, truly. The *donai* were killers by design, but the stag and the wolf were his first. The stag was prey. The wolf was not. One predator to another, he felt regret for the wolf. They had enough in common to be kin, so he dug a hole and buried it. It was something sentimental that Calyce would have done.

Andret used the stag's hide to wrap up the cooked meat and left the remaining bones for the wolves. It made him feel less like a thief. The stag would have been their kill.

He headed back to the hill where he'd buried the containers, and started digging. About halfway through, he took a break to drink from a nearby stream. When he returned, the amber-eyed wolf was sniffing around the hole.

She stuck her head in and dirt came flying out. Strange. He'd have expected her to go for the sack of meat he'd left by the opening. The breeze told him that three other wolves were nearby. When it shifted, he scented two others.

"So, you're the brave one."

Dirt continued flying out in steady spurts.

"Or maybe just curious."

She backed out of the hole, dragging one of the carriers by its handle.

Andret took a deep breath, ready to run after her, but she set it down instead and went back into the hole. She dragged the second carrier out, dropped it, and circled them, sniffing.

"They have no scent, do they, curious one?" With the seals intact, they would have none.

She went into the hole a third time and came out with his backpack. Her tail wagged as she sniffed it.

"Yeah, that one's going to have lots of scents." Sweat for one. And the lingering scent of past rations.

He lowered himself to a crouch. She dragged the backpack to him and backed off.

Andret extended his hand. She sniffed it but backed away when he tried to touch her.

"Fair enough. I wouldn't trust me either."

He took the survival blanket out of the bag and wrapped it around the meat. The containers went in next. He headed for the stream to fill the canteen.

As he ran for the mountains, clouds drifted in and settled on the horizon.

A yip behind him brought him to a halt. The curious one was panting with exhaustion. He'd been running into the wind and had missed that she'd been following.

Damn.

He stopped and turned around. "Go back to your pack."

She closed the distance between them and howled. The pack answered. Five wolves came over the hill.

Andret blew out a frustrated breath. He could run much faster than they could. They would slow him down.

Tante would remind him that he'd been bred with the need to bond. It was as much a part of him as his eyes, his elongated cuspids, his nanites.

Lone *donai* became unreliable, went mad. Other *donai* were tasked with capturing and beheading them, using swords designed specifically for that task.

The other wolves approached, less cautious than before.

You need them. And apparently they needed him.

He laughed.

"Well, if we're going to be a pack, you're going to need a name," he said to the gray female.

She sat and panted, her tongue swollen from the heat.

"Ena for you, I think."

The rest of the pack had caught up. They, too, were tired, and lay down to catch their breaths.

The splash of water against rock came from the west. He'd have to parallel a stream if they were going to run with him. And they'd have to hunt.

Andret let them rest a bit and then headed for the stream. They waded in to cool off and drink.

"Better to travel at night, right?"

Ena returned to his heel, still wet, and shook her fur dry, spraying him. Well, if he was going to adopt them, he might as well smell like them. He knelt and extended his hand. She gave it a curious lick and headed for the shade of the trees.

Andret sat down next to her, back propped up against a fallen tree trunk. Ena set her chin on his thigh and fell asleep. The others settled in around him, some close, some still wary enough to choose distance.

He drank from his canteen, and settled in to wait, watching the cloudless sky with its naked, unfamiliar stars.

Three of the wolves stopped along the crest of a mountain ridge. Ena called to them, as did the younger, more trusting males, Thunder and Raven. Their howls filled the air as the sun set on their twenty-first day together.

That night, as Ena settled against Andret, she whimpered herself to sleep as he stroked her bristly gray fur. Stroking her gave him a sense of peace, a sense of calm that rivaled his memories of when he'd been young enough, and light enough, to sit in a human's lap.

Of the faces of all the women who'd taken care of him, it was Calyce's that he remembered the most, although she had not been the one who spent the most time with him. Like the wolves who'd come along and then decided to leave, he suspected the strength of the bond just hadn't been strong enough. There were bonds forged of duty, and bonds forged of love. Calyce had loved him in a way the others had not.

Ena, Thunder, and Raven loved him.

That night, Ena went into labor. Thunder and Raven paced nervously but kept their distance. By dawn she'd delivered four wolf pups, three alive, and one stillborn. He'd tried to take the stillborn away from her, but she'd bit his hand, puncturing his skin and drawing blood before he let go.

He drew his hand back, horrified.

Your blood is poison to us. It was one of the first things a *donai* was taught.

But Ena wasn't human, and the fact that her fangs had pierced his skin erased any doubt that she was engineered as well.

The punctures on his hand sealed within seconds. Within minutes, his nanites had erased any trace of injury.

With wary eyes, Ena licked the stillborn pup well into the next day as her live ones nursed. It wasn't until she fell into a deep sleep that he took the stillborn pup from her.

He cradled the tiny female to his chest and padded away, just as Thunder and Raven returned with the carcass of a young doe. They always gave Andret first choice, but this time they dragged it past him as if he wasn't even there.

Andret ran deep into the forest, far enough that when Ena woke, she wouldn't be able to find her stillborn pup. He dug a small hole.

He'd never seen anything so still. Oh, he'd seen death. Accidents were not unknown in the creche. Humans were so fragile and didn't have their own symbiotic nanites. But he'd never seen death like this—one not preceded by life.

What had gone wrong?

He shifted his vision, looking at the small body in a way no human could. The pup was small, far smaller than the others. He compared its anatomy with that of the adults. His untrained eye saw no anomalies.

There was something unspeakably wrong with not knowing the reason this one had died and the others had survived.

His chest hurt as he placed the pup into its grave and covered her up with dirt. He knelt there for a while, the hole made in his soul by the loss of Calyce widening just a bit.

Humanity no longer seemed like something to hold on to.

It hurt too much.

They could not travel until Ena was ready. She wouldn't let Andret take her pups and carry them. Not after he'd taken the dead one. She growled and snapped and looked at him with distrust.

He should leave her to her pack. It was the logical thing to do. It was the right thing to do. He had forty *donai* lives to protect.

Every day he told himself that Thunder and Raven would take care of Ena. They hunted and fed her so she could feed her pups. But he couldn't leave. He'd made it as far as an hour's run and turned back. Along the way, he hunted and brought back anything he'd come across. But he'd always return.

"I don't suppose you can tell me how long this is going to take?" he asked as he reached to pet one of the milk-drunk pups that had dozed off and slipped off her nipple.

She answered with a growl.

Either he or Raven or Thunder would stay with Ena while the other two hunted. At night, he'd watch the sky. He knew exactly where the system's phase-points were. Some were close enough to shimmer if he shifted his vision to the right part of the spectrum. But he never saw any signs.

He was growing. He could tell by how tight his clothes were getting. The boots were the first to go into the backpack. The shirt and jacket second. He made slits in his trousers, all the way up to his thighs.

Thirteen days later, Ena's pups opened their eyes. A few days after that, they started to walk. One wandered close, and he picked it up and Ena didn't growl or come take it away from him.

In another week they were playing, barking, and bringing the wolves so much joy that sometimes Andret's heart ached with a different kind of hurt. He'd look away.

Still too human.

A week later, the pups nipped at his heels and Ena came up to cuddle with him. She licked the hand she'd bitten.

"It's all right," he said. "I heal fast."

She kept licking.

"All right, all right, apology accepted."

She huffed and nuzzled into his neck.

An odd kind of peace, of contentment, flowed through him.

"We have to keep moving, you know."

Ena's gaze settled on the mountains ahead of them as if she'd understood him.

The next night, he made a sling out of his jacket, and she let him place her pups in it. They headed toward the mountains.

Andret knelt on the shore of a still mountain lake, washing his face. Two winters had come and gone. The points of his ears had come in. He sported a dark beard and long, black hair. An animal pelt hugged his hips. He'd torn the straps off his backpack and made a belt to keep it in place.

The change wasn't quite complete—he would be larger by the time it was over—but it had gone far enough that no one would mistake him for human.

Ena's reflection joined his in the water's surface. She leaned into him like she always did when given the opportunity.

Happy yips and growls in the distance told him that their pack was playing. They'd encountered no other wolves here. There was not enough game. But his pack had him, and he was a far better hunter. With him, the wolves took down larger prey than they could otherwise.

That night, lying under the stars, hands laced behind his head, he saw it—the shimmer of an activated phase-point. His layered irises had matured and extended far beyond a human's visual spectrum. They allowed him to clearly see not only the phase-point but the small dot that came out of it—a ship. It was accelerating at speeds no human could survive, and it was headed for his planet, not merely passing through. It made several course corrections for a re-entry that would take it to the site where he and Calyce had crashed. It might still have been a probe.

There was only one way to find out.

Ena, who'd been cuddling up against him and snoring, picked her head up, attuned as ever to his mood.

The time had come. He'd thought the hole in his soul, in his humanity, healed, or at least well scarred over. But now it tore anew.

He'd had two years to discover who and what he was. Two years to understand where the change was taking him. He was more pred-ator than soldier. That part was still to come. And he yearned for it, dreamt about it. When the adult *donai* had come to the creche to take custody of the children, he'd seen what he would become, where he belonged. He still wanted to be with his own kind.

The creche staff, including the armored combat instructors who trained the children to fight and fly, feared the adult *donai* the most. Calyce had been the only human that didn't fear them. He had to go to his own kind, to honor her last wish and sacrifice, to save the lives with which he'd been entrusted.

He petted Ena's head. She whimpered, pushing into it.

"It's all right, little sister."

He would miss her. He would miss them all. They had been his family, his pack, the bonds of love that had kept him sane.

He knelt in front of Ena, and the pack surrounded him. He pet-ted them in turn, the aging males, the young pups.

"My word as *donai*, I will return."

He didn't realize there were tears on his face until Ena licked them off. How strange. Grown *donai* did not cry. Humans cried. Perhaps those tears were the last vestiges of his humanity.

When Andret had first chosen this meadow as their home, he'd done so because of the nearby cave. He'd placed the containers deep within, where the metal of the mountain would shield them from most sensors.

Accompanied by the wolves, he returned to the cave and emerged with the container marked "male."

Save the container marked "female," Calyce had told him.

Even without weapons, his speed, his strength, had defeated the strongest, best-armed humans at the creche. But he could not defeat other *donai*. Mature, trained, and armed, they would be wary of a solitary *donai* coming out of the forest. The container would be his bargaining chip, the proof that he was still sane. They must see him as a young *donai* who'd been given a mission and was still worthy of trust and respect.

The pack ran with him, following him until their strength gave out. Their howls trailed behind him as he outran them. They were a strong, intelligent pack. If he didn't return, they'd descend to richer hunting grounds. They'd survive. He was certain of it. He needed to be.

For the second time in his short life, he left his family.

First, a family of one named Calyce, a woman who had been his mother, a child of her heart if not her body. How different were they, as a species, if a *donai* could think of a human as his mother? If he could love her in that way? If she had loved him as a son? If she'd trusted him with the lives of forty others?

Second, a family of wolves. Ena was as much a sister to him as any of the *donai* at the creche. How different could they be if they could bond like they had, if they could adopt him and accept him as their leader?

He hurt. Not from the burn of muscles taxed to their limits, not from loss. Joy had done this to him, let him feel loss as intensely as he had love.

If he could hold on to it no matter what was to come, he could become the best of both—human and *donai*.

Andret crouched on a branch, high up in the trees overlooking the crash site. Rain and wind had swept Tante's funeral pyre away years ago. The damaged fighter shone in the sunlight, impervious to the planet's vegetation.

He didn't recognize the markings on the ship dwarfing his own. The design was definitely Ryhman; the markings were not.

Three *donai*, two males and one female, emerged from the ship. They were all at least a head taller. The larger male was twice as wide as any *donai* Andret had ever seen. They wore uniforms opaque to his enhanced vision. Sidearms and short blades rode their hips. They wore their hair in the short, cropped style of *donai* troops. The large male's was black like his own, the female's blond. The smaller male's was white, but not with age.

"Come down," the female said, her contralto voice strong and clear as she looked straight at him.

He stilled, patting the container strapped to his chest.

"Come down, or we'll come for you."

The males sprinted, racing to his position.

Before he had a chance to leap, the tree he'd used for conceal-ment fell to the ground. He rolled away, arms crossed over his chest, protecting the container.

It cost him, kept him from escaping. The males pinioned his arms back and dragged him out of the forest. He struggled, yelling at them to let him go.

When they did, it was at the female's feet.

Cruel hands grabbed at his hair, yanked his head back. The sharp edge of a blade cut into his neck, forcing him to stillness.

His gaze locked with the female's.

"Your designation?" she asked.

The blade was too deep in his flesh to let him speak, although he tried.

A quick flick of her hand, and the *donai* holding the blade eased up on the pressure.

Andret coughed up blood.

"She asked you a question," the dark-haired *donai* with the blade said.

"My *name* is Andret."

She smirked. "Is it now?"

"Yes," he said, making another attempt to free himself. The hands holding his arms tightened, digging in deep, making him wince.

The female tore the container off his chest, her nails leaving trails of blood as they ripped through his skin.

Andret's face hit the ground. A knee pressed into his back. He arched his back enough to get his face out of the dirt before his head was pushed down again.

"Strong for his age," the *donai* holding him down said.

The female's eyes widened as she examined the container. She lowered herself to the ground. Her layered irises swirled, contracting and expanding as she looked him over.

"What are you doing here, Andret?" There was a note of amusement at his name.

"Protecting my *donai* brothers." And sisters. But they didn't need to know that. Not yet.

She ran her hands reverently over the container as a predatory smile revealed her cuspids.

"Let him up," she said, rising. She handed the container to the white-haired male.

The knee on Andret's back pushed him down as he made to rise.

"We don't need him," the deep, harsh voice above him said.

"I said, let him up." Her voice harmonized with something inside Andret. The compulsion to rise, despite the pain in his pinioned arms, the weight on his back and head, became unbearable.

The *donai* above him let him go, releasing his hands, easing off his back and head. Andret pushed up, pivoted, and struck with all his strength. Four bones in his hand broke, but his target staggered back, blinking in surprise.

"Stand down," she said.

The dark-haired *donai* obeyed, hands clenched, body positioned to strike, but still nonetheless. The look on his face was not one of obedience though. Bared teeth and a pulsing jaw muscle promised retribution.

The white-haired male looked on, amusement on his face. "Oh, he is young," he said, tightening his grip on the container.

"Turn around, Andret," she said.

He did. His body didn't give him a choice. Chills ran through him, different from the ones that had given him calm efficiency before. Tremors pursued the chill, chasing it through his skin, down into his muscles and bones, creating a resonance of pleasure mixed with an eagerness to please.

She ran her hand over his chest, along the healing furrows she'd left behind, baring her teeth as she did so. A deep breath at his neck pulled at his scent. She closed her eyes, a lioness savoring the aromas of her prey.

She twisted her hand into his hair, giving it a tug. "Why are you protecting your brothers?"

"I gave my word as *donai*."

She leaned closer, her scent wrapping around him, sweeter than anything he'd smelled before. Better than a kill. Better than anything. For an instant there was no forest, no other males, nothing but her and a sense of purpose mixed with the joy of being with his own kind.

"He'll do," she said, letting him go and spinning on her heel. "Bring him."

"Do what?" Andret asked, unsteady as he followed, his head slowly clearing.

"Fight for our freedom. What else?"

On the planet now called Serigala, a slab of white marble stabs into the sky like a sword with its hilt buried in the soil beneath. Light from two moons shines down on a wolf's head carved into the monument, along with an inscription:

> *This is the final resting place of Calyce, the only mother I ever knew. Let it be known that every* donai—*male and female—who bears the name Dobromil owes their life to the love and bravery of a human woman.*
>
> —ANDRET, FOUNDER OF HOUSE DOBROMIL

ZOMBIE DEAREST

AN ANITA BLAKE, VAMPIRE HUNTER STORY

LAURELL K. HAMILTON

"You got my daughter pregnant," the woman said.

I settled a little more comfortably in my office chair in my business skirt outfit. I wasn't a cross-dresser, or trans-anything, so being a woman with only girl parts I couldn't have gotten anyone pregnant, which meant she was crazy, but like a lot of delusional people she looked sane. In fact, Mrs. Herman Henderson looked like she should be sitting on the PTA board of a nice school where they still had bake sales to raise money for band uniforms.

The man sitting beside her looked like the male version of her, someone who still read the paper for his news, maybe smoked a pipe, hunted once a year, or maybe went fly-fishing with the same group of men he'd gone to college with, but they still kept in touch. They looked like churchgoers, the conservative wet dream that people would assume voted Republican but actually voted Democrat because of certain issues not to be discussed at church. Too bad they were crazy.

"Mrs. Henderson, I assure you that I had nothing to do with your daughter being pregnant."

"You had everything to do with it," she said, voice getting a little shrill.

I debated pressing the button on the complicated phone on my desk that let the office assistants know to interrupt me. It was meant to be an intercom system, but hitting the button so the office staff could hear crazy talk or screaming usually got reinforcements pretty quick.

Mr. Henderson tried to pat his wife's arm, but she jerked away from him. "Julie, I don't think Miss Blake has any idea what you're talking about."

Normally I'd have corrected him to Ms. Blake, or Marshal Blake, but he seemed to be the sane half of the couple and I didn't want to insult him. *Miss* was okay if he helped get his crazy wife out of my office.

"She should know, she should know what her black magic does to people."

"Now, dear."

"Don't you 'now, dear' me, Herman Henderson."

"I don't know what you think I do here, Mrs. Henderson, but I don't do black magic."

She looked at me then with brown eyes so angry they were almost black, the way mine could get sometimes. Her hands clutched the handbag in her lap so tightly the skin was mottled. If she opened her purse and reached inside it, I was going to draw my gun just in case.

"You raise zombies, that's black magic."

"No, as a matter of fact, it's not."

"You sacrifice animals to raise the dead. That's evil." Her purse began to shake, and I had a moment of wondering if bombs shook like that, then realized it was just her hands shaking. I really had to stop jumping to the worst possible conclusion all the time. If there was anything in the purse, it would be a gun. See, not the worst possible thing.

"So you're a vegetarian?" I was betting money she wasn't.

The question caught her off guard enough that she frowned and forgot to be furious with me for a second. "No, no, I'm not a vegetarian. What has that got to do with anything?"

"You eat meat then."

She nodded, her hands relaxing a little around her purse. "I just said that."

"Does it make you evil to eat meat?"

"Are you making fun of me?" she asked, and the anger started to climb back into her hands and eyes.

"No, just pointing out that the fact that I kill a few chickens or the occasional goat to raise the long dead isn't any worse than slaughtering animals for food. If one doesn't make you evil, then neither does the other one."

"Eating a good steak or baked chicken isn't the same thing as slitting their throats to call the dead from the grave." Her hands were starting to mottle again.

"I don't see the difference," I said.

"That's because you're evil!" She shouted it at me. If the office hadn't been mostly soundproof, it might have brought our daytime office staff to the door, but for help to come that way I'd need her to yell louder. If we made that much noise, then it would probably be from me handling it myself.

"So, you don't want me to raise a zombie for you."

"Of course not!" She stood then, shaking with her anger and other strong emotions I couldn't even guess at.

"Do you have a vampire or shapeshifter problem?" I asked, keeping an eye both on her husband and on her hands clutching the purse. It was big enough that she could have hidden anything from a .380 to a small .45. Maybe all that was in there was her wallet and an understated lipstick, but I'd never gotten in trouble being paranoid. I was a U.S. Marshal for the Preternatural Division; it wasn't paranoia if they really were trying to kill you.

"No, no, none of that," said Mr. Henderson. He tugged on his wife's arm, trying to get her to sit back down, but she stood there ramrod straight and glaring at me. He wasn't going to shush her or make her sit down. In fact, I wasn't sure I could count on him for any real help. If I had to shoot her, he'd probably lie and say I shot first. Screw this. I reached for the button on the telephone.

"Please, Miss Blake, we don't know who else to go to."

I hesitated over the button. "The note by your appointment said 'zombie,' so I assumed you needed one raised, or maybe laid to rest."

"You defiled our daughter!"

I pressed the button and smiled at the crazy woman while I counted slowly in my head. Before I got to twenty, there was a knock on the door and Mary, our daytime receptionist, poked her head in. "Sorry, Anita, but you've got an emergency call."

It was now up to me to decide how serious the fake emergency would be. Was it a small one, so that she could escort the Hendersons to the lounge for coffee, tea, and some calming down, or was it a big one, so I was done with appointments for the day and she'd escort the would-be clients out of our offices for good? They would then find that my calendar would be full for them for, like, ever.

"Julie, sit down or they're going to think we're crazy."

"I'm sorry but I really do have to go," I said, standing up.

Mary walked into the room to help herd them out.

"You raised a zombie and it got our little girl pregnant."

"And we're done," I said, making shooshing motions at them

toward the door, while Mary made come-right-this-way motions on her end.

Mr. Henderson stood and took his wife's arm, pulling her away from me but not exactly going for the door. "Miss Blake, you raised Thomas Warrington for the historical society our daughter belonged to."

I stopped shooshing, because I did remember raising Thomas Warrington from the grave. I remembered because he'd been one of the most perfect zombies I'd ever raised. He'd not only looked alive, but he'd felt warm, had a pulse. He'd felt alive even to me, and it was my psychic ability, or magic, or whatever you want to call it, that had raised him. It had been creepy as hell.

"I can see it in your face, you remember now, don't you?" Mrs. Henderson said, and she sounded triumphant.

"I remember Thomas Warrington. I put him back in his grave when the historians were finished with their interview. He's still dead and gone and in his grave."

"Our daughter told us that you knew they'd had sex, that you knew what he'd done to her."

"I don't expect to have to warn my clients that they shouldn't fuck the zombies I raise. If they want them for that kind of shit, they can go somewhere else, because that's a hard limit for me."

"My daughter did not plan on having sex with that creature, he seduced her with your magic."

I shook my head. "When I realized that barrier had been crossed, I put him back in the ground. I remember your daughter, she was over twenty-one and a consenting adult. It's not my fault she made a poor choice, but he was centuries dead, which means that if she got pregnant, it wasn't from my zombie."

"Are you calling my daughter a whore?" She almost lunged at me, but her husband grabbed her arms and started backing her up.

"We didn't believe it, either, Miss Blake, but according to the blood test, our grandson is related to the closest living descendant of Thomas Warrington."

"That's not possible," I said.

"Blood tests don't lie, Miss Blake."

"Then you need to double-check the test."

"We did."

I stared at him, and something on my face made the woman say, "You really didn't know it was possible, did you?"

I shook my head. "It's hard for any undead to father children, but zombies . . . it's impossible."

"Our grandson is real enough, Miss Blake," he said.

"Impossible," I said, but softer.

"Our daughter is dying, Miss Blake."

"What? Of what?"

"The doctors don't know."

"She just lies in the bed," Mrs. Henderson said, "and no matter how much they feed her through the tubes, she just keeps dying." She started to cry softly.

"That can't have anything to do with a zombie from almost two years ago."

She rallied her anger one last time, eyes blazing at me from between her tears. "She's wasting away, the doctors said it's like a vampire victim except there are no bites, but something is draining her to death."

"Zombies don't do that, can't do that."

"The doctors brought in a witch to consult," he said.

The mother glared at me, tears drying on her face. "The witch said it's something dead that's trying to drag her down into the grave. She asked if there were any malevolent spirits associated with our daughter, or our family, and there aren't except for your zombie."

"When I realized he wasn't a normal zombie, I reopened the grave. He was burned to bone and ash and scattered in running water. That's as dead and gone as it gets, Mrs. Henderson."

"Then what is killing our daughter?"

"I don't know."

"Will you help us, please," he said.

"I don't know how to help your daughter."

Mrs. Henderson jerked away from her husband and poked a finger into my upper chest hard enough that it pushed me back a little. I could have stood my ground, but it would have hurt us both. She didn't need a jammed finger.

"Your monster got our daughter pregnant. Justine didn't want to date ever again, because she'd had a perfect love and their love child. She was so happy that she just closed herself off to anything or anyone else, and now she's dying."

"I'm terribly sorry for what's happened, but it's not my zombie. I destroyed it almost two years ago."

The anger drained away and she started to cry again. I'd have preferred her yelling at me. "You owe us," she whispered.

Justine Henderson lay in the hospital bed, hooked up to more tubes and wires than you ever want to see on someone. Her hair was still straight and brown, but I remembered it thick and shiny. Now it was dry and lifeless like the rest of her. She was painfully thin. The doctors said that no matter how many nutrients they pumped into her through tubes and needles, she just kept losing weight. I wouldn't have recognized her if her parents and the doctor hadn't assured me that this was the same woman I'd met that one strange night nearly two years ago.

The doctors were stumped, so they'd researched supernatural

diseases and come up with a wasting illness associated with old-time vampirism, as in the last case reported in America was in the 1700s. It was why I'd brought Jean-Claude with me. He'd arrived in this country from France around the same time, though that "epidemic" of wasting illness hadn't been his doing. I was hoping he would know something the modern doctors and witches didn't about whatever the hell was happening to Justine Henderson.

"Was she very thin when you met her?" he asked.

"No, she was a good, normal weight, not one of those women that starve themselves."

"Then she has lost a great deal," he said, fingers smoothing down the front of his white shirt in one of his nervous gestures, but there was no lace for him to toy with, just a plain shirtfront. His fingers went to the mandarin collar, but it was too plain for him to have anything to play his fingers over and soothe himself. He was actually wearing a tailored black suit with thin satin lapels so that it was vaguely tuxedo-like. It was the simplest clothing I'd ever seen him in, and his fingers kept trying to find something to fuss with, to no avail. Until this moment, I'd never realized how much fussing with the lace and complicated bits of his clothes helped him deal with stress. He'd dressed to meet the family and the doctors, saying, "It would be unseemly for me to look festive in the face of their grief."

I took his hand to let him run his thumb over my knuckles to see if that would help. It was odd to think of the master vampire, ruler of all the bloodsuckers in America, as nervous. He was my fiancé, which made me feel like I should have understood what all the fancy outfits meant to him sooner than this.

"She looks skeletal," I said softly.

"That is fitting since she is dying."

"Do you agree with the doctor that this is some sort of vampire-caused illness?"

His hand went very still in mine, as if he were holding his breath, but that wasn't it; he'd just stopped breathing. He didn't have to breathe except to talk, but he usually did it anyway. Now he went still in that way that the older vampires could so that if I hadn't been holding his hand, I would think he'd left the room.

"The illness the doctor refers to is when a newly risen vampire began to prey on their family. They would lure them out and drain them dry. Some would turn into vampires, but most simply died." His thumb started moving over my hand in small circles and he began to breathe again, as if a switch had been turned back on. If he'd been human, he would have needed at least a bigger breath, or maybe a gasp, but he wasn't human. "They preyed on their family because they could gain entrance to the house without permission," I said.

"*Oui*, we can enter public buildings without being invited, but private homes are safe from us unless they were once our homes."

"Shouldn't the vampire who made the new vamp stay with them and make sure the family massacre doesn't happen since it draws attention to them?" I asked.

"They should, and in Europe they would, or some older vampire would, but many of the ones that fled to America did not hold with tradition. They did not understand that some traditions weren't whims of the council but logical precautions."

"You heard the doctors—there are no marks where a vamp is taking blood from her."

"There are other ways for vampires to feed, *ma petite*, as you know."

I lowered my voice because it wasn't common knowledge that some master vampires had secondary ways to feed. "I know you guys can feed through your human servants, like literally take some of the nutrition when we eat if you're trapped in, like, the hold of a ship. It makes sense for long voyages, but if you drain your human servant to death, that could mean you'd die with them."

"Harm to one can be harm to both," he said. His fingers had found my engagement ring and he was now sliding his finger over it. I guess any fidget object would do.

"So, no vampire would do this to his own servant."

"You are correct."

"I'm missing something, aren't I?"

"There are even rarer ways to feed from a distance, *ma petite.*"

I shook my head. "Feeding on fear, or anger, or whatever emotion usually requires touching skin to skin."

"Not if they are ancient enough."

I filed that away for later, because I hadn't known that. "So, some ancient vamp is doing this?"

"*Non, ma petite*, I would sense such power, and even the very ancient among us would need some connection to the woman. It would not be random."

"So, what is it?"

"I have seen this happen to humans for only one cause from my kind. The *ardeur* can drain someone to death."

"Only if you're feeding on them continuously, and no one is coming in here and fucking Justine to death."

"Once a human is addicted to the *ardeur*, if they do not get regular feedings, they can stop eating and waste away from want of its touch."

"She's not starving herself to death by not eating, Jean-Claude, she's starving while the doctors are pumping her full of food. She should not still be losing ground."

"Belle Morte, who was first gifted with the *ardeur* so she could feed from lust, could drain a human from a distance like this."

"Are you saying it's Belle doing this?"

"No, no."

"Then what are you saying?" I was getting angry or impatient or both, and I wanted to stop holding hands. I must have thought it too loudly, because he let go of me.

"Sorry, I'm just . . . I want to help Justine and her family."

"You feel responsible," he said.

"Yeah, I guess I do."

"Does the baby truly belong to the zombie you raised?"

"They really did trace down a descendant from Thomas Warrington's brother. He didn't have any children personally. The descendant shares genetics with the baby Justine gave birth to, enough to be family, so yeah, it looks like Warrington really is the father."

"It is difficult enough for an older vampire to have children. I have never heard of a zombie being able to do so."

"Me either. I guess I'll be doing another write-up in the professional journals." Though honestly I didn't want anyone to know I could raise a zombie this alive. The government had looked to me to raise a recently dead world leader just temporarily, or so the rumor had said, but luckily the zombie they spied on had been the shambling dead and wouldn't pass for human. That had been a few years and a few power levels ago. If the same government agencies realized I could raise something this "alive," I'd be back on their hit parade. No thanks. I could just see Bert Vaughn, the business manager at Animators Inc., trying to schedule me to raise dead husbands from the grave to get that one last baby. Yeah, Bert was an unscrupulous bastard and would think it was a great idea. No. Just no.

The one thing helping me stay out of the news and off the radar of the unscrupulous was that the Hendersons didn't want anyone to know that their little girl had had sex with a zombie. They didn't want their grandson to be all over the Internet as the zombie baby. If we all worked hard, maybe we could stay out of the news on this one.

"Unless Belle Morte snuck into this country and targeted Justine for some reason, it can't be the *ardeur* being fed from a distance," I said.

"Not Belle, no, but the woman was seduced by our bloodline."

I looked up at him. "What do you mean by that?"

"Your zombie may have looked alive, *ma petite*, but this girl saw him rise from his grave, correct?"

"Yeah."

"Yet despite seeing that fearful sight, she still had sex with him within an hour or two of his rising."

I nodded. "It was freaky quick."

"She professed her love for him and he for her within hours, is that not also correct?"

"Yes," I said. I really didn't like where this was going.

"Belle's power was lust, mine was more than that, but it was only after you gained the power that it turned into love."

"Yeah, I accidentally bound several people to me in true love." I rolled my eyes as I said it, trying to make light of something that scared me. To be able to make someone accidentally fall in love with you—real love—was not a power I wanted.

"Belle could cause lust in hundreds, thousands, and be unmoved if she wished it, so it was her weapon of power. I saw kings give up their kingdoms for one more night with her. In me, it became a two-edged blade. I could cause casual lust, but for more, I could only cut as deeply as I was willing to be wounded myself."

I nodded. We'd realized a while back that some of our love might be the *ardeur*, but if it was, we both felt it now. What do you do when your happy-ever-after may be magically induced love? Do you fight it? Ignore it? Find some witchy therapy? I'd have been pissier about it if I hadn't bound several people to me by accident, too. It made it harder to throw stones at him. My house had too much damn glass in it for me to bitch at him. Lust isn't love, and my version could even cause true friendship, because that's a type of love, as well. The learning curve was still ongoing.

"You're explaining in detail things I already know, because you want me to think about them."

"Yes, *ma petite*."

"You're saying that the zombie, Thomas Warrington, used a type of the *ardeur* on himself and Justine here. You're saying that's what made them fall in love."

"I believe so."

"That's not possible. He was a zombie, not a vampire, for a start, and even vampires don't come into secondary powers like the *ardeur* as soon as they rise from the grave. It takes decades, or centuries, to come into that kind of power."

"I do not believe it was his *ardeur, ma petite*, but yours. He was your creature, after all."

I really didn't like the term *your creature*, but I let it go, because it couldn't be true, or maybe because I didn't want it to be true. "But he's dead, Jean-Claude. We let the exterminator crew burn him to ashes and bones after he went crazy and tried to attack us."

"He turned into a flesh-eating zombie, if I remember correctly."

"Yeah, it wasn't in his history that he'd gotten trapped in the mountains in winter. The group he was with turned to cannibalism when one of their members died from the cold. Cannibalism in life is on the list with people having psychic ability or magical ability, voodoo practitioners, witches, sorcerers, devil worshippers, murder victims, and clergy. Because any one of them can come back as a flesh eater. They look good at first, but unless they eat the flesh of the living, they start to rot."

"You told me his time in the mountains was a deep secret that he and the men with him never shared with anyone. You could not have known, *ma petite*."

"I know, but damn it. We were just lucky he didn't hurt anyone."

"Are you sure he was reduced to ashes?"

"And bigger bones. I mean, the flamethrowers couldn't get hot enough to turn the bigger pieces to more than charcoal, but that's dead enough for a zombie. I treated him like a master vamp and put some of his ashes in different bodies of running water. Thomas Warrington is as dead as I could make him, Jean-Claude."

"But there were larger bones left?"

"Stop pussyfooting around and just tell me what you're hinting at, please? I'm out of patience for your usual soft delivery."

"If his skull and a few other bones remained intact and he was a powerful enough vampire, then there might remain enough power for him to reach out to someone addicted to his power."

"First, he wasn't a vampire, he was a zombie. Second, no, they went to a crematorium and were turned to ashes, then those were scattered in water."

"Did you see the bones burned to ash?"

I stared at him. "What are you saying?"

"If you did not see it done, *ma petite*, then perhaps someone took a souvenir rather than do their duty."

"Are you honestly telling me that if the skull and some of the skeleton survived, it could reach out to Justine like this?"

"Not without help."

"What kind of help?"

"Magical help."

"Are you seriously saying that just the bones of this guy are draining Justine's life away?"

"It is possible."

I stared down at Justine Henderson dying in front of our eyes and realized that her mother was right: I owed them one.

I'd gotten enough ashes back from the crematorium to make up a body the size of Thomas Warrington, so how did I prove that it hadn't been his ashes? They were scattered in a stream near the original cemetery and in two different rivers, so even if it had been possible to get DNA to prove identity, it was too late, the ashes were gone. If we'd had more time, I'd have reported my suspicions through normal channels and an investigation would eventually start. Justine didn't have "eventual" in her time frame. If we were going to save her life, it had to be now.

I needed another cop that I could trust implicitly, and I needed supernatural backup. The cop was easy. Sergeant Zerbrowski was my unofficial partner when I worked with the Regional Preternatural Investigation Taskforce. It had been the Regional Preternatural Investigation Squad then, but they'd changed it recently to reflect how many cross-state-lines and multi-agency cases they'd been handling for years. They were handling supernatural cases before the government had forced the U.S. Marshals Service to have a preternatural branch. *Taskforce* covered what they did a lot more than *squad* or *team* had.

Zerbrowski had also been at the graveside when I had to roast Thomas Warrington's zombie. He'd seen how dangerous the zombie was, and how different it had been from any other zombie we'd seen. All I had to do was tell him, "Remember the flesh-eating zombie that we had to roast at the graveside?"

"Hard to forget that one."

"Someone may have done a switch at the crematorium and kept some of its bones. I think someone is using them for black magic, and if we don't stop it, a woman younger than I am is going to die."

"I'll clear my dance card, just tell me when and where." See, the cop part was easy, and once I thought about it, so was the supernatural backup. Nicky Murdock had been one of the guards that helped us fight and finally kill the zombie. Zerbrowski would accept that I'd want someone with me that knew what we might be up against, and he and Nicky got along, which wasn't true of all of the guards on Jean-Claude's payroll. Besides, Nicky was one of my lovers and a blood donor for Jean-Claude, so it meant he got along with all of us. The older I got the more I valued that in a partner, whether romantic or police. Why didn't I take Jean-Claude with me? It was daylight and all the vampires had to be a snooze in their coffins—or bed, in Jean-Claude's case.

Nicky and I pulled into the parking lot of the crematorium to find Zerbrowski waiting for us in his new car. I wondered how long it would take him to trash the interior of it under fast-food wrappers and other debris. I knew for a fact that his wife, Katie, made sure he was neatly dressed when he left the house, but he got out of his car with his tie crooked and a food stain that I could see from feet away. His short curly hair was almost completely salt-and-pepper now, which made his silver-framed glasses blend in more and his brown eyes stand out, as if they and his eyebrows were the only dark colors left on his face.

"Hey, Anita, hey, Nicky."

I said, "Hey, Zerbrowski."

He grinned up at Nicky, who towered above me and looked massive even beside the detective. "Jesus, Murdock, did you put on more muscle?"

"No, I just look bigger standing next to you." Nicky gave the line completely deadpan. He was one of the few people I'd ever seen get the better of Zerbrowski's constant teasing. The only people he didn't tease were the ones he hated, and he didn't hate many people.

Zerbrowski grinned and patted his belly. "Hey, it was doctor's orders that I get smaller. My cholesterol is in the normal range now. I get to eat junk food once a week." He rubbed his stomach as if just thinking about it made him happy.

"Congratulations on the lower cholesterol and the cheat day," I said, and smiled.

"Thanks. How do you want to play this?"

"You be nice cop, I'll be cranky cop, and Nicky will be scary cop."

"He's not a cop."

"No, he's a special consultant that I've brought in for this case. As a U.S. Marshal with the Preternatural Division, I can do that."

He looked up at the bigger man, taking in the short blond hair and the one blue eye. "Glad you got rid of those club kid bangs, hard to see to shoot people when your hair is over your eyes like a shaggy dog."

"Not 'eyes,' Zerbrowski, just 'eye,'" Nicky said, again totally serious.

"Yeah, I see you rocking the eye patch, never seen you in one of those."

"It's new."

Zerbrowski looked at him as if waiting for more, and when it didn't come, he let it go and turned to me. "Okay, I'll ask nicely who would be in charge of emptying the ashes into containers and giving them back out to people."

"You be nice until it's time to not be nice, and then it's my turn."

"And what will scary cop do when it's his turn?"

"When Anita gives me the signal, I'll tear off my eye patch and let them see the scar. If they don't piss their pants, I'll think of something else."

Zerbrowski looked up at him as if not sure whether he was serious, then nodded, trying not to smile. "You could always yell boo when you rip off the eye patch."

"Great idea," Nicky said, and even I couldn't tell if he was serious.

Not only did Harold Ramon clean the crematorium but he was the go-to guy for putting the remains in containers for loved ones and the police. He worked late and alone, a lot. He had to be our guy.

He was friendly, shook all our hands as if he was really sincere about working his way out of cleanup and into customer service. His eyes flicked to take in the serious muscle development that no amount of clothes could hide on Nicky, but I couldn't hold that against Harold. Nicky's size made a lot of people nervous.

He denied everything, until Zerbrowski took a step back and made a small, go-ahead gesture at me. It was my turn at bat.

"The woman in the hospital, who's dying, is named Justine. She has a baby and parents who love her. She's their only child."

"I'm sorry that she's sick, but I did not do what you're accusing me of."

"If you help us find the remains and stop the spell before she dies, then maybe all this goes away, maybe you don't even get written up for abuse of a corpse."

"I did not . . ."

I held my finger up and went, "Shhhh, but if you don't help us and Justine dies because we couldn't stop the spell in time, then you will be as guilty under the law as the practitioner who cast the spell. Do you understand what that means, Harold?"

He frowned at me, eyes darting around the room. He'd stopped wanting to make direct eye contact somewhere in my little speech. His hands were clutching the chair arms, and he was leaning back in the seat because I'd moved forward to invade his personal space.

"I . . . I don't know. I'm innocent. I didn't do anything wrong."

"It means, Harold, that if Justine dies because of this spell, then I'll have a warrant of execution for the magical practitioner, or practitioners, that cast it or caused it to be cast. That includes anyone that sold them illegal ingredients for the spell, like illegally obtained human body parts."

"I'm just plain ordinary human, you can't kill a human being like you can a monster or a witch. I know my rights."

"Normally, you'd be right. If you were the owner of an herb shop, or a new age store, and you sold someone books or crystals or what have you, then you'd be safe under the law, but it's illegal to sell human remains outside of very special circumstances. It's also illegal to fuck about with the remains of people's loved ones. It could mean that this entire place gets closed down, all because you got greedy."

"I didn't . . . I would never . . ."

"Would never what, Harold?" I asked, voice almost a whisper, leaning so close that our faces almost touched.

His eyes got frantic for a second, and I thought he was going to tell us the truth, but then something harder and more stubborn filled his eyes, and I knew I'd lost him.

"I do my job, that's it." He sounded angry.

I sighed and stepped back. "We don't have time for you to be stubborn, Harold." I motioned Nicky forward like I'd given up a partner on the dance floor so he could cut in.

He moved like the mountain of muscle that he was, and almost growled, "My turn."

Harold stayed stubborn and firmly innocent, until Nicky put his face next to his and ripped off the eye patch. Harold made a *yip* sound.

"I can smell that you're lying," Nicky growled, and meant the growl now. The warm, prickling energy of his inner lion trailed off him and made me shiver.

"I didn't do anything illegal." Harold's voice was a little high pitched, but he was standing firm.

The heat of Nicky's beast ramped up, spreading through the room like invisible bathwater, hot and ready for a soak. I had to take some deep breaths to keep my own inner beasts from rising to the surface. We didn't have time for my metaphysics to get out of hand.

Harold screamed.

His boss stood up from his chair behind the big desk. "What did you do to him? Even if he's guilty, I won't let you abuse him."

"I didn't touch him," Nicky said in a voice that was almost too low to understand. "Not yet."

"Get him away from me! Get him away from me! I'll tell you who I sold it to, I'll tell you everything, just don't let him hurt me."

"No one is going to hurt you, Harold, I'll see to that," his boss said, all indignant.

Nicky stood up and looked at the other man with an eye that was pale gold with an edge of orange around the pupil. "Sweet Jesus, what are you?" the boss asked.

Nicky opened his mouth to show the very beginnings of pointed teeth to match the eye. Boss Man screamed and put his chair between them, as if that would help.

Nicky gave a little bow and let me step up and take Harold's information, while he found a bathroom so he could get himself back together. Eyes go first for most shapeshifters, but sometimes when the teeth start to change it's harder to stop the process. Nicky would be fine, but teeth meant the bones started to reshape, and that can be a little weird to watch the first time. No reason to scare the civilians.

Harold told us everything we needed to know and more, and none of us had laid a finger on him. Let's hear it for teamwork.

We thought Zerbrowski would have to stay behind with Harold to make sure he didn't warn anyone, but when Zerbrowski called for backup, a uniform showed up in moments. Maybe luck was on our side, or maybe it was on Justine's side. I said a quick prayer of thanks and for her to hold on. Right now I owed the Hendersons a debt I could pay; if she died, I'd owe them forever.

The address Harold had given us was only a few blocks away from the Fabulous Fox Theater, where Broadway traveling companies dazzled audiences, but on the street we drove down, nobody's name was up in lights. There weren't even many working streetlights, but lucky for us there was daylight and we didn't need them. There were boards on some of the windows and bars on others, along with graffiti that might have been gang tags, or it might have just been wild art running free across the buildings, the canvas of urban artists. We'd driven past the building that matched the address Harold had screamed at us. It didn't look any different from the rest of the block. Nothing made it stand out.

We parked a block away from it so no one in the building would see us put on our body armor, which for those of us outside the military is usually just the vest. I readjusted where I carried my sidearm and switched up to the .45. I was too short and too curvy to wear it concealed, but once I put the vest on, concealment was over, so the .45 got a drop holster on my thigh. I had a 9mm Springfield EMP, which had become my usual concealed carry at the office when I had to wear girl clothes, because it concealed better than anything else I'd found, except for the Sig Sauer P238. I kept the little .380 as a backup, because I could conceal both it and the Springfield under female office attire with a reinforced waistband on the skirt at least. Today, I didn't have to hide anything, so they were as visible as the .45. I got the AR-15 rifle with all the customization for my shorter reach and preference for close-quarters fighting. Nicky's rifle was customized for his very different needs. We both had the rifles on tactical slings so if we needed to switch weapons, we could let it swing out of the way but not lose it. Nicky had handguns strapped to him, too, just bigger ones for his larger hand size. We both had knives; I just had more of them.

"I suddenly feel inadequate," Zerbrowski said. He had his vest and his handgun, but that was it.

"Do I say, 'It's not the gun'?" I asked, smiling.

He grinned. "Katie loves me anyway."

I laughed. "Yes, she does."

Nicky shook his head at both of us, and we started the block walk to the building.

"Always the awkward part. Do we knock and announce, or just bust the door down?" Zerbrowski asked. "I mean, we don't really have a warrant yet."

"I've got a request in for one, but magical malfeasance is harder to prove than vampire or shapeshifter attacks, so it takes more time to get a warrant issued."

"Does the girl in the hospital have enough time to wait for the warrant?" Zerbrowski asked.

I shook my head. "I don't think so."

"If only there was a metaphysical equivalent of smelling smoke," he said.

"Anita, can you sense it?" Nicky asked.

"Sense what, the bones?" I asked.

"Yeah."

"I don't do just bones."

"They are the bones of the most alive zombie you've ever raised; wouldn't your magic linger on them?"

I shook my head. "It doesn't work that way."

"How do you know until you try?"

I started to argue some more but finally shrugged and tried, because if I could testify to sensing evil magic inside the house, then it could be the magical equivalent of smelling smoke, or hearing screams, because a police officer can enter a home without a warrant if they think lives are at risk. I could have lied later and just busted down the door, but Zerbrowski might get in trouble, and he was here as a favor. Why wasn't I worried about getting in trouble? Because I was part of the Preternatural Division. It would take a hell of a lot more than busting down a door ahead of a warrant to get me in trouble. The people that say we are basically assassins working on American soil with the government's approval aren't entirely wrong.

I opened my metaphysical shields just a bit, like opening a window just a crack to see if you can catch a breeze. I caught something, but it was too faint to be certain. I thought about opening my shields more, but if we were about to go up against an evil practitioner of some kind, I didn't want to lower my shields, because it would be very much like lowering a shield in battle. You can see over your shield better, but so can your enemy, who will happily plant an ax between your eyes.

If I didn't want to drop my guard, what else could I do?

"Try using your necromancy," Nicky suggested.

"I thought that didn't work in daylight," Zerbrowski said.

"If I was trying to raise a zombie that could think and answer questions intelligently, then you're right, but I'm just trying to sense the dead, or the undead, or maybe Nicky is right and the bones will have some sort of power signature that I can sense."

"And if you know it's in there?" he asked.

"Then a life is at stake and we break down the door and save that life."

"Sounds like a plan," Zerbrowski said.

Almost any other metaphysical ability I had was something I had to coax, or call, or raise inside me, but not my necromancy. It was always there just below the surface, eager and waiting for me to drop my guard so it could spill out of me and into the nearest dead body. I put my fingers against the cool brick of the building the way I sometimes touch the dirt over a grave.

I hesitated for a second because if it had been a grave, I would have sent my power searching through the dirt for the body I wanted to raise, and then I would have called it to me. I didn't want to do that, did I? Was there enough left of Warrington to come to my call? Was there enough of my magic left on the bones to call it to me? If we wanted to make an arrest, we needed to catch him red-handed. If we wanted to come back with a warrant and execute him, same thing, but was that really my goal? No, my goal was to save Justine Henderson's life so she could see her little boy grow up, so her parents could have holidays with their child and grandchild. I didn't give a shit about legalities; in that moment I just wanted to save a life.

At first it was just my hands against the cooler roughness of the bricks, and then distantly I felt an echo or a taste of familiar power, my power. I closed my eyes and trusted that the two men with me would keep me safe from any physical danger while I gave myself to my magic and let it lead me through the brick and the wood and the paint and the tingling of the electricity in the walls, and until I could hear a voice in my head that was thinking one word over and over like a heartbeat: *Justine, Justine, Justine.*

Thomas Warrington had died not only in love with her but

bound to her with a version of *ardeur*-induced true love. I didn't
know what the other magic user had done to make Thomas aware
enough to think of her, or powerful enough to reach out and start
leaching energy from her, but as I heard her name breathed through
my mind, constant as a pulse, I knew that was what was happening.
The practitioner that had done the spell didn't give a rat's ass about
Justine—he just wanted a powerful relic like the bones of a flesh-
eating, very alive zombie. I wondered if the bones had stopped working as well for him once Thomas started longing for his ladylove.

Let's go find out. And I hadn't realized I'd said it out loud until
Zerbrowski replied, "Go where and find out what?"

Our buyer was named Robbie Curtis. When I'd asked Harold if
Robbie was short for Robert, he didn't know. Robbie lived on the
third floor, not even a creepy basement or a scary attic, but just an
ordinary floor. Nicky broke the door to pieces for us. He and I had
our rifles snug to our shoulders, looking for danger. Zerbrowski had
his handgun up and ready, too. We all knew the drill and, pointing
safely away from each other, we searched the dingy living room for
someone who wasn't us, but it was empty of everything except sag-
ging furniture and a rug that was so threadbare I thought it was part
of the floor, until it moved under my boots.

There were two doors at the back of the room. Nicky pushed
through the one to the right, putting the door flush against the wall
so nothing could hide behind it. A small kitchen looked white and
tired in the light from the single window. It was cleaner than the
living room, neat and tidy, all the dishes put away. I went to the last
door, and before I even touched it, I felt the thrum and pull of that
longing: *Justine, Justine, Justine, Justine.*

I motioned, letting them know it was behind door number two.

Nicky held up a finger and then pointed it at the door. He could either hear or smell one person in the room. I motioned and mouthed the words *one inside.*

Zerbrowski nodded that he'd understood.

We were all already standing to one side of the door just in case our bad guy had a gun to go with his creepy magic. It was just standard not to stand in front of a door when you didn't know what was on the other side. Until it was time to kick it in, and then you sort of had to stand in the danger zone of the door, which was why SWAT and other special teams had heavy shields and body armor. Of course, they were only human, and Nicky wasn't. There was a time in my life where I might have argued about which of us got to kick the door in, but it was just good physical math to let him do it. Zerbrowski and I came at his side, sliding around the door to either wall like there was enough of us to cut the pie. Nicky did follow along the wall behind me like I'd learned in SWAT and he'd learned somewhere less formal. That left Zerbrowski on his side of the room alone, but the room wasn't that big, so we could still cover each other and the room.

Only when we were in place and could keep each other as safe as possible did I let myself really look at the room. I mean, I'd seen that there was a small bed in one corner against a heavily draped window. There were two more windows in the far wall, but they'd been covered with plywood and then painted black so that the entire far wall was black. Between the boarded-up windows were the top and lower half of a skull nailed in place, or maybe screwed in place; it was hard to tell from here. The skull and jawbone seemed to be trapped in a nightmarish scream. Part of a left arm and then the pelvic bone were all pinned in place like some evil butterfly on display. The sound of *Justine* in my head was so loud I wasn't sure I would hear anything else in the room.

There were symbols painted around the bones that I didn't recognize, but then I didn't do this kind of necromancy, the kind that used the dead to power your magic instead of using your magic to empower the dead. It was almost the polar opposite of what I did. The symbols went all the way to the floor on either side of a small altar that was directly below the bones.

"Where is he?" Zerbrowski asked.

It took me a second to understand he meant the person that Nicky had sensed in the room. The bones were so loud, the magic so overwhelming, that I'd forgotten that there might be a living danger in the room. It was too careless for words; I knew better than to let my power deafen me to other safety concerns. *Stupid, stupid, stupid,* I thought, until I realized that I was saying it to the same beat as *Justine, Justine, Justine.*

I closed up my power like folding it back into a tight fist that I wouldn't let go of again. When I did that, I could hear other things, feel other things besides horror at the fact that Thomas Warrington was somehow still attached to his bones, still aware of himself enough to reach out to the woman he loved. He was gaining power as he drained her life away, not what he meant to do, but when you're just a few bones nailed to a wall for a black magic ceremony, you probably don't think too clearly.

Nicky and Zerbrowski were already moving toward the bed in the far corner. I caught up with them and was blissfully alone with my thoughts instead of with Thomas's one thought. Zerbrowski and I trained our guns on the bed, while Nicky took a one-handed grip on the footboard and lifted, his gun still in his other hand as if the bed weren't heavy at all.

I stared down the barrel of my rifle at a short, dark man who looked up at us with wide eyes. Robbie Curtis looked terribly ordinary and harmless huddled there. I didn't have to be a wereanimal to smell the fear on him, but just because someone's afraid doesn't mean they aren't dangerous. Cornered animals fight harder. He had his hand wrapped around a small bag tied around his neck like a necklace. He pointed his other hand at me like it was a blade. I felt something go out from his hand to me, but it split around my psychic shielding like water around a boulder.

Zerbrowski yelled, "Put it down!"

I wasn't sure what he was telling him to put down, the bag, his hand, what? The man sent energy at me again, but I was a boulder and his power could not move me, or crack me, or do shit to me. I stopped looking down the barrel of my gun at him and let the AR-15 hang from its tactical sling while I reached down and grabbed the arm he was pointing at me and jerked him to his feet.

"Anita, be careful," Zerbrowski said.

He was right, but I was too angry to care. I hadn't let my temper get the better of me at a crime scene in years, but fuck it. He pointed his finger at me and again there was that push of power rushing around my shielding. "What is that supposed to be doing to me? Huh? What the fuck is that supposed to do? Hurt me? What?"

He did it one more time, but this time he pointed at Zerbrowski. I heard him make a noise, not a scream, but not a good sound. I fought the urge to look behind me at him, but I had to make sure Curtis didn't hurt anyone else; secure the weapon, then tend the wounded, otherwise you get more wounded. I grabbed the man's pointing finger with my free hand and broke it. He screamed, knees going weak so that he helped me take him to the ground. I kicked his legs out from under him and put him on his stomach on the floor. Nicky started to help me, but I said, "I've got it, help Zerbrowski."

Nicky didn't argue, he just left my side, and I knew he'd do what I told him to do. I didn't dare glance over but concentrated on putting the man's hands behind his back and getting the handcuffs out of their holder. I killed more people than I arrested, so handcuffs weren't my best thing when someone was wiggling on the floor. I had to secure the prisoner, had to make him safe so he couldn't hurt anyone else. If I'd done that first thing instead of being an arrogant, angry shit, Zerbrowski would never have been hurt.

"He's alive," Nicky said from behind me.

The man who was struggling with my knee in his back said, "You're hurting me!"

"Good," I said and finished getting the handcuffs around his thin wrists. The cuffs were designed to withstand the strength of a shapeshifter. A human, even one that could cast spells, wasn't getting out unless he could unlock them with magic. Shit, I didn't know if that was even possible. I couldn't do it, but that didn't mean he couldn't. "You shoot magic at us with the broken finger, I'll break it again. If you use magic on us at all, I'll start with your fingers and keep going until you can't cast spells anymore. Are we clear on what will happen if you use any more magic?"

"You're a cop, you can't do shit like that."

I put my face down so he could see me. "I'm a marshal with the Preternatural Division, you're casting death magic, I can do a hell of a lot worse than break your bones."

"Jesus, no, please, don't kill me."

Funny how they always get religious when they think they're going to die. I was half lying to him. If I'd had a warrant of execution for him in my pocket, then I could have done whatever I wanted to him, but we hadn't waited for the warrant, so I had to play by cop rules, not executioner rules. Handcuffs in place, bad guy subdued, I let myself glance behind at Zerbrowski. He was sitting up and leaning against Nicky, but his eyes were open and he had his gun in his hand pointed in a safe direction.

"The magic worked on him. Why didn't it work on you?" Curtis asked in a voice that was thick with pain.

"What should have worked? What were you trying to do to me, asshole?"

"Drain you a little, that's all. I wasn't using the full spell. I wasn't trying to kill any of you."

I had a moment to realize that he'd done the equivalent of trying to wound us instead of killing us, and if he'd been aiming to kill, then I'd have had to explain it to Katie and the kids.

"Anita," Zerbrowski said, "I'm okay. Chill, okay?" He meant *don't hurt him any more*, but didn't want to say it out loud in front of the prisoner in case we needed to threaten him with violence to get information. I didn't feel bad about the finger. If he was green enough or weak enough to need to point to work magic, then he deserved what he got. And I was pissed at myself for not realizing that I wasn't the only target in the room. I'd been so busy being immune to the magic and angry that it was my own magic being shoved at me that I hadn't thought it through. It was a rookie mistake, one that could have cost Zerbrowski everything.

I ground my knee harder, one hand staying on him so I could feel if he moved. I did not want my carelessness to hurt anyone else today. I glanced back. Zerbrowski was on his knees, but he looked steadier. His gun was still out, but I was blocking any shot he had at the bad guy. Nicky was still trying to help him up, and Zerbrowski pushed him away. "Go help her with the perp."

I realized that Nicky couldn't stop helping Zerbrowski until I told him to stop. My metaphysical ties to Nicky have some weird consequences, like if I give him a direct order, he must obey it. "Nicky, it's okay."

Nicky stopped fussing with Zerbrowski and came to kneel by me.

"Hold him while I pat him down," Nicky said, and just like that I felt foolish again. I'd been so busy concentrating on the magic that it hadn't occurred to me to search him for a gun or knife. I helped Nicky pat down his back and then I rolled him over on his broken finger, which made him complain—okay, he screamed—but we searched him for weapons anyway. There wasn't anything to find, but I hadn't known that when I jerked him up off the floor the first time. How could I have been so careless?

"He's clean," Nicky said.

"No, he's not," Zerbrowski said. "The bag around his neck isn't harmless."

"You're right," I said and reached for the bag. He tried to fight us off, handcuffed, broken finger and all. I finally had to cut the leather thong that held it around his neck, and only Nicky's hand on his head kept him from cutting himself on my knife.

Nicky kept his hand on Curtis so he couldn't get up while I opened the bag on the floor near the bed. The bag held a small bone, some herbs, some grayish powder, and a small stone. I looked at the bone for a long time and then finally at him. "It's a bone from the skeleton on the wall." I said it like I was sure.

"I bought the bones through legitimate sources." Talking from the floor handcuffed with Nicky almost sitting on him, he still managed to sound like he meant it.

"Your legitimate source gave you up," I said.

"You're lying."

"How else did we find you?"

Curtis looked uncertain then.

"Did you actually try and use some sort of necromancy or death magic on me? Was that all the finger pointing and clutching your juju bag?"

"You broke my fucking finger!"

"You're lucky that's all I broke."

"This is police brutality."

"Remember I'm not regular police, Curtis."

"I didn't see a marshal's badge, I think you're lying. I think you're just regular cops, so it's police brutality. I'll press charges."

"Oh no, breaking your finger wasn't brutal, you haven't seen brutal yet."

"Is that a threat?" he asked indignantly.

"Yes," I said.

My simply agreeing threw him, so he didn't know what to say. I got my badge off my belt and held it down so he could see that it was a U.S. Marshals badge with the banner across it that read Preternatural Division. His eyes widened, his breathing got faster.

"See, preternatural marshal, which means I do not have to play by regular cop rules."

Zerbrowski spoke from closer to the skeleton on the wall. I was just happy he was feeling well enough to stand and move around. "Have him take down the spell or whatever it is."

"Take it down," I said as I put my badge back on my belt. It was harder putting it back than taking it off with the body armor on.

But Curtis shook his head. "I will not dismantle it for you, and I warn you if you touch it without my help, you could be seriously hurt or killed."

"Fuck this," I said. I left Nicky to guard Curtis and went to the wall with its mystic symbols and bones.

Zerbrowski asked, "What are you going to do?"

"Take it down."

"Shouldn't you wait for one of the police witches to look at it first? Some of this stuff can be pretty nasty."

I looked at the wall with something other than my eyes, some people would call it the third eye, and whenever I looked at the symbols, they had a faint glow, which meant active magic. I didn't recognize the symbols, though, so I had no way of knowing what they meant. I didn't do a lot of magic symbols, because mine was more innate psychic ability than outside magic. There was some weight and power to the altar, too, but more of the ordinary energy that any physical item can gain if it's used in regular magical practices. It was when I looked at the bones on the wall that it flared brightest. They had power. They glowed with a gold fire that nothing else in the room could match. Jesus.

"You're using the bones as a sort of magical battery. That's why you have part of it in that bag that was around your neck and why you held it so tight. The magic you tried to use against me is mostly from the bones."

"I am a sorcerer."

"Most sorcerers get their magic from somewhere outside themselves—demon, genie, elemental, but it's always an outside power source."

"You have to have willpower to control them, that is the true power," Curtis said. He tried to sound smug, but he was still lying on the floor, so it lost some of its smugness, but he still sounded pleased with himself. I didn't want him pleased with himself.

"If I told you that your spell here was draining the life out of a young woman, would you give a damn?"

"I don't know what you're talking about."

"I bet you can't even hear what the bones are saying, can you?"

He frowned and looked puzzled. "They can't talk. They're objects of power, not alive."

"Just because you can't hear it doesn't mean it's not saying something."

"I don't understand," he said.

"I know you don't." I prayed for guidance and got that little warm push that I sometimes got when a prayer gets a thumbs-up. That was good enough for me. I started to ask for a hammer and then realized that it wasn't nails or screws, at least not through the bone. He had little racks that the bones were sitting on, with clamps holding them in place.

"Zerbrowski, go stand over there by Nicky."

"Why?"

"I'm going to take one of the bones down."

"Anita, just because you were brute enough to withstand whatever he did to me doesn't mean you can touch this stuff with impunity."

"Impunity, really?"

He grinned at me. "Hey, Katie reads to me and the kids at night, okay?"

I smiled and shook my head at him. "You go watch over Curtis, and let Nicky be my lovely assistant."

"I'd usually argue that I'm your lovely assistant, but one magic whammy was enough for today." The fact that he just did it without arguing meant it had hurt him or scared him even more than I thought. Crap. He was going to need to see a witch and a doctor to make sure he was okay.

"If you touch the bones, I cannot be responsible for what happens. They are powerful magical relics and I cannot control what they will do to you."

Zerbrowski said, "Are you threatening us again?"

"No, I used magic to ensure my safety when I touched the relics. She's about to touch them with her bare hands. It's dangerous."

"Maybe he's got a point," Zerbrowski said. "Maybe we should wait for some more magical backup."

"This is death magic, Zerbrowski. I'm who they'd call for backup."

"Just be careful, okay?"

"Okay," I said. I looked at the bones with that inner sight, and the golden glow was there, but I realized that my hand was glowing with the same glow, except mine was thicker, shinier. What was on the bones was like golden cotton candy—light and full of air. What was on me was more like caramel or the whole apple. It was my magic. I'd never looked at my energy when I raised the dead like that. I'd felt it before but never seen it shine like this.

I laid a fingertip against the arm, and the shine of it merged. The voice was a little louder, *Justine* over and over in my head, but slower, not as frantic.

"If you take the bones outside the ritual area, you will be struck down," Curtis said from the bed where Zerbrowski had sat him down. It wasn't for his comfort; Zerbrowski didn't want to have to stay on the floor with him. I didn't blame him.

I picked up a piece of the arm and lifted it off the wall. The glow on it melted into the glow of my power, but it didn't hurt. It felt right. I carried the arm piece away from the altar and the symbols, and I felt fine. The arm was in the most pieces, some of them still showing the burn marks from the flamethrowers that had been used on them in the cemetery almost two years ago. I carried the pieces back and forth to lay them on a clean sheet that Nicky had found somewhere. With each bone that left the ritual area, the murmur of *Justine* lessened.

"You should be hurt. You should be screaming. Why aren't you screaming?" Curtis asked from the bed.

I lifted the big rounded pelvis off the wall and carried it to rest beside the arm bones. The voice in my head was less frantic now, not a plea for help but a lover's murmur of your name against your hair. I got the jawbone next, and the energy quieted more.

"You should be writhing in pain, or dead. Why aren't you dead?"

I had to stand on tiptoe to reach the top part of the skull, but I finally laid it beside the other bones, and the constant cry of *Justine* paused, and then it was like a long-contented sigh and then silence. Maybe they weren't just bones, but they weren't his magical battery anymore either.

"That's not possible, no one could dismantle my spell without repercussions."

"It may have been your spell, but it was my zombie."

"I don't understand," he said.

"You tried to use death magic against me. I'm a necromancer, you can't use death magic against me. But you especially can't use death magic against me that's fueled from my own power."

"What are you talking about, your power?"

"Those were my zombie's bones on the damn wall."

"That zombie was a flesh-eating zombie—they have no master. They belong to no one."

"This one belonged to me, because I raised him from the dead. He was *mine* and something you did to the bones is killing the woman he loved. Do you even care that you've almost orphaned a little boy? Do you give a damn about anything besides personal power?"

"I have no idea what you are talking about. I did not cast a spell to harm anyone."

"You harmed me and tried to harm Anita with that bag of bones of yours," Zerbrowski said.

"You were attacking me. I was merely defending myself."

"Tell it to the judge," I said.

"I did nothing wrong!"

"Like I said, tell it to the judge."

"I did nothing wrong. I'll be out on bail before you finish the paperwork." Normally he'd be right, and his knowing that meant I was betting he had a record.

"If I were a regular cop, you'd be right, but I'm not, remember?"

"No, I'm human. You can't execute me like I was some undead or half man."

"Watch the half-man comments," Nicky said.

"You're a human sorcerer that stole body parts to perform death magic that almost killed an innocent woman. The magical malfeasance law was created just for humans like you," I said.

"No, no, you can't do this to me, I'm human. You only kill monsters."

"If you think you're not a monster, you need to get your third eye checked."

Robbie Curtis got a warrant of execution issued for him, but I wasn't allowed to be the instrument of justice. I was too personally involved, so another of my fellow marshals got to do the honors. Fine with me, as long as he can't hurt anyone else ever again.

Justine Henderson is out of the hospital and home with her parents and baby. She's hoping to get a place of her own in a few months. I wish her well and hope that she finds someone to love the way she loved Thomas. I hate the idea of her pining for him forever.

I took the bones to the crematorium and watched them go in the oven. I leaned against the wall and read a book until they were turned to ash, no chance of getting the ol' switcheroo this time. I dumped the ashes in different bodies of running water. That is finally the last anyone will ever hear from Thomas Warrington. Jean-Claude and I have talked more about how my zombie could have gotten a version of the *ardeur*, but we don't know why it happened, and if I don't know why, then I don't know how to keep it from happening again. He turned into a flesh-eating zombie because he'd been a cannibal in real life. It wasn't in any written history on him,

he literally took the secret to the grave, so no fault of mine techni-
cally. But what really bothers me is that the loving, charismatic zombie was so full of my version of the *ardeur* that he made himself and
Justine fall in love with each other. The zombie was alive enough to
get a human woman pregnant with a perfectly normal baby, as if he
had been real. That was impossible, even I wasn't that good, but the
baby was happy and normal and a strong argument that maybe I was
that good, which scared the hell out of me. I raised the undead, I did
not do resurrection, no one did, but Thomas Warrington had been
close. I didn't know why he'd been so . . . human. I didn't know why
any of it had happened, which made my skin run cold if I thought
too hard about it. But one problem at a time, right? We saved the girl
and killed the evil sorcerer, and my breaking his finger was deemed
reasonable use of force. All's well that ends well, until next time.

ABOUT THE AUTHORS

KEVIN J. ANDERSON has published more than 165 books, 56 of which have been national or international bestsellers. He has written numerous novels in the Star Wars, X-Files, and Dune universes, as well as unique steampunk fantasy novels *Clockwork Angels* and *Clockwork Lives*, written with legendary Rush drummer Neil Peart. On his less-than-serious days, he likes to adventure with his character Dan Shamble, Zombie PI, who has appeared in five novels and numerous short stories. He has edited numerous anthologies and written comics, games, and the lyrics to two rock CDs. Anderson and his wife, Rebecca Moesta, are the publishers of WordFire Press.

GRIFFIN BARBER spent his youth in four different countries, learning three languages and burning all his bridges. Finally settled in Northern California with a day job as a police officer in a major metropolitan department, he lives the good life with his lovely wife, crazy-smart daughter, and needy dog. *1636: Mission to the Mughals*, coauthored with Eric Flint, was his first novel, and 2020 will see the publication of another collaborative novel, this time with Kacey Ezell, titled *2nd Chance Angel*. Despite considering himself a novelist, he's also had some success in the last few years penning short stories set in various universes across the many subgenres of SF. "Broken Son" is one such.

PATRICIA BRIGGS is the #1 *New York Times* bestselling author of both the Mercy Thompson series and the Alpha and Omega series. She resides in Eastern Washington near the Tri-Cities, home of Mercy Thompson; yes, it's a real place! When not working on her next book, she can be found playing truant out in her horse pastures, playing with the newest foals.

LARRY CORREIA is the *New York Times* bestselling and Dragon Award–winning author of the Monster Hunter International urban fantasy series, the Grimnoir Chronicles alternate history trilogy, the Dead Six military thrillers (with Mike Kupari), and the Saga of the Forgotten Warrior epic fantasy series. Larry lives in Yard Moose Mountain, Utah.

KACEY EZELL is an active duty USAF instructor pilot with 2,500-plus hours in the UH-1N Huey and Mi-171 helicopters. When not teaching young pilots to beat the air into submission, she writes sci-fi/fantasy/horror/noir/alternate history fiction. Her novels *Minds of Men* and *The World Asunder* were both Dragon Award finalists for best alternate history in 2018 and 2019, respectively. She's contributed to multiple Baen anthologies and has twice been selected for inclusion in *The Year's Best Military and Adventure SF* compilation. In 2018, her story "Family Over Blood" won the Year's Best Military and Adventure SF Readers' Choice Award. In addition to writing for Baen, she has published several novels and short stories with independent publisher Chris Kennedy Publishing. She is married with two daughters. You can find out more and join her mailing list at kaceyezell.net.

MONALISA FOSTER won life's lottery when she escaped communism and became an unhyphenated American citizen. Her works tend to explore themes of freedom, liberty, and personal responsibility. Despite her degree in physics, she's worked in several fields, including engineering and medicine. She and her husband (who is a writer-once-removed via their marriage) are living their happily ever after in Texas.

ROBERT E. HAMPSON, PhD, turns science fiction into science in his day job, and puts the science into science fiction in his spare time. He has consulted for more than a dozen SF writers; written informative articles ranging from the fictional depiction of real science to living in space; and written short fiction published by the US Army Small Wars Journal, Springer, Baen Books, and Seventh Seal Press (Chris Kennedy Publishing). Dr. Hampson is a professor of physiology/pharmacology and neurology with more than thirty-five years' experience in animal neuroscience and human neurology. His professional work includes more than a hundred peer-reviewed research articles ranging from the pharmacology of memory to the effects of radiation on the brain—and most recently, the first report of a "neural prosthetic" to restore human memory using the brain's own neural codes. He is a member of the SIGMA Forum and the Science and Entertainment Exchange, a service of the National Academy of Sciences. Find out more at his website: REHampson.com.

JOHN G. HARTNESS is an author, publisher, and podcaster from Charlotte, North Carolina. He is the author of multiple novel series, including the award-winning Quincy Harker, Demon Hunter series.

He is also the cofounder and publisher of Falstaff Books, and a member of the *Authors & Dragons* live D&D podcast.

JONATHAN MABERRY is a *New York Times* bestselling author, five-time Bram Stoker Award and Inkpot Award winner, producer, and comic book writer. *V-Wars*, a Netflix original series starring Ian Somerhalder (*Lost*, *The Vampire Diaries*) and based on Maberry's vampire apocalypse book series, debuted in 2019. And his young adult postapocalyptic zombie series, Rot & Ruin, is in development for film by Alcon Entertainment. He writes in multiple genres, including suspense, thriller, horror, science fiction, fantasy, and action; and he writes for adults, teens, and middle grade. His works include the Joe Ledger thrillers, *Glimpse*, the Dead of Night series, *The Wolfman*, *The X-Files Origins: Devil's Advocate*, the Pine Deep series, and many others. He is the editor of high-profile anthologies, including *The X-Files*, *Aliens: Bug Hunt*, *Out of Tune*, *Baker Street Irregulars*, *Nights of the Living Dead*, and others. His comics include *Black Panther: DoomWar*, *The Punisher: Naked Kills*, and *Bad Blood*. His Rot & Ruin books are being produced as webcomics for Webtoon. Jonathan is the editorial director of the new incarnation of *Weird Tales* magazine. He is a board member of the Horror Writers Association and the president of the International Association of Media Tie-In Writers. He lives in San Diego, California. Find him online at jonathanmaberry.com.

L. E. MODESITT, JR., is the *New York Times* bestselling author of more than seventy novels—primarily science fiction and fantasy—including the Saga of Recluce and the Imager Portfolio series, and more than fifty stories. His novels have sold millions of copies in the US and worldwide, and have been translated into German, Polish, Dutch, Czech, Russian, Bulgarian, French, Spanish, Italian, Hebrew, and Swedish. His first story was published in *Analog* in 1973. His most recent book was *The Mage-Fire War*, the twenty-first book in the Saga of Recluce series, and his next book is *Quantum Shadows*, a far-future science fantasy to be released in July 2020 from Tor.

JESSICA SCHLENKER is a professional geek with an MS in information security and a BS in biology. Her interests include homesteading, gaming, and reading (and dissecting) scientific papers in various fields. She lives with her husband, Michael Z. Williamson, and their children, cats, and her various homesteading animals.

SHARON SHINN has been part of the science fiction and fantasy world since 1995, when she published her first novel, *The Shape-Changer's Wife*. Since then, she has produced more than twenty-five additional novels, one collection, a graphic novel, and assorted pieces of short fiction. She has written about angels, shape-shifters, elemental powers, magical portals, and echoes. She has won the William L. Crawford Award for Outstanding New Fantasy Writer, a Reviewers' Choice Award from *Romantic Times*, and the 2010 RT Book Reviews Career Achievement Award in the Sci-Fi/Fantasy category. Three of her novels have been named to the ALA's list of Best Books for Young Adults (now Best Fiction for Young Adults). Follow her at SharonShinnBooks on Facebook or visit her website at sharonshinn.org.

Under the names **M. C. SUMNER** and **MARK SUMNER**, he's the author of a whole scad of novels, and short stories, and nonfiction of all sorts. He has also ghostwritten enough books to be an official ghost. His novel *Devil's Tower* was a nominee for the World Fantasy and Nebula Awards, and his mystery novel series News from the Edge became a television series that appeared on the Sci Fi Channel (as it was called at the time) in 2000. His most recent book is *On Whetsday*.

PATRICK M. TRACY lives in Salt Lake City and works as a network support administrator. His most recent publications include a contribution to the *Noir Fatale* anthology and the release of *Sakura: Intellectual Property*, which he coauthored. He was also one of the principal creators of the Crimson Pact universe, of which there are five anthologies. When not writing or fixing someone's computer, Patrick enjoys archery and playing the bass guitar. Visit him online at pmtracy.com.

MICHAEL Z. WILLIAMSON is variously an immigrant from the UK and Canada, a retired veteran of the US Army and USAF, a nationally bestselling and award-winning SF author and editor, and a consultant on disaster preparedness. When not doing these things, he is a bladesmith, a gunsmith, and a reenactor who favors the Viking era. He lives near Indianapolis with his wife, Jessica; children; and a variety of animals that are staff or livestock.

ABOUT THE EDITORS

LAURELL K. HAMILTON is the author of the #1 *New York Times* bestselling Anita Blake, Vampire Hunter series and the Merry Gentry series. With more than thirty books published, Laurell continues to create stories inspired by her lifelong love of monster movies, ghost stories, mythology, and folklore. Never one to rest on her laurels, she is currently working on a new novel set in yet a third fictional world and hopes to add to her list of short fiction soon. She lives in St. Louis with her family, two spoiled Japanese Chins, a house panther, and a house lion. In her free time, Laurell trains in Filipino martial arts with a specialization in bladework and enjoys reading, nature observation, and scuba diving.

CONNECT ONLINE

LaurellKHamilton.com
🗗 LaurellKHamiltonOfficial
🐦 LKHamilton

Photo by Jennifer Erickson

WILLIAM McCASKEY is a veteran of the United States Army who traded in the hot and sandy for central Florida with his family, dogs, and a very demanding feline overlord. In his free time, he enjoys honing his martial arts skills while imparting a few of them, traveling, and scuba diving. William made his debut with the science fiction novel *Dragon Two-Zero*.

CONNECT ONLINE

🅵 TheWmMcCaskey
🅾 TheWmMcCaskey
🆇 TheWmMcCaskey

COPYRIGHTS

#1 *NEW YORK TIMES* BESTSELLING AUTHOR

LAURELL K. HAMILTON

"Hamilton remains one of the most inventive and exciting writers in the paranormal field."
—#1 *New York Times* bestselling author Charlaine Harris

For a complete list of titles,
please visit prh.com/laurellkhamilton